
DOWN TO URSA

LISSA SHARPE

BAYOU ROSE PRESS

CONTENTS

Content Warning

The novel contains reference to emotional and physical abuse (not between the FMC and MMC). For more detailed information, please visit the author's website.

Reader, I don't write science fact.
I write science *fiction*.

A Foreword by Dr. Minerva Eloise Smithe-Canfield

I was one of six prisoners rounded up by the Brethren of Blood that week. They found me on Elba, dwindling on my last few days' worth of rations—from one sure death sentence to another.

We were held in the ship's bay for four days before being taken to the air lock—enough time for them to search through our possessions, run background checks, and ascertain if we were worth the rations it would take to keep us alive. Apparently none of us made the cut that week. Collecting us had been a waste of fuel and resources, and it showed in the set of the crew's faces.

Most of the Brethren had gathered to watch as we were sucked out into the void. They made their bets as to whom would last longest as our bodies twisted and jerked and gasped for air. This behavior might sound harsh, and it is, but I knew, too, how desperate for entertainment they would be after so many weeks and months adrift in space. The life of a pirate, I had learned, was 10 percent heart-racing excitement and 90 percent drab monotony. Anything that could enervate the dark silence of space was always a welcome distraction.

The quartermaster lined us up at the door.[1] Some of my fellow prisoners were weeping, some had shat themselves. By some miracle, I had done neither—not due to any innate bravery on my part, but because of the face in my mind, as vivid as if he stood there before me, silently urging me with his dusky blue eyes to find some way to survive; this was not the end, this could not be the end.

"Now's the time," the quartermaster bellowed to our motley lot, "for any of you godforsaken souls to make your case as to why you should live."

As others around me begged and bargained, wept and pleaded, I confess I scarcely heard them. My mind was racing, formulating a plan.

In my life, I have discovered three natural talents. The first is an aptitude for science. The second, and perhaps related, is the ability to make the perfect scone—not too moist, not too dry. Though both impressive feats, neither of these seemed promising as vehicles to rescue me from my current predicament.

The third, however, might very well do the trick. I have always, from a very young age, been an accomplished talker. Beyond the usual babbling noises of babyhood, Mother said I didn't speak a word until I was twenty-eight months old, when all at once I began speaking in full sentences. Since then, Mother also liked to say, I had scarcely stopped, even in my sleep.[2] On the surface, the ability to babble might not seem

---

1. I rightly assumed he was the quartermaster, since the captain would likely be far too busy and important to waste time on such a mundane task.

2. I have been known to suddenly and spontaneously recite the St. Crispin's Day Speech in my sleep, which is particularly strange as I am unable to do so awake.

like the most auspicious skill, but it had saved my life at least once thus far. There was every reason to hope it might do so again.

As the eyes of the crew turned to me, waiting for me to stake my claim to life, I took in a shuddering breath, whetting my cracked lips. I could feel the hostility in their gazes, along with some curiosity, but as I was the last to speak, this latter emotion was far outweighed by irritation. They were, most of them, eager to begin the killing by this point, and hoped I would get on with it.

"I won't beg for my life," I said with as much dignity as I could muster while being unshowered, unkempt, and with what I suspected to be flea bites covering my legs. "But I do offer something to make it worth your while to keep me alive." I gave a dramatic pause, just long enough to pique their interest. "Entertainment."

Some scoffed openly. Letting no doubt show on my face, I just barreled on. "If you release me out into the black abyss of space with these other poor souls, how long will I even last? Minutes?"

"Fifteen seconds," someone called from the back. "On average."

Good God. That was both a very short time to live, and a very *long* time to suffocate. I swallowed. "But if you keep me alive, I'll keep you entertained until we get to the Havens."

There. That had hooked at least a few of them. Some still looked skeptical, but I saw the raised eyebrows, the exchanged glances, which gave me some small hope. "How will you go about doing that?" one of the Brethren asked finally.

"Two stories," I promised them. "Both love stories, in their own way. One of love gone terribly wrong—deception, betrayal, even murder. And the other, a love so true that no length, no time, no distance could dim its brightness."

The words hung in the air as I waited for the Brethren to make their choice. Fearing it might not have been enough to sway them, I cleared my throat and added, "Plus some, you know, sexy stuff."

They deliberated amongst each other for a few moments, but soon enough it was decided. I was temporarily reprieved from death, along with one other prisoner named Babcock, who had promised that he could guide them to hidden fuel stores on Mars. The other four prisoners, I'm sorry to say, were not. We all watched from the safety of the deck as the air lock doors opened, releasing the twisting, twitching bodies of those poor souls into space.[3]

Not long after, I was summoned to the galley to begin my first night of storytelling. After partaking of my allotted share of food and drink, I offered the crew their choice in which of the two tales I would begin first.

"One is called 'Mina and the Mad Scientist,'" I told them. "The other, 'Mina and the Man-Bear.'"

Some in the crew demanded to know which was the one with murder, while others were more keen on the story with all the naughty bits. To preserve artistic integrity, I refused to divulge anything about the plots of the stories and how they would unfold. This may seem

---

3. In the unlikely circumstance that this account should survive after me, my guess is that some may wonder at the identity of these other four passengers. I'm sorry to say I can give no further information as to their names or where they were picked up along the route to the Havens. We were all held in separate cells, and for such a short duration, we hadn't devised ways to communicate with one another. My apologies to any families who may have hoped to finally gain some closure. As to the success of Babcock in fulfilling his promise to locate fuel, that remains to be seen. I will keep you updated if I learn anything new.

unnecessarily priggish of me, especially in the face of the raucous debate that occurred afterward—which resulted in more than one black eye amongst the men and a knife being held temporarily to my throat—but I had my reasons. Like any good storyteller, I knew the importance of mystery and surprise in sustaining interest in my tale. And, perhaps more than most storytellers, I needed to rely upon that sustainment, which could very well mean the difference between life and death. After all, if my story ended prematurely, or if it didn't keep them sufficiently entertained, there was no reason to keep me alive until we reached Haven 3—and I had to reach Haven 3. Everything depended on it.

After no small argument, it was finally decided that I will start with "Mina and the Man-Bear." I thought it prudent to write down my stories here, to keep track of the order of things and to plot out the best way to make the tales last as long as possible while still retaining their entertainment value. Ideally, these two stories will satisfy the Brethren until we reach Haven 3, at which point they will see fit to grant me my life.

But, since I must acknowledge that is an unlikely outcome, my hope is that by writing this account down, it might someday find its way back to you, my love. If you're still alive. If you've managed to escape the fate I fear must have befallen you. One way or another, whether in body or word, I will come back to you. I promised once to never leave you, and I never shall.

—Dr. Minerva Eloise Smithe-Canfield, December 2143

Part One

Mina and the Man-Bear

1

It is so difficult to think where to begin. I suppose I shall have to go back quite a ways for everything to make sense. On the one hand, that might drag out a few more days' worth of storytelling, a few more days to avoid the air lock. On the other, if I don't get to the good bits quickly enough, the Brethren of Blood might get bored and decide to kill me prematurely.

Hmm. Quite the conundrum.

I suppose I shall have to go over the key players first: Myself, naturally. Ursa, though he won't come until much later, if I really am starting from the beginning. Rawley, my fiancé, the man who wanted me dead. Meridian, his loyal assistant, who would do whatever Rawley asked, without reservation. My mother, though she'd been gone long before we came to Earth . . .

No, for *that* story, I'd need to go back even further, and I doubt the Brethren will have that much patience.

The trip from Haven 3 to Earth will be too tedious to cover, I think. It was tedious to experience, after the first exciting week of venturing out into space. Months upon months of reading, playing games, looking at the stars, and plotting and planning. I could have opted to go into cryo-sleep, as many of the other passengers did, but I was too worried about what might happen to me in such a vulnerable position. So I remained awake. I read. I paced the ship. I went over the notes given to me by Tobago, the maps, the time frame, our coordinates, checking and double-checking to make sure I had it all right . . .

I shall probably have to explain Tobago, too. But is that going too far back . . . ?

No. No. It will all get too muddled if I try to explain all the pieces before we can begin. I'll just have to start with us arriving on Earth, then fill in the details as I go through it all. That will be the best way, I think. Always start at the moment of change, or at least that's what Madame Zhang used to say, back at the academy.[1]

Yes, then. We will start there. The day we arrived on Earth, at long last. The place I'd always dreamt of visiting, but certainly never under these circumstances. Ooh, yes. That sounds nicely important . . . I'll definitely use that . . .

At long last, we arrived on Earth. It was the place I'd always dreamt of visiting, though never under these circumstances. It was the opportunity of a lifetime, to return to the source of all life and study the fungal species I'd read about in textbooks, now at last in front of

---

1. At least I won't have to explain who Madame Zhang is. It's doubtful she'll ever come up in this narrative again. But that's the difficulty of encapsulating one's story, an entire life, isn't it? There are details that are irrelevant to the whole that still make up its shaping, in however small a way.

me—living, organic matter, not just a holo on a screen. I should have been elated.

Instead, I was terrified.

Terrified that Rawley would have somehow discovered all my careful plans.

Terrified he would get to me before I could enact them.

Terrified he wouldn't, and that I might succeed.

It was rather difficult to narrow down the terror to one specific source, truth be told. My entire body was on high alert as I stepped out into that blinding sun, which was unlike anything I'd ever experienced before. I'd been warned during our EET that the sun would be brighter on Earth because of the lack of domes.[2] The rational part of me knew the sun wouldn't harm me, even though at the moment it felt otherwise. Earth was *meant* to be lived in by humans, after all, and thus it didn't need to be contained within an artificial hemisphere to keep us from being poisoned by its natural atmosphere, unlike in my homeland, the Havens.

But knowing about a hypothetical possibility and experiencing it for oneself are two very different things, aren't they? I staggered down the ramp, blinking against the sun's unfiltered brightness, so surprised by this initial attack on my senses that it took me a moment to process some of the other stimuli simultaneously occurring—the cool, dry air on my skin, the sound of insects and bird calls.

Grinning, I turned to share my observations with the passenger nearest to me, a tall, thickish and darkish fellow. "Isn't is fantastic?"

"That's a post," someone spoke up from behind me with a thick Australian accent.

---

2. Earth Expedition Training

"Oh." Frowning, I blinked through the brightness and saw that I had, indeed, been speaking to one of the posts supporting the landing bridge. How embarrassing.

With what was probably not an entirely convincing smile, I turned to face whoever had spoken to me. "Hello. I'm Dr. Minerva Smithe-Canfield."

A warm hand gripped my shoulder, steadying me. "Jay Coulson. I'm guessing this is your first time on Earth?"

"How could you tell?" I returned wryly, still blinking furiously. Things were beginning to take more shape for me as my eyes slowly adjusted. For instance, I could tell that Mr. Coulson was a tallish, medium-ish-sized blur. Possibly with brown hair, or maybe a hat. So, progress!

"Don't worry. You'll adjust. I'm one of the guides here, and I can vouch that almost no one goes permanently blind."

"Almost no one?" I echoed faintly.

He chuckled and clapped my shoulder again, which I chose to believe meant he was only joking. "I'm from Haven 1. Been on Earth for about four months now. This expedition will be my last round before I return and hand off the reins to some other bloke. Whereabouts are you from, then?"

"Haven 3," I returned.

I felt the shift in attention more than I saw or heard anything in particular. After a too-long pause, Mr. Coulson spoke louder than was necessary. "Haven 3? Really?"

I heard some low snickers coming from nearby; blinking, I thought I could make out some figures standing not too far off, probably watching all the newcomers as they arrived. I knew without needing to see them what the joke was. Haven 3 was known for having the most beautiful people in the galaxy, due to investing in some of the best genetic engineers in the universe.[3] I should know, since my own mother had been one of them—a pioneer in gene manipulation and one of the most revered scientists in her field.

Nonetheless, I was rather painfully normal. Not ugly, not even plain, but certainly not the spectacular beauty that one might expect to meet from my home settlement. I didn't have topaz eyes, or sunset-colored hair, or perfectly balanced proportions. My hair was brown. My eyes were hazel, which is really just a fancy word for brown-adjacent. My proportions tended toward pear-shaped. I had an ever-so-slight overbite, though at least my teeth were fine and straight after several years of braces. The only really distinct thing about me was that I wore glasses, which in a settlement where everyone was genetically modified to be perfect, was a rarity indeed; though outside of Haven 3, I'd since discovered, it was far more common.

So. Normal.

Feeling rather less kindly toward Mr. Coulson now for making me the butt of his joke, I pulled free of his hand on my shoulder. "Yes, *really*. Now are we going to just stand here all day, or—"

Before I could finish the thought, I felt someone roughly grasp my elbow. My sight was getting better now with each blink, but even without looking, I instinctively knew that grip. Rawley.

---

3. I'd assumed the Brethren of Blood would be familiar with Haven 3's reputation, but on reflection, I don't know if that will be the case. They might have been raised off the Havens, at some of the moon stations or other small settlements. And if so, they wouldn't have had much call to spend time at a place like Haven 3, since the primary exports are very beautiful people and genetic manufacturing, and it's obvious by looking at them that the Brethren have very little use for or experience with either. (No offense.)

"Move along, Minerva. You're not the only one waiting to get her first glimpse of Earth."

I was shoved forward—not too roughly, but none too gently, either. Mr. Coulson caught me before I could fall flat on my face, and now I could see his own face a bit better—middle-aged, swarthy, and lined from being in the sun, and if I was not mistaken, looking chastened for having teased me earlier. "Careful, Dr. Smithe-Canfield. Non-artificial gravity can be a bit tricky until you get used to it."

He knew, of course, that it wasn't gravity that had caused me to fall, but I recognized his words as a peace offering. I gave him a wan smile of thanks. When I looked beyond him, I could see that most of the people who were lingering at the ramp to watch the new arrivals looked fairly similar to Mr. Coulson, at least from what I could make out of them. Many in their forties, most darkened from being in the sun, all men.

I took in a sharp breath, suddenly conscious of just how much testosterone there was in the air. I reasoned with myself that these onlookers were all likely Earth survivalist guides, like Mr. Coulson, which was naturally a profession that might lean more toward employing men, as it required one to be single, childless, and content to live outside of family or community structures for long periods of time. Surely there would be other scientists, like myself, who were also women.

Though as I thought back on the passengers who I'd seen boarding, I realized with a sinking heart that only a handful of them were women.[4] It made sense why this group of men would be standing at the ramp, waiting to see who the "fresh meat" would be, so to speak,

---

4. I'd have to make some allowances for those who began cryo-sleeping before we even departed.

with our kind so outnumbered. It made sense, but it also made me feel rather desperately uncomfortable, bearing the weight of so much scrutiny. It was bad enough being one of the only women in my field; being one of the only women on the entire planet felt . . . ominous.

You won't be here long, I reminded myself, taking strength from the thought, even as a frisson of fear passed through me.

I sensed the shift in mood before I noticed her approach. The men lining the ramp suddenly drew up to their full heights, puffing out their chests as they murmured to each other. Mr. Coulson dropped his hold on my arm, stepping past me.

Sighing, I turned to see Meridian emerging onto the ramp.

Meridian was the sort of woman one expected to be from Haven 3. She was tall and slender, though still with a perfectly rounded, gravity-defying figure. She had bronze skin that seemed to shimmer in Earth's light, juxtaposed by bright blonde hair that cascaded in coiled curls down to her shoulders. Her features were delicate and flawless, despite months of space travel and no makeup. She glided more than walked down the ramp, her amber eyes—

No, wait a minute. She was wearing strange glasses with tinted lenses, presumably to protect her eyes from the bright sunlight. *She* did not stagger blindly down the ramp, like I had just moments before, but glided confidently forward, a vision fit for a holocard.

Oh, come now, that just wasn't fair!

Blinking over at Rawley, I saw that he, too, wore the strange glasses to protect his eyes. Of course he'd thought ahead but never mentioned such a tool to me, though he'd apparently procured a pair for his favorite assistant.

It wasn't the worst thing, by far, that Rawley had subjected me to during our long engagement, but it still irked me. I pretended not to notice, holding my chin up high. I might be painfully normal. I might have staggered onto Earth like a drunken sailor. I might have to bear the perpetual, intentional humiliation orchestrated by my fiancé, the man who was meant to protect and value me above all others.

But I could still have my dignity.

"How will we get to the base?" I asked in my most queenly, prim tone.

It rather lost its effect when I had to repeat myself, twice, just to get Mr. Coulson to tear his eyes away from Meridian and pay attention to me. She was, as usual, oblivious to everyone but Rawley, the two of them leaning their heads together to whisper conspiratorially.

"Right this way, miss," Coulson answered finally, when he was able to fit his tongue back into his mouth.

"Doctor," I reminded him.

Rawley spoke up before we could make it too far. "I'll need to be the first to make it to base, since I'm the expedition leader. And I need to ride in the same car as my fiancé. My assistant can follow behind if there isn't enough room."

Mr. Coulson released me quickly and stepped toward Meridian. "Right this way, miss."

"No." Rawley's response was curt and unamused. "Meridian is my assistant. *She's* my fiancé."

The *she* in question was, of course, me. I felt Mr. Coulson's embarrassed surprise; I was surprised, too, for different reasons. I would have thought Rawley might make me wait behind, just to try to humiliate me further in front of all these new people. It was one of his favorite games: embarrassing me in small, subtle ways everyone would notice but no one could really object to.

His reasoning became clear as soon as we were seated in the jeep that would take us to the base. Rawley stretched his arm along the seat, gripping the back of my neck in a gesture that might seem protective to anyone watching. Only I felt the insistent pressure of his thumb and fingers, the menace in the arm he now had caged around me.

"I wouldn't want to let you out of my sight, Minerva," he murmured to me. "Not in such a wild, dangerous place like this. Who knows what might happen to you?"

My heart raced as we sped across the rocky dirt roads toward the base that would be our home for the next few months.

He *knew*.

. . . Did he know? Had he somehow guessed what I was planning?

I'd waited years for my first real glimpse of Earth, but though my eyes were now clear enough to see, my mind was racing too quickly to take anything in. There was only one word running through my mind, beating through my heart.

Escape.

Escape.

Escape.

2

We'd been on Earth for nearly a week before I spent any substantive time outside. I know that might sound absurd to those living in terraformed environments who've never gotten a chance to return to the mother planet. Between overcoming my ship-lag, attending training meetings, plotting my escape, and setting up my lab, there just hadn't been much time for it.

But no, that isn't entirely true. Like everyone else, I'd always dreamed of seeing the place that all our terraformed environments were meant to echo. Earth was the ultimate adventure, the wild, untouched frontier, the stuff of adventure novels and science fiction. I know some people think it's unfair that only scientists are granted permission to explore it, but you cannot imagine the paperwork that must be completed to get approval. We go on these expeditions not for an exotic vacation, but for the love of knowledge! Even knowing that Earth might not have been entirely cleansed of the toxins that drove mankind away, we are still willing to risk our lives to progress our research. So, save your censure for those rule breakers who thwart intergalactic sanctions and illegally land on Earth to plunder its re-sources, not for the scientists who get official leave![1]

For myself, I could not have been more thrilled to be going to Earth for the first time. I'd seen pictures, watched vids, read everything I could get my hands on in preparation for coming to the home I'd never before been to—and still, it was nothing at all like I'd been expecting.

How to explain . . . ? I'd grown up in the Havens, meant in many ways to replicate an Earth experience: sunlight, soil, rivers. Yet every-thing there was artificial, and it felt, for lack of a better word, safe. There was no chance of wildlife wandering into the city, because the only wildlife that existed had been bred for a specific purpose, from which the creatures were genetically incapable of deviating. The river would never overflow, because it was man-made, monitored and reg-ulated to stay at the ideal temperature and flow rate year-round. The sun provided the optimal amount of warmth but couldn't burn our skin through the dome covering; there were no creepy crawlies waiting to bite our tender flesh if we spent too much time outside.

Twenty minutes spent in the great outdoors on Earth, between leaving the ship and being transported to the base, had told me enough to know that I was no longer in a simulation. The air was dry, the sun scorching in the afternoon heat. I had three unaccounted for bugbites on my arm within the first twenty-four hours of arriving on Earth. On the drive from the landing pad to the research base, I saw cities overgrown with vegetation, trees puncturing abandoned vehicles, and a wall of green that seemed frighteningly impenetrable. Nature was

---

1. On second thought, as my audience will be one of those groups who illegally trespass on Earth, perhaps I ought to not share this sentiment . . .

alive here in a way that was foreign to me. It felt almost . . . sentient. Like the land was just as aware of me as I was of it.

So, yes, I'd been adjusting to the new climate and atmosphere, but in truth, I was frightened to do any real exploring, even though the base was the safest place imaginable to do such things. A laser perimeter encircled the walled enclosure, in addition to guard towers and barbed-wire fences. Something would *really* have to want to get inside the base to breach all those barriers, and it would have to be a terrifically intelligent *something* to figure out how to do so.

Oddly, that thought wasn't as comforting as I'd hoped it would be.

"You are being a ninny," I'd told myself in the mirror the evening before I decided I would have to confront my fears. My reflection nodded back at me in solemn agreement.[2] Yes. Tomorrow would be the day.

I told my fiancé of my plans over breakfast the next morning. "I think I'll go out on the grounds today. Do some exploring."

Rawley snorted with laughter, choking on his coffee.

I hadn't expected him to offer to come along or anything of the sort—in fact, if he had, I would have certainly found a way to change my plans as quickly as possible. But still, I hadn't anticipated such a derisive response. He pounded on his chest until he could breathe again, still blinking back tears of laughter. "Out on a great adventure,

---

2. I'm afraid I'm taking a bit of an artistic liberty here. Just to be clear, my reflection couldn't nod at me if I weren't nodding and necessitating that my mirror image reflect the same movement. However, having read many novels myself, I know I must occasionally use figurative language to enrich the story and thus hopefully ensure the Brethren remain suitably entertained.

Minerva? Make sure to pack some rations. Take an armed guard with you in case you get lost in the ten acres of land."

Across the table, Meridian laughed into her cup of coffee.[3]

I straightened primly, refusing to be goaded. "I hardly think that will be necessary, thank you."

Mother had always told me it was important to go high when others went low. But as Rawley and Meridian continued smirking at each other while I quietly finished my breakfast, it became enormously difficult not to flick a forkful of scrambled egg into Meridian's face and drop my hot coffee into Rawley's lap. Sometimes I thought it might be rather fun to go low, just once.

When I left the table and was able to calm down, I realized it was only to my benefit for Meridian and Rawley to scoff at me venturing into the outdoors on my own. Perhaps then, once I put my plan into action,[4] their disbelief would buy me more time. They were always underestimating me. *He* was always underestimating me. But I would soon show them what I was made of.

After breakfast, I put on my sturdiest walking shoes, a hat, and a fresh coat of sunscreen and insect repellent, then stepped outside.

---

3. Yes, Meridian was there. Meridian was *always* there.

4. I realize this is an enormous tease, to not spell out what my plan was right away, but I must slowly parcel out this information to the Brethren, to keep them intrigued. Foreshadowing, et cetera.

The brightness of the sun accosted me, much as it had when I first stepped off the ship. I raised a hand to shield myself against its intensity, half tempted to scuttle back inside like a rat, but I held my ground. *You will adjust*, I told myself sternly. It was a bit like grief, I imagined—blindingly overwhelming at first, but then slowly, gradually, it became the new ordinary. The weight that was always pressing down on your chest. Or in this case, perhaps, the light that was always glaring in your eyes.

Sure enough, after a few moments, the brightness became bearable enough that I could keep moving, and a few minutes after that, I scarcely noticed it anymore.

See? I told myself jubilantly. *You are capable of this! You are remarkable, Mina! You can accomplish anything!*

Whenever I slipped into these kinds of self-affirmations, I realized how much my inner monologue sounded like my mother. It had been happening for so long that the recognition of this had shifted from painful into peaceful. I would need her with me, here of all places, my greatest advocate and champion at my side, encouraging me to be my best, believing me capable of it.

Some previous researchers at the base had created walking paths leading through the thicket of woods surrounding the building, so I happily set off on the trail. This would be a good way to build up my fortitude. I wouldn't always be able to rely on the paths made by others, but one had to start somewhere.

Now that I'd begun adjusting to the environment, I was astonished at how beautiful the wilderness was. At first, it had simply been overwhelming in its newness. But now, at the leisure of my own pace, I could fully take the time to appreciate what I was seeing. Majestic trees towered up into a bright blue, open sky unmarred by dome enclosures. These trees were not all uniform, either, but each had its own shape and texture, and each housed life of its own—from moss to insects to birds. Birds! Flying freely in the sky, chattering and singing to one another up in the branches.

This environment was different, very different, from what I was accustomed to. But the more I looked, the more I was beginning to see its beauty.

I became so confident, so complacent, in my abilities and the natural wonder surrounding me that I decided to test my boundaries a bit. Bracing myself, I stepped off the path and set off into unmarked wilderness.

It was thrilling to be truly out on my own for the first time, on a wild adventure. And, considering the plan I was soon to put in motion, I felt inordinately proud of myself for my bravery in exploring the great unknown.

That is, until I heard the noise.

It was unlike anything I'd ever encountered before, coming from somewhere deep in the forest. It sounded almost like . . . a wounded animal? But it wasn't crying or bleating; rather, it was making a strange wheezing, grunting sound.

My adrenaline spiked at the thought of a bogeyman lurking in the shadows. "Silly girl, jumping at every strange noise," I muttered to myself, determined that my logic should overcome my anxiety. How such a fanciful ninny had spawned from my ultra-practical mother was something I would never understand. She had been so staunchly pragmatic, so fearless, and I was always being swept up in one flight of fancy or another.

How *she* was dead and I remained was perhaps the only bigger mystery.

Aiming to summon some of her unflappable courage, I decided I would have to face my fears and see what was making the sound. We were perfectly safe within the laser perimeters, after all. And there was no such thing as monsters. I was perfectly safe.

I edged forward as silently as possible, even holding my breath so I wouldn't alert whatever it was of my presence.

As I drew nearer to the sound, it took me a moment to realize what it was I was seeing. Once I pieced it together, my mouth fell open in a silent gasp, and I could only stare.

Rawley's naked back and buttocks were turned to me, and he was thrusting in and out of someone who was blocked from my view by his body, though it took very little deduction to surmise it was his assistant, Meridian. Her identity was confirmed when I heard her emit those odd gasping, panting sounds again as he continued groaning and thrusting.

After my initial shock wore off, I realized I needed to retreat as quickly as possible before I was discovered. I had no idea how long this sort of thing would last, and I knew that I could not let Rawley know what I had seen.

I moved quietly at first, so as not to draw attention to myself; and then, when I was confident I had put enough distance between myself and them, I fled for the safety of the path.

It had been foolish of me, I realized now, to believe for even a moment that I was safe anywhere on the base. The perimeter might be able to keep creatures *out*, but what was there to protect me from the very real dangers that already existed within these walls . . . ?

As I reached the marked path, I took in a few bracing breaths, trying to calm my racing mind. I would have to leave now, surely? There was no choice. I could put it off for no longer. I'd thought I might have some time, that I could prepare a little longer, but now I realized—

The loud noise of a branch snapping nearby startled me from my thoughts. I looked toward it anxiously, my heart hammering as I searched the woods for the source of the sound. "Hello?"

For the first time, it occurred to me just how far I'd wandered from the main building. I was still on the path, but there were no structures, no vehicles, no *people* in sight. I was out here all on my own—except for Rawley and Meridian. But they were too far away, and too preoccupied, to have followed me so closely.

And I could feel someone watching me.

I tried to tell myself it was simply my imagination, that I was new to this place and jumping at every little sound. But there is a certain animal instinct that takes over when one is aware of being watched. My entire body tensed. My skin prickled. My senses became fine-tuned to every noise, every movement, searching for whomever, *whatever*, might be watching me.

"Hello?" I tried again. It was not, I must admit, the most clever response when faced with the strong likelihood that I was being stalked by something big enough to set all of my senses on alert.

But nothing happened. No one spoke. Nothing moved in that thick canopy of green. I stood very still for quite a long time, tense and waiting. I felt with absolute certainty I was not alone, but whatever was watching me was not making itself known.

As time ticked on and nothing happened, I decided the best thing to do would be to retreat, walking backward so as not to turn my back on whatever was in the forest. So, slowly, I retraced my steps in reverse, my eyes darting from tree to tree, rock to bush, searching and never finding anything.

Then, when I felt moderately confident I was close enough to the building to outrun anything that might chase me, I bolted toward the doors.

Later, of course, in the safety of my quarters, I convinced myself that I must have been imagining things. Seeing Rawley and Meridian had set off my alarms, and I'd been primed to see danger in everything around me. But it was all just a distraction, really, from the immediate threat right in front of me.

I would have to escape. And soon.

If you haven't been able to piece it together yet,[5] gentle reader, let me spell it out clearly now: My plan was to abandon the excursion and disappear into the wilderness. Not forever, but until I could meet with the illegal transportation I'd arranged. It would mean living on my own without human companionship for weeks, maybe even months; but it would also mean escaping a sadistic fiancé who meant, I was certain, to kill me. Faced with a choice such as this, you can begin to understand why I would have come to such a momentous decision.

You might be thinking to yourself, *But this awkward, babbling girl is a scientist, not a survivalist! She won't last a day on her own in the wild!* If so, then I take that as a compliment, because I have succeeded thus far in tricking you, just as I was attempting to trick Rawley during my first few weeks on Earth! I had known for quite a while that my fiancé planned to murder me, so I had made my own plans. Back on Haven 3, before the excursion left, I began training with a survivalist

---

5. Please don't be hard on yourself if this is the case. Not all of us are gifted with the ability to read subtext and pick up on contextual clues. I'm sure you have other talents that are equally impressive, but I did feel it important to spell this out for those, like yourself, who might need a little extra help in this particular area.

knowledgeable in the ways of Earth-living—but I'm getting ahead of myself, I'm afraid. That will be a story for another day.

Suffice it to say, I was not so inept as I let on, but I wanted everyone around me to *think* I was clumsy and awkward so they wouldn't suspect what I had planned. There is nothing quite so easy as turning peoples' own preconceived notions against them. Rawley, in particular, had to be convinced that there was no chance of my leaving the safety of the base, since I would have been so terribly helpless on my own. All the while, I would be planning my route through the forest, deciding the best area to create shelter, and yes, distributing supplies that I could gather once the time was right.

That had been the idea, anyway, but after seeing Rawley with Meridian, I knew I would have to expedite my plan.

*I am coming back with an addendum, since I was interrupted in my storytelling by an unrelated fight that broke out over the last bowl of stew.[6] It became clear to me, before I was interrupted, that the Brethren were confused by my reaction to finding Rawley with Meridian in the woods. It seems most of the Brethren thought I should be more shocked about him having sex with another woman than by him having sex at all. I often forget that not everyone in the universe follows the same cultural practices as on Haven 3. I should rehearse explaining it here, to make sure I can phrase it in a way the Brethren will comprehend. They get easily frustrated, and their frustration often leads to violence, which I would obviously like to avoid if at all possible.

---

6. One man was killed, which was, naturally, very unfortunate. Although presumably, that means there will be more stew to go around, so hopefully less fighting.

For the last fifty years or so on Haven 3, Pleasure Machines have been used as a viable alternative to sexual intercourse for anyone who can afford them. In fact, sexual intercourse is considered so common-ly coarse for the people of my social circle that I expected Pleasure Machines to be a universal practice, even on other settlements, but I suppose that is rather classist of me. I know some people continue to prefer copulation, claiming that it is more natural and less artifi-cial. This may be so! However, there are legitimate reasons to prefer Pleasure Machines. They eradicate sexually transmitted diseases and unwanted pregnancies—the latter of which is a necessary requirement on a planet whose main industry is shaped by genetically modifying one's offspring to one's own idea of perfection, *before* conception.

Of course, there are always those couples who choose to entertain more carnal physical relations, and I must admit that in my younger years I may have given into the temptation to test the waters, so to speak, as teenagers are so prone to do. These things happen, and so long as people are discreet and there are no lasting consequences,[7] there's a sort of unwritten "don't ask, don't tell" policy.

But as Meridian and Rawley are neither horny young teenagers nor in a committed relationship, the fact that they would choose to completely flout our Havenian ways now that they were on Earth was . . . unsettling. I mean no offense, of course, to other settlements who behave differently, but on Haven 3, it was ingrained in us that this type of physical passion was beyond vulgar. Just as one might be judged for being slothful or gluttonous or unable to control one's desire to sing in public, the lack of willpower to refrain from engaging in

---

7. I.e., unplanned, unmodified pregnancies

bodily intercourse when Pleasure Machines exist as a viable alternative showed a considerable weakness—a lack of moral fortitude, really.

So yes, I was more shocked to see Rawley engaging in copulation than in the fact he would choose to do so with another woman. It was true that he'd never approached me, his long-term fiancé, about entertaining this sort of dalliance. I clearly did not wish to dilly or dally with that man, though there might have been a time, I suppose, when I would have been more amenable to the suggestion. But by now, I was no longer under the misconception that Rawley truly desired or loved me. He had only ever wanted me for one thing, and I feared what would happen to me now that we were outside of civilization, where he could plausibly concoct any number of reasons for me to suddenly disappear.

And now that I knew he and Meridian were copulating, my position was even more precarious. If Rawley was letting his control slip in this aspect of his life, then it would only be a matter of time before he allowed his irritation and abhorrence at my existence to reach its natural conclusion.

The time had come. I would have to act, and soon.

The difficulty would be finding a way out of the base without being noticed. I have already detailed the measures taken to keep unwanted intruders *out* of the base, but these also had the unfortunate consequence of making it very difficult to leave. Not that I imagine many persons who had come on expeditions to Earth were eager to escape the safety of the base. We had food, we had shelter, we had companionship, we had our work. What need would there be for anyone to *escape* into the wilderness?

Yet, that was very much the position I found myself in. Luckily I still had the upper hand, since Rawley didn't know I was onto him. I still had the element of surprise.

Only . . . how to find a plausible excuse to leave the base?

This worry was so much at the forefront of my mind that I didn't dwell too much on the other being I'd encountered in the woods. Much. It was all just nerves, I told myself, a figment of my imagination. There was no way anything could have breached the perimeter; better to keep my focus on the dangers *inside* the base than outside of it.

That was what I told myself, then. But now I do wonder, my love, if that was you? I never got a chance to ask you about it. I hope I will. I hope we have the chance to do a great many things together that we never got to do.

3

B y a pure stroke of luck, my problem of how to leave the base resolved itself the very next day. I say luck, though perhaps it was more like fate.[1] Regardless, after a night spent tossing and turning, deliberating my options, I was handed the very solution to my problems the next morning during breakfast.

Dr. Shangrit was a kindly man who was a well-respected field researcher. Before this trip, I'd known him mostly through reputation. Like everyone else on the expedition, I knew that he had been to Earth twice before and was thus considered one of the experts on Earth science. Rawley, the titled expedition leader, might have had the funding

---

1. I don't believe in fate, of course, since I am a scientist and the concept of our destinies being predetermined for us is, in a word, nonsense. However, keeping my audience in mind, I think throwing in the word *fate* might be a wise appeal to hold their interest. Pirates are traditionally quite a superstitious bunch, perhaps because their brains have been addled by so much time staring into the black void of space. Though I won't be sharing that theory with them, naturally.

and the ambition to put together the expedition; but privately, it was understood that Dr. Shangrit was the true authority. He was also a kind, soft-spoken, genteel man, belying all the stereotypes about positions of power necessitating one to become a complete dictator. And, personally, it pleased me to no end to witness Rawley occasionally having to bite back his pride and defer to the older, more experienced man who had effortlessly earned everyone's respect in a matter of days.

It was an unexpected pleasure, but delicious all the same.

I'd had a few conversations in passing with Dr. Shangrit, usually as part of a group, and I'd said nothing to notably distinguish myself. So I was quite surprised when Dr. Shangrit approached me at breakfast that morning, smiling at me in his kindly way. "Dr. Smithe-Canfield. Do you mind if I join you?"

My thoughts were still racing over my unsolved dilemma of how to escape unnoticed; this, coupled with a poor night's sleep, meant that it took me a full three seconds of blinking uncomprehendingly at Dr. Shangrit before I realized he was addressing me. By my own name. "Yes, of course. Please!"

I pulled my tray back toward me, making room for him. I'd scarcely touched my protein gruel,[2] but I knew I ought to finish it to put up a good show of seeming normal. Rawley would certainly notice if I began acting strangely, and I wouldn't want to do anything to tip my hand.

---

2. This is not the actual name for the food we were served, but it might as well have been. Disgusting mushy nonsense. Of course, after my stint on Elbis, I would happily eat a whole pot of it and still ask for more. Perhaps I ought to take the opportunity here to praise the Brethrens' cook in comparison, in hopes he will develop a fondness for me? Everyone enjoys a compliment, after all!

Scraping a large helping of the food, I shoveled it into my mouth in a most unladylike fashion. "Mmm. Good mash this morning."

"Is it?" Dr. Shangrit asked hopefully, sniffing at his own spoonful. "I usually just try to drown out the taste with my coffee. Which is also quite disgusting, mind you, but more tolerably so."

"I think it's the texture," I agreed with him. "Not so many foreign bits floating around in it."

We smiled in commiseration with one another. He took a bite and grimaced. "Hmm. Perhaps I can see if the medic will numb my tongue before morning meals."

I laughed quietly, warming to the topic. "Or perhaps just permanently for the duration of our stay?"

"Oh, there are a few treats to look forward to. Just wait until they make the banana pudding. And there's always—"

"Taco Tuesday,"[3] I finished for him with a grin. "You're right. I wouldn't want to miss out on that."

We were interrupted by the arrival of Rawley, who announced himself by slamming his tray onto the table with a loud thud. As he did so directly next to me, I jumped in surprise, spilling a spoonful of mush onto my lap.

"Dr. Shangrit, what an honor." Rawley was always his most affable, charming self in front of the people he thought it mattered to impress. I had once been one of those people, but that time had long-since passed. Case in point, he glanced down at the mess on my trousers with a patronizing shake of his head. "Sweet Minerva. Always so clumsy."

---

3. Taco Tuesday meals used the same protein gruel as a base but added salsa and cheese, making it infinitely more palatable.

Sliding into the seat next to me, Rawley took his napkin and wiped rather forcefully at the stain on my lap, hard enough that I'd likely bruise. I pressed my mouth shut, schooling my face not to react; if I did, he would make sure whatever he did to me away from an audience was far worse. Our gazes met briefly, his charming facade shifting with terrifying quickness as he glared a silent threat at me. *Don't embarrass me*, that look said.

I looked down at the table, vaguely aware of Meridian sliding in soundlessly across the table from Rawley.

"Did you need to speak to me?" Rawley asked, turning his focus back to Dr. Shangrit. I couldn't see his face, but I could hear in his voice that he had shifted right back into being affable, as efficiently as a kaleidoscope being twisted into place to change the image.

"Actually, it's Dr. Smithe-Canfield I need."

I blinked in surprise, startled into looking back up. "Me?"

Dr. Shangrit's gaze was kind and steady across the table. "I'm putting together a small group to do some field research in our Olympus Camp." Was it only my imagination, or did his smile tighten as he looked back at Rawley? "You know the one from the base documents, I presume. It's only a few miles away, but it would be an invaluable experience for those interested in plants and fungi and the like. I believe that's your field of study, is it not, Dr. Smithe-Canfield?"

"Y-yes," I stammered. "I'm a mycologist, specializing in mycorrhizal fungi."

Rawley shifted next to me, knee bumping against mine. "I'm afraid I won't be able to leave while we're just getting set up."

"That's all right. It would be a good fit for Dr. Smithe-Canfield's research, but not as much for your own, I'm afraid." Dr. Shangrit's tone was perfectly friendly, but I noticed some steel had entered into his tone. "You wouldn't have access to the machines you'd need for genetic engineering out in the field. But Dr. Smithe-Canfield could manage fine with some portable equipment for her research, couldn't you?"It was astonishing to hear someone speak to Rawley this way. Nothing Dr. Shangrit was saying was rude or demanding, but the simple *confidence* with which he spoke, as though assured that Rawley would have to concede, was breathtaking. It took me a few moments to gather myself well enough to answer. "Yes, I-I think so."

Dr. Shangrit waved over Mr. Coulson, the field guide I'd met on my first day on Earth. Far more gregarious than most of the introverted researchers, Coulson's booming Australian accent had quickly become a staple at any gathering, even in our short time here. This was his second expedition to Earth, despite looking to be only in his forties or so, meaning he was probably the second-most experienced person in the expedition, next to Dr. Shangrit.

Naturally, Rawley quietly loathed him, though he'd never explicitly said so. I felt Rawley's entire body tense as the man who was *truly* genial and not just pretending to be sauntered over. "More recruits for our expedition?" Coulson asked good-naturedly, clearly having been filled in already on the upcoming trip. "You're gonna love Olympus Camp. Real outdoor Earth experience, none of this indoor plumbing nonsense." He eyed Meridian hopefully, but when she remained completely stone-faced, he gave me a nod and a grin. I smiled back feebly.

"Only Dr. Smithe-Canfield will be joining us," Dr. Shangrit said, as if it had already been decided. "She's a mycologist."

Coulson scrunched his face as he reached forward to shake my hand. "God bless you."

I laughed, somewhat nervously, resisting the urge to glance over at Rawley. Perhaps if I followed Dr. Shangrit's lead and just pretended it was all settled, Rawley would have no choice but to go along with it. "That means I study fungi."

"Well, what a coincidence. I happen to be a pretty fun guy." Coulson waggled his eyebrows at me.

Normally I'd roll my eyes at such a pedestrian joke—believe me, I've heard every variation of "fun guy" puns that you can imagine!—but I found myself almost giddy with hope. This was it! This was my way out of the base, away from Rawley.

Freedom. I could almost taste it.

I playfully wagged a reprimanding finger at Coulson. "I'm going to have to demand that's the only bad pun about mushrooms you make around me, Mr. Coulson."

"Now that's a promise I can't make, I'm afraid—"

"Minerva stays with me."

Rawley's sharp tone severed the good-natured camaraderie being built, as we all fell into immediate, uncomfortable silence. For my part, I stared at the floor, partly embarrassed at causing a scene, but mostly feeling foolish for having hoped, for even one second, that I might catch a glimpse of freedom.

Though my gaze was downcast, I could see Dr. Shangrit and Coulson exchanging glances. The affable Australian was the first one to speak up. "Don't worry, mate. We'll get her back to you in one piece."

Despite his friendly tone—or rather, because of it—I flinched, knowing Rawley would take it as a challenge. He smiled thinly. "You don't know my fiancé, but she's chronically clumsy. If I let her out into the forest, she'll at the very least sprain her ankle and at worst get distracted by a field guide and walk straight off a cliff."

Rawley sounded like he was joking, poking gentle fun at me, but a chill ran through me at the words. I knew what he was doing. He was setting the stage, so when I inevitably came across some terrible fate, it would be well-established that I was accident-prone and that I must have brought it upon myself.

"Better to keep her here," Rawley continued, gripping my upper arm tightly, "where I can keep an eye on her."

I thought that would be the end of it until Dr. Shangrit cleared his throat—so quietly that at first I scarcely heard him, though he drew the table's attention as if he'd just let off an atomic fart.[4] Even Rawley had to pause midway through leaving, because one simply did not walk out on the universe's premier geologist.

"It's difficult, you see," said the doctor in his quiet but firm voice. "We can guess at the samples that would most benefit Dr. Smithe-Canfield's research, but it would be much more efficient to have her there to select the samples for herself. And we wouldn't want to stall the progress that we all came here to achieve, would we?"

Rawley hesitated; I could tell he desperately wanted to argue but couldn't come up with a plausible excuse.

Dr. Shangrit continued, "We will, naturally, have a full security detail accompanying us. And I will be a particular companion to Professor Smithe-Canfield, if that will put your mind at ease."

A long stretch of silence passed, in which I stayed completely still, scarcely daring to breathe.

"*Dr.* Smithe-Canfield," Rawley said at last. At Dr. Shangrit's blank expression, he continued, "She's only ever worked in her mother's laboratory. Never published academically or taught at a university."

It was a rude point to get stuck on, but I didn't much care, since I knew what it meant: Rawley was conceding a reluctant defeat, but he didn't want me to escape wholly unscathed. He wanted to get in

---

4. Not the most dignified comparison, granted, but I think you'd have to agree it's an effective metaphor.

one last parting shot, one last humiliation, since he felt that I was responsible for this very public loss of face on his part.

I tried my best to quell my smile, to not look too ebullient, for fear of encouraging some greater retaliation. Rawley turned me to face him, holding on to my shoulders in a grip that was unnecessarily tight as he looked deep into my eyes. "Be careful out there, Minerva. If anything were to happen to you, I would never stop looking for you."

The words sounded banal enough on the surface, maybe even romantic, but I understood them for the true threat they were. It was no effort, now, not to smile. "It will only be a few nights, darling. You'll barely have time to miss me."

Dr. Shangrit's expedition was such a boon, such an incredible stroke of luck, that I was giddy for the rest of the day. I smiled more that morning than I had on any of the earlier days of the trip combined. I made small talk in the line at the canteen and even hummed to myself as I worked in the lab. Freedom was so close I could taste it. Everything had been set into motion perfectly, and not even Rawley could stop me now.

In retrospect, I suppose I was too free with my happiness, too careless with letting my excitement show. I ought to have known that my behavior would be a challenge to Rawley, like a matador waving a red flag in front of a bull and daring it to charge at me.[5] I suppose my happiness was intended as a taunt to him, even if I hadn't consciously chosen to behave that way. He'd tried so very hard to control me, to keep me under his thumb, and here I was, about to escape him, and there was nothing he could do to stop me!

Or so I thought.

I woke in the night, startled out of my sleep by a presence in my room. A man was standing next to my bed, looming over me.

Rawley.

Even in the dark, I knew it was him. I could feel the hatred emanating off his body.

Instinctively, I remained completely still. I suppose it was possible that he'd only come there to frighten me, but somehow I didn't think so. I sensed that he was warring with himself, deciding whether or not he should kill me right then. For a very long time, we had both known that day would come. The only real question that remained was, would it be today?

I don't know if he knew I was awake. I doubted he could see me any better than I could see him. Still, time slowed for a moment as we regarded each other unseeing, two nebulous figures in the dark. Watching. Waiting.

And then, just as silently as he'd come, he let himself out of the room.

---

5. I make reference here to the popular virtual reality game *Torero*, in which one attempts to outmaneuver a very angry bull. It's unclear if this game is as popular outside of Haven 3, so I may need to explain it to the Brethren.

I waited until I was certain he was gone before I stumbled out of bed and turned the lock on the door. It was likely a futile gesture, since I was certain I'd locked it before I'd gone to sleep, but I did so nonetheless. Then, sinking to the floor, I trembled, and wept, and wished with all my heart that my mother was there.

When I'd managed to calm myself again, I moved to my trunk, to the hidden compartment I'd hollowed out inside, and found the item that had been one of my last purchases before leaving Haven 3: a gun.

I was loath to own the thing, even more loath to use it, but it had seemed only practical to bring it with me if I were planning on forging a life on my own in the wild.

After my nighttime encounter with Rawley, I realized I might very well need to use it sooner rather than later. I put it in the pack I'd be taking with me to Olympus Camp, vowing to always keep it with me from here on out. Rawley had caught me without it tonight.

I would not make that same mistake again.

4

As soon as we left the gates of the base, it was as if a huge weight had been lifted off my shoulders. I didn't realize, until we were already well on the road, that I'd still been anticipating Rawley finding some way of ruining things, canceling the expedition or just prohibiting me from going. Whether it was Dr. Shangrit's ethos or some other factor that had caused Rawley to back down, I couldn't be sure. I knew there must be some strategy on his part in allowing me to leave on the expedition; we were constantly playing a game of nine-dimensional chess, my fiancé and I, and each of us was always striving to stay one step ahead of the other.

So, while I couldn't be certain why Rawley had allowed me to leave, I could be grateful for the reprieve. Freedom, true freedom, awaited me outside the base. I would be setting off into the wilderness before the expedition was through, but even now, I could talk freely. I could laugh. I could exist without the weight of his hateful, domineering presence pinning me down. Since my mother's death, the hasty engagement, and the long journey to Earth, I'd scarcely been allowed a moment to myself, and it had taken its toll. Among this smaller expedition group, I was free to make eye contact, to speak my opinion, even to laugh, without feeling Rawley's warning grip on my arm or seeing his glare warning me I was being too free, too familiar, too embarrassing.

As we made camp, Coulson took aside a few of the scientists, including myself and Dr. Shangrit, to explore the designated safe areas that had been assigned for our study. The camp itself would have a laser perimeter surrounding it to ensure we didn't receive any unwanted visitors in the form of wildlife; however, the same couldn't be said for the areas in which we intended to study—we were there to observe the same wildlife from which we would be sequestering ourselves at camp.

"Make no mistake," Coulson told us curtly. "There is a reason it is called *wild*life and *wild*erness. This land is rough and dangerous. There are species designed to kill you with just a touch. And that's only the plants."

"And the fungi," I chimed in cheerfully.

He frowned at me, clearly not liking being interrupted. "Like I said, plants."

It was my turn to frown back at him. "Oh, but fungi aren't plants. Although the symbiotic relationship between the two is utterly fascinating—"

Dr. Shangrit placed a gentle hand on my shoulder. "Perhaps we can let Coulson finish his presentation, and you can instruct him later on the different classifications within the fungus kingdom."

I'd thought this was basic knowledge that children learned in primary school, but apparently not. It was a little alarming, I must say, that a wilderness-survival guide didn't seem to know the difference between plants and fungi, but there was no time like the present to learn! "I'd be happy to share some of my findings, though we might need a few hours to really do it all justice."

"Can't wait,"[1] Coulson returned dryly, before jumping back into his speech about how everything in nature wanted to kill us. "As I was saying, out here in the wilderness, even the inanimate life-forms like plants and *fungi* are out to get you."

I appreciated his inclusion of fungi, really, but I had to grimace at the word choice. Inanimate? Was he joking? Some of the most sentient and communicative life-forms in the universe, *inanimate*? But a shake of head from Dr. Shangrit persuaded me to hold my tongue. I really had some work to do that evening to catch Mr. Coulson up on mycorrhizal relationships between so-called inanimate species, that was for certain!

Oblivious to my internal monologuing, Mr. Coulson continued, "And that doesn't even touch on the animals and whatnot living out here in the wild. Once was, they had a healthy respect and fear of humans, so that even a whiff of our scent might scare them off. But now? These beasties have been in charge for the last half a century. They don't know to fear us anymore, and that means we need to fear them. Even a cute little Bambi coming to sniff around your site might decide to trample over you or run you through with its antlers. So if you see anything, best to back away slowly and send off a flare with your radar signal, so I can come and extract you safely. Understand?"

I looked around for any sign of one of the animals Coulson had described. Living on Haven 3, the way Earth was spoken of, I'd assumed we'd have bears and deer and all kinds of wildlife on top of us all the time. So far, though, I hadn't seen anything. Well, unless one included that strange encounter I'd had on the grounds, where I'd felt so certain I was being watched. But I'd probably imagined that. Most likely.

---

1. I have to assume this was sarcasm, so . . . rude.

Still, I couldn't help but notice the particular phrasing Mr. Coulson had used in his description. "'Animals and whatnot living out here'?" I echoed. "You've already listed plants and fungi, so what else besides animals are meant to be living out here, exactly?"

Unlike my last interruption, when he'd seemed annoyed, Coulson leveled me with a devilish grin. "Caught that, did you? Tell you what, Doc. You tell me about your mushrooms, and I'll tell you about my Yowie. Tonight, at the campfire."

I had no idea what a Yowie was supposed to be, but if it meant I'd get to talk about toadstools, I'd agree to just about anything!

"It's a deal," I said, shaking his hand.

The next few hours were spent in pleasant research. You have no idea the vast array of fungi species found in this mountainous, rocky climate—it was unlike anything I'd ever seen in the hothouses on Haven 3, I'll tell you that! Within a few hours, I'd spotted a beautiful artist's conk,[2] a fruitful yield of porcini,[3] and a small crop of lovely *Amanita muscaria*. And if that's got you excited, I haven't even mentioned the absolutely stunning varieties of mold I was able to collect.

However, I have been informed, rather rudely, by one of the Brethren that "no one wants to hear about weird mushrooms." I would be more offended by the note, I suppose, but recalling the restless irritation that most of the Brethren of Blood exhibited during

---

2. *Ganoderma applanatum*

3. *Boletus edulis*

this part of my story, I feel I must concede that it doesn't seem to be a topic generally interesting to many people.

So I will skip ahead a little, to when the action picks up again.

True to his word, Dr. Shangrit remained as a companion to me through most of the expedition, though he was a much more lenient guardian than Rawley or any of his goons. His was such a gentle, unassuming presence, in fact, that I nearly forgot about him as I went about my work—freely, without anyone hampering or criticizing me!—until the end of the day.

He cleared his throat. "Tell me, Dr. Smithe-Canfield, how are you finding Earth?"

I looked around at the bright blue of the sky and the greens and reds of the foliage, unlike anything I'd seen in any of the Havens. I found myself wishing I were living another life—one where I'd never met Rawley and I really was just here on an expedition to study mushrooms and their variations. How happy I would have been, surrounded by my fungi and my books. I supposed I would still be achieving that outcome, once I set out on my own, but for the first time I realized I would miss the companionship of my little group of like-minded researchers, here for the love of knowledge. "It's lovely. I've seen images, of course, but nothing can quite prepare one for the reality of it."

He tsked his agreement, so I asked him, "It's not your first time, I've heard?"

"My third, and final. I have been very lucky to make so many expeditions, but the travel and time does take its toll."

"Ah, yes. I can imagine. I'm not looking forward to the return journey."

My return journey would be quite a different experience, since I would be on a smuggler's ship instead of an official charter vessel, but there was no need to mention that.

I was looking down at my feet as I made my reply to ensure I didn't stumble over a dense growth of tree roots, but when I glanced back up at Dr. Shangrit, I was surprised to find him watching me with a concerned, penetrating gaze.

My smile faltered, then broadened—overcorrecting because I feared I had somehow said too much and warned him of my plans. Dr. Shangrit didn't smile back at me, though his gaze softened. "I was acquainted with your mother, you know."

"Oh?" I hadn't known that, actually, and for some reason the thought made a lump rise in my throat.

"An uncommonly intelligent, moral woman. She is very missed."

The words hung between us, and in that moment, looking into Dr. Shangrit's eyes, I understood what he was trying to tell me. That I had a friend in him, if I needed it. That he would try to find a way to help and protect me if he could.

For that moment, too, I considered it. It would be such a relief to have a friend, someone I could trust. Someone who would do for me what my mother would have done, had she been able.

But as I looked into Dr. Shangrit's kind face, I knew that while he, like my mother, meant well, he had no true conception what a man like Rawley was capable of. My mother had underestimated him, and she had died for it. I could not let the same happen to Dr. Shangrit.

"That's very kind of you to say," I told him, and I meant it. But I didn't quite meet his gaze. Instead, I determined that I would keep my distance from him for the rest of the trip, until I at last made my escape.

5

As per Coulson's instructions, we returned to the camp well before dusk, to avoid all those allegedly scary beasties lurking in the dark. At nighttime, it felt far more likely that ravenous animals really were just lurking around the next corner, hiding in the shadows, waiting to pounce. I have to admit, in my excitement to escape Rawley, I hadn't considered just how frightening it might be, being encamped deep in the dark woods, the sound of wild creatures filling the night around us.

It didn't help that the others in Olympus Camp seemed to sense my fear. They detoured every attempt I made to talk about fungi to instead take turns telling tales of poisonous snakes that had slithered into tents, run-ins with bobcats, and spiders the size of a grown man's hand. It was all in good fun, though I still missed the company of Dr. Shangrit; he had turned in early for the night, but I sensed that he would have put an end to this kind of talk if he'd remained at the campfire. Dr. Shangrit did not strike me as the sort of man who feared the unknown things that went bump in the night.

Just when I thought the group had run out of deadly species with which to tease me, Coulson met my gaze across the fire, eyes glinting with mischief as he took a long swig of his beer. "Wildcats, spiders, snakes—they're all nasty beasts, I reckon. But none can hold a candle to the Yowie."

He spoke with an impressive hush to his voice, and I might have been suckered in, if the name hadn't caused me to involuntarily smile. It sounded like something made up by a toddler with a speech defect.[1] "A Yowie? Really, Mr. Coulson, you'll have to do better than that if you want to frighten me."

Coulson looked momentarily taken aback by my lack of awe and fear, but he soon recovered. "Laugh all you like, *Dr.* Smithe-Canfield"—he made this emphasis on my name with a slightly mocking tone, pointing out my unnecessary formality—"but the Yowie has its roots going all the way back to the nineteenth century in my ancestral land, Australia."

Giving me the term's history was one sure way to garner my interest, so I obligingly shut my mouth and listened, even though I remained skeptical.

"The aboriginals used to tell stories of the Yō-wī, a spirit that haunted the Earth. But the Yowie was no spirit—it was a living creature, part man and part beast. It lived in the Australian outback, only rarely coming into contact with man. Stories ranged from the Yowies being gentle and innocent to being wild and violent." He let the silence hang for a moment before locking onto my gaze. "And a few weeks ago, I saw one. Here."

---

1. "Mama, I bumped my knee and now I have a yowie," for example. (I believe this is a fairly close approximation of how toddlers speak.)

He was a good storyteller, I would give him that, but I was hardly impressed by such a far-fetched plot twist. "It migrated here, to the American Rocky Mountains, did it? How clever this wild man-beast is. I suppose it learned how to carve a canoe? Build a plane? Or, I'm sorry, can Yowies sprout wings and fly?"

Coulson ignored my obvious sarcasm—at least, I assumed he was ignoring me; it was possible he was too unintelligent to understand that I was making a jest at his expense. (I didn't actually believe the Yowie capable of spontaneous flight, you see, nor any of the rest of what I had just said, in case that was unclear.[2]) Either way, he continued on as if I hadn't spoken: "The Americas have their own legends about a Yowie-like creature. Some called him Bigfoot, some called him Sasquatch."

I pressed my lips into a line, raising an unimpressed eyebrow. These names all sounded like bogeymen from children's stories. Bigfoot? Really? What was supposed to be so terrifying about this creature, pray tell? That it had to order larger-than-normal shoes?

With what struck me as practiced indifference, Coulson pulled out his knife and began carving along the edge of a branch. "The thing I saw was big—bigger than any man I've ever laid eyes on, even on

---

2. Note to self: I will have to make sure the Brethren understand I am being facetious here with my delivery. They really don't seem to do sarcasm.

Haven 2.[3] Covered in dark hair, thick as a wolf's. Eyes that gleamed in the dark."

Despite myself, I was intrigued by the evocative picture he painted. "Where did you see it?"

"A campsite about a mile or so from here, where we were collecting algae. It was a night not so different from this one. We set up camp, ate dinner, talked around the fire. I must have had one too many beers, though, because in the middle of the night, sure enough, nature called."

Unfamiliar with the phrase, it took me a moment to infer that he'd needed to urinate, not that the forest had literally *called* to him. I nodded, encouraging him to go on.

"I figured we had a good fire going, men on watch, a laser perimeter set up so nothing could breach the camp without us noticing, so it would be safe enough to step outside my tent and take a piss."

Normally I might have wrinkled my nose at such an unsavory phrase, but something in Coulson's tone had finally caught me up in the spirit of the tale. I felt like I had as a child, reading through my collection of ghost stories, terrified of what I was about to encounter but also unable to stop myself from turning the next page. "And?"

"There I am, standing with my johnson in my hand, minding my own business, when I hear a shuffling in the underbrush. Well, it

---

3. The tallest man on record in Haven 2 was modified to be eight feet tall, as it was believed to give him an advantage in athletic competitions. His seventeen gold medals, in various Intergalactic Olympic events, certainly seems to suggest this to be true, though I heard anecdotally (never confirmed) that he had an enormously difficult time with his digestive tract.

spooks me good, but I'm laughing at myself, expecting to see a rabbit or something hop out. I'm peering forward, trying to see what it is.

"Then all of a sudden, I sense something in my peripheral vision. Mind you, nothing moved that I could see, I don't hear a single sound, but I *feel* something there, watching me. So I turn my head, slowly, slowly, and there it is. Big. Strong. Not a man, I clock that right away, but something else. Something smart but wild. All I can really make out are its eyes, almost human. Watching me."

Somewhere in the story, and I'm not quite sure where, I'd begun to hold my breath, waiting to hear what would happen next. "What did it do?"

"Nothing. Fucker just stared at me, and I was scared too shitless to do anything but stare back at it. Then it blended back into the dark, and I turned tail and ran as fast as I could back into my tent. You better believe, I didn't sleep another wink that night. And as I'm lying there awake, I realize the scariest thing isn't how big it is or how quietly it can move. It's not even how it somehow managed to get through the perimeter without triggering the alarm. It's that trick it pulled at the beginning—distracting me by rustling something ahead of me, so I wouldn't be paying attention to it coming up beside me. That Yowie isn't just big and mean and wild. It's smart, too."

I shuddered, then conceded with a small smile and nod of my head that he'd managed to spook me. "Well told, Mr. Coulson. It sounds like you were certainly lucky to have lived to tell the tale."

The others also chimed in with their appreciation for the story, but Coulson didn't take his eyes off me. He grinned, leaning in closer and lowering his voice so only I could hear what he had to say next. "I could always sleep in your tent tonight, if you're too scared to stay there on your own."

I blinked at him, frowning. The concern was touching, I suppose, though wholly unnecessary. "Oh, I'm not scared. It was a good story, but I'm not too frightened to sleep on my own. Thank you for the offer, though."

Coulson just stared at me for a long moment before sighing. "Well, all right then." And he turned and didn't speak directly to me again for the rest of the night.

Strange. I suppose I didn't show quite as much fear at his monster story as he would have hoped. I could have offered him a few pointers on how to make it scarier, but I didn't want to rub salt in the open wound, so to speak, and so shortly afterward, I excused myself to go to bed.

To my surprise, I continued thinking about Coulson's story as I readied myself for bed. It was the sort of tale that gave me a good thrill as it was told, but it didn't seem like it would have any lasting effects. I knew that Coulson was trying to initiate the "new kid," that he would exaggerate whatever may or may not have happened to him in the woods to try to get under my skin. Added to that the knowledge that he had admitted himself he'd had too much to drink with dinner the night of the alleged incident, and it was easy enough to dismiss his story altogether.

Easy enough to dismiss, that is, when I was still sitting at the campfire, surrounded by my colleagues, with a clear distinction between our civilized company and the wilderness beyond us. Less easy to dismiss, I discovered, when I was on my own in my tent—altogether too close to the apparently penatrable perimeter of the camp for my liking.

I jumped at every sound, felt my heart lurch with every boot crunching across gravel and every animal shrieking from the darkness. "You are being ridiculous," I told myself exasperatedly as I brushed out my hair. The only thing to do about my nerves was to put out the light and go to sleep as soon as possible, before the rest of the camp dimmed and I could no longer console myself with the comfort of others around me, awake and going about their business.

This plan worked well enough, until I woke sometime in the middle of the night with a bladder ready to burst.

I did my best to ignore it, I really did. I rolled this way and that. I attempted a variety of sleeping positions, counted backward from one hundred, even tried imagining a cow.[4] When it became clear that there was no getting around it and that I would have to pee, and soon, I tried to convince myself to simply stay in the safety of my tent and pee on the floor. It was mostly dirt and rock, after all, and likely some other creature had done the same at some point.

But I was not some barbaric animal that could just relieve myself inside of my own quarters, however temporary. There was also the issue of the urine's smell, which would doubtless permeate all of my things.

No, there was nothing else to be done about it. I would have to leave my tent and step out into the woods.

There were many perfectly reasonable things I reminded myself of as I did so. The laser perimeter around the campsite. The armed guards patrolling said perimeter. My tent being only a few feet away from where I was currently squatting in the underbrush. All things

---

4. In hindsight, I recognize this is the colloquial advice given to get rid of hiccups, but I was quite desperate in the moment.

considered, though, what would my tent *really* do to protect me if a wild, man-eating creature decided he wanted to kill me?

But then, that wasn't a particularly helpful train of thought, as it turned out.

I took comfort in the fact that I'd worn a billowing white nightgown. They'd recently come back into fashion on Haven 3, though I've since been informed by the Brethren that this is not the case in other settlements. To your own detriment, I say! Not only are loose, billowing nightgowns incredibly comfortable nightwear, but as an added bonus, they also allow for relative ease should one find oneself needing to discreetly squat and pee in the forest.[5]

As I did my business, so to speak, I decided to sing the first song that came to mind: "Good King Wenceslas." Apparently, it's a tune that has gone out of fashion in most settlements much like my beloved nightgown. However, it was one I'd sung as part of my madrigal ensemble while still in the academy.[6] Even *I* didn't sing it much in my day-to-day life, but for the moment, it seemed the best tune to serve the specific purpose I had for it—namely, something to dispel my fear of the dark open forest surrounding me. Many a tale has begun with someone being snatched from a dark forest and gobbled up by something dark and fearsome, but I had yet to hear any stories of people being attacked while singing "Good King Wenceslas." It was such a cheery tune that

---

5. An added bonus that I have yet to see in any of the promotional materials. Should I make it back to Haven 3, I shall have to suggest this as a strong marketing strategy for the product.

6. What larks we had! But the Brethren have assured me—quite rudely, I must say—they are even less interested in hearing about my madrigal ensemble than they are in hearing about my mushrooms.

it seemed impossible anything bad could happen while it was being sung, and thus, I trusted it to keep me safe.[7]

I had nearly finished both song and bodily function when I heard it: the sound of a branch cracking in the dense wilderness, not far from me.

I froze, staring into the dark, both willing myself to see something (if *something* were there) and willing myself, more ideally, to see *nothing* there (since, by the same logic, that would mean there was nothing to see).

The silence stretched on, but it was not a comforting silence. It was a weighted, heavy silence, punctuated by the uncanny sensation that something, or someone, was watching me.

The feeling was so marked that I couldn't even talk myself out of it or tell myself it was only my imagination. I swallowed, my throat thickening with fear. "Mr. Coulson," I tried to say sternly, though it came out as more of a strangled whisper. "If that's you, I'm going to be terribly cross."

No reply. A part of me was hoping that it was Coulson, since if this turned out to be only a prank, I would be irritated but at least I would be safe. But the longer the silence stretched out, the more I realized, with a sinking heart, that it couldn't be Coulson; the man didn't have the intelligence, or the capacity for cruelty, to draw out my terror for so long.

"Mr. Yowie?" I tried this time, too frightened to feel as ridiculous as I probably ought to have for saying such a thing. "If that's you, and you have any sense of decency, please don't show yourself to me. I don't

---

7. I know, I know, not the most logical train of thought, but it was late, and I was desperate to "heed the call of nature," as Mr. Lowry might say.

want to see you. I don't want to know you're there. I just want to go back to my tent."

Silence. Nothing moved in the wilderness. Nothing made itself known to me. Taking this as a confirmation from the Yowie, I rose to stand and hurried back to my tent, my heart pounding long after I'd closed the flap behind me.

6

I n the morning, I felt like a real ninny and was grateful no one
had seen me racing back from the woods like my feet were on fire.
With the sun shining and birds singing in the trees overhead, I realized
that Coulson really must have just been having fun at my expense. At
least seeing how hungover and irritable he was at breakfast satisfied my
wounded pride a little.

We would be leaving Olympus Camp in only a few days; I was
running out of time to make my preparations. I'd been putting it off
for too long, but now was as good a time as any to disappear into the
forest. I needed to distribute more supplies, so I could come back and
collect them after the expedition had moved out. Clearing my throat,
I made my excuses. "I think I'll head out first thing." No one really
seemed to be paying that much attention to me, but I felt compelled

to continue, nonetheless. "I need to get more of the true blusher,[1] just in case I've accidentally gathered some false."[2]

"Would you like some company? I'd be happy to join you if you don't mind waiting a few minutes," Dr. Shangrit offered.

That outcome I had not anticipated. Curse the nice old man and his manners! "Oh, no," I demurred, "you've just sat down to breakfast, and I wouldn't want to rush you."

"It's no bother. I wouldn't mind a brisk morning walk."

If Dr. Shangrit came along with me, there would be no point in going at all. I flushed, blurting out the first thing that came to mind. "Only, you see, I have some personal business I wanted to attend to on my own. In the woods." I gestured behind me, in case Dr. Shangrit somehow didn't know what the woods were.

The entire table fell silent as everyone stared at me. There were obvious connotations to what it was that I might need to be doing on my own out in the woods, but my desperation was such that I didn't mind if people jumped to the wrong conclusions, even if they were *those* conclusions.

Dr. Shangrit blinked at me. "Oh, yes, my dear. Do what you must."

Coulson perked up from his hangover, apparently finding my discomfort irresistibly funny. "Stay within shouting distance," he told me through a mouthful of eggs. "So patrol can find you if you run into any, you know, trouble."

I hurried from the commissary tent, not wanting to give him the chance to elaborate. I was overcompensating a bit, considering the other researchers could not have cared less if I started out early that

---

1. *Amanita rubescens*

2. *Amanita pantherina*

morning or not, but I didn't want there to be anything suspicious or out of the ordinary about my behavior. Nothing that would get back to Rawley. Just silly, scatterbrained Mina "heeding the call of nature." Nothing to see here, folks!

Obtaining my bag from my tent, I continued my quick pace out into the woods. I wouldn't go beyond the perimeter—not only to keep myself safe, but also to keep from tripping an alarm and bringing any more scrutiny to my activities. With all luck, by the time anyone realized there had been anything unusual about my behavior on this excursion, it would be far too late.

The trick to finding the right place to store the pack would be to find someplace no one else would think to look, but also somewhere that would be easy for me to find once I retraced my steps. I decided on a hollowed-out tree trunk I remembered seeing down by the stream, and I deposited the bag quickly, turning to hurry back to camp so no one would mark that my absence had been any longer than necessary.

No sooner had I done so than I heard a distinct thud in the grass behind me. I was not as frightened as I had been the night before, but my senses were still on high alert, and I let out a not-very-ladylike shout as I whirled around. "Who's there?"

Only silence met me. Warily, I scanned the surrounding area for a long moment before looking down to see what could have caused the thunk. My eyes widened.

It was a large stone, about the size of my palm, that had been completely smoothed so that it was almost soft when I picked it up. It was a distinct gray-blue color and very beautiful. Nonetheless, I looked about myself warily once more. "Is someone there?"

The question was somewhat rhetorical, since I could think of no other explanation for how a perfectly smooth stone could have landed in the grass right behind me. But then, neither could I fathom why someone would toss a rock at me and remain hidden. As far as pranks went, this one was somewhat lacking.

Unless—was someone warning me? Letting me know they'd seen me drop off the pack? But I couldn't fathom why anyone would do that, either; if someone wanted to talk me out of my plan, why not just come out and speak to me? And if they were going to tell Rawley what I was up to, it seemed strange to prematurely tip their hand.

Still uneasy, I bent down, never taking my eyes off the tree line, and put the rock back where I'd found it before slowly retreating toward the camp.

In the hours since I'd had my encounter, with whatever it had been, out in the forest, I'd managed to convince myself of any number of plausible explanations for that rock falling at my feet.[3] Yet being the rationalist that I am, I couldn't suppress the most likely explanation: that someone in the camp had somehow deduced my plan and was warning me that they were on to me.

I'd hoped to use the full week to discreetly smuggle out my supplies to various locations around the campsite. Now it seemed prudent to move my timeline forward considerably.

I would need to be ready to leave civilization—by that night.

Not wanting to indicate that anything was amiss, especially at this crucial moment, I went about my daily tasks as usual, and with relish. I did my assigned chores; I collected some absolutely gorgeous samples

---

3. My particular favorite theory was that some large bird had been flying overhead and accidentally dropped the stone at my feet. Better than at my head, eh, Aeschylus?

in the field; I played cards with the group and told stories over dinner. As much as my time on Earth had been filled with terror and torment, out here, free from the threat of Rawley, I truly had enjoyed my time. I wished it didn't have to end, though I knew it was for the best. Still, I savored each moment on this last day, knowing I would miss this camaraderie once I was on my own.

The responsible thing to do that night would have been to make some excuse, go to bed early, and get a sound night of sleep so I could awake refreshed the next morning, ready to take on my new life alone in the wild. But I was also keenly aware that this would be my last night of civilization, conversation, and companionship. Soon I would be forging out into the wilderness, with only my own company and a few fictional companions stored away in my carefully hidden packs to ward off loneliness and perhaps even insanity in the weeks I would be alone.

So, I indulged myself that night. I sat up late with Dr. Shangrit and Coulson and the others, discussing life and the universe and politics and music. And yes, as you may have gathered from that list of conversation topics, there was a great deal of alcohol involved. I wouldn't be taking any with me into the wilderness as it might compromise my reasoning capabilities, so I figured it was my duty to indulge one last time. But, since in vino veritas,[4] I determined to exercise some restraint. Nevertheless, I somehow wound up stumbling toward my tent and falling into a blissful, boozy sleep.

---

4. In wine there is truth. Or as my mother always said, "Full glass, loose tongue."

A few hours later, I awoke to the sounds of screaming and thrashing. Mangled shouts of horror, and then silence—all of this punctuated by the low, persistent thrum of the alarm and the intermittent pulse of the red emergency lights.

Something had breached the camp.

7

Even inebriated as I was, I was instantly on high alert, especially since the sounds of shouting, running, and near pandemonium were only increasing, not decreasing. My first thought was that I should just stay inside the tent, hide from whatever was causing so much chaos—since, as the Brethren have likely already discerned, my skills were much better suited to hiding than fighting.

But as the screams continued—heightened, even—my alcohol-addled imagination began to get the better of me. What if a wild animal had breached the camp? A bobcat or a boar or something of that sort? Surely that would be the only thing that could cause so much terror. And if that were the case, my flimsy tent would offer no protection. Hiding would do no good, either, since the creature would be able to smell me out.

No, better to seek out the security team, with their big muscles and even bigger guns. Most likely, they were already en route to intercept the threat, whatever it might be, and I was one of the few idiots still cowering in bed, too frightened to move.

That decided, I ran. Barefoot, in my rumpled clothes from the day before, hair askew—none of it mattered, so long as I didn't get eaten by a mountain lion. I did at least think to stop and pull my gun out of hiding. I debated about the sense in this, since it might raise unwanted questions about why I would have such a thing in my possession when I was meant to be a hapless field researcher. But better that, I figured, than coming face-to-face with a wild, man-eating animal and having my gun safely tucked away in my trunk.

It was madness outside, people running this way and that, eradicating my quiet hope that this was all just a drill. "What's happening?" I tried to ask not one but three men, all of whom shoved past me—either away or toward something, it was impossible to say—without answering.[1] Overhead, the laser perimeter crackled, a gentle reassurance that it was unbreached. Only, maybe not so reassuring, suspecting as I did that whatever was causing this mayhem hadn't torn its way through but slipped in, undetected.

Then I heard it—a bloodcurdling roar, echoing through the dark night.

Heart hammering in my chest, I twisted this way and that, trying to discern where the sound had originated. But the pulsing red of the alarms was the only light in the otherwise nearly pitch-black night, and there were bodies running in both directions, making it impossible to tell where the danger lay.

"There it is!" someone shouted, and several men turned to fire into the tree line.

I covered my ears, my eyes searching the dark forest canopy for the shape of whatever they were firing at. I could see nothing. "What's

---

1. Quite rude, really.

happening?" I screamed. Not the most sensical thing I've ever done, I know, to shout at the top of my lungs when we were under attack from some unseen force, but I was terrified, sleep addled, and still a little drunk.

At last the shots began to die down, one or two last stragglers asserting themselves before all was silent. As a collective whole, the group held our breath, our eyes scanning for any sign of movement.

And then something emerged from the woods—something big and loud and angry, a bulky, hairy shadow that roared and charged straight for us. A few men shot at it, but either they missed or the creature was impervious to harm, and soon all the men around me were screaming, running, and crashing into each other in their haste to escape. "Sasquatch!" they shouted, and the word went up like wildfire around the camp, echoing to the far reaches. The creature got hold of one of the men and dragged him back into the shadows; the soldier screamed, cried for help, then all at once, fell silent.

If I hadn't been in such mortal terror, I might have been chagrined at being proven so wrong: There could be no other explanation for that monstrous, almost demonic figure that had appeared from the shadows. The Yowie was *real*.

For my own part, I did not run, I did not scream. I merely backed slowly away, eyes wide, afraid to blink. Afraid to draw any attention to myself, afraid to close my eyes for even a moment, for fear of what I might see when I opened them again. I had this idea—senseless even in the chaos—that I could just slip away, unnoticed, back into my tent, and crawl into my bunk while hell broke loose.

Then quite suddenly, there was no one left around me. I was alone out in the opening between the tents, my own ragged breath the only sound filling the air. Even the alarm had gone inexplicably silent, though the red warning light continued to flash, blinding me with its intermittent bright blare. I raised my hand to block it, heart racing as I tried to make sense of the darkness, the quiet.

Something heavy dropped to the ground in front of me. I jumped, giving out a sharp cry that surprised even me in its forcefulness. "Hey!" Then, as the sweeping red light illuminated the figure in front of me, I blinked in surprise.

It was not, I could see now, an animal. It was a *man*—but no one I had seen around the camp, and thus no one who was part of our expedition. Even amidst my terror, I'm afraid I gloated to myself in the brief millisecond it took me to process this information, because of course the idea of some cryptid haunting the woods was preposterous, and I'd been correct on insisting so at the campfire the previous night! But by the next millisecond, any triumph faded as I really took in what I was seeing. I will catalog it here, to the best of my memory, as any self-respecting scientist would:

A man, enormous in both height and body composition. Approximately six feet, five inches. Broad, with massive limbs the size of tree trunks. Hair long, near down to his waist, and tangled, filled with bits of branches. Impossible to tell the color in the intensity of the red light. Same for his thick beard, which reached his pectorals. Around his head and shoulders he wore a thick bearskin, which perhaps accounted for the misperception that he was an animalistic creature, though underneath, for the record, he was completely naked. Further, in addition to the bearskin he wore, he also had hair on his arms and chest and legs, which likely contributed to the confusion; most men (on Haven 3, at least) had genetically bred out body hair for aesthetic purposes in the last few generations, so it was a jarring sight to see. Bright eyes peered out of an impressive nest of facial hair.

And those eyes were rooted on *me*.

His stare was so intense that I fell back a step, swallowing heavily. He—whoever this man was—was *staring* at me. No, I'm sorry, that isn't the right word. I can't think of one to accurately convey what was happening in that moment. Glaring almost seems closest? Although that implies some level of anger or hostility, and there was none of that. But it was that same level of concentration channeled into some other emotion—though that, too, felt difficult to name. Curiosity, I think, would probably come closest, along with (and believe me when I say, this surprised no one more than it did myself) no little amount of what appeared to be sexual desire. He was, if you'll recall, completely naked, and it was . . . evident.

A moment passed in which he stared, and I stared back, too stunned to do much more now that I'd come face-to-face with this wildman. His features pulsed under the bright red light. My own, I supposed, did the same. Then he advanced toward me, shoulders raised, body big and imposing—testing me, I think—before at last coming to a stop directly before me.

All at once, I remembered the gun tucked into my waistband, and I reached for it with trembling hands. I don't think I meant to use it, but instinct took over. I very much did not want to be dragged off screaming into the forest or . . . whatever else this man intended to do with me. Without appearing the slightest bit frightened, the wildman batted the gun out of my hands with little effort, knocking it into the dirt, where it skidded and disappeared underneath a jeep.

"Oh, drat!" I hadn't meant to speak, but it was going to be really irritating, trying to find that thing before anyone else did. Or worse, starting my trek into the wilderness in the morning without any weapon. The wildman tilted his head at me, and without thinking, I scowled back at him, my tone chastising. "I really needed that!"

Then I remembered that I was face-to-face with this wildman, who might very well kill me and eat my brains or something horrid like that, and feeling put out about the inconvenience of the gun began to feel silly. I fell a step back, and the wildman followed, keen, it seemed, to maintain our overly close proximity. He was near enough that I could smell his aroma—not as bad as one might think, all things considered—and it seemed only logical he could do the same for me.

"I usually freshen up more before I go to bed," I heard myself saying to him. "But I may have had one too many last night, so. You know how it goes." Looking at his blank face, I saw that perhaps he did *not* know how it goes. I gestured toward my mouth. "That's the, um, smell on my breath. Alcohol. It's quite fun going down but not so much, you know, afterward."

Good God, why was I saying all of these things to this man? Even now, I have no idea. Strange as it seems, I felt I could prolong this stalemate between us by continuing to babble. So far he hadn't knocked me unconscious, like all the people around me, after all, so maybe there was something to my instinct to talk instead of scream at the top of my lungs. In fact, I felt quite certain that if I didn't keep talking, I *would* be screaming at the top of my lungs.

"Are you, um, from around here?" I motioned to the dense wilderness in the shadows beyond us. "I'm assuming you must come from nearby because of the whole—" I gestured to his nakedness, then realized that might cause some offense. "Not that I mind! I just wasn't aware anyone else had a scheduled expedition? It takes so many permits and things, you know, that I thought we would have known if someone else was here. But, here *you* are, so . . . Oh."

Somehow amidst my babbling, I'd backed myself into a corner, up against the hard surface of one of the jeeps. Now that there was nowhere to go, the wildman's closeness felt all the more invasive, his eyes even more disconcerting up close. In the darkness, it was hard to tell their color for certain, but they were rimmed with the darkest, most beautiful eyelashes I'd ever seen.[2] For a moment, I felt almost hypnotized, unable to look away or move or breathe, not even when he leaned in close enough to touch me.

He dragged his nose along the length of my face, stopping as he reached my hairline. Grabbing a fistful of my dark hair (none too gently, I might add), he pulled me toward him, fixing his nose to the top of my head and inhaling deeply.

"Oh," I said again, for lack of anything better to say. "I'd, um, appreciate a little space, if you wouldn't—"

Over his shoulder, I saw a group of dark-clad soldiers approaching stealthily. I tried not to do anything to give them away, but the wildman must have felt me tense, or maybe his ears were trained well enough to hear them approaching. Either way, he turned to face them, spreading his arms and pushing back against me. Trying to crush me, I thought, as I began to panic and thrash against him, though later I reflected he probably thought he was protecting me.

Either way, he was too late—too distracted by me to get away in time. The soldiers tased the wildman, collapsing that great, massive body into a jerking, twitching heap on the ground. Despite my terror, it was horrid to watch. "Stop it," I begged them. "Surely there's another way—"

There was, apparently. At closer range, the soldiers injected something into the wildman's neck. I watched those dark-lashed eyes—still fastened on me—as they blinked, blinked, blinked, then closed.

---

2. Especially impressive, considering all the genetic modifications I'd witnessed in my lifetime!

8

There was no sneaking off into the shadows after that. Because of my encounter with the wildman, I was suddenly the center of attention. Those who weren't assessing my welfare and taking my vitals were demanding answers about the wildman, what he'd said, what he'd wanted, where he'd come from.

I had to repeat several times that he hadn't harmed me in any way, that I had not so much as a scratch on me. Apparently the others who had encountered him that night had all suffered broken bones or concussions, or both. I didn't know why he hadn't done the same to me, and I repeated this numbly to everyone who asked. *I didn't know, I didn't know.*

"You're very lucky," one medic informed me gravely, and I found myself nodding along.

But the more I thought about it, the more that didn't sit right with me. Despite the chaos that he'd caused in the camp, I'd sensed no danger from the wildman myself. I didn't know why that was, what separated me from the others, but I couldn't shake the instinct that the wildman had meant me no harm.

"Lucky," I repeated nonetheless, smiling shakily as I was given a cup of warm tea to help calm my nerves.

But as the early morning drew on and on, and more people came to ask me questions about what had happened, and more rumors began to circulate about my encounter with the wildman, I realized that "lucky" was the very opposite of what I was. Being singled out by the wildman had made me something of a celebrity, and this on the very night before I'd meant to make my escape.

Bugger all, it was inconvenient, that's what it was.

Camp was packed up quickly, and we made a hasty return to the base, with the tranquilized wildman in tow. There was no time to gather my hidden packs; I barely had time to get dressed before I was hustled into a vehicle and on my way . . . back to Rawley.

The man in question found me shortly after we returned. Another minor flurry had erupted back at the main camp as a new set of people marveled over the still-sedated wildman, then interrogated me to reveal everything I knew about him.

Forced to play the dutiful fiancé with so many people watching, Rawley kept his face blank as he approached me. For a moment, the two of us stared each other down, and I know it must have been only my imagination, but I felt as if he could tell, just looking at me, what I'd been planning to do.

Or maybe it was simpler than that. Maybe that furious loathing that flashed through his eyes had nothing to do with his ability to read my guilt, and more to do with his irritation that I should be singled out in this way, given any attention or praise. Keenly aware that I was the woman of the hour—the woman who had faced down the wildman and survived—Rawley embraced my stiff, unresponsive body.

"My darling girl," he murmured into my hair, loud enough for everyone to hear. "How lucky I am that you escaped unharmed. Whatever would I have done if anything happened to you?"

He took me in his arms, stroking my hair with unsettling gentleness, and it took everything in me not to recoil. "I never would have stopped looking for you," he said, once again loud enough for our audience. But the expression in his eyes was meant only for me, so that I alone could understand his true meaning.

Shivering, I remained immobile in his embrace, allowing him to hold me close as my mind whirred frantically, searching for a new plan, a new method of escape.

It might have all turned out differently if people had focused on my bravery in standing down the wildman or my cleverness in trying to distract him with my words.[1] However, after the security footage had been recovered and a group had gathered to watch it like it was the latest blockbuster, complete with popcorn,[2] the focus of the base turned to another aspect of my encounter with the intruder.

---

1. This hadn't been my intention, of course, but I was glad to take credit for this nervous impulse that had overtaken me.

2. Truly, I cannot stress enough how starved for entertainment our group had become. So far from the luxuries of our home settlements, our evenings mostly consisted of storytelling, card playing, and the occasional ribald limerick.

I grimaced as I saw myself projected onscreen, wondering why no one on the excursion had mentioned to me how unkempt my hair was. Goodness. Watching myself now, I tried to run a discreet hand through it without anyone noticing. Honestly, did it always look like that in the back . . . ?

Naturally, no one else watching the footage of my encounter with the wildman was as focused on my hair as I was;[3] they were all watching the massive naked man as he approached me, all muscles and hair and scars, even in the grainy video capture. I winced as I saw my mouth running, grateful that there was no sound, and squirmed at the laughter as the wildman grabbed a fistful of my hair and leaned in for a sniff.

Beside me, Rawley reached out to hold my knee. Others might have seen this as a gesture of comfort, but I understood it for what it was: A warning to stay still, stop drawing attention to myself.

"Looks like the Yowie has a crush," Coulson teased from across the room, giving me a good-natured wink to show his comment was in jest.

But as soon as the words had been uttered, they took on a new life in the room. "He *did* single her out," someone said, talking about me as if I weren't there. "Everyone else, he breaks a hand or a leg, but with her, he just sniffs her hair?"

I remembered the way the wildman had advanced on me, the long drag of his nose across my face and over my scalp. He'd attacked others in the camp, but with me he'd been almost gentle. Try as I might, I couldn't shake the feeling that he'd been coming for me. Claiming me. But that was absurd. Why single me out, of all people?

---

3. Presumably.

Others began to take up the idea, rewinding and pausing the video to discuss if the wildman's posture suggested he was attracted to me, others loudly dissecting the position of his feet. Some suggested that maybe it was just the scent of my shampoo that had drawn him in, since he'd sniffed my hair, and then demanded to know what brand I used. Blushing, I admitted that I used what had been given out at the dispensary, nothing special, and when pressed, further admitted that it had been a few days since I'd last washed it.

"I was on an excursion, you see," I grumbled, shifting some more. "And anyhow, it isn't good for the natural oils of the hair to wash it too frequently—"

Another harsh squeeze of my knee, and I fell silent.

"It must be something like that, though," insisted an especially unpleasant man who'd been giving me disgusted once-overs most of the night. "What else could be the appeal?"

It was one thing for me to ponder this question privately, but another to hear others speculate loudly and persistently as to why the wildman had chosen me.

"Most of the people on the expedition were men. Maybe he hasn't seen a woman in a long time . . . ?"

The idea that the wildman only reacted to me so strongly because he was starved for female companionship was repeated so often and so insistently that it was impossible for me not to take offense. Never in my life had I been mistaken for a great beauty, but it's not as if I had a third arm growing out of my forehead! However, as even my own fiancé did not come to my defense on the subject, it was at last agreed upon that the wildman should be introduced to Meridian.

I've already described Meridian's extraordinary beauty, so I don't need to do so again here. But just in case anyone thought I was being hyperbolic the last time, let me reassure you that I am not overstating

Meridian's attractiveness. You know how it's said that on Haven 3, the most divine women ever born are so plentiful that they all begin to blur together into an indistinguishable mass of beauty? Meridian's attractiveness was such that even in a sea of beauties, she still stood out above the rest. If the wildman had destroyed half of the camp just to get another glimpse of little old me, imagine what he might do to get closer to such a goddess.

Again, there was no way to avoid being insulted by this comparison, but from a scientific perspective, I could distance myself enough from my wounded pride to see that it made sense. In some ways it would even be better if the wildman spontaneously orgasmed at the sight of Meridian, because that, I assumed, would be enough of a distraction that I might be able to carry on with my plans to escape.

At the appointed hour, Meridian was brought to the wildman's cell. To avoid distraction, I—along with several others who would be observing and taking notes—would watch from a live vid-stream to see how the wildman responded to her presence.[4]

With no little interest, I watched as Meridian approached the glass cage containing the wildman. To everyone's surprise, after a few hours of futile pounding and raging against unyielding walls and doors, he'd become quite docile in captivity. No, docile wasn't quite the right word. Listless, perhaps. He was lying, inert, in one of the corners of the cell, his great, hairy, dirty, muscular body in repose. I remembered all too vividly the previous night, the terror of bones snapping and men screaming and that powerful body looming in front of me, his

---

4. Note, of course, that this is not my usual field of research, but I imagine I was given special license to participate because of my particular relationship with the wildman.

intense, almost-inhuman gaze. But here, now, lying so still, one could almost be lulled into believing he was harmless.

On the other side of the glass cell, Meridian made her approach. She was dressed plainly with no makeup, her hair pulled back. Hers was the type of beauty from which adornment detracts rather than enhances,[5] and she would be on best display, at her fullest powers of attraction, in this simple fashion.

When she came to a stop in front of the glass wall, the wildman raised his head. In the room from which we observed, there came a sort of collective holding of breath as we watched and waited to see what would happen. Unmoving, except for the ever-so-slight parting of her naturally plump lips, Meridian held the wildman's gaze.

A long moment passed as they stared at one another. Then the wildman lifted a haunch, scratched it, and lowered his head once more into a supine position. The message could not be clearer: He was, emphatically, uninterested.

"I don't know what happened," Meridian stammered afterward to those of us in the partitioned room. "We were looking at each other—really *looking*—and then he just . . ."

She glanced about the room, seeming almost desperate for one of us to provide some explanation of what had happened that could make sense to her. In all the time I'd known her, I'd never seen Meridian as anything but supremely confident, with the natural ease of someone accustomed to having all eyes on her, always. This interaction with the wildman had shaken her to her core, I could plainly see, and though I did feel some sympathy for her in that moment, another meaner, much shallower, and more petty part of me, could not help but gloat.

---

5. Yep.

"I could try contacting him again," I suggested, all innocence. If I'd thought it through, I would have reminded myself that the smart thing to do would be to turn the focus *away* from me. Alas, my stupid, fickle vanity could not pass up the opportunity. "Just by way of comparison. It may be that he's lost any sexual interest in captivity."

"That must be it," Meridian agreed eagerly, and several others chimed in the same. They were sort of annoyingly insistent, actually, that there was *no way* any man in his right mind would show more interest in me than her.

It was all I could do to keep from scowling. They didn't need to be *so* quick to agree. "Well, let's just see, shall we?"

I looked to Rawley for confirmation. He was staring at me, lost in thought, as if piecing some great puzzle together. At last he nodded. "All right."

Unlike Meridian, it was suggested that I take some time to freshen up, put on a more alluring outfit, perhaps some lipstick, but I refused. The wildman had first seen me, fresh-faced, disheveled, and in a rumpled nightdress. No need to put lipstick on the pig when he'd already been eying the hog.

I did, however, pause to run a hand over my hair, fix my glasses so they weren't crooked, and—when no one was looking—unbutton the top button of my blouse. I had integrity, but I was no saint.

Then, steeling myself, I entered the room.

9

It seemed to take the wildman forever to notice me. Perhaps he thought it was Meridian returning or one of the guards bringing rations. For one terrible moment, I feared I would get no reaction at all. Maybe that first encounter really had been some bizarre fluke, and the wildman would find me about as exciting as a lamp. How the others would all congratulate themselves on this categorical proof of my unattractiveness!

I cleared my throat. "Um, hello."

At the sound of my voice, the wildman jerked to immediate, intense attention, rolling to his feet in one swift, fluid motion.

From a purely scientific standpoint he was . . . impressive. More so than I'd noticed the first time, in all the screaming and chaos and whatnot. Then, I'd been distracted by his sheer size and brute strength, but there was more to him than that. It was really his imperfections, I realized after a moment's careful observation, that made him so remarkable. The broken nose. The smattering of freckles across his body. The aforementioned body hair that had been all but bred out of Haven 3's inhabitants. His skin was dry in patches, his feet practically grotesque with how callused and hardened they were. His skin bore tales of long-healed blisters and scars, and some that were fresher. There was a patch on the underside of his skull where it looked as though a chunk of hair and skin had been torn out and never fully healed.

These were the things that truly singled him out. On Haven 3 or one of the other outlying settlements, anyone with enough funds could have been genetically manufactured to be strong, tall, and muscular. But these imperfections proved the wildman *hadn't* been fully genetically manufactured, that some of his features might be natural to him, though just how much, it was difficult to say.

Up close, too, I could see the color of his eyes behind his dark lashes. They were dusky blue, like the sky right before it shifts into night.

Trapped in the intensity of those eyes, I felt deeply conscious of each breath, each movement, however slight. I hadn't been imagining it, I saw now as I was gripped in his gaze. He had come to the camp for me—to find *me*.

Our mutual stare was so intense, the electricity between us so potent, the glass so transparent, that the wildman seemed to forget the cell. Leaning forward to try to close the distance, he bumped his forehead into the wall, reeling back in surprise.

For a moment, he blinked, dazed, holding his head. An embarrassed look flashed across his features as he checked to see my reaction. I couldn't help it—I laughed. The moment had been preceded by so much tension, it was a relief to remember he was human, *just* human, not so very different from me.

The laugh drew another sharp stare from him, but a more probing one this time, as if the sound had surprised him and he was suddenly on guard. But after meeting my eyes again, he seemed to sense that the laughter was good-natured, and slowly his jaw unclenched, his hands unfurling. A begrudging smile pulled at the corner of his lips, softening his face and making him look less fearsome.

The silence stretched out between us, as again we were locked into a strangely intense staring session. In response, I felt my own discomfort churning up words. Something, anything, just to fill the quiet. "Nice to see you again. How have you been? Is the food . . . ?" I looked down at the uneaten pile of bland beige rations and decided on a different tack. "You're looking well. I hope you didn't get too much of a—" I brought my hand up to touch the spot on my side that mirrored where he'd been tased.

Almost trancelike, the wildman reached up to do the same. As he touched the tender spot, he grunted—a short, curt sound that somehow relayed his displeasure as clearly as if he'd articulated it aloud.

I winced sympathetically. "I'm sorry about that. You can see why they thought it was necessary, though. You can't just go around tearing up camps and breaking people's limbs."

No response from the wildman—whether because he didn't agree or he didn't understand, it was impossible to say.

I decided to change topics again, imagining that reprimanding him right off the bat might not be the best way to build a bond between us. "Who are you?" I asked. "What's your name?"

No response.

"Where are you from?" I tried again. "How long have you been on Earth?"

I imagined he must have been part of some expedition that had come down here—illegally, no doubt, since no one seemed to have anticipated he should be here. Perhaps his ship had crashed or something had gone terribly wrong, and he'd been stranded on his own for months or maybe even years. No wonder he seemed a bit feral. I wondered what he must have gone through to survive in this place on his own.

The silence stretched on. Thinking perhaps he didn't understand me, I tried again in Chinese, then Spanish, then the butchered bit of Arabic I knew. Still no answer. Perhaps he was willfully ignoring me, trying to teach me a lesson for getting him caught—but then I saw the furrow of his brow, the frenzy of blinking afterward as he struggled to make sense of my words.

He was trying to understand me, but he couldn't. Not in English or Chinese or Spanish or Arabic. And he was making no attempts to speak back to me in his own language. Perhaps he had forgotten. Perhaps . . .

"Can you speak?" I prodded him. "Do you not know how?"

But he had ceased listening to me by this point, that much was clear, his eyes intent upon my lips, watching the way they moved as I spoke. I trailed off self-consciously, one hand coming up to cover my mouth. For Meridian, this level of devotion would have probably been par for the course, but to me it was still unfamiliar, and I couldn't help but fear his interest was really focused on a piece of spinach in my teeth or a low-hanging bogey.

But the wildman watched the movement of my hand just as intently, his eyes locking on to my own once more as he brought his palm up and pressed it against the glass.

He was waiting for me to do something in response, I could tell from the expression in his eyes, though I couldn't fathom what it might be. "I'm sorry," I said, shaking my head, "I can't let you out."

The wildman grunted, removing and then replacing his palm on the glass between us. His eyes were fastened so intently on mine; I've never felt anything like it before, nor since. It was like the rest of the world became dimmer somehow, like no one was watching us on a vid-stream. Like it was just the two of us standing there facing one another, drawn to each other like magnets.

Slowly, almost hypnotically, I raised my own palm, reaching out to touch his on the glass.

The door opened behind me. Startled by the sound, I turned to see Rawley, silhouetted in the light from the hall, his face unreadable. "Minerva." No question in that tone—it was a command.

Flustered, embarrassed, apologetic, I cast one look back at the wildman before obediently retreating to where Rawley stood waiting.

Behind me, the wildman shouted in protest, banging both palms against the glass with such force that the entire room shuddered. I turned back, trying my most reassuring smile. "It's all right. I—"

Rawley grabbed me by the upper arm before I could finish, dragging me through the door and closing it behind us to drown out the wildman's roar.

10

"**L**ooks like you've found yourself an admirer."

It was the first thing Rawley had said to me since we left the wildman's cell, though his fuming silence had been a message of its own, loud and clear. That he had waited until now—in the mess hall at dinnertime, with all these people around—and that he was trying his best to sound amused told me I would need to tread very carefully.

The others at the table laughed, oblivious to the undercurrent of tension in my fiancé's tone. "Yes, he does seem quite smitten with you, Dr. Smithe-Canfield," Coulson agreed jovially. "A case of love at first sight!"

I knew he was trying to make light of the situation, and I did my best to smile at him, though it was difficult with Rawley watching me like a hawk.

"I'd hardly call it love," Rawley spoke up when at last it became clear I wouldn't be saying anything. "Lust, more like it. Did you see that massive erection? Disgusting, filthy creature. You're lucky that glass was between you two, Minerva."

Farther down the table, Dr. Shangrit made a sort of choked, embarrassed tutting noise, tugging at his collar.

"No. I don't believe he meant to hurt me." I hadn't realized I believed this until I spoke the words aloud, but as soon as I did, I knew it was true. The wildman might be rough around the edges, even a little crude, but I'd felt no ill intent from him. Curiosity, perhaps longing even, but no danger or harm.

It was a mistake to say so out loud, though. I knew this, too, before I'd fully finished speaking. When I looked up at Rawley again, his eyes were furious, though he managed a tight smile. "Sweet, innocent Minerva. That's the thing about wild animals. You can never turn your back on them for even a moment."

Hearing the threat in the words, I felt my blood run cold.

As I should have anticipated, the interest (and yes, let's put the less dignified name on it, *popularity*) that surrounded me after my close encounter with the wildman made it impossible to sneak off, unnoticed, into the wilderness. People who had never paid me any mind, and some who had even looked at me disdainfully, now wanted to sit with me at the mess hall, walk with me down the corridor, even chat with me in the bathroom stalls. I noticed, with no little amount of amusement and *be*musement, that some of the women had taken to wearing their hair like me.

And yes, all right, the attention went to my head. Who wouldn't be flattered by so much notice, and for such a thrilling reason? The praise wasn't because I'd won a spelling bee or discovered a new strain of fungi,[1] but because I apparently had a savage man-beast under my thrall. It was quite a feather in my cap, and even though I was still in as much danger as I ever had been, I couldn't help but enjoy myself.

"What's his story?" Coulson prodded me at lunch the next day. He was only one of many interested hangers-on, interested to pick over any tidbit of gossip that hadn't already been passed around and dissected. "Did he tell you anything?"

It wasn't the first time the question had been asked, but still everyone held their breaths, waiting, as if I might suddenly remember that the wildman had announced he was the Baron of Cheese Town and that we must all serve as his dairy underlings. I shook my head, trying to soften the negative with a smile. "He doesn't seem to be able to communicate. Or at least, not much. Perhaps if I could spend some more time with him . . ."

It wasn't the first time I'd floated this idea around, hoping it would catch some steam and be brought to fruition by popular demand. As the head of the expedition, Rawley would be the one ultimately making the decision on what to do with the wildman. I knew that nothing I could say would persuade him in my favor—if anything, my asking to spend more time with the wildman would ensure that it never happened.

But if everyone else was clamoring for it? On the surface, Rawley might not seem like the type to give into peer pressure, but he cared enormously about public perception. Reputation. He wouldn't want to be known as the person responsible for stopping progress.

---

1. Though both accomplishments, I think we can agree, would be worthy of more than a little excitement!

And if I wouldn't be able to sneak away from the base, then I would need to ensure all eyes were on me. Perhaps that would make it more difficult for Rawley to do . . . whatever it was he planned to do to me.

"Did he tell you his name?" someone else at the table asked.

I shook my head again. "No, nothing like that." Afraid I might lose their interest with my nonanswers, I added quickly, "I'm not sure if he even has one."

Naturally, I could know nothing of the sort, but once the idea had been suggested, I could see it taking hold in the minds of the people around the table. "How could he not have a name?" one woman asked.

Relieved they'd taken the bait, I sat forward. "Think about it. He doesn't seem to speak any language. Not only did he not understand any of the dialects I tried, but he also made no attempt to speak back to me in his own tongue."

"He could be mute," Coulson pointed out.

"Yes, I suppose that's a possibility. But what if he didn't answer me because he *couldn't*? What if he's had no one to communicate with for a very long time—or maybe even ever?"

The words hung in the air for a moment before someone toward the back of the group scoffed. "So he just sprouted up from the forest?"

"Obviously not," I snapped back, irritated by the stupidity of the hypothesis. "All I'm saying is, he might not have a language because he's had no one to speak to. And it holds that if he's had no one to speak to, then he might be nameless."

Another long beat passed, as everyone seemed appropriately impressed by the gravity of this statement. Then, some idiot blurted out, "We should call him Tarzan."

I glowered at the suggestion. "No, we should *not* call him Tarzan."

"Why not?"

"Because . . ." I don't know why this idea offended me so much—on the wildman's behalf, naturally—but it did. I enjoyed Tarzan stories as much as anyone, but they were just that—*stories*, about a fantastical man who was raised by apes but miraculously had no facial or body hair and intuitively knew to cover his genitals with a loincloth! To lump in my wildman with that felt like shortchanging him, even infantilizing him—trying to turn him into something soft and cuddly when he was something rugged and raw and truly wild. "Do you see him swinging on any vines, hmm? He has nothing in common with Tarzan."

"What would *you* call him, then?"

I tried my best to think of other literary figures that were more in keeping with my wildman. Enkidu sprang to mind, but I couldn't imagine saddling the wildman with that name; Mowgli, maybe, but that didn't feel right, either. Coulson's "creature stories" from our expedition all had ridiculous names, as has been previously established, so those were out of the question. How would anyone take the wildman seriously if we called him Yowie, for goodness sake?

The crowd was turning restless, which meant they might soon turn against me. So I blurted the first name that came to mind. "Ursa."

A long beat. "Ursa?" Coulson repeated.

It was difficult to tell, from his tone and the expressions of the others around me, if this was an acceptable offering or not. But if this decision was taken from me, I might lose any of the authority I'd gained over the wildman, which might in turn lead to me being less of a person of interest, which might then lead to the expediting of my untimely murder. So, I did what any intelligent person would do.

I doubled down, hard.

"Yes, Ursa." I lifted my chin, meeting everyone's gaze and daring them to contradict me. "Like the constellation of the Great Bear. The wildman *was* wearing a bearskin, after all, but he presumably comes from somewhere in the galaxy—so part Earth, part sky. He's hairy, he's strong, he's aggressive when provoked. He's elemental and wild, timeless and strong. And he smells a little like fish. So, yes, Ursa is obviously the best choice, until he can tell us for himself what his name should be."

Another long beat. Then gradually, everyone began nodding, and I heard the name being murmured, weighed. Accepted. It would soon spread like wildfire across the camp, and that would be that. His name would now be Ursa, and I had been the one to choose it for him.

I was still smiling to myself as I began walking toward the lab. How I was meant to focus on yeast at the moment, I had no idea; as exciting as yeast is, my mind was still with my wildman, Ursa, and wondering when I would get to see him next.

With some surprise, I discovered that my interest in him wasn't merely for the attention he garnered me. Like everyone else, I was curious about where he had come from, who he was, why he had come to the camp. But even more than that, and something I hadn't been quite able to articulate to the others—or perhaps, that I had kept close to myself, as my own private memory—was the strangely intense connection between us. It was more than just his evident curiosity in me. I'd felt a sort of understanding pass between us in our short time together, one that baffled me as much as it did everyone else. I wanted to know what it was, and why we seemed to be so drawn to one another.

These thoughts preoccupied me, perhaps accounting for my lowered guard. As I passed a darkened stairwell, I was suddenly grabbed by the back of the neck and thrust forward, so that I stood at the very edge of the top step, my feet scrambling to stay rooted on the ledge. The staircase was steep and wide, meaning the handrail was out of reach, and I could easily see that I would topple down at least one or two stories if whoever had hold of me decided to cast me down.

My captor was, of course, Rawley. Even if I hadn't known his intentions already, I could smell his cologne, feel the familiar pressure of his long fingers tightening down on my bones.

Neither of us said anything. Above my own shaking, ragged breath, I could hear his only slightly more controlled exhales through his nostrils, feel the hotness of his breath against the back of my neck.

Moments later, he pulled me back to safety, releasing me. I fell to the floor in a heap, clutching on to the wall and trying my best not to cry.

"Careful, darling," Rawley said, in a perfectly controlled, even tone, cloying with its false concern. "You were so close to the edge, and we all know how clumsy you are."

I didn't look at him, just measured my breath. He watched me for a long moment before abruptly turning and walking away.

He didn't have to say the words to make me understand. No matter what games I played, no matter how many eyes were on me, he could still find a way to get to me. I was not safe from him so long as I was here.

He would find a way to kill me, once he was ready. And he would enjoy it.

11

No formal announcement was made, but by the afternoon, everyone in the base knew that Rawley would be attempting to make contact with Ursa on his own. No one could quite seem to piece together what a geneticist like Rawley hoped to accomplish by studying the wildman, and though I had my ideas, I kept them to myself.

It was clear that, amongst other things, Rawley was attempting to remove me from the narrative surrounding Ursa. If Rawley could bring the wildman into his confidence, take him under his wing and make him his pet project, people would stop paying attention to me. As many threats as Rawley might make about the kinds of terrible accidents that could befall me, I knew he was too cautious to try anything with all eyes on me.

But if Rawley became the center of attention, the source for all information about the wildman, then I could be relegated to the background again. And if there were to be some tragic accident then, well . . . it would be awful, but not anything to draw too much suspicion.

It was a sobering thought. The only thing that brought me any peace of mind—or really, if I'm being honest, perverse pleasure—was that the name Ursa had caught on. I'd witnessed for myself someone correcting Rawley when he called him "The Wildman," and I'd had to quickly hide my smile.

Removing me from Ursa's story wasn't going to be as easy as he'd hoped. I would make sure of that.

Like everyone else not on shift, I gathered around one of the monitors in the mess hall to watch as Rawley made his approach to Ursa's cage. Though the monitors had no sound, I could see that he entered the room with his usual easy authority, flanked by two of the biggest and strongest soldiers on staff. Rawley carried a large metal tin in his hands.

"What's he got there?" asked someone near to me. It was a purely rhetorical question, as no one could guess the contents of the box. But it was helpful, I suppose, for someone to voice what we were all wondering. I was only glad that I didn't have to be the inane person saying it out loud.

From the grainy footage, I could see that Ursa was in his usual prone position on the floor, his back to the entrance of the room. Even so, it was clear he was fully alert and aware of Rawley and the soldiers. Rather like a great cat in captivity, his languidness might trick some into believing he was benign. But no one who had experienced his power and presence firsthand would be lured into any false sense of security.

I wondered if Rawley was clever enough to recognize this. He had always had a rather inflated opinion of himself and his prowess; I wondered if his pride would allow him to realize that he had more than met his physical match.

Rawley approached the cage door, the two soldiers in tow. I could see from the slight movements of his head that Rawley was saying something. Still no response from Ursa. I probably only imagined the irritation in the set of Rawley's shoulders, but it gave me pleasure nonetheless.

After a moment of this, Rawley reached forward to open the door.

It was only then that Ursa showed any signs of life. He sat up, body alert, watching the door warily.

Rawley entered, one hand raised, the other holding out the box. Showing no signs of fear or trepidation, he continued talking to Ursa. The two guards tried to follow him into the cage, but he cut them off with a sharp word before returning his focus to Ursa.

For a long moment, the two men in the cage regarded each other. I caught myself holding my breath, waiting to see what would happen.

Rawley opened the box, moving slowly to set it on the floor. He pushed it closer to Ursa, who inspected it carefully. He sniffed its contents, pushing at the outer frame of the tin before at last reaching in and pulling out something. It was hard to tell from the camera angle just what exactly he was holding, but it was clear it was some kind of food. Ursa held some of it up to his nose, sniffing again before he began to eat. He dragged the rest of the box closer to him, digging into it with both hands and all but shoving it into his mouth.

Remembering the ignored food from the other day, I realized Ursa must have been starving, and I felt a pang of remorse. I'd been so heady with all the attention I'd been receiving, I hadn't even considered that Ursa must be hungry, disoriented, maybe even frightened, though he certainly didn't look it now. I felt a trickling of unease, knowing how much this gift would ingratiate Rawley to him, especially if Ursa began to associate him as the person who brought him his sustenance.

The same thought seemed to cross Rawley's mind. On the monitor, I saw him rise to his feet again, turning a brief glance to the camera. I don't think it was my inflated sense of self-importance that made me imagine that look was for my benefit, to gloat at his victory. Venturing a step closer, Rawley watched Ursa eat for a moment longer before he said something else and reached out to clasp Ursa's shoulder.

Without even pausing to look up, Ursa grabbed Rawley by the side of the head and shoved him against the glass wall, hard.

It was very lucky for me that the gasps and shouts of surprise drowned out my snort of laughter. That would have been quite an awkward thing to have to explain, as Rawley's supposedly doting fiancé!

Rawley wasn't too badly injured, it seemed, since he stirred and tried to crawl away on his own. The soldiers rushed into the cage, weapons drawn and pointed at Ursa as they hurried to Rawley's side. I felt a frisson of fear for what they might do to Ursa, and I was not alone; others around me called out in protest.

Luckily Ursa showed no signs of further hostility. He kept his head down, continuing to eat out of his tin, as the guards took Rawley by the arms and half supported, half dragged him out of the cage.

Along with providing me endless amusement, Rawley's injury meant I didn't have to look at his face for the rest of the day. Rumor was that he had a concussion and would be out of commission until tomorrow at the earliest. I suppose, as his fiancé, I should have volunteered to keep watch on him overnight, but I didn't offer and Rawley didn't send for me, so it was an evil that was mutually avoided.

I'd had hopes that Rawley might continue to convalesce the next day, so it surprised me when I looked up from my breakfast to see him standing over me. I stiffened instinctively—wary, as always, whenever he was near, but even more so when he was looking at me as he was now: smiling solicitously, with gentle eyes.

"My love," he said, loud enough so that everyone around us would be able to hear, but not so loudly as to make this showmanship obvious. "I had hoped to prevent exposing you to the wildman's capricious moods and keep you safe, but it seems that for whatever reason, you're the only one in this camp he trusts."

He was a very good actor, but it could still take me by surprise, sometimes, just how sincere he could sound when he had the proper motivation—in this case, the proper audience.

"Are Ursa's moods capricious?" I asked, feigning innocence. "I've always found him to be so gentle."

I'd intentionally used Ursa's newly given name, and I could see this annoyed Rawley, though he covered his irritation quickly. "Which is why, my dear, I'm afraid I'm going to have to ask you to take on some risk. Would you be willing to see him again?"

I stalled, chewing my toast. "To what end?" Seeing Rawley's blank face, I pushed on. "I would need to know what the purpose of my visit would be. I wouldn't want to do anything to needlessly annoy or badger poor Ursa. And certainly nothing that would harm him."

I realized it was true as I said it. Though Ursa had proven to be an unexpected pawn in my ongoing chess match with Rawley, I truly didn't want to see him come to any harm. If Ursa's moods were capricious, then Rawley's were downright volatile, and I didn't want to see anything happen to Ursa in retaliation for what he'd done the day before.[1]

Rawley lowered his voice a touch so that it would be harder to hear. "I don't know if you'd be able to keep yourself from annoying Ursa, even if you tried." With that dig thrown, in his perfectly pleasant tone in case anyone *had* overheard, he continued, "But the purpose of the visit would simply be to set up communication. We want to know where he's from, why he's here. How we can help him."

Rawley knew there wasn't any way that I could refuse that offer, especially with everyone listening in. But I was skeptical that his intentions were entirely benign. There was no way he would allow me the victory of being the only one to communicate with Ursa, unless he really wanted something out of the exchange.

Still, I found I couldn't resist the opportunity. And anyway, I reasoned with myself, at least if I was around, I could offer Ursa some measure of protection—perhaps even think of some way to thwart Rawley in whatever he was planning. "Fine," I said, rising to my feet. "Take me to him."

Rawley's expression was amused, though I could see from his eyes that he was deeply irritated. "I didn't mean right this moment, Minerva. Though you certainly do seem to be in a rush to get back to your wildman."

I felt a blush rising, but I was determined not to let my embarrassment show. "Anything in the name of scientific discovery."

"Hmm," was all Rawley said.

---

1. That is to say, smashing Rawley's face into a glass wall. It still hasn't gotten less funny, even after all this time!

I wondered if he'd regret his decision and decide to snatch the opportunity away from me, just to teach me a lesson; that was most certainly something Rawley would do. But at the agreed upon time, I approached the door to the room where Ursa was being kept and entered.

Rawley was already waiting inside, along with a group of guards—six this time, instead of the two he'd had on hand before. Just like yesterday, Ursa was lying on the floor, staring at the ceiling, as unbothered by the guards' presence as if they were little bunnies who were frolicking around him. Perhaps to him, these men did seem as weak and pointless as little fluffy woodland creatures—at least, individually. En masse, he had to know that they posed a threat to him, especially with their weapons, which had already proven able to neutralize and even harm him.

But this was all part of his alpha display, I was to learn later. One of the ways Ursa had been able to survive so long in the wild on his own was by meeting other animals with a display of dominance. If he showed nervousness or fear, the other creatures would sense this and think he was weak and vulnerable. If he met them as their equal, they would believe he was capable of defeating them and would usually give him a wide berth.

I can say, firsthand, that this behavior worked well with humans. Even though he was weaponless and vastly outnumbered, Ursa still had the six armed guards in the room shifting anxiously, watching every breath, every twitch of muscle, waiting to see what he would do. Rawley put on a better display of pretending not to care, but the very presence of the soldiers indicated that he, too, had learned not to underestimate Ursa.

My beloved fiancé looked up as I entered the room, a barely perceptible sneer tugging at his lip. "You're late."

I was no such thing, and he knew it. Like any self-respecting mycologist, I prided myself on being not only on time, but also at least five minutes early. It was a habit that made me not especially popular at parties, I'd found, but it was very much appreciated in a lab setting. So, knowing he was merely trying to bait me (perhaps hoping that if I approached Ursa in a flustered state, it might somehow disrupt my connection with him?), I ignored the jab. "Six men?" I challenged instead. "That seems like overkill, don't you think?"

At the sound of my voice, Ursa suddenly became fully alert, rolling into a squat in one swift motion. His gaze collided with mine, with its usual fierce intensity, and I couldn't help but blush, even knowing that Rawley (and probably every other person in the room, as well as those watching on camera) were sure to take note of it. "Hello, Ursa."

With an irritated intake of breath, Rawley drew my reluctant attention back to him. "The soldiers are for your protection, darling."

Men and their fragile egos. I barely repressed the urge to roll my eyes. "Has Ursa found a way to break through the cage?" Maybe I was pushing Rawley's buttons too hard, especially considering he had all but threatened to kill me the day before. Still, I couldn't help but feel emboldened in Ursa's presence—like a fiercer, stronger version of myself—even though it was hard to define exactly why.

Rawley smiled at me, and the sight made my heart sink. His smile was never a good sign. "Didn't I tell you, dearest? You're going into the cage today."

Over Rawley's shoulder, I was vaguely aware of Ursa rising to his feet and pacing, watching our exchange closely. I dared a glance at him, seeing his physical presence with new eyes after learning I was going to be in such close proximity, without bulletproof, industrial-strength glass between us.

I did my best to keep any traces of concern out of my voice, however. "The soldiers are going to come into the cage with me?" It was probably futile, but I thought I'd at least throw the idea out there.

"That sounds a little crowded, don't you think? No, they'll simply be on standby. Don't worry. You saw how quickly they were able to come to my aid yesterday."

Rawley was being facetious, of course, knowing that I'd been watching as Ursa smashed his head into a glass wall before the guards could so much as bat an eye. As the possibilities of what Ursa could do to me before anyone intervened raced through my mind, Rawley fought a grin, stepping closer to me and lowering his voice as he leaned in to whisper into my ear. "Don't worry, Minerva. I'm sure there'll be time to stop him *before* he rapes you."

Vile, vulgar man! Ursa seemed to agree, since he gave a warning grunt and slammed his palms on the glass. Or maybe, more likely, he seemed to dislike Rawley stepping in so close to me, noticing the obvious distress it caused me.

Great—just what I needed, a shouting, riled-up wildman right as I was about to enter his cage. I stepped away from Rawley, willing myself to be calm and collected. Calm. Easy. Relaxed. I hoped that if I exuded these things, Ursa would pick up on them and emulate my behavior.

One of the guards unlocked the door for me as I approached. I sought Ursa's gaze once more, smiling and giving an awkward half wave. "Hello, again! Do you mind if I . . . ?" I gestured into the cage. "Is now a good time?"

I was being terribly awkward, but it was difficult not to be with so many people (and Rawley) watching, and under Ursa's usual intense attention. He looked at me like he could tear me limb from limb, but perhaps not in a way that would be entirely unpleasant. I know that sounds absurd, but I truly don't know how better to describe it. All I could do was sincerely hope that he meant me no harm, and to make myself as little a threat as possible to ensure this.

Ursa didn't answer my question, obviously, but he didn't look opposed to me entering his space, so I took a tentative step inside, then another, until I was fully inside the cage with him. I held his gaze the entire time I did this, searching for any sign of hostility so I could make a hasty retreat if needed. Ursa seemed receptive to my approach—confused, but curious, and maybe a little aroused. So, yes, I'd say receptive overall.

I was startled out of the intense deadlock of our gazes by the sound of the door being closed and bolted behind me. Surprised, I turned, my eyes widening in alarm as I saw that I had, in fact, been locked in the enclosure.

Rawley grinned at me from behind the safety of the glass wall. "So he doesn't try to escape."

Not wanting to give him the pleasure of knowing how panicked I was, I refrained from reminding him that he'd left the door open when he'd come into the cage yesterday.

Swallowing, I cast a glance up at the camera in the corner of the room, certain that those watching on in the mess hall were titillated by this new development. Regardless of what happened to me—if Ursa decided to assault me, or eat my flesh, or have a lengthy discussion about the rules of pickleball—at least it would provide entertainment to the peanut gallery. I tried to take some meager reassurance from that. No one could say Minerva Eloise Smithe-Canfield didn't put on a good show!

At last, I turned back to Ursa, who was now, suddenly, much closer to me. Not touching me but close enough that he could certainly do so if he took a mind to it. I yelped in surprise, then covered it with a nervous laugh, not wanting to be rude but also not wanting to rile him up by screaming in his face. "Oh, hello! You surprised me."

No response, naturally. Ursa was studying me with his rapt attentiveness, and I couldn't help but do the same. Up close, his eyelashes were even more impressively dark and thick than they had appeared in our previous encounters. Under the scraggle of his thick beard, I saw he had nice full lips and a strong jaw.

These were all aesthetically pleasing features, and I was impressed that whoever had selected his genetic modifications had done so in a way that seemed somehow both striking and natural. I wondered, though, why they hadn't chosen to breed out his body hair, too. And was that a mole I spotted on his left shoulder? How fascinating!

I ventured half a step closer to better inspect him. Though his beard and head hair were thick and lush, there wasn't as much body hair as I'd thought there might be for someone potentially unmodified; there were men I'd seen in pictures from the twentieth century who looked like they had carpets on their abdomens, after all. Ursa had only a relatively light smattering on his pectorals and torso, and the hairs were dark and rather curly.[2] From a purely scientific standpoint, I was curious to know if they would be soft or coarse, and I unthinkingly reached forward to touch them.

I caught myself before I made contact, reminding myself that I was locked in a cage with this man and needed to enforce clear physical boundaries. But Ursa had recognized my intention, and he grunted

---

2. I have been asked, and feel for transparency's sake I should mention, that there was hair in, shall we say, other areas of the body, which has similarly been bred out of most men on Haven 3. However, I did not feel as free to observe these areas in such close proximity.

in what sounded like displeasure when I stopped short. I hesitated, unsure of how to proceed. I didn't want to open the door to lots of unprompted touching (!), but it also seemed unwise to offend a giant man-beast whose bicep was as thick as my head.[3]

Ursa ended up making the decision for me, as he clasped hold of my wrist and held it against his chest—his pectorals, to be precise. The hair was soft, for the record, not coarse. And also for the record, the skin underneath was quite . . . taut. I could feel the steady thrum of his heartbeat under the skin, as well as the heavy weight of his eyes on me.

I swallowed and did what I always do when I'm nervous. I babbled. "How interesting. Thank you for the honor of letting me touch your pectoral." It was only through sheer willpower that I was able to resist the urge to blurt out "man boob," as my nerves had urged me to do.

After a moment of inspecting the chest hair, I removed my hand again, speaking up quickly so as to distract Ursa and not allow him time to growl any irritation. "I realize that we haven't been properly introduced." I touched my own (hair-free!) chest. "My name is Min-erva Eloise Smithe-Canfield. Most people call me Mina."

These words seemed to do the trick, since Ursa just watched me in silence, following the movement of my lips closely with his eyes.

Emboldened, I continued, "Since you couldn't tell me a name be-fore, I've taken the liberty of calling you Ursa. Is that permissible?"

A blank stare didn't precisely seem like a confirmation, but at least it wasn't a denial. To make sure he understood my meaning, I touched my chest again. "Mina." Then, once more, his own as I gestured to him. "Ursa."

---

3. Hyperbole, but only slightly.

Admittedly, yes, this might have been something of a cliché moment, but I knew of no better way to convey the information. And, apparently, Ursa was either fine with this decision, or he had determined that the time for talking was past. With my hand on him once again, he seemed to feel emboldened to reach out to touch me.

Just as I had been fascinated by his hair, Ursa seemed equally interested in mine—or in my lack thereof. Like the last time I'd visited him, I confess I had left my blouse unbuttoned a bit to allow for some mildly titillating exposure of my clavicle.[4] Ursa now seemed to feel at liberty to push aside the fabric of my shirt so he could explore the skin of my upper chest, apparently fascinated by how smooth it was. By upper chest, be reassured that I truly do mean *upper*—no breasts were exposed or fondled in this exploratory mission, mostly because I held a firm grip on the material of my blouse so it couldn't be opened any further.

Ursa did find my bra strap, however, and seemed perplexed by it, pulling and tugging at it. Afraid that this might cause him to venture further than I cared for him to, I thoughtlessly reached up and slapped his hand. "Stop that!"

It wasn't a harsh slap, but when the man was nearly twice my size and we were locked in a cage together, it was still a slap. I'd seen him slam a man's head against a wall for less just the other day! Taking a step back, I stammered, "I mean, I would prefer that you not, that is, if you don't mind . . ."

I doubt very much that he understood the words, but whether because he sensed from my body language that I was uncomfortable or because he had simply grown bored, Ursa released my bra strap and

---

4. A truly underrated body part, in my opinion.

circled behind me. He took hold of my sensible plait, grunting as he tugged at the wayward curls that had managed to escape.

Nervous with him now out of sight, though still deeply aware of his looming physical presence behind me, I cleared my throat. "Curly hair really is such a nuisance in this atmosphere. Yours seems fairly straight. Is that natural, or do you use a tonic . . . ?"

The question remained, obviously, unanswered. Ursa seemed to have discovered the binding that held the plait together and pulled it free, undoing all the work I'd done to restrain it that morning. With my long hair loose, he began to run his fingers through it, pushing it back and forth, not seeming to mind the snarls he encountered.

As strange as it was to have my hair being pushed every which way—and, I'm sure, becoming even more wildly voluminous in the process—I have to admit it felt rather nice. Relaxing. No one had played with my hair since I was a child, and it is a most soothing experience, is it not?

After a moment of this, Ursa circled back in front of me and nudged my head with the side of his, encouraging me, I believed, to do the same to his hair. Fair was only fair, I supposed, and I didn't want to be rude, so I reached forward and began fondling and tossing his hair around like he'd done with mine, running my fingers along his scalp.

Ursa grunted with what sounded like pleasure. Grunted is maybe the wrong word, since that sounds, well, sort of sexual. This was more of a purr, a contented rumbling in his chest, and there was something very unthreatening about the sound that didn't put me on my guard like a *grunt* might have. For once, his eyes were closed, not locked on my face, and I found myself smiling as I reflected that he was like a big dog. Dangerous, perhaps; powerful, certainly; but even the most ferocious beast just wanted a nice petting every now and then.[5]

I was still smiling when Ursa opened his eyes again, meeting my gaze. Seeing my expression, his lips slowly mimicked mine, curving tentatively upward. His hesitance made me wonder if it was the first time he'd encountered such a seemingly common thing—this signal of shared human amusement, happiness, joy.

The thought was interrupted as Rawley cleared his throat. "If the two of you are done playing with each other's hair, we have something more important to take care of."

At the sound of Rawley's voice, Ursa's smile instantly disappeared, his body tensed, and his face took on an expression that could only be termed aggressive; let your imagination make of that what you will, I truly don't know how else to describe it. It was clear Ursa had no love lost for Rawley, and I couldn't help but be pleased by this. I had always suspected, in the very short time we'd known each other, that Ursa had impeccable taste.

Reluctantly, I turned to face my fiancé. "What is it?" Normally I would never dare speak to Rawley in such a way, but somehow behind an impenetrable glass wall with a wildman at my back, I felt emboldened.

"I'm going to enter the cage now. Your job is to keep the wildman calm. Do you think you can manage that?"

I frowned at Rawley. "Why do you need to enter at all? That's only going to upset him."

It was then that I saw the syringe in Rawley's hand, and I quickly pieced together that he intended to draw some of Ursa's blood. That

5. Oh, get your mind out of the gutter. You know that's not what I meant.

had most certainly not been part of our plan, and it had not been discussed with me beforehand.

I could think of only one reason why Rawley would need to take a sample of Ursa's blood, and it was something I wanted no part of. My eyes locked on the sharp tip of the needle. "What is that for?"

"We need to make sure he isn't carrying any diseases." Rawley said this to me as if explaining something to a very small and exceptionally stupid child. "A blood sample will give us the most thorough results—unless you know of a better way, Minerva?"

What he said made sense, but I couldn't shake the fear that the sample of blood would be used for other, more nefarious purposes. Still, I couldn't very well deny the sense of testing Ursa for communicable diseases, though I did wish we'd had this conversation before I'd been placed into such close proximity to the wildman in question.

"You're going to upset him," I said again, lamely this time, because I knew there were no real grounds for me to protest.

"Which is why you'd better do a good job of keeping him calm."

Swallowing, I turned to Ursa, who was glaring at Rawley, his entire body rigid. I reached out, tentatively touching Ursa's arm to draw his attention to me. "Ursa."

It worked, at least in terms of his gaze, though I sensed that Ursa was still keenly aware of Rawley and the men opening the cage door. I couldn't help but notice that, despite what he'd claimed previously about not wanting to crowd Ursa in the cage, Rawley made sure to bring in three of the armed guards.

"Ursa," I said again, keeping my voice as calm and soothing as possible. "These men are going to take a sample of your blood. There will be a little pain, but it isn't meant to hurt you. We want to make sure you aren't sick, so we can treat you if you're unwell."

The words likely meant nothing to him, but Ursa once again seemed to be able to read my tone and expression. He was alert but not hostile as the men approached.

Instead, I was the one to take umbrage as two of the men flanked Ursa on either side. "What are they doing?"

"They're going to pin him down so he doesn't lash out at anyone," Rawley said matter-of-factly.

I knew, just as matter-of-factly, that this would not end well for anybody. "Don't touch him," I instructed the guards, firmly but not sharply. Again, trying to stay calm so Ursa would remain calm. "He will retaliate if you try to hold him down."

I don't know how I knew this, but I knew it with certainty, even having had so few encounters with him. The guards looked to Rawley, who shrugged. "Then you hold on to him, Minerva. But don't come crying to me if he bashes your face against the wall."

"Let's hope my face isn't quite so bashable." Again, it was only Ursa's presence that made me bold enough to say something like this to Rawley. I saw his gaze narrow, and Ursa apparently saw it, too, since all at once he let out a low, menacing growl and stepped between me and my fiancé.

The message was as clear as if Ursa had said it out loud: *Don't threaten my woman.* Even Rawley seemed capable of deciphering it, since suddenly his expression shifted. He smiled, raising both hands, including the one that was holding the syringe. "We're all friends here," he said, all charm now. When Ursa didn't growl again, Rawley seemed to take that as a good sign and took another step forward. He bent down, offering the top of his head. "Would you like to touch *my* hair?"

Ursa responded by smacking him across the top of the head.

It was by no means the same forceful aggression as he'd used yesterday when he'd smashed Rawley into the wall—it was not even hard enough to knock Rawley off his feet, though he did stumble, more from surprise, I think. But the head-smack made clear, nonetheless, what Ursa thought of all his schmoozing.

I choked on a laugh, turning my face away so Rawley wouldn't see my smile. But Ursa saw my amusement, and he returned it with a grin of his own, looking pleased with himself. Almost smug.

That was an interesting new flavor of Ursa I hadn't expected. I was fascinated by how he could convey so much with so little communication, at least in the traditional sense. And, if I'm being honest, the sight of that grin did something quite unexpected to me physically, making my heart increase its tempo.

Scowling, Rawley retreated. I could see he very much wanted to rub his head, though his pride wouldn't let him. "I suggest if you don't want him restrained, then you find a way to keep him from assaulting everyone."

It wasn't *everyone* that Ursa was assaulting, just Rawley; but this hardly seemed productive to point out. "Give me the syringe. I'll do it."

Perhaps the hit to the head had been harder than I thought, because Rawley handed over the equipment without any protest. I turned back to Ursa, seeing the way his eyes narrowed at the sight of the needle. His gaze met mine warily.

I felt wary, too, as I considered what I'd just volunteered to do. How to explain to a wildman, who seemingly couldn't communicate, that I was about to jab a sharp needle into his skin . . . ?

"Listen, Ursa. I won't lie to you. This won't be pleasant. But I am very good at this, if I may say so myself. In my old lab, they called me

"One-Try Mina," I'll have you know.[6] All that to say, I'll try to make it as efficient and painless as possible. All right?"

Some of the wariness seemed to fade from Ursa at the sound of my voice—which was odd, since that was the very thing that was usually so off-putting to others. Or maybe it was my no-nonsense manner or the extensive eye contact I kept making, all of which was designed to let him know, *I am not here to hurt you. I am your friend*. I wouldn't say Ursa was exactly thrilled with the process, all things told, but at least he didn't hit anyone else, myself included. I did with him what I'd done with all the skittish patients who'd come to my mother's lab, talking him through each step:

"I'm putting on the tourniquet—it might feel a little tight, especially around such a big bicep. Do you mind me asking what your arm routine is . . . ?"

"Now I'm feeling for your median cubital vein. Ooh, it's a nice juicy one, you should be very proud . . ."

And so forth.

Ursa grunted his displeasure at the various small pains of the procedure but was otherwise a good patient. He seemed interested in the process, and afterward he kept poking at the wound, even though I told him to leave it alone. "It won't heal if you keep picking at it," I scolded him, softening my words with a smile.

He smiled back at me, more easily this time, though it still didn't seem an entirely natural expression for him. Nevertheless, the smile transformed his face, made it softer, less threatening, his eyes a big and guileless blue.

---

6. I agree, it isn't the most terribly catchy or clever nickname, though one usually has little say over these things.

And there again came that strange fluttery feeling, like I suddenly couldn't quite catch my breath.

Rawley interrupted the moment by all but snatching the syringe from my hands, like a petulant child. The smile instantly fled from Ursa's face, and he likely would have charged Rawley if I hadn't instinctively placed a staying hand on his arm. Not for Rawley's sake, mind you, but because of what I feared the guards might do to Ursa. "Don't pay any attention to him. He's just being rude. Maybe he missed his lunch. It always makes one a bit cranky, doesn't it?"

Rawley didn't look up at that, his gaze down on the syringe full of Ursa's blood. "I'd better get this to the lab."

Seeing the way he looked at Ursa's blood gave me a tiny frisson of worry. I had a feeling I knew what that look meant; and if my suspicions were correct, I might have just betrayed Ursa terribly by helping Rawley get that sample.

"Minerva, with me," Rawley snapped from the cage door.

But I wouldn't be. With *him*. I vowed this to myself even as I followed Rawley and the guards out of the room. I wouldn't let Rawley get away with it, not again.

Pausing at the door, I met Ursa's gaze, giving him what I hoped was a reassuring nod. "I'll be back," I promised, not knowing how I'd be able to do so, but vowing to myself I'd find a way.

However, my efforts to calm him ultimately proved to be as ineffective as my attempts to speak to him earlier. Ursa's face twisted with belligerence and fear as he brought his palm to the glass, again and again. He looked positively indignant at my abandonment, and as I paused in the doorway to meet his gaze, he looked at me expectantly.

"I won't leave you here," I tried, but I saw almost immediately it was futile. Any understanding that had passed between us before seemed to have dissipated. All he saw now was that I was leaving him in a cage, alone.

Overcome with guilt, I exited the room, wincing as I heard Ursa's roar of anguish following me down the hall.

12

Now that he had what he wanted from Ursa, Rawley no longer deemed it fit for me to visit the wildman. It was suddenly far too dangerous for me to be in even the same room as Ursa; my mere presence seemingly caused too many emotional outbursts from our "guest."

I suppose when someone like Rawley is in a position of such undisputed power, one doesn't need very good justifications for shitty decisions. Especially since there was no way for me to circumvent his authority. Only Rawley could decide who saw Ursa, and he no longer seemed to care that so many people had become so invested in my relationship with our resident wildman. That, more than anything, made me worry for what Rawley had planned for Ursa.

That, and the fact that the monitor in the mess hall had been disabled.

There were still security cameras filming Ursa, though; that much became clear when I "accidentally" took a wrong turn down the hall-way leading to his room, only to be briskly led away by two guards within the first three steps. So, along with the camera in his room, there had to be at least one in the corridor recording the movements outside.

Ursa must have something that Rawley wanted, desperately. And I was beginning to have a sinking suspicion I knew exactly what it was. Or rather, I felt my suspicion being confirmed with each new security measure taken. I feared that in handing over Ursa's blood sample, I had unwittingly signed his death warrant.

I have, in the past, been known to have a flair for the dramatic. My mother always said I had the brain of a scientist but the heart of a galaxy-net reality star.[1] It would be just like me to burst into the mess hall and proclaim that Rawley was intending to use Ursa as a lab rat, when in actuality, the reason for all the hidden cameras was something completely benign. Such as . . . he was planning on throwing Ursa a surprise party and didn't want to spoil it, or some other such nonsense. And yes, I know that was a rather poor example, but in truth, it was difficult to think of a motive for Rawley's behavior that wasn't ill-intentioned. Still, I would have to find proof before I confronted Rawley.

It came to me, suddenly, what I should do. There might be cameras monitoring Ursa, but there wouldn't be any monitoring his blood sample. If I discovered that the sample confirmed what I feared to be true, then I would know Ursa was truly in danger. And if it didn't confirm that, well, then I was worrying over nothing. Perhaps I had mistaken Rawley's intentions.

---

1. My mother and I were obsessed with reality programs on the galaxy-net, like *Freshest Face in the 'Verse*, *Undercover Captain*, *Haven 1's Next Top Singer*, and *Bachelor in Haven 7*. This was a rather strange quirk for one of the universe's most accomplished geneticists (and her daughter), I agree, but we all have our guilty pleasures.

But when I thought about the room full of cages back on Haven 3, the smell of blood and feces, I knew I hadn't.

Getting hold of Ursa's sample would be easier said than done, though. I wasn't a pathologist or a geneticist. My specialty was fungi,[2] not DNA or genetic modification. I fretted over what reason I could possibly give for requesting the results, and came up with nothing.

So, I finally just decided to ask.

St. John, the lab technician, was someone I'd known in passing on Haven 3, primarily because he'd worked with Rawley. Asking him about Ursa's results directly would be a bit of a risk, since I didn't know if he was an innocent colleague of Rawley's, or if he was complicit in the underground experiments Rawley had been running. The fact that he was here on Earth leaned toward the latter, since Rawley would want to have his trusted allies on hand should the need arise. Then again, maybe St. John really was just an efficient technician.

As far as Haven 3 citizens go, St. John was not the most attractive of the bunch.[3] He'd had most of his superficial modifications done post-birth, before post-birth modifications had become wildly controversial. Fortunately for him, he had not suffered any of the worst side effects of some of the early PBM experiments, such as death and permanent disfigurement; unfortunately for him, his enhancements hadn't entirely taken to his original genetic material, and the result was a weird conglomeration of features, rather than the seamless combination one came to expect from the upper echelon of Havenians.

---

2. Perhaps a less flashy, but just as important, branch of science!

3. Apologies, St. John, should you happen to be reading this. I mean no offense, I'm only stating my completely subjective opinion. I'm sure there are plenty of people who find you quite handsome. Just not me.

His crystalline eyes were a bit too bright, and his too-white teeth were rather ghoulish. Strangely, I'd always found him to be much ruder than others of my acquaintance about my own lack of modification. I believe he felt that his few modifications made him superior to my complete lack. By way of comparison, most of the truly attractive specimens on Haven 3 were usually quite benevolent in their interactions with non-mods such as myself, perhaps secure as they were in their clear superiority.

Nonetheless, I tried for my most friendly smile as I approached St. John at his desk. "Hello, St. John! How's Earth life, buddy?"

The *buddy* was a mistake, I realized it right away.

St. John glared at me. "Oh. It's you."

I laughed like this was friendly banter. "Anyway, I just thought I'd drop in to see how things are. Catch up. All that."

"Why? We're not friends, non-mod."

Oh honestly, the prejudice was staggering! All because I'd been born and not manufactured, for goodness sake! I dropped the fake smile, glaring back at St. John to show him I meant business. "Listen up, weak chin. This can go one of two ways. I can drop in here every single day and ask you inane questions and tell you every single last detail about my day. Or you can tell me what I want to know, and you'll never have to see me again."

St. John hesitated, clearly intrigued by this promise of no longer having to suffer my presence.[4] "What do you want to know?" he asked warily.

---

4. Rude. And really, St. John, if you are reading this, this type of supercilious behavior is exactly why no one likes you. And for the record, I did mean offense before about how strange looking you are, you botch-mod buffoon.

"Ursa's bloodwork. What did Rawley find? Any contagious diseases?" If Ursa was being quarantined because he might infect others, then all of my fears were unfounded; no nefarious schemes were at play. I could go on with my plan to disappear into the wilderness without a backward glance, and Ursa would provide the perfect distraction to take all the focus off little old me!

"No, he was completely healthy. It was a pretty boring lab day, honestly. I was hoping he had syphilis. I've always wanted to study syphilis . . ." With that said, St. John turned back to his instruments, obviously expecting me to immediately keep my promise of no longer speaking to him.

Heart in my throat, I stepped back into his line of sight. "What about his genetic makeup? Were there any abnormalities?"

"I answered your question already, non-mod."

St. John started to swivel his chair back around, but I grabbed his shoulder, halting him. "Please, St. John. This is important." Realizing that appealing to the goodness of a man like St. John, with a moral compass apparently as soft as his chin, was rather futile, I tried another tack. "Or I can always read aloud to you from my findings on the Japanese umbrella.[5] Some really fascinating stuff."

I wasn't being facetious—my findings were truly fascinating!—but my threat of incredibly interesting knowledge seemed to do the trick. St. John visibly shuddered, wrenching his shoulder out of my grasp. "Fine. There were no genetic abnormalities. Happy?"

"What alterations were made to his pre-birth material?" I pressed. "It has to be the eyes, right? The eyelashes?" Nobody was naturally born with such vividly colored eyes, framed by such perfectly dark

---

5. *Parasola plicatilis*

lashes. Those had to have been genetically manufactured—or so I had told myself as I paced my room at night, worrying about what Rawley had planned for Ursa.

"No. Nothing. His genetic material was completely untouched." St. John shooed me off, like I was vermin that had scuttled into his workplace. "Now off you go. Don't let the door slide shut on your huge non-mod ass on the way out."

I was too aghast by what I'd just learned to be offended about the disparaging comment about my normally proportioned, completely healthy-sized posterior region. It was just as I had feared. I knew with a sinking, one-hundred-percent certainty what Rawley had planned for Ursa.

And I knew, in that same moment, that I would have to find a way to stop it.

To my non-Havenian listeners, I will likely need to explain why it was so rare that Ursa had no modifications. Haven 3 is known for taking genetic modifications to extremes, chasing the latest fads in beauty, trying to push the envelope on what is most rare and exotic. Other Havens, and other settlements, might consider themselves to be non-mods in comparison, but the truth is, it is extremely rare for a child to be born in this day and age with no genetic modification whatsoever. Other settlements sometimes tend toward prioritizing other qualities over beauty, like athleticism,[6] intelligence,[7] or kindness.[8] Even parents who can't afford much will usually choose to modify certain genetic factors—susceptibility to conditions or diseases, things along that line.

Among the already rare group of non-mod individuals, it is even rarer to find an individual whose genetic material naturally produces superior, desirable qualities. I've already detailed, and had detailed to me many times throughout my life, how unremarkable I am, not only in physical appearance, but also in my relative unexceptional intelligence compared to my brilliant mother. To put it bluntly, no one is really all that surprised to hear that I'm non-mod when they meet me. It's fairly obvious at first glance.

But despite his physical abnormalities and defaults, Ursa's lack of genetic modification was surprising. His unusual size and strength, his aesthetically pleasing facial features (underneath his massive beard), and his rather large . . . masculine attributes all suggested he must have had some modifications chosen for him. That would be the obvious assumption made upon seeing him. The fact that he was not only a non-mod, but such an impressive specimen of a non-mod, made him truly special.

And truly vulnerable, now that Rawley had figured this out.

---

6. Haven 2

7. Haven 1

8. Haven 4

But perhaps this all requires some more explaining. I can sense the Brethren were frustrated last night at the breadcrumbs of information I've been doling out so slowly, trying to prolong the story. I suppose I'll have to pause briefly now and explain why it was so alarming to discover that Ursa was a non-mod, just like me.

Part Two

Mina and the Mad Scientist

T his story does not have a happy ending, I'm afraid.

There once lived a girl named Mina on a settlement called Haven 3. It was a place renowned for its impossibly beautiful people—and impossible was not an exaggeration in this place, because almost no one was made by nature alone. Haven 3 thrived on genetic manufacturing, the ability to choose the perfect combination of features—height, eye color, bone structure—to create a prepackaged, perfect person.

Two of the pioneer geneticists, Rosalind Canfield and Miles Smithe, were both brilliant, both very much in love, and both believed they had a vision for a society in which children wouldn't have to be born with genetic abnormalities, chronic illness, or fatal conditions. Miles had been born with one such disease that ended his life far, far too early, but Rosalind was determined to carry on his fight.

Yet when Rosalind saw what her research was really being used for—not to correct disease, but to make superficial, aesthetic alterations meant to create "flawless" people—she decided she would have no part in it. When Rosalind was artificially inseminated, she bravely left her child unmodified, creating a rare non-mod in a settlement full of genetically modified beings.

Mina grew up always surrounded by perfect, beautiful people, each more special and breathtaking than the last. She was not bad-looking—some might even say she was mildly attractive and grew on you the more you saw her—but in a sea of special people, she would always be normal.

There were a few rare others who were also non-mods—people who had moved to Haven 3 after they were born, or people whose parents couldn't afford the treatment, or most frowned upon of all, people whose parents had carelessly produced their offspring outside of a lab. Yet new research was being pursued to allow even these non-mod nobodies to significantly alter their genetic material post-birth, so they, too, could be special.

As a teenager, Mina begged her mother to let her test out the new treatments. She wanted to be special, just like everyone else. Rosalind forbade her on two counts. First, the treatments were still being tested, and no one knew what the side effects would be. More superficial treatments, like eye color and hair color adjustments, had resulted in some mild early success; but no one could predict what would happen when PBMs attempted to take on larger changes, such as bone structure, height, body shape, or skin color. Second, Mina was perfect just the way she was. She didn't need violet eyes or aqua hair or any other silly accouterments to make her special—that could only come from within.

Rosalind's words were wise, but Mina was young and headstrong, and she foolishly believed she would have her mother at her side forever. She mistook love, real love, for a cage, and beat herself tirelessly against it, trying to escape.

But with time, Rosalind's warnings turned out to be prescient, since many of the early successes of PBM treatments turned into catastrophic failures. As the years passed, and Mina grew into adulthood, then on into spinsterhood, she let go of her dream of enhancing herself and moved on with her life. She was content, mostly, with her mushrooms and her Mother and her friends.

But everything changed, the day Mina met him.

Augustus Rawley did not seem like a mad scientist when Mina first met him. He was handsome. He was charming. And best of all, he seemed enthralled by her lack of modification. He had been ruined, he liked to bemoan, by some minor modifications made by his parents—fuller lips, a stronger jaw—and he envied Mina's pure, unaltered state. For the first time in her life, Mina felt special.

Rawley was a colleague of Rosalind's, and at first she seemed pleased by the match. After all, her daughter had finally stopped threatening to potentially risk her life by trying new genetic modification procedures.

But as more time passed, Rosalind grew warier and warier of Rawley. Why was he so adamant about the superiority of Mina's untampered genes when he had devoted his own research to post-birth genetic modification? Why were so many of his findings undocumented, and why did so many of his research logs go mysteriously missing?

Mina didn't listen to her mother's concerns at first. She was in love, or so she thought. Rawley was handsome, intelligent, considerate. It was strange that he always had his research assistant, Meridian, shadowing him everywhere he went, and that Mina had seen him coming out of the Lower District at such odd hours, a place where so many non-mod girls had gone missing . . .

Then Rosalind was dead. There had been no symptoms, no warning. One night she went to sleep, and the next morning she simply did not wake up again. Mina's world was turned upside down. The shelter and safety she had taken for granted, even resented, was gone forever. For the first time, her eyes were opened.

She remembered how irritated Rawley seemed to be with her mother's professional and personal complaints. She remembered how he'd often bring Rosalind tea at the lab, and how once that offering began to be refused, she'd caught him coming out of their kitchen, where her mother kept her tea leaves. A terrible suspicion began to bloom in Mina's heart, but she told herself she was grieving, that she likely wasn't in her right mind. She would have to find proof.

As Rawley's fiancé, Mina had been given free rein of his town-home—except for his lab in the basement. There were sensitive materials there that couldn't be disturbed, he'd informed her with unusual intensity. She must never go down into the lab, not ever.

The Mina before Rosalind's death would have never even considered breaking that promise. But the Mina left behind without her mother was adrift, unsafe, vulnerable. She had to know what her fiancé was hiding.

She went into the lab.

Mina never found proof that Rawley killed Rosalind, though it remained a strong suspicion in her heart, especially after what she saw that day. Because what Rawley was hiding in his lab proved that he would not hesitate to harm, to maim, even to kill—whatever it took to feed the insatiable monster of his own greed.

The lab was full of cages. And inside those cages were girls—all of them terribly mutilated, all of them wailing in agony. Mina recognized many of them as the girls who'd been reported missing from the Lower District. Like her, they were non-mods, whose genetic material was un-

tainted. Rawley had been experimenting on them to try to advance his techniques in significant post-birth genetic modification, but clearly his methods were not effective. These poor women were suffering inhumane cruelty, their own genetic material destroying them from the inside out.

It was too late for rescue. All they wanted was merciful death, and despite Mina's pleas, they took it for themselves, along with their revenge: setting fire to the lab so Rawley would be unable to use his research. Afterward, Mina had no choice but to pretend she had never been there. He would suspect, most certainly, but he couldn't know for certain, and that might buy her some time.

Mina had seen her future. Rawley hadn't singled her out and courted her because he loved her. He'd recognized her as a non-mod who might make a useful test subject someday. Unless she devised a plan, it would be her in one of those cages, probably sooner rather than later now that she'd destroyed his secret lab and all of his blood-earned findings.

Rawley couldn't make accusations when he wasn't sure how much, if anything, she knew; and Mina couldn't bring his crimes to light without endangering herself. There were plenty of rich, powerful people on Haven 3 who cared more about Rawley successfully completing his trials than any damage he did to human life, especially poor non-mod girls from the Lower Districts.

With Rosalind dead, Mina had lost her family, lost any connections that might keep her safe. Rosalind had been someone important in Haven 3, but Mina was just her non-mod, mycologist daughter, with no special skill set or knowledge to make her valuable in a settlement that revolved around manufacturing beautiful people.

As luck would have it, Rawley was offered a research expedition to Earth. It was the one piece of news that could curb his disappointment about the destruction of his lab and research. Perhaps there was something on Earth that could help him resolve his difficulty with significant-

ly manipulating genetic material post-birth, some untapped resource on the planet that would solve all his problems.

Mina hoped Rawley would leave her behind, but she wasn't surprised when he insisted she come with him. She would be his test subject, after all, if he did have some miraculous breakthrough. He couldn't afford to let her out of his sight.

But Mina had an ace in her pocket that Rawley hadn't anticipated—a friend of hers from childhood who had spent significant illegal time on Earth. His name was Tobago, and he captained a smuggling ship that made frequent unauthorized trips to Earth. He helped Mina devise a plan for how she could escape, how she could survive on her own in the wild, until they could meet up for a scheduled rendezvous. He would smuggle her from Earth and help her start a new life somewhere else—Haven 4, perhaps, since they were said to have very good cheese. Using an old comm channel they'd abandoned when they were children, Mina and Tobago brainstormed and trained and plotted together for weeks, until Mina thought it might even be possible she could succeed.

It was a risky plan, potentially even crazy, but what choice did Mina have? It was either escape into the wild, or die in a cage.

PART THREE

MINA AND THE MAN-BEAR

(AGAIN)

13

From past experience, I knew that the corridor outside of Ursa's rooms was heavily monitored. Usually. But I also knew that on Taco Tuesday, the queue started forming well before dinner time. I'd once noticed in passing that every single person on base seemed to be in that line for the one decent meal we got throughout the week. I was very much hoping that this included the people who were meant to be monitoring Ursa's visitors.

When Tuesday evening came around, instead of hurrying out of my lab to try to be one of the first fifty or so people to get served my supper,[1] I made my way to Ursa's rooms.

I waited for somebody to stop me in the hallway, shout at me that I didn't have the proper clearance.

Nobody came.

---

1. This was important, since after the first twenty minutes or so, the "meat" began to get rather...crusty.

Perhaps someday, someone would teach Rawley the importance of ensuring that his security guards had their dinners delivered, especially on taco night. I was exceedingly glad, though, that it had not happened before that evening.

Reaching the door to Ursa's rooms, I quietly let myself inside.

My plan to save Ursa was perhaps not the best-formed scheme of all time. It may come as no shock to learn that mycologists are not generally renowned for their tactical maneuvers and strategies. All of that to say, while I knew what I was about to do was a bit foolhardy, it was the only thing I could think of.

I was going to let Ursa out of his cage.

That was it, really. I didn't know what we were going to do after that point. I suppose I hoped he'd be able to beat up anyone who tried to stop us from leaving. I could also maybe bluff my way through some of our escape, claim I was taking him to do some extra testing. Everyone knew how connected we were by now, so maybe they would buy it? And if not, then yes, I would encourage Ursa to give them a little wallop. Nothing too damaging, ideally no broken bones. But maybe a concussion or something of the like.

As much as I hadn't considered most of the plan, one detail plagued me relentlessly: Releasing Ursa from his cage would put me in very close proximity to him. No glass barrier between us. No armed guards standing by in case he became violent . . .

Yikes.

On the one hand, I felt as though Ursa and I had developed a real bond. Without any words, we seemed to almost communicate with one another, which was remarkable, really. He was obviously quite interested in me, for reasons that I still didn't entirely understand, and I felt rather protective toward him. I know that might sound ridiculous, seeing as he was so much bigger and stronger, but he was all on his own. He trusted me, and I very much wanted to be worthy of that trust.

On the other hand, I'd literally seen him slam a man's head into a wall and break a bunch of peoples' bones. Granted, it had been rather funny to watch him knock Rawley around, but I instinctively felt it would be less funny to have him bash my head into a wall if he decided I was a threat, or if he outgrew whatever fascination he had with me. As much of a bond as I felt I'd developed with Ursa, he was a bit like a wild animal. He could turn on me at any moment. And he was bigger, and stronger, and faster, and if he wanted to hurt me, there was really nothing I could do to stop him.

Perhaps the wise thing to do would be to leave him where he was and use him as a distraction to sneak off on my own, as I'd always planned to do.

But knowing what Rawley had planned for Ursa . . . I couldn't do that. Not after what I'd seen. I wouldn't wish that fate on my worst enemy, and I certainly didn't wish it on him.

That settled it. Self-preservation be damned! I would have to let Ursa out of his cage.

At least if Ursa tore me limb from limb and ate my corpse after I freed him, Rawley wouldn't get a chance to murder me. There was some consolation in that.

As I approached the cage, Ursa seemed unusually alert, restless. I think perhaps he was picking up on my body language, sensing my anxiety. He was an excellent reader of people, for someone who seemed to have little practice in interacting with them. His eyes roved my face, and he opened his jaw wide and growled in agitation. I did my best to smile, to drop my shoulders and try to look relaxed. "Everything's fine, Ursa. We're just going to try something a little different today, that's all. I'm going to open your cage and let you out. Exciting! Please don't eat my face off, haha."

Ursa remained unconvinced by the jocularity in my voice. He paced the cage, butting his head against the glass, rolling the top of his head against the wall as his shoulders and back bunched and flexed. Even without a shared language, it was easy to understand he was ill at ease.

Well. It certainly wasn't a very fortuitous beginning. I wondered if I was making a mistake by letting him out, if he really was just a wild animal who'd happened to take a shine to me.

"Ursa." I raised my hand to the glass, pressing my palm against it, and held my breath as I waited to see what he would do.

The frantic pacing slowed, then stopped altogether. Ursa stayed with his forehead pressed to the glass wall perpendicular to where I was standing, watching me through a curtain of hair. Slowly, slowly, he pushed away and walked toward me, stopping just short of the wall. His eyes met mine, a question.

"Trust me," I said.

After a moment's pause, Ursa raised his palm, pressing it to mine.

I smiled at him sincerely this time, both reassuring and reassured. Ursa wasn't just some wild animal in the body of a man. There was a soul in there, reason, intellect. We had bonded, in some strange, inexplicable way. I could trust him, I felt intuitively, with my life. And I would need to very, very soon.

Looking into his eyes, I wondered how I'd ever thought for even a moment that he might be capable of hurting me.

Then all at once, Ursa rose to his full height in front of me, chest puffed out, jaw opened and teeth bared as a low growl emanated from his throat.

I winced away from him, and briefly, I thought I'd been mistaken, that all this time I'd been seeing intelligence and kindness in what was simply madness.

Until I saw Ursa looking just over my shoulder.

I turned to see Rawley in the open doorway. For a second, our gazes locked and held—just as mine had with Ursa's moments before, only with a very different undercurrent running beneath it.

Then at once, we were both running for the door to Ursa's cage. I barely heard Ursa's frantic roar over my own heartbeat pounding in my ears. Rawley was faster, but I was closer, and in triumph I closed my hand over the release button that would unlock the door.

"Stop!" I ordered Rawley. "One more step and I'll open it."

Rawley froze in place. I could see him calculating, quickly, if he could reach me before I could press the button. If he could close the door again before Ursa managed to break free.

Behind me, Ursa paced frantically, growling in a low, agitated way that indicated he would very much like to be out of his glass prison. There was no question of whose side he would take—and even as I registered this, I saw the same realization dawning in Rawley's eyes, too.

"You stupid bitch," he muttered. "I should have killed you on Haven 3 when I had the chance."

14

"Hello, fiancé," I replied. "Nice to see you, too."

It was easy to be so blasé in Rawley's presence, with my hand on that release button and Ursa on the other side of the door. His taut, flexed muscles on full display and his open aggression toward Rawley made me bolder than I might have otherwise been with my homicidal fiancé in the room.

I ought to have just opened the door then. I don't know why I didn't, except that I was still afraid. I'd wanted a chance to talk to Ursa, to coax him into calmness before I removed that glass barrier between us. Now, with Rawley in the room, there was no chance of that. I didn't know what Ursa might do in such an agitated state. I didn't want to believe he'd hurt me, but what if he got carried away? What if he'd been docile with me in his cage only because there were men with guns waiting just outside?

I watched Rawley with a close and careful eye. Even though I had the upper hand now, experience had taught me not to underestimate him. If he lunged at me, if he pulled out a weapon, I had to be prepared to press the release button, consequences be damned. "You probably *should* have killed me on Haven 3, dearest. I think you'll find it's harder to do so now."

"Perhaps," Rawley acknowledged, not moving from his position a few feet away from me, where he'd frozen in place. "But not impossible."

"Why don't I open this door, and we'll see how impossible it is?" I challenged.

"Wait! Wait." Rawley held up his hands, as if in surrender, before he forced himself to add another "Wait. Please."

He was silent for a moment, taking stock of the room, the distance between us, and Ursa prowling his cage, glaring at him through the glass. Rawley grimaced, in what was probably an attempt at a smile. "So you've been making friends with the brute. Earning his loyalty. Giving him his first taste of real human pussy, I'd wager."

I didn't deign to respond, knowing he was likely trying to goad me into some rash action. If he was here now, he'd doubtless been watching the security footage, which meant he knew there'd been no tasting of any kind whatsoever going on. Crude, vulgar man! I couldn't believe I'd ever thought myself in love with him. If I'd had Ursa's strength, I would have crushed him with my bare hands.

As if in response to that thought, Ursa growled, baring his teeth at Rawley and pounding his palms against the glass.

"Your new boyfriend will kill me if I do you any harm. I somehow doubt I can persuade you to get him to play nice with me and go along with my experiments as planned." Rawley didn't bat an eye, though the tightening of his jaw indicated he wasn't insensible to the threat Ursa presented. "So what are we to do?"

I shrugged. "If only I didn't loathe you so completely, I might be more sympathetic to your plight."

"He's useless to me with you around, that much is clear. I could just let you leave with him, let the two of you fuck like rabbits out in the forest—much like Meridian and I have been doing all this time behind your back."

Doubtless he meant to wound me with those words. I only rolled my eyes. "Yes, well. You weren't very discreet about it. I've known now for ages."

More like a week, but still. I liked having the upper hand for once.

Rawley covered his surprise quickly. "But then," he continued, as if I hadn't interrupted, "I would lose my new prize guinea pig. And you know I never lose, Minerva. So, what to do?"

The words hung in the air, a taunt. A bribe. An offering. All at once, I understood what he was proposing to me. "You're going to let me go, on my own, and you won't bother me—if I leave Ursa behind for your experiments."

Rawley smiled. "What can I say, darling? You've always been cleverer than you look."

I could lie and say it didn't tempt me, but I've promised to be forthright with this account, and in truth . . . I was ready to turn Ursa over to him. Even having seen what I'd seen, even knowing firsthand what would become of him in Rawley's clutches, I saw a glimpse of freedom—an outcome to this story where I wouldn't wind up poked, prodded, tortured, dismembered. Dead. I'm not proud of it, and I don't mean to make excuses for it, truly. It remains one of my deepest regrets. I can only say in my defense how completely I feared Rawley, and that somehow to me, Ursa wasn't quite real yet. He was flesh and blood, I knew, but I didn't grasp that he could feel the same as me, hurt and fear and want and hate and love.

I swallowed, my mouth suddenly sweltering. "Swear. Swear to me that you'll let me go, that you won't try to follow me."

"I swear."

But already I was shaking my head. "I don't believe you."

Rawley started to step toward me, but a warning growl from Ursa kept him in his place. "Honestly, Minerva, what would I even do with you when I have the perfect specimen here? I may be many things, but wasteful isn't one of them."

The words sounded right, but how to trust a man like Rawley who was incapable of putting anything before his own self-interest? Rich condemnation, I know, coming from a woman contemplating turning over another living being to save her own skin.

"Leave Ursa here," Rawley instructed me tersely. "Keep that cage door shut, and I'll let you go, I swear."

It was too good an opportunity to give up. But my conscience, feeble and weak as it was, wouldn't let me accept it so easily. "Promise me you won't kill him, or torture him like you did those girls on Haven 3. Just take enough samples for your experiments and then leave him be."

"Of course," Rawley said quickly. Too quickly. I saw the sneer of contempt cross over his face, but I told myself it was because he thought my request was stupid, not because he had no intention of keeping his word.

I had to tell myself that, didn't I?

A long beat. Then I glanced back at Ursa. He was still pacing agitatedly, and I knew he wasn't going to be pleased when I left the room. I did my best to offer him a reassuring smile, but I found I couldn't quite meet his gaze. "It's going to be all right."

"Calm him down again," Rawley instructed me. "Don't act like you're afraid of me. I don't want him to think I'm the enemy."

You are the enemy, I snapped back mentally. Frankly, I didn't see why I should do anything to make Rawley's job easier for him. Wasn't it bad enough that I was going to leave Ursa behind?

"Tell him I'm here to help him. Tell him to trust me, Minerva. Or the deal's off."

I reluctantly lifted my gaze to meet Ursa's. There was no way, without understanding our language, that he could comprehend what was being decided at that moment. But somehow, through the thick bramble of beard and hair, those dusky blue eyes told me he knew what I was about to do. His agitation at Rawley's presence had shifted into something else altogether. He grunted at me indignantly, and for the first time, I sensed his anger *toward* me instead of *for me*.

He pressed his palm flat against the glass, as we'd done just moments before. His eyes implored me to do the same. It was a small gesture, but in it was defeat, disappointment. Hopelessness. Resignation. It was so utterly human, I wanted to weep.

"Trust me," I tried to say, but choked on the words. "Everything will be . . ."

I couldn't finish it.

Then all at once, Ursa's eyes widened as he tracked something behind me. I'd allowed myself to become too distracted.

I turned, scrambling to press down on the release button, but it was too late. Without warning, Rawley had me by the back of the neck, and he slammed my head against the glass, hard. "Unfortunately for you, I'll no longer be requiring your services." This was said in an affable tone, as if he were speaking to a customer service agent. "As a fiancé, or as a lab rat."

Using my disorientation to his advantage, he turned me to face him, then raised his other hand to take me by the throat. I scraped at his fingers with my nails, gasping, choking, twisting my body every which way to try and escape him, but to no avail. "Rawley," I heard myself saying in a choked, grated voice, over and over again, stuck on a loop from which I could not escape, until it no longer even sounded like his name. Not that it would matter. There was nothing I could say, nothing I could do. He wanted me dead, that was all, and he wouldn't stop, he wouldn't stop . . .

"You burned down my lab, you bitch," Rawley seethed at me, and there was nothing amiable in his voice now. "Seven years of work, gone."

Gradually, I stopped thrashing, stopped gasping, as his thumbs dug deeper into my windpipe. It was only then I became aware of the din going on in the background—Ursa's wild, bellowing roar, a frantic pounding, or maybe that was only my own heart, the blood rushing in my ears . . .

And then all at once, I was dropped to the floor, gasping for shuddering breaths that burned all the way down. I may have passed out, must have passed out, for when my eyes managed to open once more, Rawley's back was turned to me. My head lolled to the side—where I saw a crack in the wall of Ursa's glass cell, meant to be impenetrable.

Rawley tilted his head, observing this show of strength with scientific detachment. He looked at the crack in the glass, then down at me, and back again at the glass. "Interesting."

And then I blacked out.

15

“**M**inerva.”

I gasped, then awoke, hands fluttering to my throat, which still burned on the inside and felt tender to the touch.

It took me a moment to become aware of my other senses. It was dark. The floor was wet. As my eyes adjusted, it appeared as though I was in some kind of . . . warehouse? Overhead lights flickered from metal beams and low-hanging air conditioning vents. Open pipes gushed out a slow stream of what I hoped was water onto the concrete floor. Exposed electrical wires poked out of gutted portions of the wall, where the plaster had been half demolished to reveal a thick block of cement beyond.

“Minerva.” Rawley’s voice caused me to jump in panic, but my brain caught up a moment later, processing that he wasn’t nearby. His voice was coming from a speaker. I searched the room until I spotted it—mounted next to a camera, which swiveled to follow me with its blinking red eye. “Good morning, darling.”

Even without seeing his face, even with the distortion of the speaker, I could hear his amusement.

Whatever he had planned for me, it was going to be very, very unpleasant.

"As you can see, we've made some new arrangements for you. You may be wondering why we bothered to go to the trouble, since you've proven to be such a disappointment. God knows, I ought to have killed you long ago, and up until about a week ago, not a single living person would have cared. I will admit, you put me back a few years when you destroyed my lab. But necessity, as they say, is the mother of all invention. And in a way, you helped bring me here, to a solution that will ultimately be more beneficial to mankind. So I thank you for that, Minerva. I truly do. And because I'm so very grateful, I want to give you one last parting gift. Something to remember me by."

From somewhere else in the building, I heard a loud roar, the sound of something heavy banging against metal. Though the cry sounded animalistic, I knew it came from an all-too-human source. Ursa. He was here, somewhere nearby. A terrible suspicion began to creep into my mind, but I hoped—I prayed[1] —I was wrong.

Rawley's intercom crackled again. "Ah, yes. There's our guest of honor now. Isn't he perfect?" There was real, unfeigned awe in his voice. "Can you imagine anything more beautiful?"

Despite my fear, I glared up at the camera, hoping Rawley was watching me. *An electric fence pole shoved up your ass?* I might have snarked, if my throat weren't still on fire.

Rawley went on, clearly enjoying himself too much to shut up. "We ran his blood sample. He's like you, Minerva—completely pure.

---

1. An extremely rare occurrence on my part, but in this case I believe you can agree, warranted.

Not a hint of genetic manipulation on him. Though he's a far more impressive specimen, I think we can both agree."

Trying my best to tune him out, I searched the building for escape routes, weapons, anything that might help me.

"You're wondering how he can be so strong, so fast? That's what we're wondering, too, Minerva. And what we intend to find out. Today will begin that study, and you'll get to be a part of that. I hope you understand that we won't be able to include your name in any official capacity, for reasons that should soon become obvious."

Soon? Did this blustering idiot really think I hadn't pieced things together yet? I wanted to leap to my feet, throw things at the camera, knock it down, but I held myself back. Somewhere beyond my distress, I knew this was the sort of response he wanted, so he could revel in my fear and rage, but I had to stay focused. I tried to channel Tobago's rational, competent voice in my head. Were there any exit routes? What around me could be used as a weapon?

"You see, our wildman seems to be awfully fond of you, doesn't he? He nearly broke through two inches of reinforced glass to come to your rescue. Seems like an awful lot of fuss to me, I confess, but then, as Meridian pointed out to me, your non-mod body shape probably instinctively suggests a higher fertility rate to his Neanderthal brain, and . . . well, biology.

"Unfortunately, he'll realize just how low he's been aiming once we take him back to Haven 3 and he sees the vast variety of breedable options, but we thought we'd let you have your fun before that little revelation takes place. Every girl deserves to be the belle of the ball at least once in her life, after all. Plus, Meridian wants to see some primitive mating rituals firsthand, and I don't have the heart to tell her no . . ."

It felt like a punch to my gut. I'd already guessed where this was going, but I'd blindly, irrationally, kept hoping I was wrong. It was too grotesque, even for Rawley—wasn't it?

No, I thought grimly as a steel door, opposite me but one floor above, began to creak open, revealing the silhouette of Ursa standing just beyond. It was just grotesque enough.

They were going to trap me in here with him and let biology take its course.

I'd been in close proximity with Ursa in a room before with no glass barrier between us, and he hadn't attacked me. Perhaps now under these different circumstances—with me wounded and unable to communicate with him, without any guards to intervene, with Rawley actively egging him on—Ursa might continue to be gentle with me and follow my lead.

But I found it was not a gamble I was willing to take.

A chuckle came from the speaker above. "Consider this a late engagement present, Minerva. Don't say I never gave you anything."

Even if I'd been able to summon the perfect retort, it would have been impossible to get it beyond my swollen, fiery throat. Instead, I fixed the camera with my steeliest glare and raised both middle fingers.

Then, scrambling to my feet, I turned to the dark, winding corridor behind me and ran as fast as I could.

Hide. That would be the key now. I could not outfight Ursa. I doubted very much I could outrun him. But I just might be able to outsmart him—use all that brute strength against him, somehow . . .

I ran, searching the walls, the ceiling, for anything that might be useful. At last the hallway ended, opening into another large room that looked to be only half completed, still under construction. A ladder was leaning against one of the walls, leading up to a metal catwalk hanging over the room. And in the corner was a window, through which I could see Meridian.

Without pausing to think, I ran over to her, searching for a door that might allow me entry into the room. Finding none, I banged my hands on the glass window separating us, demanding her attention. In my desperation, I thought perhaps I could appeal to something human, something *woman* in her, something that would not allow her to stand by and watch me be attacked and violated.

Her expression flickered, and for one elated moment, I thought I'd gotten through to her, that she felt guilty for the part she was playing in this and that she might relent and find some way to help me.

Then I realized what I had misread in her gaze—she was merely irritated that I was obscuring her view of the room.

I glared at her, banging my palms on the glass again, wishing I could do more, but already I heard the sound of Ursa approaching, something clattering down the long hall behind me.

Without pausing to think, I ran to the ladder and began to climb as fast as I could.

I reached the top just as Ursa entered the room. He was not running, as I had feared, but slowly taking his time to explore the new terrain, pushing against the walls, rubbing his back against the exposed beams and scaffolding, sniffing the floor.

As his eyes found me, perched at the edge of the catwalk, he stared for a long moment. I stared, too, watching to see what he would do. Face-to-face with him again, I didn't want to believe he would hurt me, didn't want all of that trust and camaraderie built between us to be thrown away now that there was nothing physically separating us.

But when he started toward me, panic took over. Without second-guessing myself, I kicked the ladder down, covering my ears as it clattered loudly to the floor.

Ursa did not flinch, though, just watched me. And then he loped back a few steps, settling into a squat in the corner. Keeping his vigil.

I relaxed, allowing myself to sag against the railings. I was up here, safe. He was down there, with no way to reach me. If he tried to set the ladder up again, I would just knock it down every time. He couldn't get to me. I told myself this over and over again like a mantra. He couldn't get to me.

Unless Rawley intervened.

I sat there with my feet dangling over the edge, heart still pounding in my chest, as I waited to see what Rawley would do.

This wouldn't be an exciting show for him, after all. And if it didn't prove to be entertaining enough, he would find a way to make it entertaining.

16

Nearby, something clattered, and loudly.

I sat up with a start, inhaling sharply. I hadn't been dozing, had I? It seemed impossible, with how rapidly my adrenaline had been coursing through me, but my body was still exhausted and recovering from being beaten and strangled. I blinked away the film clinging to my eyes, searching for the source of the sound. Ursa couldn't get to me, I reminded myself, but I wanted to know *what* he was doing to make that noise. I searched for him in the spot he'd been keeping vigil in before, feeling a trickle of unease run through me as I saw he was no longer there.

For hours he'd stayed in the same position, simply watching me. I had been forced to begrudgingly marvel at his endurance; I'd had to shift, move about, rise to my feet and stretch, lie down across the catwalk—and all the while, he'd hardly moved a muscle, scarcely even blinked.

And now he was gone. Less composed now, and far less reassured, I searched the room until I spotted him. He was halfway up the adjacent wall, scaling one of the exposed beams and making alarming progress toward the catwalk.

I scrambled back on all fours, staring at him in disbelief, then rage. If I'd been able to, I would have screamed at him. Instead, I pounded my fists in frustration against the metal grating.

For once, Ursa's focus was not on me; it was on the building's intricate skeletal framework as he chose his next footing carefully. I might have admired his skill and dexterity, were it not being put into practice to come after *me*, for reasons I feared could only be nefarious.

Overhead, the speakers crackled. "Uh-oh, Minerva. Looks like somebody knows how to climb . . . And he's making good progress, I must say."

I ignored Rawley's taunting as best I could, taking deep breaths and focusing on my options. I could attempt to scale down the side of the wall myself, though I imagined it would be slow going, and I would likely either get stuck somewhere mid-climb. Or fall. I could stay up here on the catwalk and try to face Ursa, but that seemed like more of a suicide mission than anything else.

At last, my eyes lighted upon something hopeful: a metallic ventilation system, half a foot or so above me. There was a gap between two of the duct columns on either side. If I stepped on the edge of the railing and stretched far enough, I might just be able to pull myself up onto the edge and into one of the columns.

Visions of me plummeting to the concrete floor filled my mind. The likelihood was rather high, I had to admit. But my only other option was to wait for Ursa to reach me and hope he wouldn't hurt me. With the effort he was expending to reach me, this outcome didn't seem to have a high probability.

It's not that far, I told myself resolutely, steeling myself as I rose to my feet. It was lucky I wasn't afraid of heights, all things considered. If anything in this scenario could be considered *lucky*.

"I wouldn't miss, if I were you," Rawley's voice taunted from the speakers. "I imagine Ursa won't be averse to fucking you from behind, even if your bones are shattered from impact."

I ignored him. My mind was a tranquil pond. I was in control of my body, and the only limitations placed on me were those I placed on myself.

Rising to my tiptoes, I reached out my arms as far as they could go and leaned forward to grab onto the ducts.

My fingers made contact with the edge. I gripped it tightly, and with agonizing effort, I began to pull myself up. Thank goodness Tobago had insisted on all those pull-ups as part of my survivalist training! This was not so different, really, only the stakes were much, *much* higher if I lost my grip or couldn't hold on any longer.

Despite the intensely painful sensation it caused, a ragged scream tore through my injured throat, flushing blood up into my mouth.[1] I glanced back long enough to see Ursa looking up at me, watching my progress for a moment before redoubling his efforts to reach the catwalk.

With one last final whimper, I pulled myself into the opening in the ducts. I wanted to collapse there. Unconsciousness loomed, threatening to overwhelm me, but somehow I was making myself crawl forward, aware that any moment, Ursa would reach the catwalk, and then it would be mere seconds before he followed after me, without any injuries or wounds to slow him down.

---

1. It wasn't much, truth be told, but I hope this detail will be impressive to the Brethren.

Levering myself up on my elbows, I crawled forward. Luckily, aside from my throat, I wasn't too badly injured from Rawley's attack—earlier this morning? Yesterday? It was impossible to gauge the passage of time without windows, but my body was utterly exhausted. Still, I dragged myself forward, motion by agonizing motion. I was not a fighter, nor a survivalist, though I had played at it for a few weeks leading into this trip. I marveled now that I'd ever thought I'd be capable of surviving out in the wild on my own.

Come on, Mina, Tobago would have ordered me if he were here—no pity in his voice, just a brisk, unyielding command. *Move. Move. Fight for your life.*

I did. I fought with everything I had, crawling until I reached a fork in the system. One way led to a semi-sheer drop into some unseen darkness below, the other veered off into potentially endless yards of ducts, twisting and turning throughout the building.

Had I been at full strength, well fed and rested, I might have gambled on the latter option, hoping I could be quick enough to get enough of a head start to lead Ursa on a wild goose chase until he no longer knew up from down.

But my throat was on fire, and my body was giving up on me, and black spots were already beginning to dim my vision, and I knew no matter how many tricks I devised to fool my body into moving forward, it could only endure so much. And it was bloody loud crawling through these rusted, old vents, which would make stealth nearly impossible.

The other way—the drop—was more nebulous. I had no idea how steep the fall was or what I would be landing on at the other end. I could break something, or end up trapped somewhere.

I might have debated the pros and cons for a moment longer, had I not felt the dip of the metal underneath me, indicating that Ursa had reached the duct and let himself inside.

That decided it. I launched myself forward toward the drop. As the rumbling of the thin metal drew closer and closer, I pivoted my body so my legs would take the impact of the landing, and then, biting down hard on my lip, I let myself fall.

In the end, the drop was probably about eight feet. I did my best to tuck and roll as I hit the ground, but I still felt a sharp sting in my ankle. I hoped it was only a temporary pain; if it was sprained or broken, I was done for.

I couldn't think of that now, though. I blinked through stinging tears and lifted my head as best I could to survey my surroundings. It would be a matter of moments before Ursa caught up to me, agile and uninjured as he was. I had to be quick.

There was an open door to the left, leading deeper into the warehouse. I could make a run for it, but it felt like merely delaying the inevitable. Once Ursa caught up to me, I would have moments, nothing more. He would overtake me, there was no escaping that. It might be time to fight and be done with it.

But how? Even if I'd been at my peak shape, even with Tobago's training, I could never physically overpower Ursa. I'd seen the way he dismantled an entire camp, the way he'd cracked reinforced glass with his bare palm. No, I would have to find another way to fight him, one that did not involve relying on my brute strength alone.

Taking stock of the room, scanning for anything useful—ideally a weapon—my eyes landed instead upon the exposed panel of wall, revealing a hive of wires knotted together beneath.

I took in a sharp, painful breath, steeling myself.

That would have to do.

It was only a few moments later when Ursa appeared. He'd somehow managed to climb down the shaft instead of falling gracelessly onto the floor, and he had only a few feet left to drop. He landed on the balls of his feet—painlessly, nearly soundlessly, as agile as an acrobat.

Lucky bastard, I thought, a little petulantly, from my position in the corner of the room, half collapsed against the wall. I would have loved to have not rolled my ankle and to have instead landed like an Olympic-medal gymnast from Haven 2, but here we were.

I didn't bother to disguise my irritation at the injustice of it all. "Showoff," I grumbled at him, too weak to give full justice to the venom I felt.

I'd thought he might charge at me mindlessly, like a wild animal. Instead he rested on his haunches—watching me, yes, but also wary, as if he sensed I wouldn't have given up so easily. He literally had me cornered, and I wasn't moving, wasn't screaming. Just waiting.

Not for the first time, I wondered if I'd misjudged him, if I should have spent all this time teaming up with him instead of running from him. Perhaps we could have found some way to work together toward our common goal of escaping from the warehouse and/or beating Rawley to a bloody pulp.

Unfortunately for Ursa, it wasn't a chance I could take. I'd already made a fatal mistake in placing my trust in the wrong person. I wouldn't do so again.

"Come here, Ursa," I encouraged him through my raspy, weak voice, attempting the tone one might use to call a beloved pet closer to receive an injection or foul-tasting medicine. "Come here. It's all right. Let's be friends."

The intercom crackled to life overhead. "What are you doing, Minerva?"

After a moment's hesitation, Ursa moved forward, cautious and tentative as he approached. Even in the position I was in, I had to marvel at his intelligence. Though it seemed he'd been living on his own for too long and had forgotten simple things like human speech, he had a keen eye for reading people, knowing when to trust and when to be wary. Despite myself, I felt a little pang that he no longer trusted me. We'd built a camaraderie back at the base; at one point, I'd even been determined to set him free. Perhaps I was being too rash, assuming he would hurt me just because that was what Rawley intended.

"I have to say, Minerva, I thought you'd have more fight in you. Perhaps you've decided to give in, make the sacrifice for scientific study? Or maybe all this time what you've really been waiting for is for someone to fuck you up the ass and make you take it like a dog."

I ignored Rawley's crude words as best I could, holding Ursa's gaze—those beautiful, dusky blue eyes framed by those dark, dark lashes. Already, I was regretting what I'd have to do, but I couldn't take the chance that Rawley was right.

"I'm sorry," I told him, more genuinely now, all the artifice taken out of my tone. "You're being punished for someone else's sins. I know that. But I just can't take the risk."

At my softer tone, Ursa moved even closer, though he stopped again a few feet away from me, toes dipping into the edge of the puddle of runoff sloped down near the drain there. The puddle that was now the only thing separating him from me.

Did he sense the danger? I wondered uneasily. Or was he merely delaying his gratification when he claimed me as roughly as Rawley had described? Was that what all men really were, stripped down to their most primitive instincts?

I would have to be more persuasive, bait him so he would come closer. I shifted, aware that the fabric of my tank strained over my breasts as I did so. Ursa followed my movements, staring without bothering to hide it.

"Come here, Ursa," I said again, holding out a hand to him and wetting my lips with my tongue, watching as Ursa followed this with his eyes, too. *Gotcha.*

The intercom crackled to life again. "Something's wrong," Rawley said, almost as if to someone else, and then to Ursa, a sharp, barking cry. "Get back! It's a trap."

But Ursa could understand Rawley no more than he could understand me, and I was there, present, in the flesh. Eyes, never so much as blinking, trained on my face, Ursa moved forward a cautious step, then another, until both feet were submerged in the runoff.

I looked away from him only long enough to find the camera on the other side of the room, offer a small gloating smile, then I pulled out the handful of wires I'd held concealed behind my back. My hands were wrapped around the insulated parts, and the tips, live and crackling, I'd held angled away from my body until now, just the right moment.

Sucking in a sharp breath, I dropped them into the water.

The result was instantaneous. Ursa jerked back, tumbling over with uncharacteristic clumsiness, body twitching, as the smell of something burning infiltrated the air.

He'd fallen backward, out of the puddle. I watched him for an anxious moment, seeing to my relief that he was still breathing, even if shallowly. He was still alive. The relief I felt surprised me, despite everything. It was possible he might have meant me harm, but he was only a pawn in Rawley's disgusting games, just as much as I was. I wish it hadn't come to this.

I rose awkwardly to my feet, using the wall for support. No sooner had I done so than Rawley barreled into the room, seething. In all our dealings it had always unnerved me how distant and remote he seemed to stay, even in the midst of his cruelty and violence; but there was nothing of that now, only pure, unfiltered rage.

"You stupid bitch," he shouted, advancing on me. "I won't let you destroy it, not again."

He didn't care about Ursa. It was the experiment he wanted, the science. I'd barely managed to raise my arms before he had me by the hair, dragging me over Ursa's body and throwing me to the concrete. My bones cried out in protest, blood flecking from my mouth.

Still, I remained silent, my body going limp. It may surprise you to learn that I have never been the most physically inclined person, and I certainly had no experience in combat. What Rawley was doing to me hurt enormously, but I think it was the shock that was more hampering—sheer disbelief kept me from fighting back, attempting to defend myself. I lay there on the floor like a rag doll, as if by this display of passiveness I could convince him to stop hurting me—or more of a stretch, even, that he might just forget I was there.

As a tactic, it had its flaws, especially now that Rawley was so determined to end my life. Relentless, he aimed a kick to my ribs, again, then again. *Oh, God,* I realized. *He's going to kill me. He's really going to kill me this time.*

I blacked out, maybe more than once. In my brief bursts of consciousness, I was vaguely aware of Rawley shouting at me, of the flickering lights overhead spinning and swimming, of a noise emitting from my throat that sounded hardly human, it was too saturated with pain. I do remember distinctly thinking, *I am going to die*. Even then, I couldn't quite believe it. Not, I think, because I still held out hope of rescue, but because it was simply incomprehensible that what I am could simply cease to exist, that everything that makes me Minerva Eloise Smithe-Canfield could just end.

And then suddenly Rawley was crying out. Maybe I was only delirious with pain, but it seemed he was being lifted—yes, *lifted*—from the floor, like he was a child, and tossed across the room. I saw Ursa, big and terrible and angry, rising to his full height.

Still slipping in and out of consciousness, I heard Rawley shouting, then screaming, then silent. The sound of fists on metal, loud and terrible, then something tearing and shouts of rage. Then being lifted, cradled, as if I were something precious.

"Mother?" I asked.

And then I slipped into the darkness.

17

T hings have taken a turn, I'm afraid. I'd no sooner finished telling this last portion of my tale to the Brethren when I discovered my audience had turned against me.

"Traitor," I heard a few of them grumble, and the looks they gave me were cold enough to freeze fire.[1]

This wasn't the first time the Brethren were displeased by something I'd shared with them in the story. They *really* didn't like it when I tried to describe a specimen of orange peel[2] I'd found on my second day at Camp Olympus, although to be fair, I think they would have been much more excited if they'd actually seen the sample I found. Anyhow, I'd known them to be restless, bored, and irritated with me in the past, but never angry. Too late, I realized I might have pushed

---

1. A ridiculous hyperbole, I agree, but I'm afraid I'm a bit shaken by the encounter, and my mind isn't operating at full capacity. Thus, my figurative language has likewise suffered.

2. *Aleuria aurantia*

them too far. But what choice did I have? I must represent the story accurately, and that means including the parts where I didn't behave as well as I ought to have.

Regardless of my dedication to complete authenticity, some of the Brethren of Blood were so outraged by my betrayal of Ursa that there was a bit of a skirmish. Some very rude things were said, which was rather hurtful, I must say; and not all of them restricted to my character. However, for a group that prides itself on utmost loyalty, I can understand why feelings may have been running high for the Brethren. Why some people may have even said things that they perhaps didn't really mean, things about one's slight overbite and larger-than-average hip width and things of that nature.

It probably would have been a good time to hold my tongue, but I wasn't going to sit by and let them tear me to shreds. "That's rich, any of you commenting about *my* appearance. Have you looked in a mirror lately, hmm? Or do space pirates not care about basic hygiene? Last time I checked, missing teeth aren't the fad in *any* of the Havens—and yes, I'm talking about you, Red Bill. There are things called toothbrushes. Ever heard of them?"

I ought to have stopped there, I suppose, but I have always had a bit of a temper, and I was irritated by their constant complaining. "And while we're at it, how dare any of you lowlife hypocrites get angry at me for gambling with someone's life. How many people have you pushed out of an air lock for entertainment in the last month alone?"

The biggest mistake, I think—beyond insulting the space pirates who were keeping me alive solely for their entertainment—was mentioning the air lock and reminding them of that possibility. Not my brightest moment, I will own to that.

Naturally, the men began debating whether they should shoot me out of the air lock on the spot. Then some of them began arguing over whether they ought to torture me first or just watch me suffocate, and some of them began to physically fight each other, and then the whole room erupted into chaos.

I was surprised when someone gripped me by the arm. He was dark-skinned with a thick beard. His hair was graying at the temples, even though he otherwise looked to be only in his thirties or so, and his eyes were dark and grim as he held my gaze.

Orion, the quartermaster.

He was the sort of man one didn't notice at first because he blended so completely into his surroundings. But then, all at once, he'll say or do something that brings him into sharp relief, and you can't imagine not having picked him out right away as different from everything and everyone around him. I believe Orion first drew my notice when I was trying to explain the significance of Ursa's name, and he recounted the story of Zeus and Callisto in perfect detail. With a name like Orion, it wasn't surprising that he was familiar with Greek myths and astronomy, but . . . in a group of belching, bloodthirsty men who could barely get through a single night of storytelling without someone shouting at me to "Get out yer tits," he was definitely an anomaly.

"Come with me," he said in a low, urgent tone that brooked no argument.

I allowed him to navigate me through the fray. Luckily by now, the Brethren were so busy fighting each other they scarcely noticed my movements through the room. Orion soon saw me safely into the corridor. I thought he meant to take me to my cell, so I was surprised when he led me to the private quarters. Having traveled a few times now on ships, I knew that only the captain and quartermaster received their own lodging.

I huffed in astonishment, wrenching my arm free from him. "If you think I'm going to sleep with you just because you helped me out of a scuffle—"

"I saved your life," Orion interrupted in that same no-nonsense tone he'd used back in the room. There was something extremely unflappable about him, as if he'd seen the very worst the universe had to offer and could no longer be bothered to show too much emotion about anything. "And I'm putting you here, just for tonight, so if the men stop fighting each other long enough to realize you're gone, you won't be a sitting duck, waiting in your cell."

Oh. How embarrassing. I'd read that rather wrong, hadn't I? "Well, I . . . thank you."

"It's no skin off my nose if you live or die, but you do keep the men calm with your stories. Excepting tonight, that is." He shook his head at me as if he thought I were a proper idiot, and I suppose he wasn't wrong. "You're going to have to get them back to your side tomorrow, you know, if you want any chance to survive."

His chastising look seemed to suggest I'd intentionally put myself in this position—to be left stranded on Elba and kidnapped by a bunch of bloodthirsty pirates, forced to tell stories to ingratiate myself to their ever-changing moods. Yes, all of my life's grand plans, finally coming to fruition!

I glared back at him. It probably wasn't the wisest decision, considering how he seemed to have positioned himself as my sort-of ally, insofar as he might suggest the other pirates not kill me but wouldn't step in to prevent them from doing so. I couldn't afford to alienate the only thing approaching a friend I had on this ship. But I was just so bloody tired of having to fight for my life. "What more do I have to do to keep these space apes entertained? Should I light some fiery hoops and jump through them?"

Orion looked unimpressed by my outburst. "Right now the only thing that's in your favor is that the men dislike Rawley more than they dislike you."

I snorted. "Great. I'm a notch above the man who kidnaps, tortures, and kills women for kicks and giggles. But just one notch, right?"

He went on as if he hadn't heard me. "The Brethren don't operate under the same moral code you do. They've also killed people, and they'll kill you if you can't keep them on your side."

"And just how am I supposed to do that?"

"The Brethren might be murderers and scoundrels, but they value bravery. Loyalty. If I were you, I'd course correct your story, and quickly."

I shook my head. "I can't just change what happened."

Orion scoffed. It was subtle, but I saw it. My eyes widened as understanding dawned. "You think I'm making the whole thing up. Rawley. Ursa. Everything."

He shrugged. "What I think doesn't matter—"

"What reason would I have to lie?"

"Staying alive," he returned simply. "Believe me, I'm not one to judge. We all do what we have to in order to survive."

I frowned back at him. For the first time it struck me as strange—this quiet, soft-spoken, obviously intelligent man, traveling with these bloodthirsty mercenaries. What had brought him to this place? And why was he here now, trying to help me?

"Keep them on your side," he urged me again quietly. It was the only time I'd seen anything like real emotion in his eyes. I thought of what a normal, moral person would have to do to survive amongst this group and how it must be easier to just shut down, snuff out whatever self still existed. "Make them believe you. Make them root for you."

I thought about Orion's words long after he was gone. I didn't know how to do it, simply put. I was no hero. I was a non-mod, perfectly normal nobody. The only special thing that ever happened to me was you. Meeting you. Falling in love with you.

I might not be a hero they would rally behind. But *you* were—are. They might not take me back to Haven 3 for my own sake, but for yours, they would. I realize now that I'll have to do my very best to help them see just how special you are, what a magnificent and rare abnormality you are to this universe.

You've saved me before. Maybe you can do it again, even from so very far away.

18

For a long time after the warehouse, there was only confusion, distortion. Fading in and out of consciousness. I know some of what I remember must be imagined, because sometimes Rawley was there, and sometimes I was back on Haven 3, trapped in the secret room with those poor, screaming, dying girls, and sometimes those poor, screaming, dying girls were *me*. Other times I saw Ursa, roaring in my face, tearing at my clothes, and other times he was feeding me some strange mash-up of leaves and what looked like roots and cooing at me like one might a small baby.

The only consistent thing was the pain. My ribs were the worst offender, painful enough to rouse me from a deep slumber every time I inadvertently shifted, moaning in agony. My throat ached, too, when I would try to call out against my visions or nightmares or whatever they were. I found myself weeping—silent tears, because the sobs hurt too much—and all I wanted was my mother to make everything better. And sometimes she was there, brushing my hair from my face and telling me everything would be all right. And then I would wake up, and she would be gone, and that was the most painful part of all.

I still don't know how much time passed or how long I was un-conscious. I had vague, scattered memories of Ursa carrying me, of him lowering me into water, of me being in unimaginable pain. Of someone tending to my wounds, someone who I'd thought in my delirium was my mother but clearly must have been my wildman. I woke groggy and absolutely parched, so thirsty it felt like I could drink and drink and never stop being thirsty.

Intending to call out, I let out a strange, raspy, gurgling sound instead. Ursa was at my side in an instant, his face hovering over my own, just a little too close for comfort's sake.

The last time I'd been conscious, I'd been terrified of his proximity, but now, aside from some residual wariness, I found my fear had mostly abated. Perhaps I was simply too tired to be afraid. I suppose I'd also realized that I'd been helpless for so long now, if he intended me harm, he'd had ample opportunity. And the truth was, right now, he was the only person who could help me, and I very much needed his help.

"Water," I rasped, making a cupping and drinking motion with my hands so he would understand.

Ursa disappeared from view again, so I took the opportunity to observe my surroundings. I was still feeling woozy, and I didn't want to overexert myself. I just slowly turned my head this way and that, cautious in case I had broken something that shouldn't be jostled. I appeared to be in some sort of cave, with light filtering in from some nearby opening, indicating it was daytime. I could hear running water from somewhere not too far off, but around me I could see only rocks, dirt, and mud.

So this was where Ursa lived. How very . . . Spartan of him.

The man in question returned shortly, his hands forming a shallow bowl filled with water. It wasn't the most hygienic solution, but I doubted he kept cups around. And anyway, I was much too thirsty a beggar to be a chooser.

Forgetting my resolve to move slowly, I lunged forward, slurping the water out of his palms like a greedy cat. "Thank you. Thank you," I gasped, lapping up every last drop, ready for more.

It was such a relief to quench my poor dry mouth that it wasn't until I'd finished drinking that I realized—

I was completely and totally naked.

As in, not a single stitch on me. As in, not even my knickers. Not even my socks. *Naked*.

I screamed, shoving Ursa away and scrambling to my feet, covering myself as best I could as I searched for someplace to hide. I did this while still screaming, if that's what it could even be called—it sounded more like a banshee shriek. There was nothing to cover myself with, only stone, stone, and more stone. At last I resorted to pressing my body into the rock wall, turning my head to glare at Ursa with all the venom I could muster as I tried, in vain, to cover my posterior region with my hands.

"You—you pervert! Waiting until I was unconscious, helpless, and then . . ." I shuddered. "What have you done with my clothes? Bring them to me this instant!"

But Ursa, looking completely bewildered by my behavior, just stared at me from across the cave. How dare he act so innocently, after what he'd done! Incensed, I squatted down, grabbed a handful of pebbles near my feet, and threw them at him as hard as I could.

The pebbles were tiny, not likely to do much damage, and anyway, my aim was terrible, but the gesture had the intended effect of running him out of the cave.

"That's right—get out! And stay out!" Buoyed by the fact I'd managed to scare him off, I felt a bit mad, greedy with the power I had. "This is my cave now!"

It was really rather fun, stomping around the cave naked, all by myself. After a few minutes of this, as the adrenaline began wearing off, I realized how strange it was that I could walk around so freely. Rawley had beaten me to within an inch of my life. I'd felt bones shattering. But now, as I stretched and twisted and experimented with my body's movement, I felt only the slightest twinges of pain, more like I'd gone a few days without stretching properly.

How utterly baffling. Just how much time had passed, I wondered, that I could be so completely healed?

With a jolt of panic, I worried I'd missed my meeting with Tobago. But my fear quickly abated. It was still warm outside, which meant it must still be summertime, and Tobago wasn't coming until the beginning of autumn in the Earth's northern hemisphere.

So then, how had I healed so quickly? As I was still alone, and naked, and in a cave, there was no one who could give me any answers. I soon became distracted by the faint sound of running water I'd heard when I first woke up. Determining that it couldn't be too distant, I ventured toward the opening of the cave.

"Ursa?" I called warily, worried he might pop up and ambush me. I adopted my sternest tone. "If you're out there, you'd better make yourself known right now, or so help me—I will be *very* cross!"

When no answer was made and no wildman reappeared, I poked my head out, making sure the coast was clear, before venturing a few steps. Outside of the cave, I didn't feel quite so powerful and free, so I used one arm to cover myself, and the other to pick up a big stick, before making my way down a slight incline to a waterfall below.

The cave opening was on the side of a gray rock wall, gradually sloping down to a pool of clear aquamarine water. The pool wasn't very deep, probably about shoulder-high. Just a small body of water formed from the waterfall that gushed down from higher up the mountainside and continued trickling down to a river that continued on over the rocky terrain and into the waiting wilderness. It was a beautiful, isolated spot, surrounded by rock on nearly every side, which no doubt kept the cave entrance from being discovered by trespassing animals.

Once I reached the pool, my thirst renewed itself anew. When I'd drunk from Ursa's hands, I'd been so overwhelmingly parched, I hadn't fully appreciated just how incredible the water tasted. I had never before, nor since, tasted anything so fresh, so crisp, so clean. On impulse, I splashed the water on my face, then my armpits for good measure, then patted myself dry with the backs of my hands.

It was only then that I noticed the familiar fabric strewn across the rocky bank. My clothes! So this was what the pervert had done with them . . .

Relieved, I made my way over to the bank. But as I picked up my shirt from the grass, I saw—with no little horror—that my trousers were absolutely drenched in dried, old blood. So, too, were my other things, and my shirt was torn to ribbons. I had a brief but vivid flashback of Rawley kicking me in the ribs again and again and again.

Retreating to the safety of the cave once more, I let myself cry. Rawley, the man I had once loved, the man who was still technically my fiancé, had killed my mother. Had tried to kill me. Now I was in a cave in the middle of nowhere with a sex-crazed wildman who didn't speak *any* language, let alone English. And I was naked.

I was having a bit of a day, all things considered.

Only the more I thought about it, the more I realized Ursa probably wasn't a pervert. My clothes were destroyed—I'd seen that for myself.

Rather than leave me in torn, blood-soaked garments, he'd taken them off and tended to my wounds, somehow so effectively that I'd completely healed in just a matter of days, judging by the growth of hair in my armpits. Nudity clearly didn't seem to be an issue for him, so he would have had no idea that I'd react so violently to it. I'd probably frightened the poor man out of his wits, screaming and carrying on like that.

By now, it was getting close to dusk, which meant night would soon be here. I had no idea where Ursa was, if he'd be returning, or if I'd scared him off for good. And though I'd proclaimed myself queen of the cave in my earlier blustering, something told me I would very much not want to be out here on my own once darkness fell.

I once again ventured to the mouth of the cave, this time much more contritely. "Um, Ursa? Are you there? You can come back now." In the silence that followed, I added, "And bring some clothes, please."

19

I have no idea if Ursa heard and understood me, or if by my earlier overreaction, he'd formed the determination on his own, but when he returned to the cave in the late afternoon, it was with an armload of clothing. Some of it smelled quite musty and mildewed, some of it appeared to be men's, some was too small, and some was twice my size. Still, I understood the gesture for what it was as he dumped the clothing at my feet and then scuttled away a few steps, watching warily for my reaction.

I'd returned to my previous position—pressed against the rock wall of the cave, with one arm slung awkwardly behind me in an attempt to cover my posterior—but I did my best to smile reassuringly at him over my shoulder. "Thank you, Ursa. How very thoughtful of you. I'm sorry about earlier. An overreaction, I agree."

He just blinked at me.

"I'm going to get dressed now," I told him.

Nothing. No movement. No response. Just more blinking.

"So if you could, um. Look away. Please." I made a shooing motion, to which he furrowed his brow. Frustrated now, I motioned turning my face in toward the rock, covering my eyes with my hands, and then again, so he'd finally get the picture.

When I looked back, Ursa was still staring at me. Only now, he was much, much closer, only a pace or so away . . . with no glass wall between us, no soldiers watching on with tasers. If he'd been intimidating to me before, he was absolutely terrifying now, a big wall of muscle and hair. Naked—and I was naked, too. My heart began to race, my palms to sweat, but I knew I could show no outward sign of fear. I'd have to be stern and firm, like a master with its dog.

And yes, even then I knew that it was a little ridiculous to make such a fuss about clothing when he'd clearly seen me naked already, but it was a different matter to have him see me naked when I was unaware and to *know* he was seeing me naked—to be very, very aware of it.

"Ursa," I commanded him, trying to maintain eye contact while still keeping the front of my body pressed against the rock wall. "Here!"

Ursa obligingly moved forward—*too* obligingly, really—stepping in so close the front of him was nearly touching the side of me. Let me repeat that for anyone not painting a clear mental picture: The very naked front of him was nearly brushing up against my also very naked skin. It took everything in me not to scream at him again.

"Face to the wall," I instructed, slapping my palm against the rocks. I repeated the overexaggerated gesture of turning my own face in toward the wall, covering my eyes, et cetera. Then I repeated it a few more times.

It took me a moment to realize he wasn't even watching what I was doing. His eyes were roaming the exposed skin of my posterior, darkening as they swept over the curve of my back, and other parts of me that also curved. I felt him begin to stir, no longer only *nearly* brushing against me.

With a yelp, I sidestepped away from him, still keeping my front pressed to the wall. "Ursa, face, wall!"

Finally giving up any pretense of modesty, I turned toward him, feeling myself flush all over as his eyes roamed the front of me. Quickly I managed to push his head so he was facing the wall.

"Stay!" I ordered him. "Stay!"

Heart racing, breath heaving, I watched him, waiting for him to turn back around, primed to run or pounce or scream, whatever was necessary. But this time, Ursa stayed facing the wall, his large, broad back and muscular legs and buttocks turned toward me.

Doubting very much he would remain this way for long, I scrambled over to the clothes, sifting through them as quickly as possible, fearing he might turn back at any moment. I hastily assembled a hodgepodge outfit, not giving myself too much time to lament the terrible options. He'd brought me clothes, which I would happily take despite the lack of aesthetically pleasing options, but there were no undergarments of any kind. Still, *some* layer of clothing was better than none, I supposed.

I rushed to cover myself again, certain that Ursa would soon turn and advance on me again. To my surprise, even when I was fully dressed, Ursa remained with his face to the wall. I knew I couldn't keep him like that forever, but I found it oddly touching that he would obey me for so long.

Still, I figured, best not to push his goodwill too far. I cleared my throat to indicate I was done. No movement. Ursa wouldn't understand those kinds of social niceties. He'd been outside of civilization for too long to understand decorum. I ventured toward him, hesitating before touching him on the arm. "Ursa."

He rounded on me, stepping—as always—just a bit too close. I fell back, fidgeting nervously with my hair as he looked up and down the length of me in my new clothes—an oversized white dress shirt that I'd tied at the waist to make it more manageable,[1] and a pair of khaki trousers (a little big around the waist, but I could find a rope or vine or something to help hold them up, I was confident).

"Thank you for the clothes," I told him, still not quite looking at him. I'd forgotten what a presence he was, this close, with no glass between us. What a force of nature. His build, his smell. The power in every movement, no matter how minute. It seemed better not to look at him full-on with him so near—like the instinct not to look into the sun, for fear of blinding oneself at its awful beauty. "You could wear some, too, if you'd like." I thrust a pair of trousers at him. "These might fit."

Ursa looked down at the garment, making no move to take it, before looking back to me again. Head tilting. A question.

"Please," I insisted, thrusting the trousers at him again. I didn't know how much longer I could go without looking at his penis, with it just *being* there, out in the open like that, and I did not want to seem like I was encouraging him in any way.

At last, reluctantly, Ursa took the trousers. I broke my resolve not to look at him directly, smiling to show my thanks. He made no move to put them on. For a moment, we just stared at one another, until Ursa made the same gesture I'd done earlier to indicate I should look away.

"Oh!" I blushed furiously, turning my face into the rock wall. "Sorry . . ."

Once we were both clothed, I enlisted Ursa in helping me get to the nearest patch of woods so we could gather kindling. It was a temperate day, but as it drew closer to nightfall, I could feel it was going to be quite cold, and I wanted to get a fire going. Ursa, for his part, seemed perplexed as to why I would want to gather a bunch of sticks, but he gamely let me load up his arms as I nervously prattled on about the best type of wood for burning and hoped Tobago's instructions would all come back to me now that I had to put this skill into practice.

Once we were back in the cave and night began to fall, I followed all the steps as best I could remember them and was relieved when I saw small sparks begin to light and catch on the dried leaves and twigs. "There." I sat back, pleased with myself, as the fire crackled to life, its hypnotic bloody embers sending out long, greedy fingers of warmth.

Ursa stared intently at the flames, grunting softly under his breath. If he'd been the religious sort, I imagine he might have crossed himself. As it was, he darted a wary eye toward me, and if he'd had the vocabulary to express it, I imagined he might wonder what strange witch he'd brought back to his camp.

"Not so helpless, am I?" I watched his stupefaction with no little pleasure. "You might well be amazed at what I can do. I was top of the class in my survival course." But lying had never been my strong suit, even when it was to someone who couldn't speak English, or maybe any language for that matter. "Well, I *was* the only student, but I did learn very quickly and—uh-uh." I tutted at him, catching his hands before he could get too near the flames. "No, no. Bad. You mustn't do that. Ouchy."

It wasn't exactly poetry, but Ursa seemed to take this as a romantic gesture, his fingers closing over mine. When I looked up, it was to that fierce, dusky gaze, intense enough it could swallow me whole if I let it.

I extricated myself quickly and shifted away from him. Thankfully he didn't follow; apparently some things translate even without a shared language. I was eager to get past the moment, so I put on a show of holding up my hands a safe distance from the flames, modeling the appropriate way to warm oneself. "Mmm. Cozy."

But when I at last dared another glance at him, Ursa was not mimicking my behavior, just continuing to watch me closely. I scowled at him, poking out my tongue for good measure. It was not, perhaps, the most mature thing to do, but really, he was making everything so unnecessarily uncomfortable.

"If you think that's flattering, it isn't," I groused at him. "I've been stared at like that before, and I was naive enough then to think it was love, but all he was after were my genes. Not very romantic, I think you'd agree."

Nothing from Ursa, just that persistent, insistent watchfulness.

I looked away, into the fire. "I suppose you don't exactly have access to gene-modulating technology out here, so I won't suspect you of the same motivations. But what you want from me"—I flushed but pressed on—"is no less mercenary, not really. I suppose there are some who'd say I should be flattered. But clearly if you think this"—I gestured to myself—"is anything to write home about, you must be pretty starved for options. I suppose I'm a step up from your hand or a mountain goat"—that was too distasteful, so I barreled on—"or whatever you've done to get by this long, but honestly, there are women out there with violet eyes and swan necks and tiny feet and giant breasts." I realized, belatedly, that I was gesturing a little too creatively on this last one, and I clamped my hands down to my side.

"So, you see, I'm nothing special. You'll discover that soon enough, I imagine. It's only a matter of time until they find us." I shivered. "Until Rawley finds us."

He couldn't understand the words, clearly—and thankfully, considering the content of the diatribe I'd just given—but something of the last bit's meaning must have translated in my tone because all at once, Ursa stood, rising to his full, impressive height. The flames cast flickering shadows dancing across his broad shoulders, the sculpted muscles of his arms, the ribbed, scarred plane of his torso, the broad tree-trunk legs. His eyes glittered in the dark, the eyes of a big predator, and he grunted, low and fierce. It was only a noise, not words, not some secret language of his own, but somehow, locked in his dark blue gaze, I understood. *You are my woman,* he told me. *I will protect you. Nothing will harm you when I am near. I will kill anything that would endanger you. I will tear it apart with my bare hands.*

Naturally, all of this was communicated in silence as his stomach rose and fell with labored breathing, his eyes still locked upon mine.

"Oh," I said at last, when I was able. There was not much more that could be said, after all.

20

W aking has always been a difficult and unpleasant act for me. Sleep is so warm and wonderful that I cling to it for as long as possible. Mother always said the most productive people were early risers—she herself was up by five every morning to do her exercises before getting an early start at the lab—but I've always thought anyone in such a hurry to get out of bed must be sorely lacking in the art of sleeping. This morning, still pleasantly warm from the remaining embers of the fire (that I'd built from scratch! With my bare hands!), I gave a satisfied sigh and snuggled in deeper against my heat-regulating blanket.

Only it wasn't a blanket, I remembered with a sudden wide-eyed lurching sensation. I certainly hadn't seen any stashed away around Ursa's cave,[1] and furthermore, in my (admittedly limited) life experience, blankets did not snore.

---

1. Though there were quite a few animal skins, I wouldn't necessarily term these as "blankets." I wasn't accustomed to my blankets on Haven 3 having had faces.

Careful not to rouse the slumbering giant, I shifted and attempted to sit up, but I found I was clamped down underneath an impressively heavy forearm. My back, I discovered as I took anxious stock of my situation, was pressed against Ursa's chest, my bottom nestled into his groin area. In addition to the arm engulfing me, one of his hairy legs had snaked over my own (less hairy, but admittedly not hair*less*) limb, and his nose was pressed firmly against the crown of my head. Oh, and so far as I could ascertain, he was completely naked again.

Good God. What a ridiculous scenario to find myself in! Here was a perfect stranger, uncivilized (at best), possibly infested with fleas or lice or both, and with a very obvious erection pressing into my bottom. Oh, and I desperately had to pee.

There were no two ways about it—I would have to free myself from Ursa, put a safe distance between us, and somehow manage to do so without waking him.

The most direct route would be to just push him off and crawl out from under his hold. But, even should I manage to lift his limbs (which, frankly, given his dense muscle mass, was no guarantee), this route seemed most likely to wake him, since I would be jostling him about so much.

No, I decided, the better option would be to leave his limbs in place but to sort of shimmy upward through the gap between the ground and the arm engulfing me. Some jostling would still be involved, but hopefully not enough to wake him if he was in a deep enough REM cycle.

That decided, my first step was to turn myself so I was facing him. That way, I reasoned, I could keep an eye on him as I made my progress and gauge how much I was disturbing him and if he seemed likely to wake. Also there was the matter of not wanting to slide my posterior over his erection—for obvious reasons, I should think.

My progress was agonizingly slow, both in turning around to face him, then in the careful, complicated move upward. For a large portion of my attempt to shimmy free, it felt as though I were making no headway at all, but finally, at long last, my shoulders emerged through the possessive tunnel of his arm around me, then my torso, then my waist.

Now my hips—the greatest challenge yet. Once I passed these through the gulf, it would be an easy matter to slip my legs through. But, as I soon realized with growing dread, there would be no guarantee of my success. The arch created by Ursa's arm over my body had been wide enough to squeeze my upper body through, but well, I had always had a quite generously sized lower body—the holidays weren't that long behind us, and one can't help a fondness for Yule logs.

Even more carefully now, I progressed. There was no real gap to speak of anymore, I was forced to admit, but hopefully if I was subtle enough in my movements, I would gently graze by him and he wouldn't stir.

The other downside in facing him while moving so slowly was that for an extended time, my pelvis would be sliding along his face. If I'd hoped to move myself out of a precarious position before he woke, that sort of seemed like an out of the frying pan, into the fire scenario now. I checked the impulse to move faster, telling myself the likelihood of waking him would only increase. *Jostling, Mina*, I reminded myself fiercely. *Jostling!*

Naturally, it was while I was in this precarious position that Ursa suddenly shifted. It was only slightly, but I froze, petrified to move even the slightest bit. Eyes still closed, Ursa grunted, then shifted, his arm grazing my thigh. I tensed, holding my breath, but he settled again with another low rumble.

And then, he sniffed.

Inhaled, was more like it. I looked down in horror as Ursa's eyes drifted open, languorous and bleary as he looked up at me from nose-deep in my crotch. He inhaled again and let out an indecent sound that seemed to indicate pleasure at whatever odor he'd encountered.

Then with another grunt, he rolled over, releasing me. I scrambled across the cave, turning just in time to see him scratch his chest, his haunches, before drifting back into a deep sleep.

I remained with my back to the rock wall, heart pounding in my chest. For whatever reason, Ursa had refrained from acting on his attraction to me, even though it was clear that he was . . . excited by my body. But there was no telling how long his forbearance would last, especially if we were always getting into situations where we were naked and/or pressed up against one another. I would have to set up some clear boundaries, and soon.

It wasn't too long afterward that Ursa woke. I'd already made a small fire to stave off the morning chill, and I sat with my profile toward him, able to keep him in my line of sight but also able to turn my attention to the flames so he wouldn't catch me staring. I did this both out of a sense of innate politeness and because I wanted to start setting the example of the type of relationship we should have as peers and comrades. No long, lingering stares. No uncomfortably charged atmosphere or obvious arousal. We were colleagues who happened to sleep in a cave together. These adherences to decorum might be unfamiliar to him after living on his own for so long, but I was certain he would be quickly reminded of the necessities of polite, civilized behavior so long as I provided the way forward.

Out of the corner of my eye, I watched Ursa stand and stretch, still naked. I held my breath and waited in a moment of silent anxiety as I felt his eyes on me. Then, with a sigh, he tugged on his trousers before coming over to join me.

The night before, in my relief that he was finally covering himself, I hadn't noticed the trousers were too small for him. They were rather comically small, really, ending mid-calf and jutting low on his hips. That last part wasn't quite so funny, actually, with the sharp angle of his hip bones and the dark line of hair trailing down from his belly button . . . but at least his manly bits were covered.

I beamed at him beatifically to show my gratitude. I had decided the best way to nudge him back into civilized behavior was to reward him with smiles and encouragement whenever he followed my rules. "Good morning, Ursa! I had a lovely sleep, how about you?"

Ursa blinked at me, looking both bleary and wary. I guessed that he wasn't a morning person, and perhaps he wasn't certain how to respond to my overt cheerfulness since I'd spent the past day screaming at him.

Even knowing he likely wouldn't understand the words, I felt it best to explain myself. "I am very sorry about all the shouting and whatnot yesterday. It won't happen again, so long as we both keep our clothes on, ha! Anyhow, now that I know we understand each other better, we're going to be the best of friends."

Ursa didn't say anything, which I suppose was to be expected. He scratched at his arm for a moment before rising to his feet and moving to the entrance of the cave. Once he was there, he turned back to me, waiting.

"Ah, yes." I rose to my feet, too, realizing he meant for me to follow. "I suppose we'll have to forage for some breakfast? There really isn't any way to store food in here, is there?" Trying for a joke, I added, "No chance of any tea, I'd wager?"

Without responding verbally or expressively, Ursa exited the cave, leaving me to scramble after him.

Thankfully he was just outside, positioned on the rocky incline below the entrance to help me climb down. My shoes hadn't been as ruined as my clothing, but they were heeled leather boots. I quickly ascertained they wouldn't be very useful for climbing or roaming through the forest. With reluctance, I left them behind, testing out the ground with my bare feet. The rocks were smooth enough around the edge of the pool—the water seemed to have worn down some of the rougher edges of the rock face—but I doubted the rest of the wilderness would be as forgiving on the tender skin of my feet. I was beginning to understand why Ursa's feet were so callused and tough.

As we skirted around the pool, Ursa gripped my arm, which I found to be a little condescending until I nearly slipped into the water and he managed to haul me back up. "Slippery!" I said, for lack of anything better to say, and Ursa just blinked at me.

In a short time, we made it to the woods. I was on more solid ground now, literally, which made it easier to move about without Ursa needing to coddle me like a toddler learning to take its first steps. The thorns and pine needles and pebbles littering the forest floor *did* make it more painful and difficult to move around, but I didn't want Ursa to think I was incapable of keeping up, so I bit my tongue each time something poked the soft flesh of my feet and did my best to grimace-smile every time he glanced back at me.

I was pleased that, between my study of mushrooms and Tobago's training, I wouldn't be a hindrance in finding food to eat. I knew how to identify edible berries and fungi, which ought to make for a pleasant enough breakfast.

At first, Ursa watched me closely in my process. Then, seeming to decide I was doing a competent job, he left me to it. After finding a promising bramble bush, I became engrossed with trying to pick out the fully matured berries, so I wasn't paying very close attention to what Ursa was doing.

It wasn't until I heard a thwacking noise that I looked up, frowning—and then looked *up*, my jaw dropping. About ten yards away, Ursa had somehow managed to climb an extremely tall tree without any branches low enough to reach from the ground, and he was sitting on a high branch, using a long stick to hit a beehive.

I continued to stare in openmouthed shock for a moment before I reclaimed my senses. "What are you doing?" I demanded, straightening in astonishment.

Ursa ceased his thwacking, then grunted at me and gestured with his free hand for me to stay back. Right. As if *I* were the one doing something dangerous in this scenario. I might have been raised on a different planet, but even I knew better than to mess with a beehive.[2] With renewed determination, Ursa managed to knock the hive off the branch. It plummeted down to the forest floor, cracking open and sending a thrum of angry bees spilling out of it.

---

2. It might be worthwhile to explain to the Brethren that beekeeping is a thriving practice on Haven 3, since honey is so renowned for its skincare properties. Then again, they seem to rather dislike my expositional tangents, so I suppose I might just wait for them to ask any clarifying questions and then respond as needed? Even though, frankly, some of them could use a good skincare routine . . .

Even though I was quite a distance away, I screamed and instinctively retreated farther, watching in amazement as Ursa shimmied his way down the tree. I know that might seem an odd verb choice, *shimmied*, but I really don't know how else to describe it. He moved quickly and surprisingly gracefully, as if he were sort of dancing his way down the tree, somehow managing not to fall, even though there were no branches to use as footholds. It was really quite an impressive feat, and I wondered where he'd learned to do it.

Ursa hopped down the last few feet, a safe distance away from the angry throb of bees. He watched their activity closely, keeping his eyes on them as he fished around behind him until his hand found a large stone. Still with his eyes trained on the bees, Ursa threw the stone into the downed hive, smashing it open.

He retreated a few more feet, watching the movement of the bees. If any part of me had thought he was antagonizing them just to be, well, an asshole, that idea was quickly dispelled by the careful intensity with which he studied them. He moved with purpose, presumably to get at their honey, though I didn't know how he'd be able to do so without the full force of the hive coming after him.

After a minute or two had passed, Ursa grabbed another rock, venturing a step closer, then another. For a moment, he remained still, watching. Then he threw the rock. At almost the same moment, he dove forward, grabbing something from the depths of the broken hive and taking off into the forest. All of this happened within seconds, without any pausing or hesitation on Ursa's part.

The majority of the hive swarmed around the rock, though some gave Ursa chase into the woods. I could no longer see him or hear him, and I watched with wide eyes to see how the entire thing would resolve itself.

A minute or two later, Ursa reappeared, looking enormously pleased with himself as he showed me the piece of honeycomb.

"Ursa, you did it!" I couldn't help but be impressed. I'd never seen such an astonishing physical feat. I'd always been taught to think that pursuits of the mind were far more valuable than any physical exertions, but there was something wholly exhilarating about witnessing what the human body was capable of accomplishing. I grinned at Ursa, and he grinned back before breaking off a piece of the honeycomb and handing it to me.

My own offerings for breakfast seemed rather paltry in comparison, but at least I was contributing. "Some brambleberries, and some hen-of-the-wood mushrooms," I told him as we sat down to eat our meager feast. "They would really be better cooked, although I suppose we don't have anything to cook them on . . ."

Not for the first time I thought longingly of my supply packs that I'd left hidden near the Olympus campsite. My kingdom for a frying pan! But at least we had food.

Ursa seemed to be of the same mind, since he took his share of the mushrooms and gobbled them raw and whole, following them with the berries, then ending with the honey. I took his lead and ate in the same order. The uncooked mushrooms were quite bitter, but I knew they weren't poisonous and would be quite nutritious. The brambleberries tasted better, and the honey tasted best of all. I'd only ever had processed honey before, and eating it in its undiluted form was almost a sensual experience. The flavors were rich and ripe and bursting, and I'm afraid I quite forgot myself in exploring the honeycomb with my tongue, trying to chase each and every last drop.

When I finished, I looked up to find Ursa staring at me. I couldn't quite read what was in his expression. Most likely he was taken aback by just how ravenous I'd been. Holding my gaze, he began to work on licking clean his own piece of honeycomb. I found myself having to look away from the sight of his pink tongue darting in and out of all those little crevices, something about it leaving me flustered and unsettled.

My eyes landed on some angry welts on his arms and torso, indicating he hadn't gotten out of the experience unscathed. Making a clucking noise of concern, I touched his arm near one of the sores. "Ursa! Are you all right? You've been stung!"

When I looked back up at him, he was giving me that same unreadable but intense look as before, and I instinctively withdrew my hand. Remembering that I wanted to keep some firm boundaries erected, I decided to double down on behaving motherly and concerned—as one might behave toward a coworker or neighbor, naturally. "You must be more careful. The honey was delicious, but there's no need to injure yourself this way."

Something in my tone must have translated, even if Ursa couldn't understand the words. He huffed at me, looking irritated at my lack of fawning gratitude, but at least he wasn't giving me that smoldering stare anymore. With a grunt, he stood and pivoted back in the direction of the cave, and I followed soundlessly behind him, wincing at the sight of more welts on his bare back and resisting the urge to fuss over them.

When we reached the cave, Ursa stopped at the edge of the pool. Without any warning or fuss, he shucked off his trousers, kicking them onto the ground.

I yelped, turning my back to him and covering my eyes. I heard the sound of him moving through the water, splashing, grunting. After a moment, I realized he was trying to get my attention. Still covering my eyes, I turned slowly and peeked through my fingers. Ursa's lower half was covered by the water, but he was still *naked*, and I knew he was still naked, so I wasn't sure what he was hoping to accomplish by trying to get me to gawk at him.

Ursa gestured to his chest and arms, watching me expectantly. I looked up to the sky instead, nodding. "Must be very refreshing. I'm glad you're enjoying yourself! I think I'll just . . ." I turned my back to him again, settling myself down on a rock to wait.

I heard Ursa's audible sigh, then some more splashing. A moment later, he stepped onto the rock next to me, dripping down in puddles that stained the light gray of the rock to a darker shade. Keeping my focus on the ground, I didn't look up, even when Ursa grunted at me again.

"I'll be happy to look at whatever you want to show me once you're wearing trousers," I informed him, cheerful but firm.

Another grunt-sigh. Behind me, I could hear Ursa pulling on his clothing, and when I turned, he was covered again. The trousers were, ridiculously, even smaller and tighter on him when his body was wet, but at least his parts were concealed. Hinted at rather transparently through the tight material, but concealed!

I beamed a smile of reward for his good behavior. "What is it you wanted to show me?"

Ursa looked down at himself meaningfully. I didn't understand what he was trying to do, and I shook my head to show it. Ursa huffed and held out his forearms to me. It took me a moment to realize the welts that had covered his skin a few minutes ago had lessened considerably. There seemed to be far fewer than before, and some were just tiny pinpricks of red irritation now.

Frowning, I clutched his forearm, pulling it closer to me for inspection. "How strange." But already, I was second-guessing myself. Maybe it wasn't all that strange? Maybe beestings on Earth healed more rapidly, or maybe there hadn't been as many on him as I remembered . . . ?

Realizing that I had broken my own rule by getting too close to Ursa once again, I released him and stepped back. "Fascinating. Thank you for sharing with me."

I'd adopted the too-bright, overly enthusiastic voice again, and Ursa still didn't seem to know what to do with it. He blinked at me. I blinked at him.

This was going to be a long and strange process, the two of us learning how to live together, how to comprehend one another.

On the one hand, I was very grateful not to be on my own, as had been my original plan. But on the other . . . there was something terribly lonely about being with someone else and knowing you could not understand each other.

21

The next morning, I woke with some great surprise and no little amount of trepidation to realize that Ursa was gone.

Sitting up, my heart in my throat, I searched the small cave more times than was really necessary to ascertain he wasn't there, just in case I'd somehow missed him. "Ursa?" I called, clutching the animal skins we'd been using for blankets more tightly around myself.[1]

When no answer was forthcoming, I moved to the mouth of the cave, peering out to see if Ursa was bathing in the pool. When there

---

1. The Brethren might be astute enough to notice the usage of the word *we* here, so I must be prepared to answer any questions about why Ursa and I were continuing to sleep next to one another, despite my resolve to keep any contact of a sexual nature from happening. The simple answer is honestly just that it was rather cold at night, even in the warmer summer months, and it was necessary to sleep together for warmth. I'm afraid the Brethren might read too much into this detail, though, and it might move the development of our relationship timeline forward too quickly if we skip over some of the other necessary steps, so I'm going to avoid elaborating if at all possible.

was no sign of him there, I told myself he'd gone out to fetch breakfast and would be back shortly.

But too much time had passed for that to be a likely scenario. It's difficult to say exactly how much time, without a watch or clock or even a good view of the sun, since I was too frightened to leave the cave on my own. It felt like hours, but that might have just been my anxiety slowing the passage of time. For the first time, I realized what a precarious position I was in. The plan had always been for me to set out on my own in the wilderness until I met up with Tobago, but now that I'd actually left the base, I understood just how ill-equipped I was to the task. Venturing into the woods by myself this morning was a daunting prospect, whereas the morning before, with Ursa by my side, it had seemed like such an easy, even fun task. Having a guide who understood the wilderness, who had already provided me with a viable shelter and knew where to find food and a good water source, was what had kept me alive this long.

What if he had been injured somewhere out in the forest? I ought to go after him, but then, what if I ended up getting hopelessly lost looking for him?

What if he'd simply realized I was too much of a burden and decided to leave me?

I paced and stewed and was afraid to leave the cave long enough to even go to the bathroom, for fear I might somehow miss his return.

Then all at once, he appeared in the opening of the cave, as unconcerned and carefree as ever. His arms were loaded down with something he'd been carrying, but he tossed the items to the ground, eyes scanning the cave until he found me.

"Ursa!" Unable to help myself, I raced over to him. I wanted to throw myself into his arms and cling onto him and tell him he was never allowed to leave me again, but that all felt a little dramatic, all things considered. Plus, now that he was back here with me and the danger had passed, I realized how silly I'd been, how carried away I'd gotten. So instead, I drew up just short of him, patting his arm and shoulder awkwardly. "Hello, there, you!" My relief shifted almost instantaneously into anger, my hands finding my hips. "And just where have you been all this time? I was worried sick!"

Ursa didn't seem to understand my words, but my tone must have translated, because he shied away as if afraid I might attack him. How preposterous. Although, I suppose the last time I raised my voice at him, I did throw stones and run him out of the cave. So, perhaps it was not *completely* preposterous. Still, he was nearly twice my size—imagine being afraid of little old mycologist me. I might have laughed if I weren't trying to hold on to the moral high ground of being abandoned.

With a grunt, Ursa gestured down to whatever he'd brought back to the cave, nudging it toward me with his feet like a peace offering.

In my excitement at seeing him, I hadn't fully processed just what it was my wildman had been carrying. "My packs!" No wonder he'd been gone so long. This wonderful man had ventured back to the Olympus campsite to find the packs I'd hidden in the woods in what felt like another lifetime. All of my most important supplies were here—cooking utensils and a microscope and clothes and shoes and food and *bras*. I couldn't remember ever being happier in my life.

This time, I did throw myself into his arms, too overwhelmed with giddiness to check myself. "All my things! Oh, you lovely man. I could just—"

I stopped myself short of finishing that expression, even though it was a common enough phrase. It felt too intimate to even say the words *kiss you*, with him so broad and half naked and *close* to me. He was already giving me that hard, intense look from our bodily contact alone, and I quickly stepped away, dropping my hand and squatting to investigate my packs and cover up any discomfort.

"What do we have here?" I clapped my hands together in delight. "Don't worry, Ursa, I fully intend to share all of my goodies." Remembering some of my more delicate items in the packs, I amended, "Most, anyway."

At my urging, Ursa squatted to help me sort through the packs. I lined up all my items into their various categories—cookware, clothing, et cetera. Ursa wasn't much help in that department, I'm afraid, since he just picked and sniffed and tugged and moved everything out of their piles, but I was too happy to mind (much).

When I was done unpacking, I folded up the empty packs, too, and set them near the cave entrance. "We can use these to gather and store edible items we find in the forest, so we don't have to make so many trips out." *And so I can have food on hand if you ever disappear like that again,* I added to myself.

Ursa was still busy rifling through various things and smelling them. When he picked up a bar of soap, he sniffed it and grunted, handing it over to me.

"No, that goes in that pile just there," I told him.

Ursa grunted again, holding out the soap to me.

We might not have spoken the same language, but his meaning was all too clear. I blushed. Ah. So that was why he'd gone to such trouble to bring the soap and fresh clothing and whatnot to me from a campsite that must have been at least a few miles away. It was his not-so-subtle way of telling me I was starting to smell. A bit offensive, really, coming from a man whom I'd seen grooming his own beard for insects.

Then again, I had caught a whiff of myself this morning, and I could see why an intervention might be necessary. I'd been avoiding cleaning myself, of course, because I didn't want to put us into a situation where we would once again be naked together. Ursa seemed to have no compunctions whatsoever about nudity, although I noticed he had taken to wearing those ill-fitting trousers during the day. I knew this was for my sake, not his own, and I tried to show my gratitude with verbal reinforcement; however, as was usual when I spoke to him, Ursa seemed less interested in *what* I had to say than in watching *how* I said it. He gave such rapt focus to my lips and tongue that I became self-conscious and flustered and often found myself babbling sheer nonsense just to deflect some of his intensity.

Now, though, with Ursa clearly hinting that he wanted me to bathe and put on fresh clothing, I waffled on what would be the best course of action. On the one hand, he *had* already seen me naked, so it wouldn't be like he were witnessing anything new. On the other hand, Ursa had a way of making me feel stripped even when I was fully clothed, so I didn't know that removing the only barrier between us was the wisest course of action. Then again, the pool looked so incredibly inviting to my sweat-soaked and bloodstained skin . . .

A few moments later, I stood at the edge of the water, still internally debating what to do as I clutched my fresh clothes and towel and toiletries to my chest. I'd hoped perhaps Ursa would let me have some privacy, but no such luck. He stood right next to me, also staring at the water, though through my peripheral vision, I caught him glancing over at me every so often, as if he was unsure what we were doing but determined to be my shadow in doing it.

I decided that now might not be the time for subtlety. "Perhaps if you would wait inside the cave," I tried. Surely I would be safe here on my own, in this remote pool surrounded by rock walls—and even safer with Ursa nowhere near me, so I could bathe in peace.

Ursa's response was to shuck off his trousers. "Gah!" I cried at the sight of his exposed manly parts, covering my eyes quickly. A moment later, I heard a splash as he dove into the water.

So much for bathing on my own. I peeked over my hands, ascertaining that his lower body was submerged before leveling him with a stern glare. At times, I thought Ursa couldn't understand a word I was saying; other times, it felt as though he understood me well enough but delighted in riling me up. As if in response to this thought, Ursa grinned at me from the water, entirely unrepentant.

He *did* look rather relaxed and cool, with the water slicking down his wild hair and beard, little droplets dripping to his broad, muscular shoulders and arms.

I averted my gaze. "I suppose there's no way I'm getting you out of that pool now?" He made no answer. When I looked back at him, he just kept grinning as he treaded water.

"Fine," I conceded, then fixed him with a level, no-nonsense glare to show him I was still queen of the cave. "Turn around."

I demonstrated turning my head, a gesture he was now well familiar with after living with me for the past few days. Ursa huffed and rolled his eyes,[2] but obligingly turned his back.

After a few minutes of watching him to make sure he wasn't peeking, I made short work of my clothing. It was a relief, honestly, to get out of those sweat-stained, stinky garments. I reflected that Ursa was unusually clean and olfactorily pleasant for someone who had lived in the wilderness for what must have been years. Perhaps this was due in part to the pool conveniently located right outside of his cave. I wondered if he also had a method of combing his hair, because

---

2. The cheek!

although it was tangled, it wasn't as matted as one would expect for someone who didn't seem to own shampoo . . .

As I'd been lost in my own thoughts, it took me a moment to realize that Ursa had pivoted back around and was now unabashedly staring at me.

My first instinct was to shriek and cover myself again, but then irritation quickly overcame any sense of modesty I had. Honestly! I thought we'd come to an understanding, but clearly there was still some work to be done. Resisting the lingering urge to conceal my womanly bits, I instead placed my hands on my hips and glowered at him. "You're a bit of a pervert, aren't you? Always sneaking around and staring. Well, go on, get an eyeful. Nothing you haven't seen before, right?"

From my tone, Ursa seemed to understand that he was meant to look away, but rather than avert his gaze, he tilted his head to the side, almost as if in challenge. It seemed he was going to take me at my word and get his eyeful. I tried to remain defiant, chin raised, but the languid slide of his eyes over my body was making me uncomfortably aware of myself in a way that I had never been before. I had to remind myself to breathe as his gaze took in my breasts; my nipples began hardening into painful little pebbles. He gaze briefly darted up to mine before moving back down, down, down. My breathing became shallow, and again I fought the urge to cover myself, determined to remain defiant and unashamed. He was no longer smiling, his dusky eyes intent and watchful, his pink tongue darting out to wet his lips.

I pressed my legs together, covering myself with my hands. "Oh, honestly," I snapped, edging myself toward the water. It was clear he'd won this little game of chicken, but that didn't mean I had to concede gracefully. "It's very rude to stare."

Plunging into the water, I stayed underneath until I felt some semblance of myself returning. When I emerged again, cool and haughty as can be, I made sure to let nothing below my shoulders show above the water.

Ursa was grinning again, wanting to let me know that he knew he'd won whatever game it was we were playing. Scowling, I turned my back to him and reached for the soap and shampoo I'd left at the pool's edge, then busied myself with the task of bathing.

"I suppose it's not your fault that you're so uncouth," I told him, still not facing him as I scrubbed myself vigorously. "I don't know where you're from, and I highly doubt it's Haven 3, but if it were, you'd understand our Havenian philosophy is really the most civilized. Imagine being at the mercy of your bodily impulses, a slave to sexual desire! When you can get all the same benefits from a pleasure machine, without the risk of disease or unplanned pregnancy, and without the need to search for a willing partner. It would be like, if every time I were hungry, I'd have to wait until I came across a deer that wanted to be eaten. It's so much more efficient to just have food ready and available for consumption, don't you think?"

I'm afraid by this point I'd lathered my scalp to within an inch of its life. Perhaps it was fortuitous, then, that I was interrupted by Ursa suddenly looming in front of me, brow furrowed in that intense way of his. At first I feared he was coming closer to examine my body again, and I tensed, raising my arms defensively and letting out a loud "Hah!"

I quickly realized, however, that it was the shampoo that had drawn him over with equal parts curiosity and consternation. He circled me in the water, sniffing and reaching out to touch the lathered foam but recoiling his hand before making contact.

My defensiveness immediately evaporated, and I laughed at his endearing naivety. "It's fine, Ursa. It's only shampoo. See?" I scraped some foam onto my fingers and held them out for him to examine.

Still frowning, Ursa tentatively leaned forward, setting his nose just above the foam and inhaling once, then again. The second time he got too close, and some got onto the tip of his nose. He recoiled, rapidly shaking his head this way and that, trying to dislodge the suds.

Laughing, I cleaned my hand in the water before raising it to wipe off the tip of his nose. Ursa scrubbed over the same spot with his knuckles, as if reassuring himself it was all gone. Seeing my laughter, his face relaxed, and he grinned, acknowledging how ridiculous his overreaction had been.

"It's harmless," I reassured him again. "But it smells good, doesn't it?"

I took some more foam from my head, holding it out for him. Ursa ventured forward more boldly this time, gripping my wrist as he leaned close to inhale the foam. He let out a low grumble of pleasure at the scent, his blue eyes seeking out mine.

The combination of that sound and that look sent an odd sensation jolting through me. I pulled my hand back quickly, but I didn't move away. I liked when Ursa and I were communicating this way, sharing and learning from each other in innocent camaraderie. I didn't want to revert to that strangely charged other way of interacting, which felt wild and heady and out of my control.

"Would you like to try some?" I asked, keeping my voice bright. I'd been so excited to wash my hair that I'd rather overdone it on the amount of shampoo, so I gathered the excess in my hands and offered it to him.

Ursa tilted his head at me again, clearly not understanding as he leaned forward to sniff.

"No," I laughed. "Here. Turn around."

I nudged Ursa so his back was turned toward me and gently administered the shampoo, rubbing it into his scalp. "There, you see? Just like that."

Ursa's answering groan of pleasure was proof enough that he was enjoying himself. I laughed again but put more distance between us, swimming around him so we were facing each other. It felt safer to have him continue shampooing on his own. I raised my hands to my own scalp, modeling for him. "So, you just sort of rub it in, until your hair feels clean. And then you—"

I abruptly ducked my head underwater.

When I reemerged, Ursa's face looked crestfallen. I didn't realize why until he reached for a lock of my hair, sniffing its end. He sighed with relief, and I laughed again. "Is that why you were worried? The smell won't be as strong, but it won't go away for a while."

Seeming encouraged by this, he dunked his own head underwater, emerging a moment later with sleek, clean hair. He offered the top of his head for me to sniff.

He looked so proud of himself that I didn't want to ruin the moment by refusing. I tentatively touched my nose to the top of his scalp, inhaling like I'd seen him do. Hmm. That did smell nice!

"Very good," I reassured him, and Ursa pulled back, grinning at me.

His expression was guileless, and we were back to being friendly with each other. So why did I have to ruin it by noticing the way his eyes brightened when he smiled, the fullness of his lower lip?

"I'm going to swim," I announced suddenly, turning my back and swimming to the opposite side of the pool.

In that moment, I understood that living with Ursa was going to be very complicated. But I was the one with the responsibility, the moral obligation, to show him the right and *civilized* way to behave.

22

How to describe the bliss I felt that night . . . ? I'm not sure if it's possible to capture it fully. After days of living in filth and squalor, caked in mud and dried blood, without proper undergarments,[1] and wearing trousers I had to tie in place with a bloody ridiculous rope, I was finally clean and in clothes that actually fit me. Not to mention the cookware I'd be able to put to use the next day, plus the stores of protein bars and other packaged foods that, along with what we could forage in the woods, would allow us to receive adequate nutrition. And the best part of all was that Rawley was

---

1. I might not want to mention this too explicitly to the Brethren. The last time clothing was brought up, they seemed overly interested in my lack of undergarments and kept interrupting the story to ask more details about ridiculous things, such as if I was able to keep my breasts in place as I moved or if they were constantly swinging about. They find *this* interesting, but not the advancements that have been made with genetically altering mushroom strains? I will never understand men.

nowhere to be found. I was clean, I was clothed, I was fed, and I was *safe*.

Sitting next to the fire in my beloved billowing white nightgown, I combed out my hair to let it dry properly. I smelled so good. It was heavenly. And it was making me feel very benevolent. So much so that when I glanced up and caught Ursa staring at me in *that* way of his, I didn't frown at him or scold him like I usually might. Smiling, I beckoned him closer.

"Come here, Ursa." I patted the space next to me on the rock. Despite all his staring, Ursa frowned warily, like he was afraid I was trying to lay some trap for him, but he did tentatively move closer.

I suppose it wasn't often that I invited him into my personal space, but what can I say? I was feeling generous. Giving him my most seraphic smile, I once again motioned for him to sit, which he finally did. "Would you like me to comb your hair? That will help it dry without all those nasty tangles."

Ursa likely couldn't understand what I was asking of him, so I held up the comb and theatrically ran it through my own hair, humming with exaggerated pleasure, before motioning toward him. He didn't respond, just continued giving me that hard stare. I decided to take that as confirmation that I could proceed, and I further resolved to ignore his gawking, especially when we were in such close proximity. Perhaps if I willfully pretended not to notice the way he was always watching me, he would stop doing it.

I started detangling the ends of his hair, then slowly worked my way upward. When I hit one particularly gnarly snarl,[2] Ursa grunted in protest, jerking his head back and taking my comb with him. The

---

2. I couldn't resist the tempting assonance!

comb dangled from his hair, making him look rather ridiculous, and it took everything in me not to laugh, knowing instinctively that it would wound his pride.

"I'm sorry, Ursa. Please come back. I'll be more gentle, I promise."

With a little more gentle cajoling, I convinced him to sit back down. I rose onto my knees to have a better angle as I attacked the tangles on his head. Ursa was a model patient after that, and soon I was able to make clean strokes down the length of his long hair.

"We'll have to remember to use conditioner next time," I told him. "Though really, it's remarkable that your hair is as healthy as it is. Were you rubbing some aloe or horsetail into it before . . . ?"

I trailed off as I realized Ursa wasn't even listening to me. His eyes were closed, a deep rumble of contentment ruminating through him as I continued to comb his hair. This time I couldn't hide my smile. Here was this massive beast of a man who had announced himself into civilization by breaking limbs and cracking heads, who knocked honeycombs out of trees and smashed them open with rocks—but he liked a little pampering as much as the rest of us. I found it strangely endearing.

Ursa's eyes opened quite suddenly, meeting mine. They really were *so* blue. I stuttered a laugh, my heart galloping in response. "It does feel nice, doesn't it?" I pulled away, comb in hand, twisting back toward my toiletries pack to retrieve something. "You know what else might feel good?" Finding what I'd been searching for, I took it from the bag and held it up into the air: trimming scissors.

Ursa reeled back in almost comical horror. I suppose the firelight was glinting off the blades in a rather menacing way, making them appear sharper than they actually were, but still. I gave him my best no-nonsense look. "Don't be silly. I'm not going to hurt you. I'll just trim off some split ends and, uh, tame that beard, I think."

The beard was the thing that really made Ursa look so wild, I'd determined the other day. Beards, as a general rule, were not in fashion on Haven 3, but on the rare occurrence that a man did wear hair on his face, it was kept very trim and tidy. I might have a better idea of what Ursa looked like underneath all that bushy nonsense on his face, and now that the idea had taken hold of me, I was determined not to let it go.

"Please, Ursa." I could see that he was still reluctant, so I may have resorted to pouting, like I might have done as a child when I *really* needed to get my way. "I promise, I won't hurt you or make you look ridiculous."

No more ridiculous than a large, bushy beard, anyhow! I added silently.

Ursa's gaze snagged on my pouty lips. He did seem to be very interested in my mouth. So, I decided I would use that to my advantage and began to talk as I simultaneously started trimming. "I remember the first time I went to get a haircut . . ."

Honestly, after all this time, I can't remember what I said, only that I knew instinctively that I had to keep chattering to keep him distracted enough to let me groom him.

Obviously, I was not unaware of how close we'd become as I was snipping and trimming away. I felt, keenly, the weight of his eyes on my lips, the magnetic sway of our bodies each time I got close enough to almost touch him. I never did touch him, beyond what was necessary to turn his head this way or that. I did wonder, though, what I might do if he reached out to touch me, to place his big warm hands on my hips, and for the first time it struck me how really flimsy this nightgown was, the material almost nothing against my skin . . .

"Finished!" I leaned back, proudly examining my work. "Ursa, it's night and day, really. You have to see it!"

Turning back to my pack, I found a mirror and handed it over to him. Ursa tentatively took hold of the frame, reacting in surprise at the sight of his own reflection. Then, blinking, he leaned in closer, touching the side of his face, then the mirror, jumping as his fingers made contact with the glass.

It was all very endearing and funny, though seeing as he had forgotten what a mirror was, it did make me wonder how long it had been since he'd been in civilized company. Out in the wild, he must have at least seen his own reflection in a still pool of water or the like, though not as clearly as he could see it here. He seemed fascinated by the sight of his own features, his blue eyes searching his reflected face with almost as much intensity as he reserved to observe mine.

Now that he was so distracted by his own image, it was my turn to stare at him. Deciding to tidy up Ursa's appearance had been more of a lark than anything, but now that I'd finished, I was amazed at the transformation that had taken place. It had always been clear he had a good bone structure and beautiful eyes; but without the distraction of his gnarled hair and shaggy beard, I could see just how handsome he truly was. It was almost unbelievable that he hadn't been genetically modified in any way. His close-cut beard showed the hard lines of his jaw and cheekbones and more clearly accentuated his full lips. Those features were a deadly combination with his long dark lashes and dusky blue eyes . . .

Which were looking right back at me now. Blinking, I snapped out of my thoughts, deeply embarrassed that Ursa had been the one to catch me staring this time. Fair was fair, I supposed, but I didn't know why the sight of his face should suddenly make me feel so . . . unsettled. I'm not sure that unsettled was even the right word for it. I had never felt anything like this before and didn't know what to compare it to.

"Very handsome," I reassured him, forcing brightness back into my voice. "You'd turn all the heads on Haven 3, I can tell you that!"

Ursa said nothing, just looked at me. So, we were back to that. I knew it was up to me to steer things back into safer territory again.

"It really is remarkable how *healthy* your hair was, despite the usual wear and tear of being grown so long." It started off as simple babbling, but as often happens when I begin to speak with no idea of where I'm going, the idea took on a life of its own. "Was it the honey? It is often used as an ingredient in shampoos, I believe, and you seem to be rather adept at gathering that—aside from a few pesky beestings."

Even as the words left my mouth, I realized that I hadn't actually noticed any sting marks on him since we'd gone bathing in the pool. A day had passed, so it made sense that the wounds would have faded. But they'd been quite violently irritated only yesterday, and now there was nothing. I examined his chest and arms again to verify that I wasn't misremembering, then crawled forward so I could take a look at his back. Nothing! Not a single welt or mark left.

Rocking back into a crouch, I frowned into Ursa's face, wishing, not for the first time, that we could communicate more easily. "How is it that you don't have a single mark left?" Another thought struck me almost right on top of it: "Or *any* marks, really? You're constantly climbing and scraping and rubbing up against trees.[3] You should be a walking wound. So why aren't you wounded?"

I recalled how when I'd been fussing at him after he was attacked by the bees, he'd seemed wholly unperturbed, simply jumping into the pool when we returned to the cave. I remembered, too, how quickly my wounds had healed after being beaten by Rawley and the vague, disorienting memory I had of Ursa lowering me into the water.

"Is it the pool?" I wondered aloud. "Does it have healing properties?"

Ursa didn't respond. He might not have even known what I was talking about. Yet once again, I was struck by the intelligence in his eyes, which made me feel like he understood me completely, even if he couldn't use words to communicate back with me.

And if it *was* the pool, I determined, I would find some way to discover where its healing properties stemmed from and how they might be used to help others.

Maybe that was the reason, for all of this—why I'd come to Earth, why I'd found Ursa, or rather, why he'd found me. Maybe, despite all his ill-intentions, Rawley had unwittingly led me toward the greatest discovery of all.

---

3. I'm not sure if I've mentioned this yet? Ursa had an odd habit of stopping at trees around our cave to rub his back against the bark. Sometimes he would even do this against the rocks in the cave, while watching me very intently. There's not much of a story around this behavior, it was just something he would occasionally do that struck me as odd. Still, this quirk of his might be worth fleshing out with the Brethren to try to extend the amount of nights that my story carries on . . .

23

I would be remiss if I didn't mention that not all of my time with Ursa was spent chasing each other around caves and frolicking in pools that possibly had mysterious healing properties. Truly, much of our time together passed rather uneventfully. We taught each other a great many things between the more exciting events that took place during those early days of getting to know one another. Some of this dispensing of knowledge was done for the sake of necessity or to enrich the life of the other person; some of it was done out of sheer boredom. Ursa taught me how to forage for food. I'd already had some idea, obviously, about what mushroom strains were edible and which were poisonous,[1] and during my wilderness-survival training, I'd learned about a few berries and roots and such. But Ursa expanded my culinary horizons by showing me how to catch fish and find fresh

---

1. I mustn't go overboard with all the mushroom talk, as the Brethren really don't seem to like it—even though they might be astounded by how interesting they'd find it if they just gave it a chance!

honey, and I vastly expanded his horizons by teaching him how to cook meat.[2] Along with these more necessary skills, I also taught Ursa how to whistle and play Simon Says, and he repaid me by teaching me how to burp on command.[3]

But by far, the most important things that I taught Ursa during our time together were the basic components of human communication. I won't catalog how long this process actually took, since without any other human beings around, or technology, or even board games, you can imagine we had an enormous amount of time on our hands. I think the Brethren might prefer to believe that our entire time was spent in a sort of mutual, half-crazed lust, each action loaded with sexual innuendo, but the truth was, we were both just human and as such, there were highs and lows in our interactions. Sometimes we avoided each other altogether, needing our time apart. But when we were together, most of my instruction to Ursa centered around speaking and reading. With no training and few materials on hand, I'm enormously proud of what I accomplished in such a short time.

However, such a thorough description of the process of teaching a wildman how to communicate would likely be considered "dull" by my bloodthirsty audience—although they will likely appreciate the few parts of the story where our interactions became vaguely sexual, which I must say I find irksome. Surely, there is an audience out there, like myself, more interested in the anthropological value of such a study, not just the titillating bits! However, it seems best not to risk it here, with the threat of air locks and suffocation always in the

---

2. One would be better served not to spend too much time imagining how Ursa had eaten animal byproducts before this instruction, I think.

3. Maybe best to leave this out, or a demonstration might be necessary.

background. And really, what more can be expected from pirates?[4] Perhaps there are readers out there who wish to learn more about my methods, in which case, if I've survived long enough to bring this manuscript to one of the Havens and get it published, I suggest you get in touch with my editors and reassure them that the reading public still craves the intellectual stimulus of discovery!

But for now, I suppose, I had best get on to the "sexy bits" . . .

Ursa's interest in learning how to speak ebbed and flowed. As someone who had spent a nebulous amount of time outside of society, he no longer seemed to value the necessity of verbal communication. Nor could he comprehend the pleasure of the written word and its ability to enlighten, enliven, and transport one from one's immediate circumstances. To him it was all gibberish. Sometimes he seemed to enjoy mimicking the stranger sounds I produced—one cannot entirely understand the bizarreness of the pronunciation of the letter *x* until one encounters a human who potentially has no concept of what an alphabet is, for example. But more often than not, he seemed confused, disinterested, and at times even downright sullen at my attempts to teach him.

I'm not proud to admit that I sometimes resorted to underhanded methods to retain his attention. Actually, no, that's a falsehood—I'm *enormously* proud of my ingenuity in figuring out how to hold his interest in those early days, before he had really grasped the concept of language and how monumentally it could open up his perspective. Some may say my methods were underhanded or unscientific, but to

---

4. I apologize if my phrasing appears insensitive to those pirates out there who might be scholars of the human condition along with bloodthirsty mercenaries.

them I'd say that I used every tool at my disposal to ensure Ursa's success, *and it worked*. So stick that in your pipe and smoke it!

By this time, I was, of course, not unaware of the...physical effect I had on Ursa. It hadn't occurred to me to incorporate this influence into my teaching methods until, quite by accident, I stumbled upon its efficiency. One day, when Ursa was being particularly obstinate and refusing to cooperate, I wetted my lips in frustration.

Ursa's eyes followed my tongue, and his demeanor changed instantly, from surly to engaged. Initially I was irritated by this, until I realized it was the first time all afternoon he was paying attention to my lessons. "Ball," I tried, over-enunciating the consonants, really putting my lips and teeth into it, letting them earn their keep.

To my utter surprise, he repeated the word back to me. Well, to be fair, it was more of a "Buh," but it was the first time he'd shown any such initiative, and it was utterly thrilling to see my methods working.

I shrieked with excitement, reaching out to grab his arm and give it a giddy shake.[5] Ursa grew very still, looking down at the place where my hand rested on his bicep.

It was understandable why this might've been a moment of some note to him, since—despite living in rather close quarters—we only touched very rarely, and it was even rarer for me to instigate physical contact. Ursa, I had discovered quickly, was quite a tactile person, and he was always initiating touch between us—picking vegetative detritus out of my hair, inspecting a stray freckle on my arm, pulling me back from a poisonous plant I was about to brush against during one of my nature rambles, et cetera. All of these were innocuous gestures,

---

5. That was the intention, anyway, though his arm didn't budge all that much, being such a heavy muscular mass, as it was.

but they still encouraged a tactile relationship between us. I, however, had not been so free with making contact. In my recollection, I had initiated touch between us precisely five times. The first time to play with his hair when we were back at the base; once to stop him from getting too close to the fire, as I have already described; once to show him how to use shampoo; once to cut his hair and trim his beard; and once to smash a large mosquito gorging on his chest.[6]

So, my grabbing Ursa's arm so freely was quite an unusual exchange for us, and I could tell he was doing his best not to spook me off, remaining completely still, all but holding his breath. Aside from his first instinctive glance down at my hand, he was almost pretending as if nothing was happening at all, which I found rather endearing, I must say.

When I continued to reward him with touch for his attempts to speak, it wasn't entirely mercenary on my part. Of course I wanted Ursa to learn how to speak and read, because yes, it would reflect well on my teaching methods—and because, frankly, it would be nice to have somebody to talk to. But, it wasn't only for me. Communicating would open Ursa's horizons and make communication between us less frustrating. I'd inadvertently discovered a new method that would make learning more enjoyable for him. We both won!

If I sound defensive about this, I suppose I am. You can't imagine the amount of criticism I've already received from the Brethren, about how I mistreated Ursa in this way or that, how I used him, or overencouraged him, or didn't encourage him enough. I suppose there are a

---

6. His pectoral, to be more precise. That had been quite an awkward encounter, as you can imagine.

great deal of things I could have done better. Especially when I think of . . .

Well, that's getting ahead of myself. And that's the point, really. In hindsight, it's easy to say I should have done this or he could have done that. But at the time, we were simply experiencing everything, reacting and interacting, as two complete strangers thrust into the unknown, together.

Anyhow, back to our speaking lessons. I'm not entirely sure how much time in total passed, but I believe we spent a matter of weeks in this way, with me teaching Ursa words when he was receptive to it. Nothing too complex, only what I could easily communicate to him. Rock. Hand. Face. Leaf. And so forth. Once we made our breakthrough, Ursa seemed more interested in learning, not only for our close proximity, but because he was beginning to understand and make his own connections.

Less interesting for him, it seemed, was actually *speaking* the words. He was comfortable in his silence, even seeming to prefer it, but he liked to listen to me talk. Maybe it was only because he didn't know how to tell me to shut up—that was what Mother might have said, if she were here. But I don't think so. He would stay so perfectly still when I spoke, watching my lips and sometimes moving his own in unconscious mimicry, even if no sound came out.

When I spoke, I got the sense that he understood me, for the most part, and so I kept talking—great big waves of verbal diarrhea, rushing out unchecked. I said whatever came to mind, whatever senseless train of thought I stumbled over, just to have something to say. I was not so comfortable in my own silence, it seems. Then, gradually, I found myself telling the entire story of Rawley and Tobago. My mother. Every detail I could think of, the words painful but healing, somehow, to have spoken aloud.

I didn't realize I was crying until Ursa bumped his forehead against mine, grunting as he rubbed away my tears with the top of his head, and I had to laugh, it was all too bizarre.

At his perplexed look, I laughed again, wiping away the lingering traces of moisture with the tips of my fingers. "Well, that's one way to shut me up," I told him, settling back against the rock with a smile. "There, Ursa, see? You've put a smile on my face."

He furrowed his forehead in concentration, an expression I now recognized him not understanding one of the words I'd used. I quickly went over in my mind what I'd just said, trying to pinpoint which word it could be. "Smile?" I asked, and he leaned forward, concentrating intently.

"Smile." I gestured to my face, brightening my voice. "Happy." Then contorted it into a frown, pantomiming tears. "Sad." Then back to smiling. "Happy."

If anyone else had seen me doing this, they would have thought I was mad, but Ursa was used to my unconventional methods by now. I don't know if my expression was contagious or if Ursa was simply mimicking it, but the corners of his mouth twitched upward. "Smile!" Reaching forward, I wiggled my fingers into the grooves of his face. "There you go—that's the spirit."

"Mina smile, Ursa happy."

It was so unexpected, so fluid, that for a moment, I could only stare at him, thinking he must have strung the words together by accident. But then he contorted his face into a goofy expression that I supposed must be a mirror of my own, and I couldn't help but laugh. Even so, I felt it difficult to meet his gaze, the moment feeling a little too intense.

"Careful, Ursa," I warned him, keeping my tone light and playful, even as a blush crept up my neck. "You could make a girl swoon, with poetry like that."

The idea was too complex for what I'd been teaching him; there was no way he could understand me. And yet, as I met Ursa's gaze, it seemed somehow he did.

24

For two people who couldn't entirely communicate or understand one another, Ursa and I got on remarkably well. We gradually settled into a routine of swimming, foraging, teaching Ursa to talk, eating, sleeping, and so on and so forth. Despite the strangeness of the circumstances, it all became rather commonplace, sometimes even dull in its repetitiveness.

Except for the times when Ursa would disappear.

It didn't happen too often. Days and weeks began to blur together during this time, but if I had to guess, I'd say it happened about once every other week or so. My only warning would be that Ursa would gather more food than usual and stockpile it in the cave. When he was about to leave, he would get nervous and evasive, pacing and stalking the area around the cave as if to make sure no hidden dangers had suddenly emerged. Then, with several grunts and gestures that seemed to indicate I was meant to stay in the cave, he would leave, disappearing for several hours before returning, without any explanation as to where he'd gone.

My curiosity was, naturally, piqued. After much speculation, the best conclusions I could come to were that (a) Ursa had a secret store of food somewhere he wasn't willing to share—which, if so, rude; or that (b) Ursa was part of another expedition, studying the scientists who believed they were dealing with a wildman raised outside of human society—unsettling; or that (c) Ursa had another woman tucked away in some other cave who he had to check up on periodically—enraging!

All three scenarios seemed unlikely, but I couldn't come up with anything else to explain his long absences, and Ursa certainly wasn't forthcoming with any information. I suppose the rational, adult thing to do would have been to ask him where he disappeared to, but as a woman who had been engaged to a man who had pretended to love me so he could harvest my genetic material for monetary gain, I hope I might be forgiven for having a few trust issues.

So, rather than confront Ursa and have a reasonable conversation on the subject, I did what any neurotic, suspicious person might do in my place.

I decided to follow him.

The next time Ursa stockpiled the cave with berries and nuts and honey, then gave me his stern, serious grunt lecture about staying in the cave, I nodded as guilelessly as I could, making every show of settling in with my microscope and some samples and one of my precious bars of chocolate. Ursa knew me well enough by now to understand that my supine position and delicious treat meant I wouldn't be going anywhere anytime soon.[1] Satisfied, he left me. I waited to the count of thirty-four before scrambling out of the cave as soundlessly as I could.[2]

Ursa was, naturally, far more experienced than I was at traversing through the forest, but I had two advantages at my disposal: the wilderness-survival training Tobago had given me back on Haven 3, and Ursa's height. I was no expert at following a trail, mind you, but I knew some basics; and I could follow Ursa's head, bobbing distinctly above the brush line.

I thought I was doing a pretty good job at remaining stealthy. Silently congratulating myself on both my deception and my tracking skills, I stepped into a clearing I'd seen Ursa walk through not moments before—and all at once, he was gone.

Gone, I tell you! Not just my view of him, but any trace of where he'd gotten off to. I could see no footprints, no bent twigs or scattered pine needles, nothing that might indicate what direction he'd moved. It was as if he'd simply disappeared.

And further, I realized with slowly percolating dread, I'd been so busy following him, I hadn't left myself any markers to get back to the cave.

I turned carefully in a circle, trying to orientate myself. I knew where I'd entered the clearing, but I couldn't quite gauge where the clearing was in relation to the cave. The path had not been a simple, straightforward one, but rather, one full of twists and turns and oh God, why hadn't I brought my compass?!

---

1. I possess an unexpected capacity for duplicity, no?

2. I meant to make myself wait until sixty, but then I began to second-guess myself, worried that I might lose his trail—hence, the randomness of the number.

As the panic fully began to set in, I decided my best bet would be to call after Ursa. Yes, he would know that I had been following him, but it was better to sacrifice my pride than to be stranded in the wilderness.

Also, for sake of transparency, *decided* is probably a misleading term. I did not rationally go through several possible scenarios and then conclude that my best option was to call Ursa. My breath was becoming ragged with panic, and I was afraid I was going to start hyperventilating. Overhead, something moved in the trees; it was probably just a bird, but I immediately became convinced it was a panther.[3]

I opened my mouth to shriek for Ursa when something pinned me from behind and lifted me off my feet. I screamed, because I was already primed to do so, but almost immediately I realized that it was, obviously, Ursa. Not only did I recognize his scent, but also I knew panthers were not prone to picking people up off the ground.[4]

By the time Ursa set me back on my feet, I was embarrassed, and so to cover it up, I immediately put on a show of being irritated. "Honestly, Ursa, you're so childish. I knew it was you." My heart pounded with a mixture of adrenaline, relief, and mortification.

When I finally calmed myself enough to meet Ursa's gaze, he was giving me a half-amused, half-irritated, half-angry glare. (And yes, I'm aware the math on that doesn't quite add up, but saying he was a third of each of those emotions doesn't quite hold the same water, does it?) He grunted at me, motioning back toward the cave. "Cave safe."

---

3. And yes, I'm aware that panthers don't reside in the American Rockies . . . but what if they do?!

4. Presumably? I suppose I've never fact-checked this. I shall leave that to any future editors who may stumble across this document.

I ought to have been impressed that he'd managed to piece together a sentence, albeit a rudimentary one. I was too peeved, however, to focus on praising him for his vocal advancement. "I know it's *safe*," I snapped back at him. "But it's also boring, and you're hiding something from me and it isn't right. I demand to know where you're going or—or, *I'll* leave once a week and not take *you* with me. Yeah. How would you like that, huh? Or maybe I'll go off to find my own cave, so I can live with someone I trust!"

It was a bit rich, I know, for me to be taking the moral high ground when I'd attempted to trick him and spy on him, but adrenaline was coursing through my veins; I was ready for a fight.

I could see that Ursa was attempting to remain stern but also trying not to laugh. From his perspective, I suppose I looked rather mad, ranting and raving when he probably couldn't understand half the words I was saying.

His response was understandable, but from my position, it was also deflating. Sometimes he looked at me like I was the most beautiful goddess in the universe, and other times like I was like a toddler having a temper tantrum or a dancing monkey, simply there for his amusement. I didn't have a lot of experience in being looked at like a sexy goddess, but I imagined those ethereal beings did not inspire a lot of mirth at their bizarre antics.

Suffice it to say, his amusement did nothing to cool my temper—quite the opposite, in fact. "What are you hiding from me?" I demanded, advancing on Ursa with my index finger and prodding him in the chest. "I think I deserve to know."

Traces of humor remained in Ursa's eyes, but I could see he was annoyed again. Another emotion I don't think sexy goddesses often inspire: irritation. He considered me for a long moment, ignoring my finger still poking into his chest for so long that finally, cowed, I let it drop back down to my side.

Then abruptly, Ursa turned, heading to the edge of the clearing. He stopped and did a jerking sort of gesture with his head that I interpreted as *Follow me.*

So, I did.

We walked in silence—Ursa slightly ahead of me, clearly modifying his movement so I wouldn't fall too far behind, but still moving fast enough that I had to scramble to keep up. I suppose that was my penance for being rude and huffy, and it worked. By the next time Ursa stopped, my anger had faded, and all I felt was embarrassed for having confronted him so abrasively.[5]

Ursa stopped just as suddenly as he'd started; I nearly ran into his back. He turned to face me, and just as I opened my mouth to give the apology I'd been rehearsing in my head for the entire walk, he grunted, motioning upward.

I dutifully followed his gesture and looked up to see a massive cliff composed of jagged rocks, a few sparse twigs and vines and greenery peeping through here and there.

It took a moment for comprehension to dawn. I knit my eyebrows together. "You want me to climb that?" I performed the overexagger-

---

5. Well, that and hungry, and a little winded, and sweaty, but embarrassment was defi-

   nitely the predominant emotion.

ated head shake I had taught him for *no* when I really, really meant it. "Not happening."

Ursa nodded back at me, just as exaggeratedly. "Yes."

Perhaps this was further punishment for how rude I'd been before. I'd hoped Ursa was just joking, but the look on his face soon convinced me he wasn't. "Ursa." I held my puny spaghetti arms out to him in all their pathetic glory. "Weak." I pantomimed climbing upward and then falling back, complete with a dramatic, gasping breath at the end. "Fall. Dead. Bad."

He squatted, motioning me toward his back. "Up."

For a long moment, I simply stared at him. "You're going to carry me to the top of the mountain?" I winced at the prospect. "The thing is, I'm still carrying some holiday weight, and I just don't think it would be wise . . ."[6]

Ursa grunted at me, reaching behind him to tug me forward. "Up."

He was being sort of appealingly commanding, and I've always had a hard time resisting authority. Fine. Let him make it three feet up before he realized how difficult it was going to be, attempting to carry me the entire way. I only hoped he didn't kill us both in the process.

"All right. But I'd just like to say 'I told you so' in advance since we'll probably be too dead for me to say it later . . ."

I doubted he understood most of that—though, judging by the eye roll, he seemed to get the gist well enough. Despite myself, I was impressed by the gesture. An eye roll! I was clearly rubbing off on him if he'd managed to pick up that social cue.

With him crouched down, back turned to me, I hoisted myself aboard. I wish I could say this was done gracefully, but I'm afraid there

---

6. Haven Day feastings are so hard to recover from, aren't they?

was some grunting and clawing and scrambling. In my defense, I have not been given a piggyback ride since I was a child, and it turns out it is *not* like riding a bicycle. Finally, my arms found their way round his shoulders, and he guided my legs to loop tightly around his waist. I guess I must have been distributing my weight strangely because Ursa reached back, grabbing hold of one thigh and one butt cheek and hoisting me up to where he wanted me to be.

Though I wouldn't call the entire process romantic, I'd be lying if I said it didn't give me a little thrill, as procedural as the entire thing had been. He was reaching behind him blindly; I doubt he even knew what he was touching, but I, for one, was very grateful he couldn't see my expression at that moment. I swallowed, holding on tighter.

With me properly situated now, Ursa reached for one of the rocks jutting above us, forearms straining, thighs flexing, and we began to climb up the cliffside.

The process up the cliff was painstakingly slow, and Ursa was lost in deep concentration, sometimes taking several moments to decide where to place his hands and feet next. Aside from his breathing, he didn't make a single sound, and I wouldn't have been surprised to learn he was concentrating so carefully that he'd all but forgotten I was there.

I, on the other hand, found myself suddenly very aware of Ursa, in a way I hadn't fully let myself be since he'd been released from that cage. I knew I should be desperately afraid—halfway, as I was, up the side of a cliff, with nothing between me and certain death but the man I was latched on to like a human backpack. And, I was. But also, from a purely scientific standpoint, I couldn't help but marvel at the sheer strength and dexterity of the man moving underneath me. It was one thing to recognize that Ursa had managed to beat his way through an entire camp of guards, but it was quite another to feel the expanse of his back and shoulders rippling underneath me, to smell the sweat on his skin and feel the fluidity of his movements. He seemed almost more element than man, like stone—no, stronger than that—like steel. Something indestructible and powerful.

And yet . . . he was man, too, in the way his skin was warm against mine. The fine hairs at the back of his neck stirring with each of my breaths, and the beads of sweat trickling down his back, sticking to the fabric of my shirt. I felt cognizant of every part of my body that was pressed to his, and I wrapped around him and tightened instinctively with every upward motion. To keep from falling, naturally. It was the most natural instinct in the world, I reassured myself, even as I clenched my legs more firmly around his torso.

It was a small eternity before we reached the top. Ursa must have felt the strain more than he'd showed it, for as soon as he pulled us up over the ledge, he collapsed belly-down with me on top of him, causing my body to rise and fall with each deep breath he took.

There was no reason for me to feel exhausted; I had only been a passenger, and yet I felt the exertion deep in my own bones.

Which was probably why I allowed myself to remain on top of Ursa, eyes closed and face pressed to his glistening back, listening to the sturdy, comforting rhythm of his heart, for a little longer than necessary.

Too long, I realized as I discovered Ursa had long since caught his breath. He seemed to almost be holding it, waiting for me. I abruptly pushed off him without properly bracing myself, and hit the rocky ground with an oof that dispelled any of the lingering sexual tension.

"So," I said, too brisk and bright to fool anyone, "what's the big secret? What at the top of this giant rock wall is so compelling that we had to risk our lives to see it?"

Ursa didn't reply as he rolled into a sitting position, but he seemed to get the general sense of what I was saying—and, based on the wry look he gave me, that I was complaining. He pushed to his feet, reaching for my hand. I hesitated only a moment before giving it to him, and he pulled me to my feet, then kept hold of my hand as he moved confidently forward.

25

It didn't take long for me to realize we were approaching the ruins of a city. Vegetation had long since begun to overgrow the abandoned streets and buildings. It was strangely humbling to stand in the face of this shell of a civilization. I'm no historian or anthropologist, but one could easily trace the lives of those who had lived in such a place, despite the city's submission to flora. Shops, automobiles, streetlights, parks, homes. The layout wasn't so different from a terraformed settlement like Haven 3, and yet it was enormously different, as though I'd stepped into a different time. And the lack of movement, of human life, made the empty buildings seem strangely ominous. A portent of something, a warning—

"Ooh, a library!" I cried, cutting across the street to the long-deserted building.

Ursa followed dutifully behind me, helping me to wrench open the door, which had rusted shut with lack of use and had some wintercreeper growing over it.[1] Inside, the building was dark and musty, but after allowing my eyes to adjust for a few moments, I spotted what I'd been hoping for.

"Books," I sighed happily, turning to Ursa with a grin.

He smiled back at me, but the expression seemed to be more at my excitement than for his own pleasure at finding the shelves still fully stocked. Obviously, given the state of the door, Ursa hadn't been coming into this particular building during any of his excursions away from the cave, so he couldn't place a very high value on books. I suppose it made sense if whatever had caused him to lose the ability to speak had also hampered his ability to read.

I could see no other reason why he wouldn't have immediately sought out the library upon discovering an abandoned city. Yes, sure, perhaps there were some food supplies that hadn't deteriorated or some useful tools that could be scavenged. I now knew the answer to where my clothing had been procured on that first day. But . . . books! Knowledge, stories, *friends*. Endless adventures, endless possibilities. It shouldn't surprise me, I suppose, that when humankind had abandoned Earth to seek life on terraformed planets, they'd left behind their most valuable treasure . . . and yet, somehow, it still did.

Luckily, all of these gems had been waiting for me, and now that I knew where they were, I could always come back for more. For now, I stocked up on some of my favorites, along with a few unknown titles that jumped out at me. The books would be for my own benefit, naturally, to help pass the time, but I could also read some of these stories to Ursa and continue his progression in learning to speak and communicate again.

---

1. *Euonymus fortunei*

When at last my pack was full to bursting, I followed Ursa back out to the empty streets. "Show me where you like to go," I told him simply.

I imagined Ursa's journeys here had to do with more than just utility. There was a reason he kept coming back to this same place, over and over again. I wanted to know what it was. I wanted to understand him, this man of few words.

He took me to a section where I imagined the city's downtown had once been, then led me to what appeared to be a science museum. These doors were easier to navigate, so I knew Ursa must come here frequently. Inside were various exhibits, some that had lasted the long length of disuse much better than others. Ursa seemed excited but also endearingly bashful as he showed me some of his favorites: The dinosaur exhibit, where he surprised me by taking a running leap to jump onto the spine of a T-Rex and climb his way up, perching atop the skull and grinning proudly down at me. The physics exhibit, where he could pull a rope to its full length, then drop it and the attached weights to send a tennis ball shooting up toward the roof. The windowless astronomy exhibit, where he pressed a button on the wall and some flickering bulbs lit up the constellations on the ceiling.

As he led me to the final exhibit, Ursa suddenly became uncharacteristically tentative, as though afraid of what my reaction might be. I tried my best to smile at him encouragingly, to show him without words that I would be receptive to whatever it was.

To my surprise, it was an exhibit on genetics. The science was rather rudimentary, seeing as how it had all been put together almost a hundred years ago, but there were displays about DNA, biological traits, dominant versus recessive genes, and so forth.

I confess, I was surprised that Ursa would be so interested in such a display. I wondered if this was his roundabout way of trying to tell me why he was here on Earth. Had he been part of a team that studied genetics—like Rawley and my mother—but become separated from them? Was he here as some sort of protest to the genetic modification that was running rampant in the Havens?

When I turned away from one charmingly outdated wall display about gene variations, I found Ursa gone. "Ursa?" I called, following the winding hallway to the next room of the exhibit and stopping short.

The room was covered, floor-to-ceiling, with pictures of people, representing all the different shapes and sizes that had once been possible before modification became so popular. My breath caught in my throat. It was really a stunning time capsule, to see human beings as they had once existed, with all their natural flaws. I moved from picture to picture, amazed at what I saw. Some people were tall, some short, some average, and all with such great fluctuations in size and weight, and such limitations on skin and eye color. They were testaments to a time before people had started requesting things like golden irises and lavender skin tones.

They were lovely, I saw with some surprise. Plain and ordinary and marvelous and wonderful.

When I turned to see what Ursa was studying, I was surprised to find him simply gazing into the eyes of a nondescript human face. There was nothing especially noteworthy about this person that I could see, except through a trick of the photograph, it appeared they were looking right back at you. Almost as if they were here in the room, too.

Ursa seemed quite moved by this, for reasons I couldn't comprehend. I wracked my brain to piece together what could have impacted
him so. Had he known this person? But these pictures had to be almost
a hundred years old, so that didn't seem likely. Perhaps they reminded
him of someone he'd once known?

"Are you all right?" I asked him quietly, touching his arm.

Ursa blinked, then looked over at me. He moved closer to me, with
a lack of consideration to personal space that he hadn't exhibited in
quite a while. His nose was almost pressed up against mine, his eyes
searching my eyes intently as he reached up to grip my face. In any
other circumstance, I might have thought he was about to kiss me, that
was how near, how intense, his closeness was. But I understood intuitively that wasn't what was happening. He was seeking something
from me, needing something from me, but I didn't know what it was.

"Ursa." I put my hands over his, not to pull them away, but to give
him reassurance. "What's wrong?"

"Mina not here," he said. His eyes darted back and forth between
mine, as if to gauge my understanding.

I frowned in confusion. "No, I am here."

"Ursa alone."

I shook my head as much as I could with him so close and holding
me so tight. "No, I'm here, Ursa. I'm with you."

He sighed, eyes drifting shut in a way that let me know I hadn't
quite understood him. But he nodded anyway, forehead pressed
against mine now. "Mina here. Mina here . . ." He made an irritated
noise, as if searching for the right word. "Now."

All at once, I understood him. Before me, he'd been alone, and these
pictures had been his closest thing to human companionship.

I had questions, so many questions. Why had he been lurking around the expedition trips but never approached anyone before me? Why was he here on Earth in the first place?

But in that moment, none of that mattered so much as what he was telling me. My heart broke for him, at how lonely he must have been. I didn't know how I could fix the past for him. But I hoped I could rewrite some of that pain. "I'm here now, Ursa. I'm here. I'm not going anywhere without you."

26

Afterward we made our way back to the cave. Ursa was characteristically silent for much of the trip, and I was uncharacteristically so. My mind was racing with a plethora of questions that Ursa seemed incapable of answering.

Incapable, or unwilling? Yet another question left between us.

We paused at the top of the cliffside, preparing ourselves to scale back down. Well, I wasn't so much preparing *myself* as preparing Ursa for the strenuous task. Ursa took a long drink from the flask I offered him, looking down at my pack, which I'd rested on the ground. He lifted it experimentally, the muscles in his forearm straining—which was saying something, since the muscles in his forearms were quite . . . considerable. He cocked an eyebrow at me.

"I suppose it is much heavier now, with all the books in it," I admitted sheepishly. Since I wouldn't be the one scaling down a cliff with a human being *and* a heavy backpack full of books strapped to me, I hadn't really considered the weight difference. "But they're important. Very important."

"Book," Ursa said, experimenting with the word and overemphasizing the consonants in that way of his I couldn't help but find endearing. "Im-por-tant."

"Very," I reassured him again. "These are full of wisdom, passed down from the ages. Full of people and ideas and stories. I have one here I think you'll like, about a man named Achilles who was a great warrior, but very arrogant, and . . . well, I don't want to spoil it for you, but it's riveting stuff. Really."

Ursa considered the pack for a moment longer before tossing it over the side of the cliff.

My wail of outrage followed after it. "Those are fragile!" I watched, hands on my head, as the backpack slammed into the rocks below. Some of those bindings were barely held together as it was.

I suppose, thinking through it rationally, I can see his point. It was a massive feat, scaling down a rock wall without any ropes or equipment. Adding a human passenger to that was doubtless enormously difficult, even for someone as strong and toned and agile as Ursa. Any extra weight or balance issues could very well get us killed.

Still. The books! I glared at him, irritated that he seemed to be trying not to laugh at my dismay. "Well, you might have warned me," I sniffed indignantly.

I was answered by the deep, throaty, rumbling growl of a bear.

Not, naturally, to be confused with the deep, throaty, rumbling growly noises made by *my* own man-bear. This sound came from an actual Kodiak bear, a massive brown blur that was charging forward.

Ursa rose to his feet swiftly, moving in front of me before I even had the presence of mind to scream at the beast's rapid approach.

The bear stopped just short of Ursa, rising onto its hind legs and crashing against him with its upper arms and claws.

I could only watch in soundless horror as the bear tried to clamp Ursa's neck in its powerful jaws—only, I realized after a belated, panicked moment, the Kodiak wasn't attacking Ursa. He was *licking* him, and Ursa was laughing, playfully swatting the bear's head away. The two of them grappled with each other, play wrestling and sort of knocking each other around. The Kodiak was clearly restraining himself, too, since he could have easily crushed and killed Ursa. When I say he was massive, I mean *massive*; he could have easily weighed a ton and was at least a head taller than Ursa standing upright.

They embraced for several long minutes. There was really no other way to describe it—they *were* embracing, like old friends reunited after a long journey. I realized, for how little I knew about Ursa's past, that could very well be true. But instead of answering any of my questions, this encounter only raised more. How did Ursa know this bear? How did they have such an easy rapport with one another? Why weren't they still together, if they clearly had such strong affection for one another?

At last, Ursa's attention returned to me. Seeing my confusion, he seemed to search his mind to find the right word, before finally landing on, "Brother."

Brother? Before I could ponder on this too long, Ursa reached for me, drawing me close to his side. I now stood face-to-face with the Kodiak bear, looking into its bronze-brown eyes, surprised at how sentient, how wise they seemed. Whatever the bear saw looking back at me, it seemed to approve, for the next thing I knew, I was being smothered by its nose, its tongue, as it sniffed and licked every surface of my head it could reach.

I looked to Ursa in wide-eyed alarm, wondering if this was an elaborate precursor to the bear eating me, but he was grinning proudly. Since I didn't think his plan this entire time had been to feed me to his brother/bear, I allowed the bear's exploration to continue, standing stock still. My God, this bear was invasive! He made all of Ursa's sniffing and poking from our early days together seem positively tame by comparison.

The bear turned its focus back to Ursa, and the two of them knocked foreheads together, rubbing their faces against each other. I saw happiness in Ursa's eyes, but also a pain that I didn't fully understand. When he pulled back, gripping the side of the bear's face gruffly, there were tears on his cheeks.

He grunted, and the bear grunted back at him, before turning and ambling off in the other direction.

Ursa watched him for a long time, his face a mask of pain. Then abruptly, he turned back to the cliffside, motioning for me to join him.

"Are you all right?" I asked him quietly, touching his arm.

Ursa didn't respond, just squatted and motioned for me to climb aboard. So, without knowing what else to do, I did.

Once back at the cave, Ursa moved to the edge of the pool to drink and splash water on his face and arms. I followed his lead, waiting to see if he would speak if given time. I was so enormously confused by what I'd just seen and by what he'd told me. As Ursa remained silent,

I intuited he might never elaborate further if I didn't at least ask the questions plaguing my mind.

"Ursa. You said the bear was your brother. What did you mean by that?"Ursa stilled but didn't look at me.

I waited a moment before trying again. "Did you spend time living with bears?"

Another beat, then Ursa nodded.

"How long?" I realized as I said it that Ursa likely didn't have a strong conception of time, living as he had been. There was nothing in his cave like a calendar or even a clock to help him keep track of the passage of time. He might be able to follow the change of the seasons, but he wouldn't know dates or any other specifics. "Months?" I tried anyway, and when Ursa didn't reply, I tried again. "Years?"

Ursa shook his head—not saying no, but expressing agitation. At last he touched himself on the chest. "Boy."

He was looking at me so earnestly, his eyes so hopeful. He wasn't keeping silent because he didn't want me to know the answer, but because he didn't know how to explain himself. "Since you were a boy?" I guessed.

Ursa nodded gratefully. "Boy." He motioned up toward the cliff-side, where we'd encountered the Kodiak. "Brother."

"You have a brother?"

"Mother. Sister." Ursa looked at me intently, gauging how much I understood.

It wasn't much to be honest. I wanted to encourage him to express himself, but there were so many missing pieces. I didn't know how to fill them in. "You have a family here somewhere?"

"Bears. Family. Bears."

"The bears . . . ate your family?" Good God. Surely *that* couldn't be right. He'd been so friendly with the Kodiak on the cliff.

Ursa huffed, then tapped his chest again. "Ursa man." He motioned back toward the cliff. "Bear big. Bear *man*. Leave. Home."

He'd really lost me now. "There was a bear man . . . ?"

Ursa shook his head in agitation. "Ursa big. Bear big. Leave. Home."

I winced sympathetically at him, feeling guilty for his frustration. I didn't want him to shut down; I wanted him to keep trying to communicate. But whatever he was saying felt too big and complex to say with his limited words. "I'm sorry, Ursa. I don't understand."

Ursa's jaw clenched. He stared ahead for a long moment, saying nothing.

And then abruptly, he dove into the water. He stayed underneath for a long time, though I could see his dark shape moving below the surface. When at last he emerged, he rolled onto his back, staring up at the sky, saying nothing to me as he floated past.

I understood the conversation was over, for now. But not forever. I wanted to understand, I did. We'd been able to communicate so many things to each other, even without words. But for the first time, we'd encountered something too big to conquer without sharing a common language.

I would have to find a way to fix that.

27

The Brethren have shown remarkably little concern for the state of my books after falling down the cliffside, but for any future readers who might find this manuscript and who might also happen to be bibliophiles, rest assured the books survived in spirit, if not all in binding. Some of the pages I'd had to group back together to the best of my ability, so there might have been a few places the stories took a sudden leap forward. Oh well. At least it would keep things exciting! I'd planned on using the books for my own entertainment and enlightenment, but since another of their primary purposes was to help Ursa with his language skills, I supposed it really didn't matter all that much if the story remained totally coherent. The sentence structures would be in place, even if the chapters were not.

Ursa seemed less excited about this new tool at our disposal to work on his language skills,[1] but one rainy afternoon when we had

---

1. So much so, that I was beginning to wonder if he hadn't purposefully tried to destroy my books by dropping them. Just joking! Mostly . . .

no choice but to huddle in the cave by a fire, I finally pulled out my copy of *The Impossible Thing*, a classic novel from the world that was. I was worried about the focus on the love story in the novel, and if that might give Ursa *ideas*, but I reasoned that since the novel also had action and adventure and time travel and historical information, it was an all-around strong candidate to spark his love of literature.

To my delight, Ursa seemed quite attuned to the story and eagerly listened as it unfolded. We spent a pleasant hour or so reading together; sometimes Ursa might tug on my sleeve or touch my leg if there was a word he didn't understand, and I would repeat it for him and explain its meaning. There was also some historical context I had to offer him, since I wasn't certain how much (if any) Earth history he'd had in school.

After that, reading became quite a regular nighttime ritual for us. Once we'd done all our bedtime preparations, I would read aloud to Ursa for a half hour or so. In this manner, we made our way slowly but steadily through the book.[2] Along with noting a distinct progress in Ursa's language patterns, I found it quite endearing how interested he was in the story. I half wondered if Ursa believed Keely and Adam

---

2. These were some of my favorite moments with Ursa, actually, but they don't make for especially riveting storytelling. The primary function of reading together was, of course, developing Ursa's language skills by broadening his vocabulary. But it was all rather wonderfully cozy. Intimacy isn't always formed in the life-or-death moments. It happened while curling up next to the fire for warmth, Ursa's face close to mine. Hearing his heartbeat as I read, the two of us feeling like the last two living souls in the universe. But we really mustn't test the Brethren's patience for plot development, must we?

were real people from the amount of concern he showed for their well-being.

One night, we settled down to read as usual. I must have been sleepy, or perhaps my mind had wandered off somewhere, because I was still reading aloud, but it took my mind a moment to catch up with what my mouth was saying.

"... he found that warm dark place between her thighs and sheathed himself in her warmth ..."

As soon as the words caught up to me, I gasped and tossed the book away from me as though it were on fire.

You see, although I'd read the book many times before, the version of *The Impossible Thing* I'd read previously had never contained so many ... explicit details. It was hinted that romantic encounters were taking place, but the narration always skirted around these parts. So far as I can gather, because of Haven 3's policy on discouraging carnal relations between people, some of the books from Old Earth must have been censored to remove the more ... *intimate* details. Thus, I hadn't known to prepare myself to read these parts aloud, since so far as I knew, these parts didn't exist.

After an excruciatingly long moment, I forced myself to glance over at Ursa, hoping against hope that he somehow hadn't caught the meaning. He was watching me intently; his eyes skirted over my face and neck, no doubt following my blush, before his gaze locked with mine.

"Sheathed?" he repeated.

I couldn't hold his eyes. I dithered, wondering whether I ought to make something up, but I found myself unable to hamper his vocabulary; what kind of teacher would I be, then? Still not meeting his gaze, I adopted a no-nonsense, brisk tone, hoping through sheer willpower to discourage him from getting any *ideas*. "It means to enclose something so it's completely surrounded."

My eyes darted to the book, still lying open on the ground. *He found that warm dark place between her thighs.* When I looked back up at Ursa, he was studying that juncture between my own thighs, his expression dark and hot.

I forcefully clamped my knees together. Then, leaning down, I slammed the book shut. "I think that's quite enough of that for tonight. Good night!"

And, turning my back to him, I pulled up my animal skins and willed myself into unconsciousness.

Sleep did not come quite as easily as I would have hoped. Even though I'd been the one who'd insisted on sleeping, I tossed and turned while Ursa had fallen into his usual heavy slumber. The fire in its pit had died down to nothing but embers, and I shivered, instinctively burrowing deeper underneath the animal skins.

Ursa remained unbothered by the chill. I suppose he'd been used to sleeping out in the elements for some time without the benefit of a fire. Plus his big body was like a furnace. In the infrequent contact we'd made, his skin was invariably warm, no matter what the outside temperature was.

Out of purely scientific curiosity, I rolled over to study him more closely, wondering how he emitted such steady heat. Perhaps his metabolism was unusually high? I had some basic knowledge of human anatomy, and I knew enough to understand that Ursa was an impressive specimen by any measure. Not only for the heat that he emitted, but for his general . . . composition.

Oblivious to my study, Ursa slumbered on. I noted that his body temperature was apparently warm enough that he could sleep with his upper body uncovered by animal skins. I observed the strong line of his shoulders, his muscular back, the faint line of scars in the dim light from the embers. I watched how his skin rippled and moved with each breath, the gentle rise and fall of his body. His face was turned toward me, the usual hard lines softened in sleep.

Though Ursa had been naked in front of me many times, I'd often averted my gaze and not taken true stock of his person. Partly because of the modesty instilled in me on Haven 3, and partly because of this obvious attraction Ursa had for me. I didn't want to encourage him by ogling him as openly as he ogled me. But since he was asleep, and since he irritatingly continued to insist on sleeping in the nude, I realized this might be an opportunity to study him without my usual restraint.

It had nothing to do with the book passage I'd just read! My interest was not remotely sexual. I simply wanted to take advantage of the chance to observe him without being observed myself, since my interest in the subject matter might easily be misconstrued.

Slowly, carefully, I took hold of the animal skin covering the lower half of Ursa's body. He was sleeping on his stomach, so it wasn't as though I would be violating his privacy by studying his sexual organs. Instead, I took in the sight of his muscular, rounded buttocks, his thick thighs. Most all of the men I'd seen on Haven 3 had been clothed, first and foremost, but in the rare instances I'd seen a man's body in any state of undress, their physical features had been similar in shape to Ursa's. And yet, there was a key difference I hadn't been able to name until now. Those men had all been bred to be muscular and strong, so they didn't have to work to achieve that stature. Their muscles, though remarkable, had borne a softness to them, a superficiality. Those men were meant to look impressive, but could they run up the length of a tree to knock down a beehive, or scale the side of a cliff with a human passenger? I thought not.

Ursa's muscles, his broad stature and strength, had been earned through effort. He might not be as aesthetically pleasing as the Haven 3 cover models, with their smooth, glossy skin over well-defined abdominals, but every part of his body was rugged, powerful. Unbidden, I imagined those thick legs spreading my knees wide, so he could thrust inside and *sheathe* himself deep inside of me . . .

Suddenly he rolled over so I was no longer looking at his posterior region, but rather his nether regions. I'd always been aware, obviously, of that part of him on full and proud display when he'd still roamed around naked, but I'd definitely never let myself observe *it* up close. It being his penis. His *cock*. They were words that had always sent me and my friend Trini into fits of giggles as preteen girls, whispering about forbidden things we didn't fully understand. But there was nothing ridiculous about it now. It was foreign and exciting and a little bit frightening, but not ridiculous. I wondered what it would feel like, to the touch. I wondered what it would feel like inside of me.

I looked up to find Ursa's eyes open, watching me in the dark. It was as if my sudden flare of desire had called out to him. Embarrassed, I dropped the animal skin so it covered his body again. Ursa didn't move, didn't speak. For a long moment, we simply stared at one another.

Without knowing what else to do, I dropped back to the ground and closed my eyes—scrunched them shut tight, actually. It was foolish, of course. He obviously knew I wasn't asleep. I knew he knew I wasn't asleep.

But he didn't say anything, and I didn't open my eyes again to see if he'd fallen asleep. Gradually, after enough pretending, I managed to drift off into actual slumber.

28

Over the next few days, I threw myself into my experiments. I was deeply embarrassed by the lapse in judgment I'd shown by peeking at Ursa that night. It was obvious that our reading had stirred some best-suppressed ideas and emotions in the both of us. I determined that I'd read the rest of *The Impossible Thing* on my own, carefully flagging any passages that might cause such unwanted reactions, so I could skip over them in the future. In the meantime, I switched our nightly reading to an old textbook on astronomy. Ursa didn't seem to be quite so interested anymore, though he did like the passage where I explained to him the meaning of his name. Considering the connection to bears I'd since discovered in his past, I had to wonder if I wasn't a bit of a prophetess . . . ? Then again, Ursa had been wearing a bearskin when I'd first met him, which is probably why I'd made the initial connection between him and the *Ursidae* family.[1]

During the day, I gathered my usual samples of fungi, as well as took samples of the pool water. I hoped to continue my work with the fungi that I'd come to Earth to research, even knowing that my work would likely never be discovered or published, at least not in my lifetime. The pool water was its own unique mystery. I gathered samples of the water itself, as well as the plant life and fungi that grew nearby and the soil underneath the water and at its banks. I also discovered an unusual algae growing in the water. Now, I'll be the first to admit that I know little to nothing about algae, as its outside of my realm of expertise; I do know that many types of algae have healing properties, such as spirulina,[2] which is used for its antioxidant and anti-inflammatory benefits, and that many other strains contribute to the Earth's oxygen. It would make sense that in the process of cleansing the Earth from pollution to eventually make it habitable again, algae would flourish.

The algae in the pool outside our cave was unlike anything I'd ever seen. Again, I'd spent little time studying this life-form, so it was possible that I was getting ahead of myself with my research; how I longed for access to an academic database, to other researchers in the field who could corroborate my findings! But in short, and because I know the Brethren of Blood will have little patience for me listing out the details in full, I'll summarize what I believe to be the most interesting findings here:

---

1. I just realized that I've never asked Ursa why he was wearing a bearskin when he seemed so affectionate with that male Kodiak. It seems a bit morbid. Yet another question I'll have when I see you again, my love.

2. *Arthrospira platensis*

At first, the algae found in the pool appeared to be unremarkable and colorless, but on closer inspection, it seemed to be infiltrating everything it came into contact with—including the other plant life in the water and the soil on the bank. I found traces of it in the roots of nearby trees, as well as in earthworms, dead frogs, and yes, even my beloved fungi. Like spirulina, this algae seemed to have strong antioxidant and anti-inflammatory benefits, but it also seemed to have found a way to be absorbed into other species and let them *borrow* its photosynthetic properties. That is to say, while trees and other plants also use photosynthesis to provide food and energy, the pool algae seemed to have sort of supercharged the photosynthetic qualities of these plants to allow them to thrive more efficiently. And other forms of life, such as my fungi and the earthworm, *also* seemed to have borrowed photosynthetic properties by ingesting and absorbing the algae. In addition to their normal methods of gathering energy, these organisms were now able to draw energy and strength from the sun itself.

The next step in my study would be to take a sample of Ursa's blood to see if I could find similar traces of the algae. I could use my own blood as well, but I'd been exposed for far less time to the pool water than Ursa. I also needed to see if this or similar types of algae populated other bodies of water, or if it were only in this pool. If the algae was not particular to this pool, then perhaps in healing itself, the Earth had somehow found a way to enable most, if not all, of its inhabiting species to grow and thrive with photosynthesis. And if that was the case, then . . .

I don't think I'll need to explain, even to the Brethren of Blood, what a remarkable find that would be.

But it was far too early in my experiments to get carried away with myself. I knew the seductive danger of allowing oneself to get carried away with a few untested results. It would take time, and patience, to sort through my findings.

Time that I might very well not have. I'd been so enthralled in my adventure with Ursa that I hadn't been paying much mind to the looming hourglass hanging over us.[3] I had a very set schedule for when Tobago would be retrieving me. I'd been keeping track of the passage of time, to the best of my ability, so I wouldn't miss my rescue . . . but somehow, over the past few weeks, it had started to feel less and less like a rescue. Despite the oddness of my life here with Ursa, I found I'd grown used to my current situation. I enjoyed the days spent out in nature, *real* nature, studying my fungi and observing the flora and fauna around me. I liked finding my food and eating it fresh. I liked ending my days by the fire, reading with Ursa . . .

Ursa.

We had a whole life here together, didn't we? I honestly couldn't imagine it any other way now.

Then again, I also couldn't imagine spending the rest of my life away from civilization. I'd made what was perhaps a life-altering discovery with the pool algae, but who was there to share it with here? I could try explaining the results to Ursa, but he likely had no comprehension of what photosynthesis was, much less how remarkable it would be if there was an algae that could enable other species to adopt its properties. The lives that knowledge could change! The people it could help.

But I determined I would worry about that later, always later. We still had time.

---

3. A metaphorical hourglass, I ought to make clear. The Brethren are frighteningly literal sometimes.

Just not much of it.

29

A couple weeks had passed since our trip to the abandoned city. Now that I knew where he was going, I no longer begrudged him his alone time. As he readied to head out again one morning, I followed behind him, my satchel in hand, intending to set up camp near the pool for the day.

Ursa frowned at me as I followed him out of the cave. I smiled back at him, motioning him onward. "Go on, enjoy yourself. Don't worry, I won't make you carry me this time. Off you go!"

Quite honestly, I was also looking forward to an afternoon to myself. Once Ursa and I had learned each other's rhythms, we got on pretty well. I knew he was a grouch first thing in the morning, and he knew I got in a mood when the humidity made my hair frizz. We worked together to find food, and he occupied himself while I gathered samples and performed my experiments. We ate and read together in the evenings. Sometimes, though, no matter how much you get on with someone, you just need some *me* time.

Despite my obvious enthusiasm for his departure, or perhaps because of it, Ursa continued to frown at me. I realized why a moment later, when he pointed to the entrance of the cave. "Mina stay."

Stay in the cave, all day? By myself? I shook my head at him emphatically. "Mina will *not* stay," I corrected him. "Mina will swim and enjoy the sunshine."

Ursa frowned.

The day could not have been more perfect, and there was no chance I was going to spend it cooped up in the cave just because Ursa wanted to worry over me like a mother hen. "Go on." I shooed him toward the opening of the cave. "Go off to have your private man time. I'm going swimming."

Warm, bright sunshine and that marvelous clear blue water—yes, that sounded like the recipe for perfect happiness. It was enough to make me glad, even, that Ursa was leaving. I was not at all irritated that he clearly needed time away from me as much as I needed time away from him.

But Ursa dug his feet in, bracing himself against my attempts to run him off. "Danger." He knitted his eyebrows together and folded his arms over his broad chest for emphasis.

"Nonsense." I picked up my copy of *The Impossible Thing* and my little bag of soaps and shampoos. "I'll just be at the pool—right outside the cave. Just as safe there as I am here." Seeing his brow was still furrowed, I gave him my most reassuring smile. "Go on. I won't get into any trouble."

The look on his face could best be described as skeptical. There wasn't much he could do, though, with me herding him so insistently out of the cave, short of carrying me back inside. (Although, knowing Ursa, this was probably a serious consideration.) Honestly, he could be such a schoolmarm sometimes.

At last, finally, he disappeared, and I was on my own—really, truly, for the first time in ages. Those earlier times I'd been cooped up in the cave didn't count because I'd felt so sheltered, almost like I'd been in a prison. Out here, I was free to do as I pleased.

I stopped at the water's edge, admiring its cool clearness. My toes, by way of comparison, were positively filthy, and I expected the rest of my body would prove to be much the same if juxtaposed so closely. I reached up for the buttons on my shirt, then hesitated, looking around.

"Ursa?" I called out suspiciously. "Are you really gone?" No response came, but this was not a convincing enough answer. "I'm going to be very cross if you're lurking around, watching me."

When the silence finally stretched on long enough to assure me I was alone, I made short work of my clothes, leaving them in a pile on the ground, and dove into the water.

It was just as crisp and lovely as I'd remembered it to be. I could feel its healing properties working on me right away, soothing the ache in my back from sleeping on the ground, the mosquito bites on my arms, the pimple under my jawline.[1] With a happy lightness, I swam the length of the water, back and forth, until I tired myself out. Then, I'm not ashamed to admit, I climbed up onto some of the overhanging rocks and cannonballed into the water, because it felt both freeing and hilarious to do this completely naked.

---

1. Yes, I know—yet another thing that could have been written out of my genetic code if my mother hadn't been so insistent upon keeping my genetic material "natural." In most ways, I can appreciate that insistence now, but whenever I have an adult acne flare-up, yet again . . . not so much.

This, too, I repeated until I was exhausted, at which point I turned on my back to float about idly. I'd sent Ursa away under strict orders, and I'd meant them, but as I drifted about the pool, my mind also drifted to a scenario where he'd stayed behind to watch me. Naked, clean, and buoyant, my natural grace and beauty would be made haunting by the water, like Ophelia or the Lady of Shalott,[2] only preferably less tragic.

At last, when my body temperature began to dip and the warm, sunbaked rocks began to look more appealing, I gave up this fantasy, rolled onto my belly, and began paddling toward the shore.

No sooner had I done so than I spotted a dark head ducking behind the rocks where they sloped down to the forest floor below. Ursa. I clenched my jaw. Did he really think I was such a fragile little thing that I couldn't swim in a pool right outside the cave by myself for an hour?

Irritation flooded me. Irritation, but also, if I'm being honest, a strange rush of adrenaline. Hadn't I just been fantasizing about him observing me, overcome with my naked beauty? It was confusing, very confusing, to figure out precisely what I wanted from Ursa, but I knew this much: If Ursa was so bloody determined to watch me, I ought to give him something to see.

Impulsively, I swam toward the shallower end of the pool to retrieve my soaps. Pretending I hadn't noticed my voyeur, I slathered a good amount of soap on my hands and then began to rub them over my body.

---

2. These women, I suspect, were not prone to cannonballing, even when presented with the opportunity.

I started in the safer zones—my arms, my shoulders, my neck. Even so, I took my time, slowly lathering and scrubbing, perhaps more thoroughly than ever before. It might have only been my imagination, but I thought I sensed a sort of taut awareness from my audience of one, still hiding somewhere in the forest. I thought. I couldn't be sure anymore. Maybe he really had just been popping back in to check on me, and he'd already left again. Maybe I'd imagined seeing him altogether . . .

If so, I was being rather ridiculous. Scratch that—either way, I was being rather ridiculous. I knew I was behaving in a most wanton, irresponsible manner, but I was making a point to Ursa. I couldn't quite remember what that point was now, but I liked this feeling of taking back the power, knowing I was being watched and deciding what to let him see.

And hear. I had never before in my life thought of bathing as a sensual experience, but knowing that I had an audience, I found myself moaning at the pleasure of having clean skin. I know, I know! Ridiculous. Strangely, though, the more I played it up, the more it began to feel truly naughty and decadent. This *was* a beautiful pool, and the water *did* feel wonderfully cool on my skin, and the scent of my soaps *was* sinfully delicious.

Up to this point, I'd been crouching, so only my shoulders and head were really visible out of the water. But now I'd cleaned everything that could ostensibly be cleaned and taken much more time than was necessary to do so. I'd reached the pivotal point of deciding whether to go on or whether to quit.

The moment stretched out in tense, silent anticipation. I truly didn't know now if it was all in my mind, if I'd merely been putting on this show for myself. I didn't think so, but I was afraid to check to see if Ursa had revealed himself again. I knew I would lose my courage if I saw him, and I found, strangely, that I was eager to continue.

Straightening to my full height, I stood with my torso exposed to the air. The waterline stopped just at my hip bones, and looking down, I could see the little shadow of a triangle just below the surface of the water.

Eyes closed, I lathered more soap and began to rub it on my body—my belly first, under my armpits, then finally up to my breasts. I covered my breasts in suds, rubbing in slow circles, up and down, testing their weight. My breasts had only ever been of mild interest to me before, but they took on a new fascination for me now, knowing how often Ursa stared at them and how obviously drawn to them he was. As my fingers found my nipples, hardened into points under the cool air and my ministrations, I slowly began to circle them, too, and surprised myself with the current of hot energy that pinged between my legs at the sensation.

"Oh," I breathed.

When I opened my eyes again, Ursa was no longer hiding. He was crouched at the edge of the pool, watching me unabashedly. His eyes followed my fingers, drinking in the sight of my breasts, before his gaze met mine and held it captive. We stared at each other, both of us unmoving. There was something primitive in the air between us, something unspoken that needed no language.

Ursa rose to his feet, then paused. He kicked off his trousers, so he was also completely naked, revealing his fully erect cock. When I didn't retreat, or shout at him, or cover myself, he dove into the water. I watched his dark figure slicing through the pool, approaching me, and I didn't know what to do. I wanted to retreat. I wanted to stay in place. The decision was made for me when Ursa's upper body emerged from the water. Rivulets ran down his face, over his broad chest and arms, dripping down toward the dark shape of his erection underneath the surface. When I looked back up at his face, expecting his gaze to also be roving over my body, I found his eyes fastened on mine.

My heart hammered in my chest; my throat ran dry. I opened my mouth to speak, not knowing what I was about to say. "Ursa—"

Ursa cupped one hand over my breast, then the other. He began to mimic my earlier motions of lathering them with soap, exploring their weight in his palms, his thumbs seeking out my nipples.

It had felt good, so good, to touch myself this way, knowing he was watching. Having him touch me in the same way, his gaze so intent on my face, was almost unbearably pleasurable. Back in my reckless youth, when I'd experimented and been experimented upon, it had been all hasty, inexperienced fumbling. I had felt awkward, embarrassed by my urges that never seemed to fully go anywhere. I did not recognize this feeling now of being overcome, of losing control of myself.

I moaned without intending to, a low and strange sound. My panicked brain told me I ought to stop this, even as my body pushed itself more intently into his touch.

We both heard it at the same time—a faint mechanical whirring sound, drawing rapidly nearer. My first thought was that it must be a swarm of bees or wasps, but realization quickly dawned. A drone.

Whilst I became frozen with indecision, Ursa hooked me around my waist and dragged me toward the waterfall, to the small alcove behind it. With one hand covering my mouth,[3] Ursa pushed me up against the rock wall, flattening himself against me.

---

3. I know I ought to have been more insulted by this gesture, but . . . well . . . he wasn't *wrong* to assume it would be difficult for me to keep my mouth shut, even when in grave danger.

By small alcove, I mean *small*. There was barely enough room for the two of us pressed together, and we were still mostly submerged with a little space above our heads to breathe. Still, it was lucky that Ursa had had the presence of mind to think of it. I wondered if he'd hidden here before and that was how he'd managed to avoid being discovered by other expeditions and the enforcers who monitored the planet and kept people from illegally poaching off the land. Perhaps the enforcers hadn't done their jobs all that well, if Ursa had managed to remain undetected all this time—and who knew if there were others like him, too, managing to stay under the radar?

Then again, I thought as I met his gaze, there was no one else quite like Ursa.

We waited, both of us holding our breaths and straining to hear the drone over the gushing roar of the waterfall. The drone's whirring was muted, but I could see a faint shadow being cast on the clear blue water as it circled overhead. Then it looked like it had disappeared, though Ursa and I remained in tense silence, listening, watching, waiting.

It must have been only a matter of seconds, but it felt like ages. Still, we waited a few moments longer, before I reached up and tugged Ursa's hand from my mouth.

"Rawley," I surmised quietly, and I could see in Ursa's dusky blue gaze that he seemed to be in concurrence. "Do you think he knows we're here?"

Even as I asked the question, I reasoned with myself that if Rawley knew where we were, he would be descending with armed men and cages. More likely, this was one of many drones he'd sent out, and it had just happened to pass too close for comfort. With a chill, I realized it would have passed right over me, if—

If Ursa hadn't been watching, even though I'd told him to leave. He'd been spying on me, but he'd also saved me. It was difficult, in these circumstances, to know just how irritated I was supposed to be.

Everything had happened so quickly that it took me a moment to catch up and process where we were—or rather, where our bodies were in proximity to one another. I was still very much naked and entangled with Ursa, also naked. He was frowning, looking over his shoulder, clearly still preoccupied by the drone and ascertaining whether it would be coming back, but he wouldn't be too far behind me in discovering just what position we were in.

Ugly, coarse shame flooded me for that little show I'd put on earlier. I'd been playing with fire, baiting a bear. Panic seized me at the thought of what I would do if he wanted to continue where we'd left off.

"Let me go," I blurted. "Let me go!"

Frowning, Ursa looked back to me, our gazes once again locking together. His eyes never left mine, though I felt the moment that he became aware of our closeness, the tightening of his jaw and the long, slow swallow. The quickening tempo of his heart, so close to mine I could feel it thrumming through the skin of his chest.

At last he released me, treading water. I pushed past him, swimming back underneath the waterfall and toward the opposite bank where I'd left my clothes. I was aware of him following me at a distance. When I reached the shore, I hurriedly dressed, even soaking wet as I was.

It was only when I reached for my book that it struck me—my things had been sitting out in the open when the drone passed overhead.

I tried to remember, in vain, the exact state they'd been in. I thought I'd put my trousers on top, and those were tan, probably almost indistinguishable from the grays and browns of the landscape around us. Someone would really have to be looking carefully to spot those.

Still, I ought to tell Ursa. I turned to him, even opened my mouth to do so, but he had just come out of the water and was shaking himself off like some great hairy dog.

I know it sounds ridiculous in hindsight, but here we were at this natural, beautiful waterfall, and there was this wildman, more animal than civilized man, and the drone had only been gone for a few minutes, but already it felt preposterous that anything could mar this beautiful, untamed world I'd unexpectedly found myself in. Ursa would only worry if I mentioned my concerns to him, I reasoned, and anyway, the clothes would have hardly been noticeable. We were safe.

Oh, God, how I wanted it to be true.

30

There was an unnerving hush tonight as I told the story of the pool and the drone. I thought the Brethren might like the excitement of almost being caught by one of Rawley's Sky Spies,[1] but as I finished telling the tale of the encounter, an unmistakable tension filled the air. Normally the Brethren are quite boisterous and eager to give me their feedback on whatever portion of the story was being told, but tonight no one would quite make eye contact with me. They all grumbled about it being late and shuffled out of the room.

I've been thinking about it for ages, here on my own in my cell, and the only thing I can surmise is that the men were angry with me for being so foolish and leaving my clothing out in plain sight on the rocks. It was a very imprudent decision, I agree, but one made out of naivety, not malice! How was I to know that Rawley would be sending out

---

[1]. The term *Sky Spies* is the trademark of Dr. Minerva Eloise Canfield-Smithe, thank you very much!

drones to try to track us down? I never made the same mistake again, I can assure you of that, although in the end, it was already too l—

Apologies for cutting off mid-sentence like that. A bit dramatic, I agree. I confess, I can hardly wrap my mind around what just happened to interrupt my writing. I'd heard the unmistakable sound of someone testing the door to see if it was locked. I suppose that in and of itself isn't too surprising, considering that I'm on the prison deck. Someone might have only been ensuring the locks were working. But then, someone tried the door again and quite insistently began banging on it, as if I were the one choosing to keep it locked![2]

If that weren't strange enough, I began to hear voices on the other side. It sounded like a small group of men, and they were quite heated. I could only hear bits and pieces of their conversation, mind you, since it is a rather heavy steel door. But so far as I could tell, one man said something to the effect of "Bitch has it coming, after a story like that,"[3] and the other men seemed to grumble in agreement.

My God, these men take drones personally!

I couldn't recognize all of the voices, since I tend to do most of the talking during story time, and, aside from rude interruptions and critiques, the men mostly listen. I do, however, think I recognized Big Red, with his distinctly deep timbre. The thought made me even more nervous than hearing the threat against me spoken out loud. I had once seen Big Red break the finger of a man who coughed too loudly during story time, so I could only imagine what he had in mind for me for . . . whatever it was he thought I'd done.

---

2. Hello—prisoner, here!!

3. Or I suppose it might have been "The hatch is incoming after rats tore eels lick cat," but that does seem far less likely.

As I listened to the continued muttering outside my door, it was starting to feel increasingly unlikely that the men were trying to find a way to break into my cell and teach me a lesson because they were upset that several months ago, I'd accidentally left a pile of clothes on a rock while I went swimming. Maybe they just hadn't liked this latest installment of the story? But then, what wasn't to like? There was romance, sexual intrigue, peril, life-and-death stakes, a cliff-hanger ending! I was a little offended, honestly, to think they hadn't responded better—pearls before swine and all that.

But they'd been so oddly tense. Not quite angry, but more as if they were restless, coiling for action. Clearly, whatever was troubling them had just been bottled up all this time until it was ready to burst.

And they were gathered, en masse, outside my door.

Then I heard another familiar voice entering the fray: Orion. "That's enough," he was saying, and something else I couldn't quite catch.

I pressed my ear to the door, straining to listen. I'm afraid the door remained too thick for me to hear properly, but once again, so far as I could tell, Orion was saying something about "calming down" and "sleeping it off" and remembering the "whores on Haven 1" in a few days, although I'm not sure what any of that would have to do with me . . . ?

Then Big Red accused Orion of trying to keep me to himself (?!), and Orion said something to the effect of they could try it, but did they want to gamble on not being the one or two he shot before they managed to kill him.

Then it was very quiet for a long moment before I heard a soft knock just above my head—still pressed to the door—that made me squeak and jump. "Mina," Orion said quietly—or maybe it was, again, just the thick metal door, "are you all right?"

"I'm fine," I reassured him, also quietly, in case there was a reason we were keeping our voices down. "Just a little confused. I'm not sure what's going on out there? Why is everyone so angry?"

I'd hoped Orion might fill me in on what I'd done, so I could know to avoid it in the future. But he was just quiet for a long moment before telling me, "Don't worry. I'll be out here for the rest of the night, just in case."

And, so far as I know, he still is. How very strange. I'm still not sure what's prompted all of this fuss, or why Orion feels the need to sleep outside my door tonight, but this was a chilling reminder that I will need to tread very, very carefully in my future storytelling. Nothing is guaranteed with the Brethren, and I must make it to Haven 3.

Back to you, my love. Please hold on, if you can. I'm coming for you.

31

After what happened between Ursa and me at the pool, I was more determined than ever to be careful—both in terms of keeping myself hidden, in case another drone came by, and in making absolutely certain I didn't do anything ridiculous again, like smother my naked body with soap in front of Ursa. Once the adrenaline of the afternoon had worn off, I couldn't believe how I'd behaved. I was ashamed of myself, honestly. It wasn't the sort of thing a scientist, a *mycologist*, from Haven 3 of all places, ought to be doing.

The fact that it had felt so incredible to have him touch me was no proof it should happen again. Opium probably felt pretty darn good the first time, too, but it was a dangerous, irresponsible habit to form.

I tried to explain as much to Ursa, once night drew on and I realized I would no longer be able to avoid him as assiduously as I'd been doing since the waterfall. "You see, Ursa," I explained primly once I sat myself a safe distance from him. "What happened earlier, when we were . . . *touching*." I dared a quick glance at Ursa's face. "It cannot happen again. Ever."

If I'm being honest, I'd expected something of a dramatic reaction—Ursa shouting, pleading, maybe even tearing at his clothing, overcome by his need for me.[1] Instead, Ursa remained silent and inscrutable; whatever he felt was known only to himself.

That was that. I ought to have just let it be. But I felt compelled to explain myself further, the words spilling out before I could catch them. "It's only that we're colleagues—dare I say it, friends. And that type of behavior is inappropriate. We ought to be above that sort of thing, don't you think? We aren't animals. We're intelligent human beings, both of us, not slaves to whatever we might feel . . . however it might feel—"

"Soft." Ursa surprised me by speaking up. When my eyes darted up to his face, I saw he was shamelessly, brazenly staring at my breasts. Which, apparently, felt . . . soft.

My breath stuttered. Then again when he looked into my eyes, something almost like a challenge in his gaze.

I looked away, rising to my feet. After pacing for a moment, I faced him with my arms folded, my expression stern. "Of course, as we are only human, there are times when I'll need to be strong and resolute when you're feeling tempted, and vice versa. Can I count on you, Ursa, not to let me give in to my weakness again?"

Ursa rose to his feet, advancing a step toward me, then another, holding my gaze the whole time. Despite myself, my eyes widened. I swallowed.

When he was only about a foot away, Ursa stopped. He looked me up and down, then gave a slow, lazy smile. "No."

---

1. It perhaps goes without saying that I'd spent rather too much time reading my romance novel by this point.

Then he turned and sauntered away, leaving me gawking after him.

"No?" I echoed, stunned at his audacity. Then, to myself, I muttered, "The cheek!"

After that, I put *The Impossible Thing* away for good, since it was putting all kinds of wild ideas into my head, which was, in turn, putting all kinds of wild ideas into Ursa's head, and I decided that I'd instead spend my free time reading about the wildlife native to Colorado.[2]

I became very interested in learning about the different species native to the mountains we now dwelt in, particularly the plant life and fungi.[3] As a result, I became more interested in having Ursa show me around the wilderness beyond where we foraged for food. I wanted to spot the birds, the trees, the insects that were recorded with such detail in my book. And, if I'm being perfectly honest, I no longer felt I could trust myself to be with Ursa in the close quarters of the cave for too long, after my behavior at the pool. I hoped if we were preoccupied with hiking and exploring, there wouldn't be time or energy for any more . . . lapses in judgment.

---

2. This, I believed, was the name of the city we now lived in. I've taken some Earth history, but I confess it's hard to remember all the names and places.

3. Naturally, the fungi section was less developed than the others, but I've grown accustomed to that lack and no longer find it surprising.

Surrounded by the beauty of the wilderness, I grew to understand Ursa's silence more. Magnificent trees dwarfed us completely, so thick and full in places that you could scarcely see the sky. Then all at once, you'd step into a clearing, and the ground would slope down to show the vastness of life, the spectrum of color—the endless blue of the sky and the greens and browns of nature—and it would take one's breath away.

I'd seen images of what Earth had become in the end, before mankind evacuated. I'd read about the destruction, the pollution, the disasters. But seeing how it had been restored, I wondered how anyone could have ever left it. Despite the circumstances that brought me here, despite the loneliness I sometimes felt with the loss of my old life, I found myself no longer able to imagine what it would be like to leave this place, to leave . . .

But no. I didn't want to think about that quite yet.

Apart from learning about the beauty of the wilderness, I also learned of its danger. Ursa showed me poisonous plants, taught me about the currents that could sweep you off your feet and drag you to a watery death, and warned me of the perils of the woods at night. The uncivilized world became a different beast when the sun drifted down behind the tree line. Its power became much clearer then, as if the forest wanted to make its true face known. I found myself infinitely grateful for the fearsome, muscular companion by my side—especially on days when we were still out exploring and dusk began settling in.

One such day, when Ursa had accompanied me to gather some interesting moss I'd found near the river, I felt the sudden shift of coolness in the air and realized time had gotten away from me, again.

"Ursa, which way is the cave?" I asked—or rather, I started to ask until I turned and saw he was no longer at my side.

I turned in a full circle, certain I must have just misplaced him for a moment, that he'd only stepped out of sight.

"Ursa?" I called, listening to the echo of my voice in the empty clearing—and beyond that, the infinite silence.

I called his name a few more times, still without answer, each repetition becoming more hysterical until finally I was forced to concede the truth: He had left me. Out here in the middle of the forest, all on my own, with sunset only about a half hour or so away.

Oh, God. I squatted, covering my face with my hands. Why hadn't I just put out when I still had the chance?

A far-off cry sounded in the distance. Ursa. I shot to my feet, searching the foliage frantically. "Ursa? Where are you?" I added a touch of the pathetic to my voice. "I'd like to go home now. I'm rather cold and hungry. Please?"

No response. No rustling of leaves announcing his imminent arrival. No broad-shouldered, hairy man watching me with hot eyes. Just silence.

Another moment passed before his call came again. This time, if I wasn't mistaken, there was a touch of irritation, as though to say, *Get up, you lazy thing.* Oh. So he wanted me to . . . follow him?

"You have got to be kidding me," I muttered. But what choice did I have, really? The sun was dipping ever lower in the sky, I had no idea how to get back to camp, and I could recall all-too-vividly the sounds of the forest at night. And I could imagine, even more vividly, what might be making those noises.

"Ursa," I called as I rose to my feet, "don't leave me. I'm coming!"

This time the cry that returned to me was encouraging, and I set off in the direction from which it had come. At least, I was pretty sure this was the direction from which it had come. It was hard to tell, with so many trees and rocks and green things. Everything looked the same—for all I knew, I was walking in circles. It certainly felt that way, since every time I thought I must certainly be coming upon Ursa at any moment, he suddenly seemed to shift positions, becoming farther and farther away.

At last, I'd had enough. I stopped in my tracks, folding my arms. "Ursa! I'm tired of this. I want to go home." I sounded like a petulant child, I knew, but at that moment I really felt as if I'd been pushed to my limit. "I'm hungry, and my feet hurt, and I stink—"

All at once, something large and strong was barreling into me, knocking me to the ground and all of the air out of me in one great whoosh. Dazed, it took me a moment to realize that my attacker was Ursa, his hands pinning my arms up over my head, his thighs straddling my torso. My God, he was heavy. I couldn't have pushed him off me even if I'd summoned all of my power. At the moment, I had no inclination to even try, more annoyed than frightened at this show of strength.

"Where have you been? Really, sending me on a wild goose chase through the forest. I have blisters on my feet, I'll have you know, and I'm weak with hunger and—oh!"

Ursa was baring his teeth at me, snarling. With one swift lunge, he snapped his jaws, stopping just short of my throat.

I'll admit, for a moment, I was really terrified. What if he'd contracted some type of quick-acting rabies . . . ?

Then I realized he was making a point. Trying to teach me a lesson. I recalled how earnestly he'd been gesturing at trees and rocks and things on our way to the clearing. He'd been trying to teach me how not to get lost. And yes, perhaps it had been rude of me to ignore him. But this . . . *display* of animal behavior was all a bit much. This simply wasn't the sort of thing that was done on Haven 3, I'll tell you that!

"Yes, fine, Ursa, I understand—I should pay more attention to where we're going. The wilderness is full of all kinds of dangerous things, and what if we got separated, et cetera, et cetera." I cleared my throat. "Do you think you could, um, get off me?"

I became cognizant midway through my little speech just how close we were, so much of him pressed up against so much of me, the heady woodsy smell of him, and me trapped underneath. My breasts were heaving like this was one of the censored scenes from my beloved classic novels, but the gritty kind, with fleas and body odor.

His eyes followed mine, taking in the sight of us together. A moment passed. He swallowed. Then he released me, sitting back on his haunches.

I scrambled to my feet, adjusting my clothes, my hair. I reminded myself—and I must never forget it—just how much stronger he was than me. How much I was at his mercy, no matter how I might trick myself otherwise.

32

I thought that would be the end of it. Lesson learned. On the rare occasions we left the cave, I dutifully paid more attention, trying to get a better grasp of direction. Gradually, as I really studied my surroundings, I could tell the difference between the individual trees and rocks, and I could even understand where I was based on the sun in the sky, the way the shadows were cast.

Just when I was becoming really impressed with myself for mastering this art of navigation, Ursa disappeared again.

One moment he was beside me, foraging for mushrooms. The next, he was gone, without so much as making a sound. Okay, so it was possible he *had* made a sound that was drowned out by my explanation of how they'd genetically cultivated mushrooms for space—fascinating stuff, really[1] —but it would have had to have been an extremely muted

---

1. The last time I offered to explain this in more detail to the Brethren of Blood, I was roundly declined, but it's always worth mentioning again to see if there are any takers.

sound, since I wasn't talking *that* loud, and he must have moved fast, since I hadn't been speaking *that* long.

"Ursa?" Like an idiot, I turned in a full circle before realizing what was happening. I rolled my eyes. "Not this again."

At least I was prepared this time. Without waiting for Ursa's call to guide me through the woods, I began to forge my own path back to the cave. Hopefully he would be impressed by how quickly I'd learned to navigate my own way back and we wouldn't have to go through this tedious exercise again.

But as I reached the tree by the stream with the broken branch, which meant that I had to take a sharp left, Ursa suddenly knocked me off my feet and into the ground, and with such momentum that we tumbled and rolled over each other before finally coming to a stop, his body pinning mine once more.

Ow. That one was going to bruise. "Ursa," I protested, shoving at him. "No fair. I was almost home."

To make my point, I shoved at him again, without budging him even in the slightest. He stared down at me dispassionately, making no sign that he planned to move at any point in the near future.

"Get off," I groused at him. "I want to go home."

He grunted back at me. "Mina weak. No skills."

Well, that was rude. Had he forgotten my fire making, hmm? My ability to decipher between poisonous and nonpoisonous mushroom species? Nothing to sniff your nose at, that!

"Who protect Mina if no Ursa?"

It was a valid point, I suppose, but at the moment, I was in no mood for that sort of nonsense. "Who cares? I'm starving. Let me up."

Ursa didn't move, didn't budge at all—just sat there with his huge, heavy body, waiting for me to somehow magically overpower him.

I could see it was pointless to try to convince him otherwise. He could be so infuriatingly stubborn sometimes. So, I summoned my full strength and attempted to push him off me. Nothing. Maybe I could squirm my way out from under him . . . and, bother, that didn't work either. Nor did any of the other things I tried.

"Just you wait," I huffed as I used both my hands to attempt to move his bicep. "I'm going to get my second wind soon, and then . . . you'll be . . . sorry . . ."

At last, taking pity on me, Ursa stilled my efforts. "Legs open, up." Then he took hold of my ankles and slowly began to slide his hands up the length of my legs.

Oh, that was . . . new. The feeling of his warm, callused fingers sliding along my calves, my knees, splaying out over my thighs and inching ever higher . . .

"Ursa," I tried to reprimand, though it came out as more of a whimper. I closed my eyes.

He stopped abruptly. I opened my eyes again to find him watching me quizzically, head tilted to one side, brow furrowed in confusion. Belatedly, I realized he'd been trying to instruct me to pull my legs up to my chest—not, uh, copping a feel, so to speak.

I hastily complied, hoping that this would distract him from the flush creeping up my neck. Situated with my legs drawn up between us, my feet pressed to his chest, Ursa showed me how to use the momentum of my legs—much stronger than my arms—to thrust him off me.

Seeing my own strength propelling him into the air was a nice, giddy little thrill, I must confess. "Again!" I cried.

It would be a request I'd come to regret, as Ursa made me repeat the motions over and over, building the muscle in my legs and offering me other strategies for using my momentum to flip him over and take the advantage. We practiced these movements, too, again and again, until we were both sweating and dirty and tired from tumbling over each other in the dirt.

It was, admittedly, thrilling to get the best of him, to roll and struggle and claw at each other but come out on top, me pinning him down now, using the force of my body. I'm sure, in hindsight, he must have been letting me win to build up my confidence. But in the moment, I was flushed, excited, proud to come out the victor.

I may, or may not, have gotten obnoxious about it—drunk with the power, if you will. "Concede defeat," I demanded, pressing my thighs into his torso to hold him in place. "Mina is the champion. Ursa is conquered!"

Smiling wryly at me, Ursa obediently tilted his head back, baring his throat—the sign of submission in the wild.

The sight of it thrilled me, made me giddy. That's the only explanation I can provide for what I did next.

I leaned forward, pressing my chest into his as I angled my face into the crook of his neck.

And then, dear reader, I licked him.

His throat, I mean.

I know, it was strange! Some animal instinct must have taken over me at the sight of him, prone underneath me, exposing his most vulnerable part to my attack. And, I did attack him, so to speak, with my mouth. My tongue, mostly, but my teeth got involved, too, I think.

Good God, this is embarrassing to write. Thank Heavens my mother is dead and will never read this. I encourage you to skip past it, as well, should this manuscript not reach its intended audience and you, gentle reader, happen to come upon it. I would love to also skip over this part with the Brethren of Blood, but as the events from the other night have shown me, I must do everything I can to keep their interest piqued to avoid being suffocated in space for their entertainment. So, I'm choosing to include what follows, but really, truly, you don't have to read it. It's just some licking and biting and rolling around in the woods. You can skip to the end of the chapter and not miss a thing. Truly.

Let's see, where were we? Well, I'd just licked Ursa's throat in a fit of excitement, and he went completely still. *Completely* still, like I was lying on top of a boulder. Except we were pressed together so close, I could feel his heart beating, racing, and I guess mine was, too.

I tried to sit up, but he grabbed my arms, holding me in place. His eyes opened, searching my face.

I tried my best to smile, like it was all a funny joke. "Mmm!" My voice was too loud, too cheerful. "Salty. From all the sweat, I imagine . . ."

Again, I tried to get up, but Ursa used one of his fancy tricks to sort of lift us up so we were both upright. I was still straddling him, but I was in his lap now, if that makes sense.[2] Proof, I suppose, that he could have reversed our positions all along and was just letting me win. A bit rude of him, really, now that I think of it. Anyway, he was looking at me so intensely that I wanted to make another joke, only my mind had gone completely blank. All I could think about was how close our pelvises were and that I could see a vein in his neck pulsing. He'd

---

2. Oh, God, I'm sweating as I write this, it's so mortifying. I don't know how I'm going to say all this out loud to the Brethren . . .

tasted more than salty, I recall, like sweat and dirt, but in a way that was somehow pleasant. More than pleasant. I wanted to do it again, even though I was afraid.

Ursa took my face in his hands, tilting my head back. My heart was hammering, and I couldn't stop talking, the words avalanching out of me. "For some reason I thought it was only wolves who showed submission by exposing their throats. The alpha dog and the beta dog and whatnot. I guess now I'm sort of the alpha, if you really—umm. Oh. Ursa . . ."

Still holding my head in place, he began lapping at my throat with his tongue, much as I'd done with him a few moments before. Only, he didn't stop there. His warm tongue followed the line of my jaw. His mouth closed over the shell of my left ear, teeth closing over my lobe and *tugging*, not too hard, but not gently, either.

If I'd been thinking clearly, I might have said, *Wait a moment, Ursa, this feels nice, but we might be getting carried away with ourselves . . .*

This would have been the smart thing to say. But my God, it felt incredible, and instead, I just sort of moaned and squirmed against him. Like a fool. A wanton fool.

I already know what the Brethren of Blood will say: *More details, Mina!* Oddly, they never care to know more about the scenery of the woods surrounding the cave or the ingenious laundry system I came up with to keep both Ursa and myself fully clothed in between washes. But whenever it has to do with *this* aspect of life, they're suddenly gluttonous for information!

Well, let's see. I was moaning and squirming—right, already said that. And then I, well, I think he must have started licking and sniffing his way down my neck again, to my clavicle. Yes. And that also felt, you know. Quite nice.

Oh, bother. That's terrible! But what am I supposed to write? It was a blur of touch and sensation. I wasn't thinking through it all, beat by beat. For the first time in a very long time, I wasn't thinking at all. It was almost like my soul had left my body. No, that isn't quite right. Maybe more like my mind had disconnected for a moment. My soul, whatever nebulous thing that might be, was still very much present—connected to my body in a way I've never experienced before. I always thought pleasure, *that* kind of pleasure, must be purely physical, but looking into his eyes, bodies pressed together, hearts pounding against one another—there was something transcendent, something sublime, in that.

But for the sake of not suffocating, I will do my very best to remember the sequence of events as they occurred.

Let's see, where were we?[3] Ursa was licking along his merry way now, tasting where my neck met my shoulder. I was making noises that I'd never heard from myself before, and at first, they embarrassed me greatly, but I found I couldn't stop, and then I ceased trying altogether once I realized how excited they were making Ursa. By excited, naturally, I mean that I could feel his erection pressing between us, although as has already been established, that was hardly anything new. The poor man seemed to be in a state of almost permanent arousal around me.

What seemed new about his excitement now, though, was his eagerness to explore and get me to continue making those sounds—and seeing that I wasn't pushing him away or halting him as he touched me. I knew I ought to be the one to keep a level head, put an end to things. But I also knew if he didn't keep touching me, I was going to

---

3. Buckle up, Smithe-Canfield! Bravely onward and upward, so to speak.

go mad. Possibly explode. It was as though the simple act of licking my skin had opened a conduit straight to my core. It felt like I had molten lava brewing inside of me, and the feeling—even at this level—was far more intense than anything I'd ever experienced with a pleasure machine. The sensations of the pleasure machine had always been . . . well, *pleasant*, a neat, contained fire in a hearth. This, whatever was happening to me now, was like a wildfire consuming the wilderness,[4] a blaze that could not be controlled.

"Ursa," I whined, pleaded, rubbing my core frantically against his leg in the hopes that the friction would be enough to satiate this urgent need inside of me. (It was not.)

With a grunt, Ursa took hold of my shirtfront and ripped it open, sending a few buttons flying in the process. His hands began to roam over my stomach and back, but I was too impatient for that and firmly guided his hands up to my breasts. He began lifting and caressing them, all while impatiently working to free them from the confines of my bra. Then, locking eyes with him for a long, charged moment, I saw the devilish glint in his eyes before he leaned forward and closed his mouth over my left breast and began to suck.

My hands moved to his hair, gripping frantically—not so much trying to guide him as holding on for dear life as the sensations coursing through my body wreaked pure chaos on me. "Ursa!"

In answer, he shifted his hips, so his erection was now pressing up against that throbbing part of me, and began to buck against me. We were still fully clothed in that region, but the friction, the sensation,

---

4. We don't have wildfires on Haven 3, as one could imagine in a constructed atmosphere with no wildlife to speak of, but I have, of course, seen the footage of the Earth that was, back before it was rehabilitated.

was incredible. All the while, he licked and sucked my breasts, my hands still tangled in his hair, both of us moaning and grinding against each other.

Then all at once, Ursa went very still, his grip on my hips tightening painfully. A moment passed, only long enough for him to meet my gaze, and in his eyes, I saw terror.

Then he was flipping me over again, so my back was to the ground, and using his broad body to block me as out of the forest, there was a blur of speed and sound, and—seemingly out of nowhere—a mountain lion pounced.

33

The cougar dug its claws into Ursa's back, jaws snapping at his neck as it dragged him toward the tree line. Ursa reached behind him, holding the big cat by the jaw, gritting his teeth against the pain as he struggled to keep the mountain lion from gaining purchase on his throat. Getting a good hold, he managed to twist around, so the two of them were facing one another directly. Then they tumbled down together, scrabbling in the dirt and pine needles.

For a moment, I sat there, completely dazed by this turn of events. Then, glancing to my side, I saw there was a skull-sized rock near my feet. Acting not out of any bravery or resourcefulness, but rather an acute panic, I took the small boulder in hand, raised it over my head, and let out a bloodcurdling shriek as I threw it at the big cat with all my might.

The blow connected, the rock striking the mountain lion's head. It growled, releasing Ursa, as I'd hoped—and turned toward me. *Not part of the plan.* I backed away, tripping over myself in my haste to escape, as the cougar coiled, preparing to pounce.

Mouth dry, I could only stare at it stupidly, looking my untimely doom straight in its eyes.

Ursa roared, launching himself onto the mountain lion's back. As the big cat lurched and writhed and tried to throw him off, Ursa scrambled to take hold of the creature's head. The two of them twisted around, locked in an embrace almost as intimate as a lover's, before at last Ursa grabbed the cougar's skull and with one swift motion, snapped its neck.

The cat collapsed. For a moment, all I could see of Ursa was his poor mangled back, rising and falling with shuddering breaths. Blood dripped down him in a great gushing avalanche.

Then he looked up at me, his eyes a dazed plea. With a start, I realized he was hurt—too hurt to move on his own.

"Ursa." I started toward him, arms stupidly outstretched, as if—to what? Implore him? Catch him? Lift him up and carry him on my back?

He passed out before I could reach him, face buried in the dead cat's neck.

What followed was sheer panic. Frantically searching Ursa's pulse to make sure he was just unconscious, not dead. Then frantically devising a way to get him back to the cave. I may not have known quite as much about surviving in the wild as I'd once, overconfidently, believed I did, but even *I* knew that all the blood and carnage would attract other animals. We had to get away from here and back to safety, soon.

What no one had prepared me for, during any of the schooling or training I'd received in my lifetime, was how to move an unconscious man who was roughly 1.5 times my size, without any tools or instruments at my disposal. What I wouldn't have given for a wheelbarrow at that moment! I knew we had some rope back at the cave, but I didn't want to chance leaving Ursa in the forest on his own, unconscious and vulnerable and exposed to the elements.

Trying to calm myself, I assessed the resources at my disposal. I could attempt to pull up some roots to use as ropes, but that seemed like a long, tedious process that might not even work. If the root was strong enough, I might not be able to pull it out of the ground, and if it was weak enough for me to pull up out of the ground, it might not hold Ursa. The root idea seemed like a dead end, unfortunately.

The only other item that might do was my own clothing. I was going to have to fashion rope out of clothing and hope it would be strong enough to both hold the weight of Ursa's body and withstand being dragged through the woods. It was time to see how well my clothing was manufactured.

My shirt was the obvious choice, since I could use the sleeves to tie the material around Ursa's body and drag. The blouse was already ruined anyway, between Ursa tackling me in the forest and then . . . well, ripping open my shirt during that other thing that happened. It already felt like a lifetime ago. I suppose one benefit of being attacked by a mountain lion and having to devise how to get my companion back to safety was not having to worry about what our heated tryst in the forest meant and what repercussions it might have. Silver lining, and all.

I was being facetious, of course, because the only other alternative was to break down crying, and I wouldn't let myself be that silly sort of person who lost her head in the midst of a catastrophe. I would find a way to prevail. My people were those of the stiff upper lip. I would find a way to keep calm and carry on, or die trying!

Unfortunately, I quickly discovered Ursa's torso was quite a bit broader than mine, and though the material of the blouse would shield his back from being dragged across branches and thorns and rocks and the like, there wouldn't be much room for me to get a hold on the material to pull him along. There was no way around it. I would have to take off my trousers, too, and tie them to the sleeves of the shirt.

Once that was accomplished, that left his poor head rather dreadfully exposed to the elements. Off came my knickers, too, which I used to fasten a sort of cap, stuffed with my socks, all held together with my bra. Hopefully that would be enough to cushion his head from being bumped around on the ground.

And yes, for those keeping track, that left me absolutely stark naked to accomplish this task—minus my glasses and my boots.[1]

"If I didn't know better," I huffed at Ursa's unconscious form, "I would think you'd orchestrated this entire thing just to get me starkers."

Ursa didn't respond, obviously, because he was unconscious. Still, worth checking. If anything might rouse him from being passed out, it might be the mention of my nudity.

After that I began the slow, incremental drag of Ursa's body through the forest. There is no way to spruce up this portion of the

---

1. Although this is a faithful recounting of what took place, so far as I can remember it, I also believe it will be beneficial to have another chapter in which I'm naked. The Brethren seem to be very responsive to these moments in the story, most likely because it heightens the sense of bodily vulnerability and frailty, and the perils of external danger.

story, I'm afraid. Even with the life-and-death stakes, it was dull, dull, dullsville. Between the rough terrain and my pathetic upper body strength, we made terrible time.

I was beginning to fear we wouldn't reach the cave by nightfall, and I did not want to be caught out in the woods in the dead of night. Stuck somewhere between panic and hysteria, I found myself babbling again, mostly just to keep from weeping.

"If there's any part of you that can hear me, Ursa, you really ought to wake up. I'm naked as a jaybird over here. Ass. Breasts. All of it just jiggling around out here in the open. You'd love it, if you weren't so wounded and unconscious. Oh, God, what would my mother say if she could see me now? The woman who used to chastise me for putting my elbows on the table—Lord! She'd roll over in her grave. You are quite heavy, you know. I don't mean that as an insult because you're obviously quite fit, and all, but that's probably part of the problem, isn't it? Muscle weighs more than fat, and you don't have much of that. You're sort of chiseled and hard all over, and hairy, and sometimes, yes, even smelly, and I oughtn't to find that appealing, yet somehow I do. Isn't that strange? There are people back home who've had most of their sweat glands bred out of them, or altered so they smell like flowers or sea air or some other nonsense, but now I get a whiff of your dirty, sweaty body and . . . I don't know. It does something to me. *You* do something to me, and not just because I like the way your sweat smells or because it was awfully nice to be licked by you. You make me smile. You make me laugh. You make me feel seen for the first time in my life. I thought I was going to be doing this on my own, but now I can't do anything without thinking about you, wondering what you'll think of it, of me. I couldn't have done any of this without you, I know that. I like to pretend that I'm the one teaching you things, but I know it's you, teaching me to stay alive. And more than that, I think. You must be all right, Ursa, because—well, because . . ."

I realized I'd drifted off, stupidly, because in the middle of whatever it was I was going to say next, I saw his eyes were open and he was looking back at me. Woozily. Blearily. He didn't seem to quite know where he was or what was happening, and I knew he couldn't have been fully alert because his eyes were on my face instead of anywhere else on my exposed body, but he was *awake.*

"Ursa!" Without thinking, I dropped my trouser-ropes and half clambered on top of him, mindful of his wounds, so I could clutch his face. "Thank God you're awake."

Already his eyes were starting to roll back into his head, drifting shut again. I shook him, not too hard, but not as gently as I probably should have. "No, no, no, Ursa, you have to stay awake. You have to help me. I'll never be able to make it back there without you."

Ursa's head lolled about. His eyes fastened on nothing, and then all at once, they were locked onto me, as beautifully intense as they had ever been. I held his gaze, gripping the side of his face, trying to impress on him the importance of staying conscious. "I know it hurts, Ursa. I promise I'll let you rest. I'll take care of you. But we have to get back to the cave first. You need to stay with me until then."

His head started to drop back, but I tightened my grip. "Ursa, listen to me. You'll die if we can't make it back."

That didn't seem to make much of an impression on him. His head slumped forward now, eyes drifting shut.

"No, no, no, Ursa. Listen to me. Listen to me. You will die if we can't make it back. I will die, do you understand? I won't be able to leave you here, but I won't be able to protect you. We will die. You must stay awake and help me get you back to the cave!"

A long moment passed in which I scarcely managed to breathe.

And then Ursa was groaning, struggling to push upward, and I was scrambling to my feet, helping him maneuver around my awkward clothing binding to loop his arms around me. "That's it, Ursa. Lean on me. I can help you. One step at a time. There we go. Not too much farther now . . ."

34

Between Ursa's incredible stamina and my persuasiveness, we were able to make it back to the cave. I'm not too humble to admit it took an extraordinary amount of ingenuity on my part. It was like corralling a very drunk, injured gorilla back into its enclosure—particularly if said gorilla could briefly be distracted from his pain and disorientation by groping one's body. Yes, I'm also not ashamed to admit that part of my ingenuity was using my feminine wiles. We were in life-or-death peril, and the situation called for it!

With a hearty mixture of *that* sort of enticement, plus my singing rousing spaceship shanties to keep him awake and occasionally shouting in his face like a drill sergeant to keep him motivated, at long last I deposited Ursa into our animal-skin bed. Even though my own body was beginning to shake as the adrenaline wore off, my task was not yet finished. I gathered whatever supplies I could find that would hold water and scrambled back down to the pool.

It was dusk now, the inky dark of night beginning to snuff out the remaining light on the horizon, and as I filled up various containers with water, it struck me anew just how close we had come to being stranded overnight in the forest. How close he had been to death, at the savage claws of that mountain lion. How close I had been to losing him.

I let myself weep for two minutes. I didn't want to delay getting Ursa the help he needed, but it also felt necessary for me to release my fear and anxiety for a short, precious amount of time so I could give him my full focus and attention once I returned.

Once the two minutes were up, or thereabouts, I wiped my eyes with the back of my hand.[1] "Enough of that now, you barmy lass."

With that, I finished filling up all of my containers, then got to work.

Even though I'd been studying the pool water and its healing properties for some time, I was still amazed to see it at work. All of my experiments had been on superficial cuts and bumps and bruises. I had deduced that Ursa had used the pool to heal me after my injuries sustained by Rawley, but I hadn't been conscious enough to properly observe the water's processes. Mind you, I would have never wished an injury on Ursa; but, seeing for myself how quickly—and yes, even miraculously![2] —Ursa's wounds were healing, I couldn't help but be fascinated.

---

1. As I was still naked, I did not have any tissues or handkerchiefs on my person.

2. As a woman of science, one can imagine how loath I am to use this word, but truly, I can think of no better way to describe it.

Deep scratches scabbed over within minutes. Overnight, new tissue began to grow, and within a day, the wounds had faded to scars. Previously I'd seen minor injuries like beestings disappear altogether, but Ursa's wounds were so severe, I hadn't known if the pool water would be enough to make a difference. A healing process that I might otherwise have estimated to take a few weeks had taken a little over twenty-four hours. It really was astonishing.

Throughout all this, Ursa slept like the dead. I knew he wasn't dead, obviously, since I could see him breathing and shifting about restlessly, as he often did in his sleep. I suppose even with the help of the pool water, his body needed to expend enormous amounts of energy to heal so quickly. Still, even with the quick improvements, I knew I wouldn't feel fully at ease until he was conscious again for more than a few moments at a time. It had been a relieving distraction to focus on the medicinal properties of the water, but now that Ursa was physically healed, I began to grow paranoid that something might be really wrong with him, something the water couldn't fix.

Late into the second night with Ursa, there still wasn't any response. Sleep felt like an impossibility, when I didn't know if he would be all right, but I reminded myself that I would need to keep up my strength to care for him until he was able to do so himself.

Sighing, I readied myself for bed in my favorite billowing nightgown. As I brushed out my hair, I glanced over my shoulder at him. "Ursa, you're wise not to wake up now. I'm wearing that nightgown you hate."

Ursa had never told me in so many words that he hated my nightgown, but a woman knows these things. After his initial curiosity in the garment had worn off, I noticed Ursa always got huffy when I put it on. I suppose it was a little matronly, but it was *so* comfortable! He likely would have preferred that I wear nothing at all, knowing the way his tastes ran.

Buoyed by the idea, I glanced over at him again. "You must wake up sometime soon though. And if you do, I promise I'll start sleeping in the buff, as they say."

No response.

"Naked," I added.

I was maybe a little delirious, coming down off the adrenaline and lack of sleep from the past few days. Still, I thought it might be worth a try to see if I could encourage him to wake up sooner. Ursa continued to sleep soundly, though, so I shrugged, sighed, and climbed into the animal skins with him.

Up close, I faced him, watching the gentle rise and fall of his chest as he slept. It was the most comforting feeling in the world, to watch someone sleep. Especially when you had almost lost them.

Especially, I realized looking at his face, when that person was Ursa. My panic at the thought of losing him hadn't just been because without him, I would be on my own. It was because without him, I would be without *him*. We had known each other for such a short time, and yet it was as if I'd always known him. I couldn't imagine a life now without him.

"You must be all right, Ursa," I told him quietly, urgently. "You must come back to me."

Ursa just continued sleeping. And not too long after, I joined him.

35

It was not unusual for me to wake before Ursa. He was rather endearingly grumpy in the morning. Most other times he was so stoic, so strong and fearless; it always made me laugh to see how bleary-eyed and grouchy he was first thing in the morning.

Ursa *was* a light sleeper, though, which was perhaps why he was always so irritable when he woke for the day. I could tiptoe around the cave, making only the slightest sound, and he would be up like a shot, eyes blazing, body on full alert. I suppose that was a natural byproduct of him living alone for so long, away from civilization. Out here on his own . . . the danger of something taking him unawares while he slept would have been all too real.

But this morning, Ursa was dead to the world. *Still.* I knew his body had been through a terrible ordeal, and rationally, I knew it wasn't unusual that he'd need more sleep to recover. I couldn't help myself from fretting over him, though, holding a hand above his mouth and nose to reassure myself he was only sleeping. Normally even this would have been enough to wake him, but still he slumbered on.

I finally determined I wasn't doing either of us any good, just sitting here and watching him and worrying myself to death. As it seemed likely he would still be asleep for some time, I decided to be proactive and go gather our breakfast. It was true that normally I wouldn't venture out on my own, and that I was still wary after being attacked by a mountain lion, but I also reasoned that if I knew anything about Ursa, he'd be ravenously hungry once he woke.

Plus, he'd been training me to find my way back to the cave, hadn't he? If I couldn't find my way back from the place we scavenged for breakfast almost every single day, I wasn't a very good pupil, was I?

That settled, I dressed, found my pack, and paused just before leaving to press my lips to Ursa's forehead—to check he wasn't riddled with fever, mind you. "Sleep," I urged him quietly. "I'll be back soon."

It didn't take long to find sufficient breakfast. I couldn't access honey on my own, but I did manage to gather many of his other favorite things. My haul, combined with the protein bars back at the cave, would likely be enough to appease him for an hour or so upon his waking before he went scavenging for his next snack.

And he would be well enough to do so, I told myself, swallowing back the lump in my throat. Very soon.

I'd started back to camp when a sudden thought struck me—I'd noticed a small growth of lion's mane[1] the other day when I was out scavenging with Ursa, not too far away. Though lion's mane wasn't

---

1. *Hericium erinaceus*

specifically known to aid with the healing process, I knew it might help in the long term if he'd sustained any nerve damage. And, all right, I felt the need to do *something*, to not just sit around uselessly and hope he healed.

Ursa would have been proud of me, had he been there. I took my time to really study my surroundings and left markers to ensure I'd be able to trace my way back. By the time I found the small outcropping of lion's mane, my own stomach was growling, and I hoped that meant Ursa would soon be hungry enough, too, that he'd wake up, even if only for a little while. I would know so much more about his condition once he woke up.

As I began the trek back to our cave, I was so distracted by the thought of Ursa's injuries that it genuinely took me a moment to realize what I was hearing: the low rumble of an engine, growing louder into a shrieking pitch as it drew nearer.

My first thought was that it must be another of Rawley's drones, and I quickly flattened myself to the ground.

But as I craned my neck to watch what was passing overhead, I saw it wasn't a drone at all.

It was a spaceship.

A smuggler's ship, to be precise. I wasn't someone who knew much about starcraft, but I happened to recognize this particular vessel.

It was Tobago's ship.

36

I watched from a careful distance as the crew began to disembark. I recognized a few of the faces, as well as the serial number embedded on the side of the cockpit. There could be no mistake. It was Tobago's ship, here on one of his regular illegal scavenging runs.

I'd gotten the schedule wrong.

My time frame must have been off; I must have been unconscious longer than I realized.

The obvious thing to do would have been to announce myself, demand to speak to Tobago. I could arrange my passage back as planned, and perhaps they would have a medic onboard who could treat Ursa and make sure he was well enough to for me to leave behind before I departed back to Haven 3.

But unexpectedly, the thought of leaving Ursa behind was like being tossed out of an air lock—like all the air was being sucked out of my lungs.

So I watched the ship silently, unobserved. It was unclear what the crew was here to scavenge for, but what *was* clear was that they would be here for some time. They were pulling out camouflaged tents, putting up a laser perimeter. They'd be here for at least a few days, I guessed, if not longer.

When I saw Tobago emerge down the ramp, giving curt, quick orders to his crew, my heart lurched in my chest. Even though we'd planned this outcome all along, it felt surreal seeing him here, my childhood friend. My ticket back to civilization. Back in Haven 3, the thought that I wouldn't be overjoyed to see him when he finally arrived had never crossed my mind. I had always been counting on Tobago to rescue me, always; I could never have guessed that his arrival would fill me with absolute dread.

Because it wasn't only myself I had to take into account now. I could always try to bring Ursa with me, but I knew it would come with a price. Tobago might be my longtime friend, but I knew him too well to think he'd take Ursa out of the kindness of his heart, especially with the risk of Rawley coming after him if he found out he'd helped us. Furthermore, even if I could persuade Tobago to take on another passenger, Ursa would never do it. *Could* never do it. Earth, the untamed wilderness—this was his home. He would be miserable in society, with all of its intricate rules, and customs, and politics, and the clothes. My God! The clothes. He would absolutely loathe them. He'd be arrested within a week for indecent exposure.

And it would ruin him. Not the indecent exposure, he probably wouldn't mind that at all, but rather, the artificiality. It would be like trying to contain a beautiful redwood in a petri dish. Haven 3, that overly civilized and monetized world, would be so small for him, so bleak and contained. No direct sunlight. No plants grown outside of a lab. No massive trees to climb, no secluded pools to dive in, no open night sky to gaze upon. Everything obscured by the glass of the dome, everything regulated and small and *cultivated*.

He would be miserable. It would destroy him.

And I found that even the thought of it destroyed me. I wanted Ursa exactly as he was—wild and honest and unaffected and free. There was no artifice about him. He did exactly what he wanted, held nothing back. He was generous and kind, protective and brave. He'd rescued me from the base when I'd been ready to leave him behind, just to save myself. He'd been so patient with me as I learned to adapt to living in the wild. And there were layers to him, too, unexpected discoveries at each new turn. There was so much pain underneath his stoic surface. But he could also be funny. His face was often hard to read, but then he'd get this expression, this wonderful, surprising look that let me know exactly what he was thinking and...

I loved him.

The recognition shouldn't have been such a surprise to me, but it was. I'd lived with him for months, learned from him, taught him how to speak and drink tea, dragged his body through the woods just to get him back to safety. We spent all our time together, but it still never felt like enough. I wanted to be with him, always. I'd been so afraid of living on my own in the wilderness, but instead he'd taught me what it was to not feel alone for the very first time.

I loved him.

I loved him, and I knew going back to civilization would destroy him. So I would stay here, with him, even if it were dangerous. Even if I might never see my friends again. Even if there was no indoor plumbing. I loved him, and I could not, would not, leave him.

Soundlessly, I slipped behind the tree line and made my way back to Ursa.

37

As I approached the final landmarks to our cave, I could hear shouting all the way from the forest. Recognizing Ursa's voice, panic gripped me as half a dozen different scenarios raced through my mind, each one worse than the last. Ursa was sick and needed help. Ursa was being attacked by another wild creature.

Ursa was being captured by Rawley.

In at least half those scenarios, there was nothing I could do to help him, and indeed, racing toward him would only put me in harm's way, too; if *he* couldn't fight off an attacker, what chance did I stand?

But then, what other choice did I have? If Ursa needed me, I had to go to him. There was no other way.

I scrambled up the small rocky embankment, raced past the pool, and hoisted myself into the cave. What I saw drew me up short, stunning me into silence.

Ursa was awake. Naked. Shouting. The pool water seemed to have worked its usual magic,[1] and any remaining injuries on his body were merely faint ghosts of what they'd been.[2] But his eyes were wild, his entire body tense, and he paced the cave with seemingly uncontrollable agitation, shouting indecipherable syllables. Roaring, more like. He'd scattered our stock of supplies around the den, as if he'd mowed through them in a rage.

I still didn't understand what was happening. He'd been sleeping peacefully when I left. What could have riled him up so terribly? I wondered if perhaps he'd seen a snake or some other vermin hiding in our things. That might explain why he had tossed everything around, but it wouldn't account for why he was in such a temper.

I'd never seen him this way before. I should have been afraid of this massive, angry man. But I wasn't. This was *Ursa*.

Still, I would have to approach this outburst, whatever it was from, carefully. I decided to use a brisk schoolmarm tone, which had sometimes been effective in the past at curbing his wilder behavior. "Ursa, honestly! What's gotten into you? This is going to take ages to clean up."

At the sound of my voice, Ursa whipped his head around to face me, staring at me in a way that made me feel almost like he wasn't seeing me at all, even though he was looking right at me.

---

1. I'm using this word hyperbolically, since of course I don't believe in magic. I do believe that the natural world has an enigmatic, unknowable, maybe even mystical quality to it, but magic? Pff. Not bloody likely.

2. See previous note. If magic is nonsense, then ghosts are pure poppycock. But as metaphors, both terms work rather effectively.

Brisk schoolmarm wouldn't do, I saw right away. Something was really wrong. "Ursa, what is it?"

Ursa started toward me like he was going to grab me. Then abruptly he turned from me and crouched, covering his face, shoulders shaking.

My heart lurched. I ran to him, dropping to my knees beside him. "Ursa, what is it . . . ? What's happened . . . ?"

"Mina gone," Ursa told me through heaving breaths. "Ursa wake, and Mina gone."

I intuited instantly how it must have been for him. He'd been sleeping for days, and he woke up feeling disoriented and vulnerable. Instead of finding me beside him, I'd been missing, along with my pack and my shoes. He must have thought the absolute worst of me. It pained me to realize it, but I also understood. He'd been alone for so very long. The thought of going back to that solitude must have been terrible.

"Ursa." Any hesitation or self-consciousness left me. All I could think about was ensuring he understood, *really* understood, just what he meant to me. I wrapped my arms around him from behind, resting my cheek against his back. "I only went to get breakfast. I wasn't leaving you. I would never leave you. I—"

I started to tell him I loved him, but I lost the courage. Instead I just repeated, "I would never leave you."

And as simply as that, it was decided.

Then I held him quietly, anchoring him as the last of the tremors wracked his body. Even after he was calm again, I held him, waiting for him to let me know what he needed, ready to do anything that would help him.

A moment later, Ursa stood. I watched him, but he didn't look at me or address me. He walked over to his trousers, tattered from his encounter with the wildcat. After he pulled them on, he moved soundlessly to the opening of the cave.

I watched him, also soundlessly, waiting to see what he would say, what he would do. I didn't know if he was still overcome with emotion, or embarrassed at his earlier display, or worse, if some switch had been thrown in his mind when he'd thought I left him, and now he was closing himself off to me emotionally to protect himself. The thought made my stomach lurch in panic. What if I'd realized I loved him, just in time for him to decide he no longer wanted me?

"Come?"

The single word drew me out of my spiral. I blinked at Ursa, who was still not quite facing me or looking at me but clearly waiting for me to follow him, wherever he was going.

What choice did I have, really?

Rising to my feet, I trailed after him.

38

We walked for some time in the forest. Instead of adjusting his pace to mine, like he usually did when we went scavenging together, Ursa loped ahead of me, pausing only when he was in danger of leaving me completely behind, and only long enough for me to be within his sight again. It's hard to say for certain how much time really passed, but it felt like hours.

I could see the purpose in his stride, the agitation set in the muscles of his back and shoulders, but without him near me, it was hard to determine what the source of his turmoil was. Was he angry at me? Teaching me another lesson about navigation? Or was he going to abandon me somewhere new in the forest and hope we'd traveled far enough I wouldn't be able to find my way back?

At long last, I saw Ursa stop up ahead of me a few paces and wait. This time he remained until I was at his side. I looked at him questioningly, grateful for the chance to catch my breath but sensing this pause was something more. "Ursa . . . ?"

Ursa was staring at the ground, hard, but he lifted one hand, pointing ahead of us. Frowning, I turned to see what he was gesturing toward.

At first glance, I'd taken the shape ahead of us to be a large cluster of boulders, overgrown by moss and other vegetation. My focus during the walk had been on Ursa; I'd cared less about what our destination might be.

But now, peering closer, I saw the large shape underneath the foliage was a ship. It looked to be an older model than the vessel that had brought me to Earth, and it was much smaller—a craft built for a small handful of passengers instead of a large group. It somewhat resembled Tobago's ship, although this one looked to be an even older make and model.

I turned to Ursa. "Is there someone in there?"

But as soon as the question left my mouth, I realized it was nonsense. There were vines growing over the hatch, sealing it shut. The windows were overgrown with mildew so thick one could no longer see inside. And there was a pervasive stillness about the craft, a lack of life, of energy. I don't know how else to describe it. It was like approaching a void.

I looked again to Ursa for answers. His jaw was clenched, his eyes hard. He drew in a steadying breath, then marched forward. In a matter of seconds, he'd pulled away all the vines growing over the hatch. Taking a steeling breath, he reached for the handle, then opened the door.

This time I didn't wait for Ursa to urge me to follow him. I was already at his heels. I didn't know what about this place was causing him so much agony, but I knew I could not let him suffer through it alone. Grasping his hand, I intertwined our fingers together, squeezing tightly to let him know I was there with him.

We entered cautiously, Ursa leading the way. He seemed reluctant to enter this place, though not out of concern for our safety. Whatever ghosts it held for him, they seemed to have a tight grip on his heart.

I saw why almost immediately. The inside of the vessel looked like a standard small interspace vehicle, the cockpit arranged to accommodate two pilots. There was a tiny galley kitchen, an even smaller water closet, plenty of storage supply built into the ceiling and wall panels, and a bedroom in the back.

What struck me right away was the obvious presence of a child—or, what had once been a child—living here with adults in this ship. Along with coffeepots and mugs were small sippy cups. A child's height was marked on the doorframe, and crudely drawn pictures were pinned to the walls. Toys were clustered with the other ship supplies—stuffed animals and toy ships and an old, broken holo with its screen cracked. Warped, dusty photographs of what looked to be a man, woman, and child decorated the space, giving it a more homely feel.

It was like peering into a time capsule, a snapshot of a life that had been abandoned without ceremony. It was as if the people living here had simply vanished.

Only, looking at Ursa's tense shoulders and strained breathing, I realized they hadn't vanished. At least, not completely.

"You came here when you were a child?" I asked him gently. I didn't want to push him beyond what he could share with me, but I knew he was trying to tell me something by bringing me here. He wanted me to understand, and I thought, at last, I was finally beginning to. "With your parents?"

Ursa gave a barely perceptible nod. His eyes were darting from place to place in the small confines of the ship, as though he were trying to take it all in at once, but somehow not managing to *see* anything in the process. Abruptly, he charged through the hatch and back to the clearing outside, all but running to escape his past.

I followed him, finding him leaning with his forearm and forehead against a tree, his breath so ragged that his shoulders shook from it. Without allowing myself to second-guess the impulse, I stepped up behind him and leaned my head into his back, lending him what comfort, what strength, I had.

When at last his breathing began to regulate again, I asked my next question, as delicately as possible. "What happened to them? Your parents?"

Ursa gave a sharp jerk of his chin—angling away from me, I thought at first, though it was more like he was almost recoiling from the memory. "Left."

"They left you here?" The thought appalled me for a moment, but not for long. Looking around this place, seeing the love in the photographs, the drawings, the little teddy bear at the center of the bed, I just couldn't believe Ursa's parents had left him behind. At least, not intentionally.

I knew now, more than ever, the danger of these woods. I'd been so lucky to have Ursa by my side, protecting me, teaching me how to survive. Most likely, Ursa's parents had not been quite so fortunate. Perhaps they'd encountered some poisonous plants, or a wild animal, or a cliffside that was not as stable as it appeared. In all of Ursa's wanderings, it was strange that he'd never come across them. But the wilderness was vast, and the Earth was very good at concealing what it wanted to keep hidden.

I wondered if it would give him hope, to tell him I didn't believe his parents had left him behind intentionally. But I sensed that conversation would need to be carefully broached, and it might take some time to convince Ursa of its truth. Besides, I could see in the set of his shoulders and jaw that he was determined to finish his story, now that he'd begun it.

"How old were you?" I asked him.

Ursa shrugged. Age probably seemed like a meaningless thing to him, after living alone so long in the wild. If the toys and the size of the boy in the fading pictures was anything to go by, I would guess he had been about six or seven. What a terribly young age, to believe you had been abandoned by your parents, to find yourself alone in the wilderness. It was truly a miracle he had survived all this time, all on his own.

Only he hadn't been completely on his own. I remembered what he'd tried to tell me those weeks ago, when we'd encountered the Kodiak bear in the woods. Ursa and I hadn't been able to understand each other then, but his ability to communicate had only grown during that time. Maybe now was the time to finally comprehend his meaning.

"When did you begin living with the bears?" I asked.

I won't attempt to re-create word for word the conversation that followed. Ursa's speaking abilities *had* improved, but there was still some need for me to interrupt him with questions and fill in the blanks when I couldn't totally decipher his meaning. I'm still not completely sure I understand the full extent of his tale, but I'm hoping when I see you next, my love, that you'll be able to tell me if this was a faithful account or not.

But for now, to the best of my ability, I will share Ursa's story.

39

Ursa's parents told him to wait at the ship while they went out to find something—Ursa can't remember what it was. He also can't recall what his name used to be, though when I asked him about a name I saw crudely written on some of the drawings—Ben—that seemed to draw some vague recollections. Ursa waited a long time for them to return. When they weren't back by nightfall, he became quite frightened; they had never left him alone for so long. When the morning came and they still hadn't returned, Ursa continued to hold out hope. He scrounged whatever food he could find and waited, and waited. But when another day passed, then another, Ursa realized he couldn't wait any longer. He needed to find food.

For several days, Ursa managed to survive by scrabbling together whatever meager items he could find. He was very hungry, but he was eating enough to survive, and he was close enough to the stream that he had water to drink.

It was at the stream that Ursa first encountered the bear who would become his "mother." She was with two of her cubs—the boy who would grow into the Kodiak I'd met in the forest earlier, and a girl cub from the same litter. Ursa was frightened—he thought maybe his parents had warned him about bears, before they vanished—but this bear must not have seen him as a threat. Perhaps it had been so long since human beings had inhabited the Earth, any fear of humans had been bred out of them; or perhaps Ursa's smallness, his obvious helplessness, appealed to some maternal instinct in the mother bear. In their first few encounters, she let Ursa take the scraps of food they found, and eventually she let him follow her back to the den.

Under the protection of his bear family, Ursa thrived. They taught him how to forage, how to climb, how to hunt. He began to forget many of his human ways. He grew alongside the two cubs, and they would play and wrestle and sometimes bicker with each other as siblings often do. The mother bear was not quite as affectionate with Ursa as she was with her two cubs, but she would let him curl up with her when he got cold and made sure he was always fed and safe. Though Ursa still mourned the loss of his first family, he believed he'd found a new one he could be happy with always.

But when Ursa and his bear brother began to transition into adulthood, their mother grew colder toward them. She still coddled her daughter, but Ursa and his brother became more and more ostracized over time. Finally, their mother would no longer allow them in the den. They lingered, trying to follow their mother and sister as they went through their usual routine of rummaging and foraging, but their mother charged at them with her teeth bared and swiped at them with her claws.[1] So Ursa and his brother ran off.

At first they stayed together, but eventually it became clear to Ursa that his brother was wandering down paths he could not follow. His brother wanted to find his own mate, have his own cubs, create his own family. There would be no place for Ursa there.

Since then, Ursa had been on his own. He'd encountered the human camps and researchers by then, but having been abandoned by two separate families, he'd grown wary of trying to approach anyone new.

Until, for whatever reason, he saw me.

Despite our gaps and occasional stumbles in communication, as we sat in the small clearing, Ursa told his story to me calmly and without much emotion. It was the lack of emotion that told me how much pain it had caused him, to be left behind. I understood now why he had become so violently reactive once he thought I, too, had abandoned him.

I let Ursa tell his story, interjecting myself as little as possible. I wanted him to feel heard, understood, and not as though I were trying to claim any of his pain as my own.

---

1. I've since done some research and discovered it is common for Kodiak mother bears to ostracize their male offspring once the mothers are ready to mate again. I don't know if this knowledge would bring comfort to Ursa or not, but perhaps it could at least provide some understanding.

But by the time he was finished, I could not hold myself back any longer. I looked at him, and I saw the boy he'd been, so frightened and so alone, believing no one would want him. I could hear in his matter-of-fact tone and see in his haunted expression that he was retreating into himself, putting up guards against me, now that he realized how badly my leaving could hurt him.

I couldn't bear it, not any of it. I couldn't stand his pain, and I couldn't stand him shutting me out. "Ursa . . ." Words failed me, though. I didn't know what I could possibly say to make things right, to prove to him I would never leave him.

Instead, I half lunged at him, clumsily climbing into his lap and throwing my arms around his neck. I felt his resistance to me, his tight shoulders and stiff spine, but I didn't care. I held on to him for dear life, my face burrowed into the side of his neck, our two hearts pressed together.

We stayed this way in complete silence for a long few minutes. He didn't push me away, but he didn't respond, either, not for what felt like a terrifying amount of time. And then slowly, slowly, I felt him soften. His arms came up tentatively. He gripped the small of my back, touched the end of my braid, sniffed the top of my head.

"I won't leave you," I murmured into his neck.

As he stiffened again, I held on tighter. "No, listen to me, Ursa." I pulled back just enough to meet his dusky blue gaze. I needed him to see my eyes, my face, to read the truth of what I was saying in my expression, not only in my words. "I won't ever leave you. And if you try to leave me, I won't let you. I'll follow you wherever you go. I'll track you through the woods, and I'll call your name, and I'll . . . sing terrible songs until you come back to me, just to make me stop."

Ursa's lips tugged upward, ever so slightly. I laughed, more out of relief than humor. Too late I realized that what I'd said had sounded more like the confession of a stalker than what I'd intended it to be. "What I mean to say is . . . obviously, if you get tired of me, you can throw me off. I'll try to respect that, though I can't promise to be very dignified about it. But as for me, and *my* heart"—I touched my chest for emphasis—"I don't ever want to be apart. We'll still do things on our own, naturally, like answer the call of nature, and whatnot . . ."

Oh, bother, why was it so difficult to speak from the heart? I was sounding like an idiot!

"But I want us to always come back together again, no matter what." I wetted my lips, bracing myself. *Courage, Mina.* "I guess what I'm trying to say is, I . . . I love you, Ursa."

His face was still inscrutable, but he tilted his head at the obviously unfamiliar word. "Love?"

My heart felt like it was trying to burrow its way out of my chest. I swallowed. "It means . . . I admire you. I care about you. I want what is best for you. And I want to be with you, always."

I watched the gears in Ursa's mind turn as he processed my words, turning them over in his precise, methodical way. Slowly, slowly, his mask fell. His face softened. He looked at me like my Ursa again, vulnerable and open and frightened and so very, very brave. "Love," he agreed, his voice thick with unspoken emotion.

I leaned forward impulsively, pressing my mouth to his. Ursa's surprise was evident. His lips were soft, but his mouth was stiff. He'd never been kissed before, I would imagine. I had only a little more experience, but thankfully not all of it had been with Rawley. Intercourse might be taboo on Haven 3, but kissing did not make un-genetically modified babies. In my youth, I'd been eager to practice with a handful of willing partners who were not too proud to try out their methods on a plain non-mod nobody.

I was by no means an expert, but I knew how to coax an inexperienced partner out of his shell. Caressing the sides of Ursa's face with my thumbs, I pulled back, then softly brushed my lips against his, once again, showing him what I wanted.

Ursa shifted, gripping me and pressing me more tightly against him. When he softened his mouth to move against mine, mimicking me, I rewarded him with a soft swipe of my tongue. Ursa growled, fisting my hair in his hand and pulling me back to him when I tried to playfully retreat. I pressed my tongue to his, and he met me eagerly, clumsy at first but quickly learning the rhythm.

By the time we pulled apart, my head was spinning. I had to lean my forehead against his to catch my breath. Panting, Ursa pressed his forehead into mine, his breath also coming fast. I felt the hard plane of his erection pressing into me, and instinct urged me to rub against him, to find some ease for the ache building in my own core.

But we could ease into all of that, my more sensible self reminded me. We had time. All the time in the world.

At the thought, I smiled at him. He smiled back, his face crinkling and softening as he looked at me. My own grin broadened; I couldn't help it—seeing him happy made me so incandescently happy, it felt like my heart would burst.

"Come on," I urged him, tugging him to his feet as I awkwardly detangled myself from him. "Let's go home."

Home. Our home. Where we would be together always.

I truly sincerely believed it at the time.

40

Though the journey to the ship seemed to have taken ages, I felt as though we were floating the entire way back home. Ursa carried himself as if a great weight had been lifted from his shoulders. We held hands as we walked. He intertwined our fingers and swung our palms back and forth in a wide arc. We grinned at each other like idiots—blissfully happy, giddy idiots. He would stop at every turn of the path to kiss me. Sometimes quick and fast and sweet, sometimes so intensely it took my breath away.

Along the way we foraged and nibbled at what we found. Then Ursa's appetite seemed to catch up with him all at once, after days of sleeping and recovering from his wounds. Luckily I'd brought my pack along, and I let him take the lion's share of provisions. I was worried that his strength would give out on him, and I kept reminding him he needed to take it easy so his body could recover. More than once, I urged him to sit and drink water from my flask, all so he wouldn't overexert himself.

Ursa seemed remarkably good-natured about my mothering, and I soon realized why. Every time we stopped to sit, he would pull me into his lap and kiss me. He was a very fast learner, I'll give him that. I tried to be stern and cross and scold him about not resting properly, but soon I would be breathless and panting and liquid with want again.

Thus, the journey back to the cave went rather slowly, though much more pleasantly this time around. By the time we made it back, dusk had begun to settle. There was still light in the sky, but it wouldn't be long before it was dark.

"Swim," Ursa urged me, tugging me toward the rocky overhang that we needed to climb to reach the pool.

I resisted, trying to keep my head. "You need to eat more. Then rest. You should preserve your strength."

Ursa just grinned at me. "Swim. Then rest."

It was probably as good a compromise as I was going to get from him. And I imagined he probably did need to rinse off, after so many days spent sleeping and healing. Plus, the pool water would help him heal more quickly, and I had some more protein bars we could eat once we got back to the cave. With how quickly it would be getting dark, eating rations would be safer than foraging for more food anyway.

"Fine," I relented with a sigh, letting him pull me toward the overhang.

I could tell that Ursa was still recovering by the slow, careful way he tested his body as he climbed, absent of his usual agile confidence. But as soon as he was near the pool, he rejuvenated, making short work of his trousers and carelessly tossing them aside before diving into the water. He surfaced a moment later, looking happy and carefree as he shook the excess water from his hair and beard. By now I was no longer surprised by the remarkably quick and potent healing properties of the water, but it was still a marvel to see how much Ursa had healed in the short time since his attack. I had almost lost him, and the realization felt like a weight pressing down on my chest. I could no longer imagine a world without Ursa. He had become my whole world.

… Or maybe that was too dramatic, but it wasn't far from the truth. There would always be other meaningful things in my life, but Ursa touched all the important parts of it. He had taken me from Dorothy's black-and-white world into a technicolor Oz.[1] He had brought color and warmth, danger and vitality into my life.

I loved him, and he loved me. We would be together always. I had lost my family but found one again, just like he had.

The realization winded me, so much so that I stood and just stared at Ursa. He looked back at me quizzically, head tilted to the side.

"Sorry," I blurted, "I was just remembering a dream I had."

I wasn't sure why I'd lied, as there was really no reason to do so, and this flustered me even more. Without really thinking about it, I kicked off my trousers, then removed my undergarments. Right as I reached to pull the hem of my shirt over my head, I paused.

I knew what it would mean to be naked with Ursa in this pool, tonight.

Acutely aware of Ursa watching me, I pulled my shirt off and tossed it aside, so I was standing on the bank as naked as the day I was born. I felt his eyes on me, touching me everywhere in the dark.

It was thrilling. It was freeing! And then all at once I became flustered, so I hurriedly dove into the water.

·

---

1. This is, of course, a reference to the early twentieth-century film, *The Wizard of Oz*, still taught in most university courses, I believe. It is doubtful, though, that the Brethren have been formally educated, so they might need some further description. Perhaps it's best to strike Oz as an example?

When I reemerged and gathered enough bravery to face Ursa, he was smiling one of his enigmatic, knowing smiles that always simultaneously infuriated me and made my heart race in one fell swoop. Wanting to wipe that expression from his face, I splashed him with as much force as I could muster. "Stop looking so smug. I've seen you naked loads more times than you've seen me."

The splash was a mistake, I quickly realized, as Ursa's eyes gleamed with mischief—challenge accepted. He treaded water, slowly narrowing the distance between us.

"Whatever you have planned, think twice," I warned him, swimming backward—not wanting to turn my back to him, but also wanting to maintain some distance. "I won't hesitate to—*ahhhhh!*"

The "ahhhhh" was not what I'd planned to say, obviously, but rather the result of being grabbed about the waist by Ursa's strong arms. Any giddiness or terror (or combination of the two) that I might've felt about being in such close proximity to his naked body was quickly dispelled as he tossed me across the pool.

I gave a rather unladylike screech, I'm afraid, as I plunged back into the water. Sputtering, I rose, snorting water out of my nose and pushing damp hair from my face as I glared at him across the pool. Ursa grinned back at me. I began swimming back toward him.

"Big mistake," I warned him, before tackling him in retaliation.

For the next twenty minutes or so we proceeded to wrestle, pounce, pummel, and just all-around attack each other. It was done playfully, for the most part, though I did take some real pleasure in dunking Ursa's head under the water, and he seemed to do the same in launching me into the air and hearing my shrieks of outrage.

By the time we called a truce, we were both winded, circling each other slowly in the water. When Ursa reached for me, I instinctively drew back, thinking he meant to tickle me or throw me again; but this time he only pulled me closer, his hands settling on my bare back and hip and sending my heart galloping. Our bodies were almost touching in the water, but not quite, not yet. He gazed at me, smiling, though his eyes were solemn, and I gripped his shoulders and parted my lips just half a second before his mouth captured mine.

The tentativeness of earlier that day was gone completely now as he moved his lips against mine, exploring my mouth with his tongue. In almost no time I was mindless, powerless to the sensation, to the way it liquefied and energized my body all at once. With a jolt of surprise, I realized we were now fully entangled, my naked body pressed against his, his thigh inserting itself between mine. When it pressed against my softness, I moaned, clutching his shoulders, his hair, resisting and then losing the willpower to resist, rutting myself against his leg, chasing that liquid fire burning deep in my abdomen.

Suddenly, I became aware of myself, what I was doing. With a gasp, I pulled away from him, swimming to the shore.

I know the Brethren will likely berate me for being needlessly prudish, but please keep in mind that I was battling against a lifetime of being told that this sort of reckless, wild want was low, vulgar, gauche behavior signaling a lack of moral character. As much as I wanted Ursa—and I desperately, urgently wanted him—it was difficult to quiet those voices from my past.

I regretted pulling away almost the moment I did it, but it wasn't as if I could just turn back, could I? My brain was at war with my body, telling me my behavior was foolish and irresponsible, while my body craved and needed more.

When I reached the bank, I was shaking too hard to pull myself up. Finally I managed, lying down on the cool, sleek rocks closest to the water's edge. I waited for Ursa to appear, to say something, but all was silent. I didn't know what to do. I didn't know how to explain what

I was afraid of, why I'd fled. I wasn't sure whether I wanted him to follow me.

"Ursa?" I called finally, my voice soft, almost a whisper in the still evening air.

He didn't say anything, but a moment later I heard him pull himself out of the water. Another long moment passed, and I thought he must have gone into the cave, or maybe out into the woods.

Then all at once, he was standing over me, a looming silhouette that blocked out the setting sun, making him the only thing I could see. My body, which had just begun to calm from its earlier fever, instantly sprang into awareness again. My breathing was shallow and panting, my core feeling tender and needful at even just the sight of him.

We stared at each other for a long, quiet moment, my gaze drowning in his dusky blue one. "Ursa," I whispered. An invitation.

He lowered himself slowly, holding eye contact as he moved over me, our bodies not quite touching, or at least not fully. Every panting breath brought us closer together, my nipples kissing his chest, alert and ready. I couldn't believe how *ready* my whole body felt.

My breathing sounded loud and obnoxiously raspy to my ears, but Ursa seemed strangely relaxed. Unhurried. Purposeful. Still braced above me, he put his nose to my hairline and inhaled, letting out a grunt of contentment before moving to one temple, then the other. Then the patch behind my ear, my throat. My shoulder, my collarbone. The valley between my breasts.

As he started to move away, I whined in protest, and Ursa laughed softly to himself, moving back up to nudge one breast against his nose, then the other. At my answering moan, he grinned, staying near but not touching me, his breath ghosting over my peaked nipple. "Please, Ursa," I begged him, not fully knowing what I was asking for but certain I would take whatever he would give me, so long as it ended this frantic, painful anticipation.

Ursa took one breast into his mouth, swirling his tongue around my nipple and making me buck up off the rocks, whimpering his name. Sooner than I would have liked, he left off his ministrations on the first breast, but I was mollified by him moving immediately to the next. The sensations were so extremely pleasant that I felt as if my body were losing its autonomy. In that moment, I had ceased being my own individual self and existed only as a conduit for the pleasure he could give me.

Continuing his journey downward, Ursa sniffed a path over my skin. As he neared my center, I was already so sensitive and *aware* that it felt like any additional sensation in that region might send me spiraling into oblivion. I both craved and feared the feeling building inside of me; I wanted to open up wide to him but also clamp my knees together in terror.

Ursa resolved this quandary for me by reaching down to firmly prize my legs open. There was no arguing with that kind of certainty. He was determined to reach that spot, and nothing would deter him this time—not a drone or a mountain lion or anything else.

I'd been the one making senseless, whimpering noises all this time, but as Ursa's nose finally found my mound and he inhaled deeply, he let out a groan of pleasure. He explored me first with his nostrils, his eyes dark with arousal as he looked up at me from between my legs, over the valley of my naked body. The sight of him only increased the pressure I felt building down there, already heightened to extreme sensitivity, almost to the point of pain, brought on by the brush of his nose, his warm breath, over my softest parts.

For a long moment, we simply looked at one another. Ursa was giving me one of his hard looks, only this time I didn't have it in me to stop what was in motion. My body craved his too entirely. My legs fell open wider, a surrender. Then, still holding my gaze captive, Ursa let his pink tongue dart out between his lips.

That was the only warning I received before his mouth was on me, exploring where his nose had just been. The resulting feeling was so intense that I gasped, then screamed, loudly enough that the birds in the canopy overhead took flight. Bucking up off the rock, I gripped him by the hair—whether to push him away or hold him in place, I couldn't have said. It felt good, so good, but the sensation was so overwhelming in its power that I instinctively felt I ought to put a stop to it.

Ursa continued his ministrations, undeterred by my vicelike grip on his skull. Just when the sensation became almost unbearably euphoric, I felt something snap inside of me, like I'd reached the crest of a giant wave and finally came plummeting back down. Elation flowed through me, a warm tingling that started low and spread to my entire body.

As my cries muted and my body collapsed with languid pleasure, Ursa looked up at me again. The look on his face could only have been described as him feeling *deeply* pleased with himself. I couldn't help but huff out a laugh at the sight of him. "Yes, yes, you did very well, Ursa. Very, *very* well . . ."

The memory of the sensations washed over me again, giving an aftershock to my pleasure. Ursa must have seen something of this on my face, because all at once his eyes intensified, the smile fading from his lips as a look of almost feral want overcame him. His body was still bent over mine, obscuring most everything of his from my view except for his head and shoulders, but he was shifting and moving oddly.

It took me a moment to realize what he was doing. "Oh," I said, feeling a flush start to climb up my neck. He was *touching* himself, seeking out that same pleasure he'd given me just moments before. And he was looking at *me* to spur on his desire as he did so.

I'd thought that, surely, as a woman of science who had always been taught to value my intellect and my education over any beauty or physicality, I would be immune to this kind of vanity. But I found, almost immediately, that I was *not*. I flushed in pleasure. I liked that he was looking at me. I liked how much he desired me—and for the first time, I could admit to myself that I had always liked it, even back from the very start. His want, his need, had awakened my own.

"I want to see you," I told him, shy but firm. "Ursa, please—I want to see you."

Ursa was not shy in the slightest. He straightened up right away, on his knees now, hand still pumping away at his fully erect cock as his eyes roamed shamelessly over my naked body. I watched the movement of his hand, fascinated and also interested in a logistical way to see just *how* he was seeking his pleasure. I watched as the muscles of his forearm and stomach rippled with each motion, let myself fully appreciate for the first time how glorious he was—his height and his strength and those eyes and that cock, but also the scars and calluses that told the story of all that Ursa was, everything he had survived so we could find each other across this vast, empty universe.

His desire for me once again awakened my own. I'd thought my body had spent its pleasure, but I found the sensations building inside of me. "Ursa," I murmured, shifting my legs restlessly. Some instinct had me spreading them apart, baring myself to him again, as I reached down and tried to imitate with my fingers what he had been doing with his tongue just moments before.

Ursa's eyes darkened. His pumping became more urgent, his expression wild as he chased the same sensation I was seeking. "Mina," he ground out. The way he said it almost sounded like a warning.

Then he was exploding out over his hand, his body jerking as his eyes pressed shut in pleasure. I watched him in fascination, forgetting my own urgency. It passed with little more than a shudder this time, fleeting then gone, but I didn't really mind, now that I'd seen Ursa peak. I'd need to practice to know myself, and I was surprised to find the thought filled me with anticipation, not dread.

When Ursa came back to himself, he washed quickly at the edge of the pool before returning to me. We curled together, our bodies fitting neatly, and the intimacy of this kind of touch was just as potent as the urgency of the other kind. Facing one another, we gazed into each other's eyes, Ursa reaching out every so often to touch my hair while I did the same with his lips. I smiled at him. He grinned at me.

"Ursa smile, Mina happy," I told him.

His grin widened. "Mina here, Ursa home."

41

Most of the evening had been lost to our *activities*, but I found it very difficult to care. What I had experienced, what we had experienced together . . . It felt much more important than the fact that we would be eating the last of my protein bars for supper. Also, I reasoned with myself, Ursa was still convalescing, so having a quiet night of leisurely activity was probably wise. And that other part of what we'd done . . . well, it seemed to be very good for his morale. Perhaps there were medical benefits, too, that would aid in his quick recovery.

And . . . if it wasn't already obvious from my inner monologue, I was beginning to spiral after our encounter down by the pool. I'd enjoyed myself enormously. *Enormously.* My entire body flushed just to think of the new sensations I'd experienced, the previously unknown intensity of which my body was capable . . .

But I had gotten carried away with myself. I ought to be the voice of reason, between the two of us. Ursa was remarkably gentlemanly, considering that he hadn't had the same upbringing as I had on Haven 3 and didn't understand why copulating with wild abandon was so base.

His urges were natural, but my own were more difficult to account for. In truth, that was the most troubling part to me—not that Ursa had wanted to do those things, but that I had. Desperately. And that, despite my better reason telling me it ought never to happen again, I was already thinking about when it might.

Rasputin.[1]

I felt fairly confident that Ursa was already considering how to persuade me to go for another round. After our first encounter, I had quickly put my clothes back on, but Ursa was still moving about naked. Granted, Ursa would always move about naked if it were up to him, but it was the *way* he was moving about naked—sort of arrogantly, as if he were very pleased with himself. And every time he caught me looking at him, he'd give me this slow, cocky smile with his eyes heavy lidded, as if he now knew he simply had to wait me out.

And yes, Ursa may have caught me looking at him, once or twice. It was hard not to be distracted by so much nudity. Especially when his form was so . . . so masculine. And exceptionally made. He was so agile, so athletic, so graceful. I liked watching the way his muscles rippled underneath his skin as he moved. I had even grown partial to

---

1. I ought to explain this, I suppose. When I was younger, Mother used to chide me for swearing, saying it was a vulgar mode of self-expression. However, sometimes one just wants to exclaim something out of the ordinary for dramatic effect! So, eventually I compromised by replacing the profanity in my vocabulary with the names of prominent historical figures who had been basically lost to the memories of those who weren't historians (or amateur historians!) of old Earth history. Thus, Rasputin. If you're unaware of this man, reader, I would highly encourage you to do some research! What a fascinating, individual—swear-worthy, indeed.

his smattering of body hair and fond of the smorgasbord of scars and sprinkles of freckles. It was just all so Ursa.

Still, I needed to get him to put on trousers again if I was going to be able to keep my wits about me. I'd even started to look at his cock, despite having always averted my eyes in the past whenever it was out on display, so to speak. I kept thinking about the look in his eyes as he'd pumped away at himself, the way he'd been gazing at me as he did it. I marveled at how much it had changed in shape and size when he was . . . aroused. I wondered, purely hypothetically, how something that big was supposed to fit inside of me, were we to enter into a primitive form of copulation, which we most definitely were not going to do.

"Time for bed!" I announced brightly. "Brrr. It feels a bit chilly tonight, doesn't it? I'm going to change into my nightgown."

I'd hoped my exclamation would passive-aggressively suggest to him that he ought to put his trousers back on. However, at the mention of the word *nightgown*, Ursa's face fell so dramatically I couldn't help but laugh. "Ursa, honestly. It's not so bad. It keeps me warm."

A look of determination came into his eyes. He advanced toward me, gaze locking on to mine, and suddenly I was no longer laughing. "Ursa will keep Mina warm."

I blinked, then my eyes widened. "Ursa, that was a complete sentence! An independent clause! Well done." His vocabulary and understanding of sentence structure was really progressing nicely! I gripped his forearm, giving it a giddy little shake of excitement until I remembered what conversation we'd been in the middle of. Oh. *Of course* he was only taking leaps in his language skills to attempt to seduce me. Still, an independent clause!

Ursa took hold of my forearm, too, so we were sort of locked together, gazing into each other's eyes. He took a moment to consider his words. "When Ursa sleep, Mina say she sleep naked."

Again, I was so pleased with his improved language that it took me longer than usual to parse his meaning. I remembered suddenly *that* promise I'd made to Ursa while he was recovering. I felt my whole body stir at the thought of it—Ursa's big, naked, masculine body, mine soft and small, the two of us huddling together for warmth underneath the animal furs. Skin brushing against skin.

Blushing, I averted my gaze. "You know it's not a good idea. I enjoyed very much what happened earlier, but we can't just . . . *Ursa.*"

As I'd been speaking, Ursa had reached for the top button of my shirt and unfastened it. I watched on as his big fingers moved down to the second button and popped it loose. My entire body woke up with that motion, a jolt of want coursing down through my belly. My breathing sounded suddenly loud and ragged in my ears. "We mustn't," I tried feebly, reaching up to grip his hand, though I didn't pull it away.

Ursa tilted his head, studying me. His eyes were unbelievably beautiful this close, an entire evening sky, darkening into night. "What is *mustn't?*"

My mouth was too dry to speak. I swallowed, trying again. "It means we shouldn't, even if we might want to."

As was probably to be expected, Ursa ignored the sensible part of that statement and focused on the part that benefited him. "Want to." He looked infinitely pleased at this, and his fingers began moving again, opening up my shirtfront as I watched on, unable to stop him.

No, that's not right. I could have stopped him, technically, at any point. I ought to have stopped him, I knew. But the way he looked at me, the nearness of his body to mine, the feelings he awoke in me, even that cocky smile . . . it made me abandon control of myself, turn it over to him entirely. Willingly.

He'd unbuttoned my shirt so gently and precisely, but now that my shirt was all the way open, he tugged it over my arms and off my body in one abrupt, almost violent movement. I gasped, surprised at how arousing I found it—that juxtaposition between gentleness and brutal strength that was so Ursa.

I felt his hardness press up against me as he reached around my torso, fumbling with my bra. His grunts of irritation might have been comical if I hadn't been feeling that same breathless restlessness, that desperation for my bra to be off so we could be closer to each other, skin to skin. "There's a clasp in the back," I tried to tell him. But either he didn't hear me, or he'd grown too frustrated to be careful, because with a groan, he ripped the clasp apart, tossing the scraps of bra onto the ground.

In the back of my mind, I knew I was likely going to be very irritated about that once I'd come to my senses in the morning, but in the moment, I couldn't bring myself to care—especially when Ursa's warm palm made contact with my skin.

I'd always known I didn't have "fashionable breasts." Left to my genetic lottery, I'd been born without the gravity-defying, large-but-perky breasts that were such a popular choice in the pre-birth packages on Haven 3. My breasts were "plums," as I'd been teased in my younger years. They'd been a source of embarrassment and no little amount of shame for the majority of my life.

Seeing Ursa's fascination with them now, his worshipful exploration of their dimensions, made all of that trouble seem like a muted, distant memory. How could there be anything shameful in something that brought so much pleasure—both for him, in his enthusiastic inspection, and for me, in being thus examined. I was lost, powerless at his hands, a willing slave to the sensations he brought out in me as he massaged my breasts, kneaded them, and caressed and teased my nipples until I was whining out his name.

When he stopped, I whimpered again until I felt him working at the clasp on my trousers. As I only had one other pair of these, I hastily reached forward to help him so they wouldn't end up torn and on the ground, too. No sooner had I unfastened the clasp than Ursa was tugging the trousers and my knickers down, making good on his evident desire to get me naked as fast as possible. To my surprise, he stopped when these garments were midway down my legs, apparently distracted by my bottom. He massaged and kneaded the flesh there, just as he had done moments before with my breasts, his appreciation evident in the way he shamelessly rubbed his cock against my now-bare stomach.

My body responded to every touch, a desperate thrumming starting up inside of me, near my core. I found myself quite keen to get naked, too, so as he continued grinding against me, I shimmied and wriggled until my trousers and knickers were on the ground.

Ursa pulled back and let his eyes rove over me, hunger in his gaze—that was really the only word to describe it. I felt like Ursa was an apex predator, and I was his chosen prey.

He tugged me down to the animal furs, so I was lying on my back. Pressing his body on top of mine, he held up his weight on his forearms so he wasn't crushing me, though strangely, probably irrationally, I wouldn't have minded. The pressing need to be closer, to be touching him more, was building an insatiable frenzy inside of me, for his nearness, his weight, all of him. He kissed me, tongue plundering my mouth, his big, hard body rubbing up against mine, and all I could do was moan and grip his hair and arch up into him, holding him close, chasing more. My body moved in an instinctive, primitive dance, one to which I hadn't realized I knew the steps. When he pressed his thigh up against my core, I bucked against it shamelessly, seeking the frantic sparks of sensation.

"Ursa, please, please." I didn't quite know what I was begging for, only that I had to voice my desperate need.

I'd hoped he might repeat his performance from earlier in the evening, when he'd lapped at me with his tongue, so I was surprised when he suddenly pulled back. For a moment, he just stared down at me, his chest heaving, his eyes darker than I'd ever seen them. He looked so powerful looming above me, his body such a force. I might have been terrified of him, if he weren't *my* Ursa.

I reached up for him, longing for him to touch me again. "Ursa," I beckoned, opening up my body to him.

With a sudden, fierce grunt, Ursa took me by the hips and lifted me up, rolling me over so my belly was flat on the ground, then urging me up onto my knees. I followed him without thought, with no choice but to be obedient in the face of such dominant authority. I felt the press of his warm torso against my back, his body rubbing against mine as he nipped at my neck, my ears. He pushed his hard cock against my lower back, grunting as he grinded against me.

Then he pulled back abruptly. I moaned in protest at the lack of contact, but it wasn't for long. He gripped my hips again, angling my bottom upward and positioning himself behind me. I was quite naive, mind you, but even I could guess where this was heading. "Ursa," I panted, not sure if I was asking him to stop or begging him to proceed.

As something bumped against my entrance, I gasped theatrically, but it was just his fingers.[2] He began to trace a teasing path over my lips, making me quiver and moan. When he dipped his first finger

---

2. *Just* his fingers, ha.

inside of me, I cried out, and when he added a second and began pumping back and forth, I dropped forward onto my forearms, offering up my posterior more readily to him. Intense sensations coursed through me at even that exploratory act. I was powerless to stop it, to resist it. I had no choice but to let it sweep me along in its chaotic wake.

When he withdrew, I knew what would be coming next. I'd thought his fingers might have prepared me, but it was still a shock when his cock breached my entrance—the sheer size of it. Ursa didn't put it all in at once but slowly coaxed his way inside, pumping in and out. After a few moments of this, Ursa was able to slide in all the way, and the sound he made when he was seated inside of me was a primal, strangled moan.

And then, it seemed, whatever self-restraint Ursa had been practicing up to this point snapped. He ground his hips in and out of me at a frantic, almost violent pace—violent in its intensity, I mean, not because of any desire to injure me. Still, it was a jarring, chaotic experience, my body being pounded into again and again. It hurt at first, and then it felt good, *very* good, each thrust only amplifying the sensation building inside of me, but it was so harried. I desperately wanted something to hold on to; the animal skins provided little of the stability I needed.

But as I peered over my shoulder, I saw his face twisted with a bliss that looked almost painful, and seeing the pleasure *he* took from our joining only increased my own. As if feeling my gaze on him, he looked into my eyes as he continued thrusting his hips against me, our thighs slapping together. Those dusky blue eyes were darkly fervent as they held mine, this long exchange of looks almost more intense than what was happening with our bodies. Until all at once, it wasn't, and the feeling inside of me surged and spiraled. My heart pounding, blood rushed in my ears, though I was still aware of his last mangled roar as he plunged into me once, then again, then one last time.

I buried my face into the animal skins, my body shaking. When Ursa withdrew himself from me, I collapsed in a boneless heap. With a groan, he joined me, drawing my body into his and nuzzling the back of my now-sweaty neck.

"Mina," he said. I loved the way he said my name. It carried so many words inside of it, when he was the one saying it.

For once, I was the one who had nothing to say. I simply nestled closer against him, letting my body speak to him, skin communing against skin.

I feel rather torn, I confess, on whether I should share this part of the story with the Brethren. They always want more details, unless I'm talking about mushrooms. I suppose I can edit out some bits, withhold some of the more intimate parts. I know the story as written will hold their interest, though, and leave them wanting more.[3] And they must want more. They must decide to keep me alive until Haven 3. It's our only chance.

But if they don't, my love, I hope these words find their way to you. I hope it will bring you some comfort, reading about that night through my memories of it. It was such an awakening for me. Not only because of the sexy bits, though those were very nice. You woke up every part of me that had long been asleep. Through knowing you,

---

3. Dirty old perverts, the lot of them.

I realized that I'd been living only half a life before. You changed me, my darling. You altered my stars.

And now I must travel across them to find you again. I will. I'll do everything I can. Please be alive. Please be all right. Please hold on, my love.

42

T he next morning, Ursa scowled mutinously at me.

I couldn't help but laugh at his expression. He was so transparent sometimes, it really was hilarious. "Did you honestly think I was going to start traipsing around naked now? No, thank you. I happen to like clothing. Aside from the aesthetic appeal, it protects your skin from sunburns and bug bites and . . . Oh, there are my trousers!"

Ursa was *not* happy about me rising promptly and immediately starting to get dressed. I could tell he'd had fantasies of recreating what had taken place the night before, perhaps many times. Truth be told, I'd had very similar fantasies, and that frightened me. I'd enjoyed myself, *immensely*, in the moment, but afterward . . . afterward it was more difficult to silence the shame that had been ingrained into my psyche from the time I was born. That what we had just done was uncivilized, base, vulgar. It was worse that I'd enjoyed myself, because that must mean I was morally deficient in some way.

I wasn't entirely sure I agreed with these ideas anymore, but that didn't mean I could immediately dismiss them. And until I could find some way to rectify what my mind was reprimanding me for and what my body so urgently wanted, I thought it best to take things slow. Besides, we couldn't just roll around like wild, naked monkeys all the time, could we?[1]

Ursa evidently disagreed. As soon as I woke, he began kissing and stroking my body, clearly intent on a repeat performance. It had taken Herculean effort for me to keep a cool enough head that I could dislodge myself. And that brought us here, to me scampering like a half-naked elf around the cave, trying to get dressed as quickly as possible.

Ursa was clearly not happy with this development, either. So far I'd only managed to put on a pair of underwear and my socks. And as mentioned, I'd just located my trousers, but I could see he'd developed an overnight loathing for any item of clothing on my body. I felt him watching me now, his eyes roaming the parts of my body that were still out on display. A confusing flush of pleasure coursed through me at the knowledge that he was watching me, wanting me. I wanted to diffuse the sexual tension between us, at least momentarily, so I could have some time to sort out my thoughts. And yet, it would be an absolute lie to say I wasn't thrilled to know he was desperate for me.

Pretending I hadn't noticed his watchfulness, I'm afraid I began to put on a bit of a show. I wasn't trying to be a tease, truly! It was only, I'd never experienced this sort of sexual power before. My whole life, I'd felt so invisible, and now here was this person who not only saw me, but also thought I was utterly irresistible, for reasons unknown. How

---

1. I confess, I know nothing about monkey species and whether or not they roll around during copulation.

could I not enjoy it? How could even the most level-headed person deny themselves this vanity?

Aware of his eyes on me, I made putting on my trousers—the most mundane of all chores—into a sensual experience. I shimmied my hips as I pulled the fabric up over my legs. I twisted and turned my torso far more than necessary, knowing it would make my breasts jiggle. I feigned that it was a struggle to get my trousers up over my hips. I turned, so my bottom was facing him, and wiggled it tauntingly as I pulled my trousers the rest of the way up.

Before I'd managed to button them, Ursa was on me, his still-naked body crowding my half-naked body into the rock wall as he licked and sucked and nipped at my neck and shoulders. Then he turned me to face him, plundering my mouth with his own, his hands urgently kneading my breasts.

I ought to have known I was playing with fire—liquid fire that began to pool low in my body, making any coherent thought impossible. Sensing he'd gained ground, Ursa grinned against my lips as one hand slid down my torso, toward that place that so urgently needed his attention.

"Ursa, we *mustn't*."

Ursa chuckled low against my ear. "Want to, shouldn't."

I shivered. Of course he'd remember that exact definition. I gripped his hand to stop its progress, knowing if he touched me *there*, I'd never be able to regain coherent thought. "We need to get dressed. We need to get food. Aren't you hungry?"

Again, it was the wrong choice of words. Ursa pulled back to look into my eyes, and I trembled at the wicked gleam I saw there. "Hungry," he confirmed.

"Oh," I breathed inanely as he dropped to his knees, the fight in me instantly gone the moment he unbuttoned my trousers.

We did, in due course, get dressed. Still, I felt I had ceded an important victory, and now that my hormones had cooled again, I worried about what it would mean.

But first matters first: food. We'd expended quite a lot of energy, and eating—true eating, not euphemistic eating—had become a necessity. We set off to look for berries and nuts and mushrooms and the like.

We hadn't been at it for very long when I found an especially fruitful thimbleberry bush. The fruit was red and ripe and sweet, and Ursa and I were both hungry enough that we didn't bother to make a collection to take back to the cave—we just stood there and shoved our faces full.

Once the intense hunger had abated, it became all at once hilarious, how feral our behavior was. Both of our hands were sticky and red, and I suppose, judging by the state of Ursa's face, both of our mouths were, too. "Here." I took out a wet wipe from my pack that I'd meant to use *before* we gathered and ate our food, rubbing at my mouth and hands before handing it to Ursa. When it became clear that he didn't quite know what to do with it and wouldn't be doing a thorough job, I took over for him.

"Crouch down so I can reach you." I wiped off his lips and beard, which weren't *so* bad—it just looked like he'd been snogging someone with dark pink lipstick on—then I moved to his hands. Those were far worse, making him look like the idiomatic someone who had been "caught red-handed." I scrubbed at his fingers and palms thoroughly, intent on my task, until I glanced up and saw Ursa looking at me.

That wasn't all that remarkable, I suppose. Ursa was always looking at me. It was the *way* he was looking at me, and after the events of last evening and this morning, I couldn't help but understand its meaning.

My jaw dropped. "Again?" I sputtered, looking down at the wipe in my hands. "What could possibly be arousing about this scenario?"

Ursa didn't reply, just smirked at me with that smoldering look in his eyes. I hated the way my body responded to him, instantly, without reservation, even as my mind quailed. "We can't just spend all of our time *copulating*." I whispered the word, though I knew it was ridiculous as there was no one around to hear us. "We ought to wait at least a week."

I'm not confident Ursa knew how long a week was; I'd been trying to explain the concept to him, but it was hard to tell how much information he was grasping when he was so monosyllabic. However, I could glean by the skeptical look he gave me that he knew a week was a long-ish period of time. Really, his face was *so* expressive, I suppose he didn't need words all that often.

"Three to five business days?" I suggested as a compromise, taking a step back to put some more distance between us. I had to remain clearheaded this time, or . . . well, something bad would happen, I was sure.

Ursa wouldn't let me escape that easily, though. He advanced toward me, settling his hands on my waist and drawing me closer. That intent look was back in his eyes. I felt my body blossoming in response, nipples hardening, my core readying. "Ursa," I protested, but without much venom now.

"Want Mina."

At first I was tempted to scoff. That wasn't much of a statement, was it, when he'd been living on his own all this time. I suppose he must have seen some other women at the base, and perhaps other women who'd come on expeditions before. I wondered how long he'd been observing, watching other people from a distance, learning our ways. But so far as I knew, he hadn't ever attempted to make contact before me. I'd never seen anything about Ursa in any of the research logs, and I was positive any other group of researchers would have been as keenly interested in Ursa as we had all been. Yet with me, he'd made contact. He'd tossed me that stone when I was alone in the forest. He'd breached the camp to come find me.

Ursa had been on his own for so long, I reasoned he would have latched on to anyone who'd show him any small morsel of affection. I'd always thought that didn't make me special. But he hadn't—he'd chosen me for some reason, and I'd never bothered to ask why.

Heart racing, I looked up at him now, trying to stay in charge of my faculties as he swept his thumb along my jaw, over my lips. "Why did you breach the camp that night, the first night we met? Were you coming for me?"

I held my breath, anxious to hear his answer. Ursa gazed into my eyes, holding my face in both of his big hands. "Want Mina."

My heart leapt. Still, my usual niggling doubts lingered. "But . . . why? Why not someone else—anyone else—instead of me?"

I'm nothing special, was the unspoken message I was too afraid to say out loud, for fear he might confirm it.

The way Ursa looked at me, though . . . the way he touched my face, his thumb stroking my jaw, my lower lip, his dusky blue eyes so impossibly soft . . . "Want Mina. Only Mina."

I melted into his touch, his words, my heart so full it felt like it would burst. "Ursa . . ."

We heard it at the same time—the whirring of the drone. For one brief, frantic moment, Ursa and I simply stared at one another. Then, almost as one, we scrambled to find cover.

"There!" I hissed, pointing toward a thick cluster of chokecherry trees,[2] with overgrown limbs that would obscure us from anything flying overhead.

Ursa and I huddled underneath, looking up at the sky, trying to spot the drone. When I saw it, I said nothing but gripped Ursa's forearm, looking up at his face. I could tell by the tightness of his jaw that he'd seen it, too, and he grimly watched its progress across the sky.

Once the drone passed out of sight, continuing north, I sighed in relief—it was short-lived, though, as Ursa surprised me by smoothly sliding out from underneath the chokecherry tree and taking off after the drone.

"Ursa!" I whisper-shouted his name. I'm afraid I was much less graceful as I scuttled out from the tree's overgrowth, hurrying to catch up.

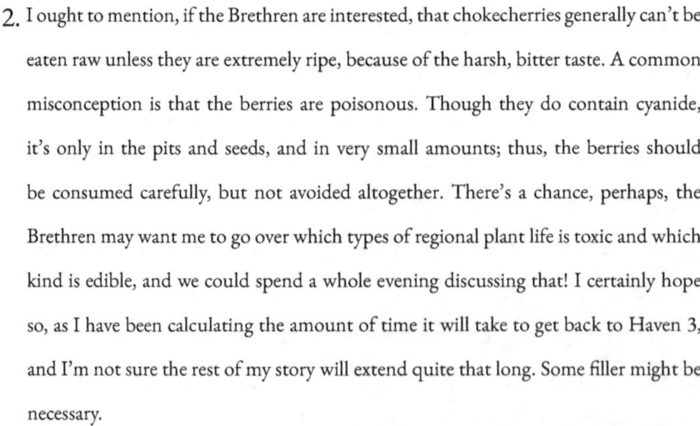

---

2. I ought to mention, if the Brethren are interested, that chokecherries generally can't be eaten raw unless they are extremely ripe, because of the harsh, bitter taste. A common misconception is that the berries are poisonous. Though they do contain cyanide, it's only in the pits and seeds, and in very small amounts; thus, the berries should be consumed carefully, but not avoided altogether. There's a chance, perhaps, the Brethren may want me to go over which types of regional plant life is toxic and which kind is edible, and we could spend a whole evening discussing that! I certainly hope so, as I have been calculating the amount of time it will take to get back to Haven 3, and I'm not sure the rest of my story will extend quite that long. Some filler might be necessary.

I wasn't sure what he intended to do. I wasn't sure what *I* intended to do, I only knew that I couldn't let him rush headfirst into danger without me. If Rawley managed to capture Ursa, I wouldn't know how to save him. I would be useless in any rescue attempt, that much was obvious. But I wouldn't be able to just let him be taken, or worse.

If Ursa was going to risk his life, then so must I. We were the same now, our fates interwoven.[3]

I caught up to Ursa as he paused at the edge of a clearing, pressing his body against the trunk of a tree as he watched the drone make a lazy arc in the sky. Without looking back at me, he seemed to know exactly when I was approaching, and he reached an arm back to shield me from going farther. Still watching the drone, he spoke over his shoulder. "Mina to cave. Ursa follow." He motioned up toward the sky, indicating it was the drone he would be following, not me.

"I'm not leaving you."

Huffing through his nose, jaw clenched tight, Ursa turned to face me. "Not safe. Not safe, for Mina."

"I won't leave you," I insisted stubbornly, refusing to cow under his commanding glare. "I won't." Seeing the shift in his eyes, I intuited what he was plotting. "And if you try to leave me behind, I'll probably just end up lost, or hurt, or in danger. Because I won't stop trying to find you."

---

3. I know I said before that I don't believe in the idea of fate and that I was only using the term to appeal to the Brethren, but the more time I've had to reflect on it, I'm not so sure I can take such a hard line. Maybe there is some scientific explanation about destiny yet to be discovered—things that are meant to happen, people we are meant to meet. I know that Ursa was this for me, and I for him. So perhaps there's something to that idea after all.

The drone had finished its arc and was on the move again. Ursa sighed in frustration before turning to race after it—though he slowed his pace, I noticed, enough that I could keep up with him. I did so gratefully, not wanting to let him out of my sight. I had a terrible foreboding that we were rushing toward danger. I couldn't bear to see him do so without me.

43

We'd wandered farther than usual to find unscavenged plants for breakfast that morning, but even so, it didn't take me long to realize where the drone was leading us. It was heading back toward the cave—*our* cave.

With a sinking heart, I'd realized my fears had come true. Rawley, or one of his underlings, must have spotted my clothing near the pool in the drone recording and come to investigate. I'd hoped the garments wouldn't be discernible from the sky, that there would be too much footage on the drone to notice such a miniscule detail . . . but there was no denying it anymore. Our home had been discovered. We wouldn't be able to stay there any longer.

Ursa seemed to have come to the same conclusion. His entire body was tense, agitated, the closer and closer we drew to the cave. I clutched his forearm, dragging him to a stop. "Ursa. Ursa. Look at me."

He avoided my gaze for a few moments. I touched his face gently. "Ursa."

What I saw in his expression broke my heart. He looked so terrified, so unmoored. To me, the cave now held precious memories; it was the home I'd known with Ursa, the safe haven after living for so long in terror. For him, though, it was the only home he'd known after being "abandoned" by his parents and cast out of his bear family unit. And now it was gone.

"I'm so sorry, Ursa," I told him. And I meant it. For so many things. For the loss of his den. For the role I'd unwittingly played in bringing Rawley's men there. For dragging him into the danger from which I'd been trying to escape. Rawley might've been interested in dissecting Ursa and turning him into a lab rat, but his vendetta against me was personal. I was the reason he would never give up, the reason he'd overturn every stone until he found us again.

"I'm sorry." I leaned my forehead against Ursa's, wanting to comfort him more but knowing we couldn't afford to stay there long. "We must go now. If they've found the cave, they'll know we're nearby. We have to go somewhere else, anywhere else."

Leaving the cave would also mean leaving behind the pool, I realized with a sharp twist of disappointment—mourning not only the memories we'd made there, but also the mysteries yet uncovered about the water's healing properties. I was beginning to develop some theories, but most of my samples were back at the den . . .

Although, I did still have a few samples stashed in my pack. I'd never properly unpacked them, with all the distractions of Ursa being attacked by a mountain lion, and my nursing him back to health, and then our copulating multiple times. And whatnot.

Taking some small consolation in the fact that I had a few remaining samples, and that Rawley would likely dismiss any work that he found of mine as boring drivel, I redirected my energy into convincing Ursa to leave. "Where can we go? Where will we be safe?"

The abandoned city we sometimes foraged in was too conspicuous, too easy to find with a drone, especially now that Rawley knew we were close by. "The ship," I realized aloud. "Your parents' ship. We can hide there for a day or two." It would only be a temporary solution, since the ship was still too close to our known whereabouts for my liking, but it would at least give us time to regroup.

Ursa's eyes were unfocused, lost somewhere I couldn't follow. I twined my fingers through his, squeezing hard. At last, he blinked, meeting my gaze, then nodding. "Ship," he agreed.

I waited for him to lead the way, but he remained still. A sinking suspicion overcame me. "Ursa, you can't."

"Go to ship," he told me, then motioned to himself. "Follow. Soon."

"Come with me now," I protested, not willing to relinquish my hold on his hand. "Whatever you're planning on doing, it isn't worth it."

Seeming to realize he wouldn't successfully persuade me to leave without him, Ursa sighed, then swiftly changed course. "Stay. Hide." He guided me to an overgrowth of Rocky Mountain junipers and arranged the branches to cover me.[1] Stepping back, he examined his handiwork with a frown, rearranging some more branches before he finally nodded to himself. "Stay. Wait for Ursa."

To this day, I don't know what he was hoping to accomplish. I don't know if he thought he could somehow convince Rawley and the others to leave the cave for good, or if his pride needed a chance to defend his home from invaders. All I knew, watching him with my heart in my throat, was that he was leaving me, and I might never see him again.

"Ursa," I hissed frantically. "Don't."

---

1. *Juniperus scopulorum*

Whether he didn't hear me or just ignored me, I don't know. I watched as he took off, running toward the den. Hands clenched tightly, I listened in tense silence, waiting to see what would happen. A few moments later, I heard the unmistakable sound of Ursa's roar, echoing through the mountainside. Then shouts, warning shots, and branches cracking as Ursa raced by, then a few moments later—too few moments, I thought with my heart in my throat—a group of men followed in close pursuit, all of them armored and carrying weapons.

They only want to tranquilize him, not kill him. They want to take him back to the base, I told myself. It wasn't much of a consolation.

I listened long after the sounds faded, trying to detect any other clues as to what was happening. Knowing Ursa, he would take them on a wild goose chase, lead them as far away from the ship as he could, then try to get them hopelessly lost. *Ursa knows these woods better than anyone,* I reminded myself uselessly. *They won't be able to catch him.*

Just when I was about to come out of hiding and make my own way to the ship, a new sound, close by, froze me in place. I watched in wide-eyed terror as a man moved past me, only a few feet away.

Rawley.

For some unknown reason, it seemed Rawley had lingered behind when the others chased Ursa through the forest. He was moving much more slowly than the other men had, his pacing deliberate as he studied his surroundings. For one heart-stopping moment, I thought he'd spotted me in the brush. But his eyes slid past me, scanning the area, and he moved steadily in the direction the others had retreated.

"He's trying to lead you somewhere. It's a distraction."

My muscles tensed in response to hearing that voice, and it took everything in me to overpower my instincts to take off running. At first I thought he was talking to me, then I thought it might be to himself; but, squinting through the foliage, I could see that he was speaking into a comm device at his wrist.

"I'll hang back," Rawley continued. "See if he loops back around. I can catch him unawares."

And he would, too, I realized with a sinking heart. Ursa would be distracted, trying to locate me. If Rawley camouflaged himself somewhere nearby, he would be able to overpower him, especially if Rawley had a weapon with him, which seemed more than likely. That was how they'd managed to capture Ursa the first time—because I'd been distracting him. I was Ursa's weakness, and they would keep using me against him.

Unless . . .

Making sure Rawley's back was toward me, I waited until he'd ventured a few more yards away before I slid out from the juniper bushes as soundlessly as possible. Rawley was almost out of sight, obscured by the trees and growth separating us. Still, I waited a few more seconds, watching him walk just a bit farther, before I finally found enough courage to use my voice.

"Looking for me?" I called.

Rawley tensed, then turned in a slow arc.

I waited long enough to make sure he caught a glimpse of me before I took off running.

I could only hope that Rawley's vendetta against me would be enough to convince him to follow after me. I could only hope that Ursa managed to outrun the men following him and lose them in the forest. I could only hope that once Ursa discovered I wasn't where he'd left me, he would meet me at the ship, as planned. I could only hope that I would still be able to find my way back there again.

The plan required quite a bit of going on faith alone, all things considered. But what other option did I have?

"Come and get me," I taunted over my shoulder, not pausing or slowing my pace even in the slightest. I knew these woods better than Rawley, but he was bigger and faster; I couldn't lose the advantage of a head start. "If you can . . . !"

44

At first, all I could do was run blindly. Even with a plan set firmly in my mind, my terror at being in Rawley's presence again drowned out any rational thought. This time I knew with utmost certainty that he would kill me if he managed to get hold of me. It wouldn't be a quick death, either—no falling down the stairs or poison in my tea. I remembered the rage in his eyes when he'd kicked me again and again, before Ursa stopped him and saved me from being beaten to death.

There would be no one to save me now. I hadn't done much right, but at least I had managed to guide Rawley away from Ursa. *It would probably be easier for Ursa to live on his own anyway, without me slowing him down . . .*

The thought elicited a sob from my throat—not for myself, but for Ursa. He had been so alone for so long. It would destroy him to be left on his own again. I could not abandon him, not even in trying to save him. I had to be smart, I had to think, I had to—

A loud crack, clapping like thunder, reverberated through the woods. I watched in horror as a chunk of a tree exploded into tiny shards, only about a foot or so from my head. It took my brain longer than it should have to catch up.[1] Rawley had shot at me—with an actual rifle, not a tranq gun. He'd almost hit me.

A second shot went wider, taking a wedge out of another tree a few feet away, but far too close for my liking. I needed to start playing to my own advantages instead of his, just like Ursa had taught me in all our sessions chasing and evading each other in the woods. In my fear, I'd run as far and as fast as I could to put distance between myself and Rawley, but that was playing to his strengths instead of my own. Rawley was stronger, faster—he would catch up to me if I kept going this way. Oh, and to top it all off, apparently he had a gun.

First things first, I had to stop making myself such an easy target.

Going against all my instincts, I slowed my pace, focusing less on putting distance between us and more on making my path difficult to follow. I found a bush to duck under , diving into the places where the foliage was the thickest, generally crawling under and going around things instead of taking the most obvious path forward. I was smaller, I reminded myself, I was smarter, I knew these woods better. I had to make him play my game instead of the other way around.

Soon enough, I heard Rawley's shout of frustration behind me—feeling far too close—and I knew it was time to implement my last strategy: hide.

"Minerva!" Rawley roared, voice echoing like thunder through the trees.

I spotted a familiar bowed tree up ahead. I'd been here before. After playing so many games of hide-and-pounce with Ursa, the woods no

---

1. For all the danger I'd been in my life up to this point, I'd never yet been shot at. I do not recommend it, as an experience.

longer all looked the same to me. I saw the patterns of the trees, noticed all the distinctive markers. I knew we were about a mile now from the cave and about another two miles from the ship.

And I knew, if I remembered correctly, there was a corker of a hiding spot up ahead.

As I neared the bowed tree, I did a little fist pump of triumph. Yes! It *was* the same spot we'd practiced at once before. The bowed tree was next to a gigantic, 150-foot Douglas fir that had been hollowed out at the base,[2] though this was concealed by a huge copse of beautiful, lush western sword ferns.[3] I'd stumbled across the space quite by accident, because unless you were looking for it, there was truly no way of seeing it was there.

I hoped.

My instinct, once again, was to prioritize moving quickly, but I knew if I just bulldozed my way in, I might risk disrupting the ferns, making it obvious someone had moved through them recently. I forced myself to slow down, to carefully pick my way through, all the while my heart pounding, my body bracing itself for the crack of the gunshot as Rawley finally took me down.

I made it into the tree. The hollow was just barely large enough to support my body if I held myself at odd angles and compressed myself as much as possible. The ferns obscured me from sight but also obscured my sight, so I'm not entirely sure when Rawley approached—I can only be sure that I heard him, tone seething with barely suppressed anger.

---

2. *Pseudotsuga menziesii*

3. *Polystichum munitum*

"Come now, Minerva. Let's give up this silly chase. We can be civil, can't we? Or have you been so busy fucking that caveman that you've turned into a barbarian, too?"

Even stuffed into the hollow of a tree, a few feet away from the man who most loathed me, I rolled my eyes at his blatant attempt to goad me out of hiding. Honestly, this man must think I was a simpleton!

"We can work together, Minerva," Rawley continued. It was hard to gauge exactly where he was in relation to me. I had no idea why he'd stopped so close—maybe because he could no longer hear me moving up ahead of him, or maybe because some animal instinct told him I was nearby, even if he couldn't see me. He didn't know where I was. I was positive on that front at least. I knew if he found me, he wouldn't be able to restrain himself long enough to play mind games with me. He'd beat me to within an inch of my life, like he'd done at the warehouse, and if I was very lucky, maybe he'd kill me before he could do whatever else it was he had planned for me. "Come back. Convince Ursa to come back, too. Think of the papers, the conferences. The discovery."

Ah, that was why he was pretending to play nice. He hoped I would help him lure Ursa back to the base. Naturally, he needed to use me as bait—whether willingly or unwillingly, I doubted it mattered much.

Silently, I raised my middle finger to him. It was obscured by the tree trunk, true, and I didn't know exactly where he was in relation to me, but it still felt highly gratifying to be able to make the gesture in his general direction.

A long moment passed in which nothing was said. But I wasn't fooled. Rawley's instincts might be able to sense I was nearby, but mine were also aware of him. And I was better at this game. The prey must always be more clever than the predator to survive. And I had managed to survive him for a very long time now.[4]

When he spoke again—from a distance farther away, though still not far enough—he let any pretense of civility drop. His tone was that of an irate, petulant child denied his favorite candy. "You stupid bitch. You fucking cunt. I will find you. You know that, don't you? I won't ever stop. I'll move mountains if I have to. There isn't a world or universe big enough to keep me from finding you."

I wished I could see him. I wished I knew where he was, exactly. If I could, I would slip out without him noticing me, find something heavy, and end his life before he could end mine. I'd never felt anything like bloodlust before, but in this moment, I loathed him with every fiber of my being.

"I'm going to find you and your little lice-infested boyfriend. I'm going to drain every drop of blood out of him I can and torture him to see what his body can withstand. And I'm going to make you watch, Minerva, before I do the same thing to you."

The thought made me sick with rage. I wanted Rawley to pay. I wanted him to suffer. And I wanted his suffering to be at my hands.

I didn't doubt that I would be capable of doing it, either. I'd never knowingly harmed another living creature, but I could murder Rawley, and I would enjoy it. It was only the thought of Ursa that kept me in that tree, hiding like a coward. If I miscalculated—if Rawley were closer than I thought, or looking in my direction when I emerged. If

---

4. In case you missed it, yes, the implication is that I'm much more clever than Rawley. And Rawley, if by some terrible fate you ever get your grubby hands on this manuscript, I hope you know it's true. I am, and always have been, smarter and better than you in every measurable way.

he could shoot faster than I could jump him. If he could kill me, or worse, use me as bait to lure Ursa to a fate worse than death . . . There were too many variables, and it was too big of a risk to take, not only for my own sake, but also Ursa's, because I knew what it would do to him if I didn't succeed.

So I stayed silent, and I waited. I listened intently to every sound, however minute. I could sense that Rawley had remained in place for a few minutes before at last he trudged on—perhaps second-guessing himself, wondering if I really had gone on ahead somewhere. Even so, knowing it might be a trap, I waited, and waited, and waited until I couldn't wait anymore. Then I stealthily slid out of my hiding spot and ran, full tilt, toward the ship. Toward Ursa.

45

Naturally, as I'm not an idiot, I didn't cut a straight path. I knew there was a possibility that Rawley had hidden somewhere and was now going to follow me to where Ursa was waiting. However, I'd considered it unlikely for one main reason: Rawley was a reactive creature, a man of spite and instant gratification. If he thought there was any chance I'd gone on ahead and he could somehow overtake and overpower me, he wouldn't be able to simply sit around and bide his time.

Even so, and even though I was absolutely exhausted, I made sure to vary my trail, to loop around, to change direction abruptly and use trees and other dense foliage to obscure my movements as much as possible. By the time I spotted the abandoned ship, I was convinced that no one—with the possible exception of Ursa—could have followed me here, and that I was going to collapse into a heap as soon as I found him. The adrenaline from the day was finally beginning to wear off, and I knew I couldn't go much farther.

It wasn't until I drew near that I saw how quiet and still the ship was. There was no trace of Ursa, no sign that he was here waiting for me.

He's trying to stay hidden from Rawley's men, I reminded myself, even as fear and unease uncoiled within me. What if I had miscalculated? What if Ursa was in danger, wounded, captured, and I'd run in the opposite direction? I should have stayed with him, I should have refused to let him leave me, I should have—

I turned to see Ursa emerging from the thicket off the ship's starboard side. His face was as stricken and etched with worry as mine. For a moment, we could only stare at one another, the fear too overwhelmingly potent, and the relief at seeing each other again still catching up.

And then we were running toward each other, and Ursa held me tight as I threw myself into his arms. We were silent for a long time, just grasping each other, the terror and the giddy relief both still warring too strongly with each other.

As we remained that way, my mind whirred. We were safe and together for now, but Rawley's words echoed in my mind. He would never give up looking. And now he knew the general area in which we were living. We could relocate, but it would mean finding a new cave or other structure to inhabit, new places to forage, new predators to fend off. Traveling on foot for days on end to try to put distance between us and Rawley. Knowing we were up against all-terrain vehicles, drones, and other technology designed to locate us as quickly as possible.

We were fighting a losing battle.

I believed in Ursa more than I'd ever believed in another human being, with the possible exception of my mother, but he was still only human. Just as she'd only been human. Rawley had killed her, and he would find a way to kill us, too. Unless . . .

As the idea struck me, I knew within moments that it was the only way. I pulled back from Ursa's tight embrace, grasping his face and looking intently into his eyes. "Do you trust me?"

I didn't know if he could even comprehend that concept, trust. It was something he seemed to intuit on an instinctive level—perhaps not a concept that could be bridged with words or promises, but by actions alone. He'd known right away not to trust Rawley, and he'd seen something in me that had allowed him to put his blind faith in me. I hoped I had done everything in my power since then to show him he'd been right to do so.

My plan now would require an even bigger plunge into the unknown. But it just might very well keep us alive.

"Trust me," I told Ursa simply. "Please trust me."

We took our time, gathering everything we would need. I filled our packs to bursting, then found a few more stashed away in Ursa's family's ship and packed those, as well. By the time we were finished, it was well into the night, so we made our camp outside.[1] First thing in the morning, we dressed, distributed the packs to carry (I'll admit freely, Ursa carried more than his fair share), and headed out together.

---

1. It might have made more sense to sleep in the ship, in terms of safety and temperature, but I knew it would be too difficult for Ursa emotionally, so we made do outside.

The trip was long, and it was made in anxious silence,[2] though Ursa and I held hands for most of the way. It was nearly midday when we reached our destination, which was, to my relief, right about where I'd remembered it being. Ursa's tracking lessons had really paid off.

To my further relief, I saw that Tobago's ship was still Earthside, though we seemed to have come upon his crew as they were packing up their camp. Perhaps we'd only managed to catch them within an hour or two of leaving. The serendipity of it took my breath away. That I'd spotted this ship in the vast Colorado wilderness; that they happened to have arrived just as we needed to escape; and that they hadn't left before we could approach them . . . All of it added up to something bigger than mere circumstance. Perhaps I would need to revisit my ideas on fate.

It had led me here to Ursa, after all, hadn't it?

Ursa's grip tightened on my hand as we approached. When the first crew members spotted us, Ursa angled his body in front of mine, chest out, posture fully erect. I squeezed his hand reassuringly, knowing that despite his show of dominance, he was terribly afraid.

"Hello!" I made my voice as bright and friendly as possible, hoping to counteract the terrifying sight that I knew Ursa must make, shirtless and barefoot and so big and broad and brave. "Could I speak to Tobago, please?"

I saw two of the crew members exchange wary looks. "It's all right," I reassured them in the same overly cheerful tone. "We're old friends. He'll be happy to see me, I promise."

---

2. More on my part than Ursa's, naturally, since he isn't much of a talker in the best of circumstances. I'm usually a nervous babbler, but even I was too riddled with worry to muster my typical chatter.

Indeed, a moment later when Tobago finally emerged, the caution on his face immediately melted into surprise and then mirth at the sight of me. "Mina?"

Ignoring Ursa's grunt of protest, I stepped out from behind him so Tobago could take me in fully. He laughed again, wiping a hand over his face before pulling me in for a hug. "You really did it, huh? And you managed to survive?"[3]

Ursa grunted again, tugging me out of Tobago's embrace. Tobago seemed to register him for the first time then, eyes widening though otherwise keeping his usual poker face. "And you found a new friend," he surmised at last, raising an eyebrow at me.

"This is Ursa." I placed a calming hand on Ursa's upper arm, trying to relay to him that all was well, that we were among friends. "Ursa, meet Tobago."

Tobago offered his hand—slowly and carefully, clever boy. Ursa just stared at it, not making any move to grasp it back. But of course he wouldn't. I took Tobago's hand instead, shaking it to show Ursa what he should do. Nonetheless, Ursa still made no move to shake Tobago's hand, just continuing to glare coolly at the other man until Tobago eventually let his palm fall back to his side, raising an eyebrow again at me.

Oh, well. At least Ursa hadn't slammed Tobago's head into a wall. This greeting might be about the best we could hope for, under the circumstances.

"I'm guessing you aren't just introducing me to be polite?" Tobago asked, eying our packs.

---

3. A bit insulting, really, that he seemed so surprised, when this had been our plan all along!

"No," I agreed. No need to dillydally around it; I knew with To-bago, it was best to be straightforward. "I want to buy Ursa's passage onto your ship."

Tobago blinked once. "This isn't a passenger ship," he reminded me. "It's a smuggling vessel."

"Well, as it turns out, we've run into some trouble, and now *we* need to be smuggled off Earth. Quietly, and preferably quickly." I set my pack on the ground and gestured for Ursa to do the same. "We can pay his way, naturally."

I watched Tobago eye the contents of our packs that we'd gathered so carefully over the past day—bird eggs, fresh produce, berries, edible mushrooms, nuts, roots, herbs for tea. All things that would make the long trip back to the Havens that much more palatable.

But that wasn't all. I'd raided Ursa's parents' ship to see what they might have been attempting to smuggle out of Earth; I figured it must have been something lucrative, for them to risk their lives and the life of their young son on an unauthorized trip. Sure enough, I'd found what they must have come for: several containers of oil.[4] I watched Tobago's face as he took this in, as well as when he opened the final small container I'd collected the day before.

"Red mushrooms . . . ?" he guessed, clearly not impressed.

"*Amanita muscaria*," I informed him. "Poisonous if eaten in the wrong dosage, but otherwise it can act as a powerful psychedelic. Shamans used to use it for ancient rituals, and the Vikings used it to . . . well, to get stoned."

---

4. Though oil is no longer the primary source of energy and hasn't been for some time, I'm sure I won't need to explain to the Brethren of Blood that there remains some lucrative black-market trade surrounding the resource.

Tobago considered the box. "And I suppose you'd know the right dosage, Dr. Mushroom?"

"I might," I demurred. "All the more reason to bring us along, don't you think?"

"All the more reason to bring *you* along," Tobago corrected. "What do I get for bringing along Tarzan here?"

I'd thought something like this might happen; luckily we'd prepared beforehand. I squeezed Ursa's hand, letting him know it was time. "Ursa, can you fetch me a pine cone?"

Ursa stepped to the base of the nearest tree and within a matter of seconds had shimmied his way to the top. I had the pleasure of seeing Tobago's jaw drop as he watched Ursa's speed and agility. "As you can see, Ursa is very limber and very fast. I imagine that might come in handy on a smuggling vessel that makes illegal stops around the galaxy?"

A pine cone dropped at our feet. A few seconds later, Ursa landed there, too—mildly winded, but not nearly as much as one might expect from someone who had just scaled a fifty-foot lodgepole pine.[5] Before Tobago could stutter a reply, I moved on. "What about that log, Ursa, could you lift it for me?"

Ursa moved to a felled ponderosa pine,[6] roughly seventy feet tall and three feet wide. Bracing his bare heels into the dirt, Ursa crouched at the trunk. The muscles in his thighs and back and shoulders flexed and strained as he lifted the base of the tree higher, higher, higher, until he was holding it aloft over his head, the rest of the tree still prone on the ground.

---

5. *Pinus contorta*

6. *Pinus ponderosa*

"He's also quite strong. Clearly."

Tobago had not managed to close his jaw again. It was a relief, and highly entertaining, to see his usually composed face so utterly expressive.

"Thank you, Ursa," I said coolly, as though this entire display were nothing out of the ordinary.

Which was not true. I'd known Ursa was strong, but I hadn't realized he was *that* strong.

At the moment, however, I couldn't dwell on it. I turned to Tobago, raising *my* eyebrow at him this time. "Some might even say Ursa doesn't need to pay his way onboard. If anything, you should be paying *him* for all the ways he'll be able to help your crew."

That, at last, snapped Tobago out of his stupor. He always did have a wallet for brains. At the impending protest I saw forming on his lips, I raised my hand. "You won't have to, though, so long as you get us back to civilization safely."

We wouldn't be returning to Haven 3. It would be too easy for Rawley to find us there. But perhaps one of the other Havens would be a suitable alternative, or one of the smaller moon colonies.

There would be plenty of time to think about it during our long journey. The first step was just getting onboard. And I wouldn't be going without Ursa, no matter what that might mean.

Tobago regarded me for a long time. I knew what I was asking of him, even if it hadn't been spoken in so many words. He wasn't a stupid man; he must have gathered we were in very bad trouble, indeed, if we needed to make such a quick escape and were willing to offer so many things in exchange. On my own, Tobago had been willing to help me out of loyalty; but to take on yet another passenger for a monthslong journey would require more food, might throw off the balance of the crew, and might draw unwanted attention and trouble on Tobago's head.

I saw him doing the calculations in his mind, deciding if it would be worth it with what we had to offer.

At last, he sighed. "Get your things loaded. My quartermaster will show you to your bunk. I think we have a spare room. We leave in less than an hour."

"We're ready," I assured him, trying not to show just *how* relieved I was. If Tobago had said no, I'm not sure what we would have done.

Leaving us to go about his preparation for departure, Tobago disappeared back onboard, the brisk, no-nonsense captain once again. I waited until I was certain he was gone before turning to Ursa, giving him a small nod and my most reassuring smile. "You did well, Ursa. We'll be safe now."

And we would be. I knew this was our best option, perhaps our only option, now that Rawley was so close on our trail . . .

But as I stood with Ursa, ten minutes before we were meant to leave, overlooking the wilderness he loved so much, watching him take in his last glimpse of it like water to a man dying of thirst, I worried. I worried I was making the wrong decision, for him, for us. I worried I wouldn't be enough.

Heart in my throat, I took Ursa's hand, squeezing it to draw his attention back to me. He looked at me questioningly, and I tried my best to smile.

"You could probably evade Rawley on your own, if you want to stay. I know I'd be the one slowing you down. If you need to be here, if it's too much to leave, I won't blame you."

They were the hardest words I'd ever had to say. I braced myself for his response like it was a blow, knowing I had given him the power to destroy me, knowing that I would never, ever let him know he'd done so.

Ursa gripped the sides of my face, pressing his forehead to mine. The gentleness of the gesture made tears spill unexpectedly from my eyes.

"Where Mina is, Ursa is home."

With a strangled sob, I wrapped my arms around him. He gripped me tightly. I felt his fear in that grasp. He was giving up everything he'd ever known, stepping out into the great unknown . . . and he was doing it for me. *With* me.

After a few moments, I wiped my eyes, sniffing as I took in my last eyeful of Earth. I'd dreamed of coming here my whole life, not knowing what I would find. It had all seemed so foreign to me at first, so impossibly wild, but what happiness I'd found here. I didn't know what waited for us next, but if I had Ursa with me, I felt like I could do anything.

"Time to go," the quartermaster bellowed from the open hatch.

I started toward the ship, feeling Ursa's reluctance, his fear. He'd been brave for me for so long. I could be brave for him now, brave for both of us. "Come, my love. It's time."

I watched him take in his last glimpse of his home, this glorious wilderness that had raised and shaped him.

And then, squeezing my hand, he followed me into the ship.

46

When I finished the evening's story, the room was completely silent. There was none of the usual complaining from the Brethren that I'd left things on a cliff-hanger, or that I'd rushed over the thing they were *most* interested in hearing about and spent too long talking about mushrooms, or that I'd rambled on for too long, as usual. Only silence. I saw a few of the Brethren exchange glances with one another. Someone cleared his throat.

These reactions, so out of the norm, felt dreadfully ominous. Instinctively, I looked to Orion in the crowd. He gave me a long, hard look, his face otherwise difficult to read. But he also wasn't quickly ushering me off to my room, away from a group of space pirates who wanted to kill me for sport, so that had to be a good sign, right?

"Is he dead?" one of the men asked flatly.

I blinked in surprise. "Is who dead?"

"Ursa." I felt the crowd shifting, everyone listening carefully for my answer.

My heart began to race. I did my best to smile, keep my voice playful but firm. "You know the rule. No spoilers!"

One of the men stood abruptly, throwing his chair against the wall. I squawked in surprise as it crashed, loudly. Orion tensed but kept himself in place, watching to see how everything would play out.

The monotone man who had, apparently, named himself speaker of the group, folded his arms and glared at me. "We don't want to keep listening to this story if it turns out he's dead. We're too . . . What's it called, Orion?"

"Emotionally invested," Orion supplied.

I looked to him, wishing he would offer me some guidance. I still didn't know what to expect from these men. I could never anticipate their capricious moods. But Orion said nothing, did nothing. It was up to me, this time, to smooth things over.

I wetted my dry lips. "We were separated . . . I can't spoil the story yet, but I promise, we'll get there. I'll tell you everything, just like we agreed." At their restless murmurs, I quickly added, "But Ursa isn't dead. He was on his way to the Havens when I last saw him, and that's why I have to get there. That's why I have to stay alive until we get there . . . I have to at least know that he made it there, that he's all right."

I hadn't meant to be so vulnerable, but the words spilled out of me of their own accord. I raised my hands, almost as if in supplication. I was completely at their mercy, I always had been. But they must have understood now, at least in part, why it mattered so much to me to find Ursa, why it was so very important that I stay alive.

Silence was my response. Some of the men exchanged a few more glances, but the rest looked at me, stony and soundless. Finally, Orion rose to his feet, gesturing for me to come with him. I crossed through the sea of pirates, all turning their heads to watch me as I passed, not knowing if they would suddenly shout at me, lurch at me, grab me by the arms and ankles and throw me out of the air lock.

No one did anything, though. When I reached Orion, he muttered quietly, "Follow me. Put your head down. Stay quiet in your room tonight."

He, too, seemed rattled by what had just taken place. If Orion didn't know how to read the mood of these men, I didn't know how I could possibly stand a chance. The last thing I saw before Orion shut the door was his solemn, rumpled face, looking back at me like it might be the last time.

An hour or so later, I was roused from my anxious pacing by a loud pounding at my door. I jumped, staring in mute horror. For a moment, I truly felt that if I remained absolutely silent, they might forget I was there.

"Mina. It's me."

The sound of Orion's voice roused me from my fear-frozen stupor. Even so, I hesitated to respond, knowing how easily he might have been coerced by the other men to lure me out of my room. Not, I reflected, that they needed to *lure* me out. They could easily storm the cell and force me out, if they were so inclined, so there was no real need for subterfuge . . .

"Mina?"

I blinked. "Yes. I'm . . . what is it? Is everything all right?"

"I'm going to open the door, yeah?"

As if it were up to me. I was the prisoner. Still, I supposed it was a chivalric gesture. "A-all right."

I stepped back, bracing myself. The door swung open cautiously. Orion peered in first before stepping inside, closing the door again after him.

I twisted my hands anxiously, waiting for him to speak. For a long moment, he simply studied me. Was he wondering how best to tell me I was about to be sacrificed for quick entertainment? Or maybe they'd devised a new, terrible way to torture me, and Orion had been sent here to explain?

"Just tell me already," I snapped finally. "What are they going to do to me?"

Orion took a deep breath. "Is all of it true? The whole story? Ursa, Rawley, the smugglers, the bear, everything?"

A short, raw laugh escaped my throat. "You still think I made it all up?"

"I think you have a very good incentive to invent a story that could keep you alive. I wouldn't blame you for it. But *they* might."

I thought of Ursa. His scent. His touch. His eyes. Those eyes. I briefly closed my own, the force of the memory staggering me. "It's real. He's real." I looked at Orion imploringly. I wasn't above begging, not for this. "Please, you have to help me convince them. I need to find him again. My life on its own . . . it's nothing special, I realize that. But our lives together, what they could be . . . I have to stay alive for that. For *him*. Can you understand that?"

Orion looked away, as if the force of my gaze, that question, was suddenly too much to face. For the first time, looking at him in profile, it struck me that he wasn't just a Brother of Blood, a sometimes ally, sometimes obstacle in my path back to Ursa. He had his own past, his own history, that had led him to this moment, just as mine had.

We all carried our secret stories hidden in our hearts.

At last, Orion looked back at me, swallowing as he nodded. "I can."

Hope flared bright in my chest, almost painful in its intensity. "Then you'll help me?"

Orion surprised me by smiling—a small, begrudging little thing, but a smile nonetheless. Ah, so his face *did* have that capability. "I won't need to. The Brethren took a vote and decided. Because of your valor, your bravery, your resourcefulness, and your desperate will to survive, you aren't a prisoner any longer."

I stared at him blankly, unable to process the words for a long moment. Even when they started to take some shape for me, they still didn't make sense. "So I'm . . . what? One of you now?"

Orion scoffed. "Don't get carried away. It takes years, *years*, to become a Brother. You have to serve and fight and prove your worth in battle—"

I waved his explanation away, embarrassed. "Right, of course."

"A Brother of Blood after a few weeks of storytelling?" Orion shook his head at me, though his eyes twinkled with mirth. "Let's call you a passenger. A valued passenger, who will hopefully continue to share her story with us, without threat of death." He reconsidered. "Well, with significantly less threat of death."

I grinned at him. "I would like that very much."

That night for the first time, I was welcomed to the galley, not to entertain the crew, but to share a pint. I didn't mention that I'm more of a wine drinker, as I didn't think that would be especially well-received and I wanted to show that I acknowledged and appreciated their gesture for what it was.

I'm one of the crew now—a guest, if not a full-fledged member. I can move about the ship freely. I can lock my door, instead of having it locked for me. I can grab something from the kitchen when I'm hungry, and I can challenge someone to four-dimensional chess in the game room if I feel so inclined.

And best of all, my love, I can return to you. The Brethren are now almost as invested as I am in making sure we find each other again. We're on our way to the Havens, and we won't stop searching until I know where you are. Until I know you're safe.

Until we're together again.

And until then, to pass the time, I'll tell more of our story. I'll start next with the raid on the lunar colony—a bit of excitement would be fitting just about now, don't you think? Or maybe I'll need to explain more about the crew of the Trojan Horse first, set the stage with the personalities who will be populating the next part of our story, or is that too much exposition right off the bat?

Those are all just details, though. The important thing is we're heading to the Havens, slowly but surely. I'm coming, my love. I'm on my way. I will find you. I will slay dragons and fight tigers if I need to. We will be together again. I promise.

Where Ursa is, Mina is home.

<hr>

TO BE CONTINUED...

<hr>

M ina and Ursa's story will continue September 2026

THANK YOU FOR YOUR SUPPORT!

Thank you for reading my book! Truly, you have no idea what that means to an author.

If you would like to continue to support this series, please leave a review!

To make sure you don't miss the next part of Mina and Ursa's story, you can sign up for my newsletter at lissasharpeauthor.com

ACKNOWLEDGEMENTS

I have been writing some shape of this idea for probably about a decade before I finally understood the full scope of the story I'm trying to tell. That's a long time to keep track of every piece of advice and helpful hand and influence along the way, but I'd like to give a general thank you to anyone who gave me feedback on any version of this book; a thank you for writing partners and instructors who helped me better my craft; and a thank you to readers for giving me the courage to finally publish this book.

I've been with Mina and Ursa for so long that I love them and am terrified to set them free into the world. Please handle with care! They are precious to me.

Some more specific thank yous – thank you to the wonderful Briana Ozor who helped to polish and fine-tune this manuscript. Your attention to detail and precision and kindness and humor is so very appreciated.

Thank you to Jen for your feedback, proofreading, and encouragement!

Thank you to my husband, Mike, for listening to me talk about this idea for years and years and years. You have the patience of a saint and the good looks of a Hemsworth. I'm a lucky lady.

Thank you to Johnny, for always being the most excited person when mama puts a new book out.

Thank you to Alexander Dreymon for providing endless hours of inspiration. (Destiny is all!)

Thank you to my Spotify playlist for helping to transport me into this world at just the click of a button.

Last but not least, thank you for reading!

About the Author

Lissa Sharpe is a mom, a wife, a professor, and an award-winning writer. She has written plays, screenplays, teleplays, short stories, songs, and everything in between. She has written two contemporary romance novels, Nun Too Soon and Nun The Wiser, and a handful of other books under other pen names. When she isn't having mental arguments with her characters or online arguments with people about Mr. Darcy, she is hanging out in the American South with her husband, son, and golden lab.

For more information, please visit her website at lissasharpeauthor.com

ALSO BY

As Lissa Sharpe
(contemporary romance)
Nun Too Soon
Nun the Wiser

As Elizabeth Gilliland
(Jane Austen-themed contemporary mystery)
What Happened on Box Hill
The Portraits of Pemberley

As E. Gilliland
(Gothic horror)
Come One, Come All

BAYOU ROSE PRESS

Bayou Rose Press is the romance imprint of Bayou Wolf Press, an independent publisher of quality fiction. If you enjoyed reading this book and would like to support the author, the best thing you can do is leave a review on Amazon, Goodreads, or wherever you review books.

If you'd like to learn more about our press, sign up for our newsletter, and stay informed on upcoming releases, please visit us at bayou wolfpress.com